PENGUIN BOOKS

Writing from Ukraine

CW00501973

Writing from Ukraine

Fiction, Poetry and Essays since 1965

Edited by Mark Andryczyk

PENGUIN BOOKS

PENGUIN BOOKS

UK | USA | Canada | Ireland | Australia
India | New Zealand | South Africa

Penguin Books is part of the Penguin Random House group of companies
whose addresses can be found at global.penguinrandomhouse.com

Penguin
Random House
UK

First published in the USA, under the title *The White Chalk of Days*, by the
Borderlines Foundation for Academic Sciences and Academic Studies Press 2017
First published in Great Britain, under the present title and with minor adjustments
and a new Preface, in Penguin Books 2022
001

Writing from Ukraine was originally published under the title *The White Chalk of Days:
The Contemporary Ukrainian Literature Series Anthology* by Academic Studies Press and
Borderlines Foundation for Academic Studies in partnership with the Kennan
Institute/Harriman Institute Ukrainian Literature Series, as part of Academic Studies
Press's "Ukrainian Studies" series, edited by Vitaly Chernetsky. *The White Chalk of
Days* was made possible in part by a major grant from the Scholarly Editions and
Translation program of the National Endowment for the Humanities: Celebrating 50
Years of Excellence, and also in part by the generous support of the Harriman
Institute, Columbia University. An open access edition of *The White Chalk of Days* is
available at https://www.whitechalkofdays.com.

Printed and bound in Great Britain by Clays Ltd, Elcograf S.p.A.

The authorized representative in the EEA is Penguin Random House Ireland,
Morrison Chambers, 32 Nassau Street, Dublin D02 YH68

A CIP catalogue record for this book is available from the British Library

ISBN: 978–1–802–06164–2

www.greenpenguin.co.uk

MIX
Paper from
responsible sources
FSC
www.fsc.org
FSC® C018179

Penguin Random House is committed to a
sustainable future for our business, our readers
and our planet. This book is made from Forest
Stewardship Council® certified paper.

Contents

Preface   ix
Acknowledgments   xiii
The Kennan Institute/Harriman Institute Contemporary
Ukrainian Literature Series   xvii

Introduction   1

A Note On Transliteration   21

ANDREY KURKOV   22
From Jimi Hendrix Live in Lviv   24

HRYTSKO CHUBAI   30
The Woman   32
and ever so slowly looms ...   33
The Corridor with Eye-Sized Doors   34
When your lips are but a half a breath away ...   35
From Maria   36
Light and Confession   37

OLEH LYSHEHA   42
Song 55   44

MARJANA SAVKA   46
Books We've Never Read   48
From A Short History of Dance   49
Easter Jazz   50
For Yann Tiersen   51
Boston, April 2007   52
Baghdad Night   53
In This City   55
Who, Marlene, Who?   56
Some woman ...   57

Organs of Sense   58
My beloved sun ...   60

VIKTOR NEBORAK   62
From Genesis of the Flying Head   64
Monologue from a Canine Pretext   68
A Drum-Tympanum (a sonnet uttered by the Flying Head)   70
She (rap performance by the Kids of the Queenie) Part 3   71
An Itty Bitty Ditty 'bout Mr. Bazio (sung by Viktor Morozov)   73
Fish   75
Supper   77
Green sounds echo ...   79
The Writer   80
The Poet   81

ANDRIY BONDAR   82
Genes   84
Slavic Gods   87
The Men of My Country   88
Just Don't Push Me Away   90
Robbie Williams   92
St. Nick No. 628   94
The Roman Alphabet   97
Jogging   99

YURI ANDRUKHOVYCH   102
The Star Absinthe: Notes on a Bitter Anniversary   104

TARAS PROKHASKO   116
Selections from FM Galicia   118
22.11   121
24.11   124
30.11   131
04.12   137
07.12   141
09.12   143
15.12   145
16.12   147
23.12   149
15.01   150

24.01   152
25.01   154
27.01   156
10.02   158

SERHIY ZHADAN   160
Chinese Cooking   162
Hotel Business   163
Children's Train   165
The Inner Color of Eyes   167
Alcohol   169
Contraband   170
Paprika   172
... not to wake her up ...   174
The Lord Sympathizes with Outsiders   176
Owner of the Best Gay Bar   178
The Percentage of Suicides among Clowns   216

IVAN MALKOVYCH   220
Stand up and look ...   222
bird's elegy   224
happiness ...   226
futile people   227
The Village Teacher's Lesson   228
Nothing is right here, you see: ...   229
An Evening with Great-Grandma   230
The black parachute of anxiety grows ...   231
There is much—I know—sadness ...   232
The Man   233
The Music That Walked Away   234
At Home   235
I gaze at my mountains ...   236
Tonight ...   237
Circle   238
an evening (goose) pastoral   239
A Message for T.   240

VASYL GABOR   244
The High Water   246
A Story About One Dollar   251

Five Short Stories for Natalie—The Fifth Story—
The Last One—The Lover   253

YURI VYNNYCHUK   258
The Flowerbed in the Kilim   260
Pea Soup   264
From Spring Games in Summer Gardens   266
   Prologue   266
   The Pilgrim's Dance, Part 1   271
Pears à la Crêpe   277

OLEKSANDR BOICHENKO   286
Out of Great Love   288
The Lunch of a Man of Letters   292
In a State of Siege   294

SOPHIA ANDRUKHOVYCH   298
An Out-of-tune Piano, an Accordion   300

LYUBA YAKIMCHUK   310
Apricots of the Donbas   312
   The Face of Coal   312
   The Slag Piles of Breasts   314
   Apricots in Hard Hats   316
   My Grandmother's Fairy Tale   318
   The Book of Angels   320
the eye of the slag heap   322
decomposition   323
eyebrows   325
I have a crisis for you   326
false friends and beloved   328
such people are called naked   330
marsala   333

About the Editor   334
Translators   336
Praise for *Writing from Ukraine*   338

Preface

Writing from Ukraine: Fiction, Poetry and Essays since 1965 gathers the writings of fifteen leading Ukrainian writers from the past fifty years. The poetry, fiction and non-fiction featured in the anthology present a wide assortment of styles—lyric, experimental, surrealistic—and cover a variety of topics, such as history, gender and nature, that provide intimate access to issues significant to the people of Ukraine.

Since 24 February 2022, global interest in Ukraine has grown exponentially. The all-out Russian invasion of the country—and the expansion of a war between the two countries that has been ongoing in Ukraine's eastern Donbas region since 2014—spurred people to learn more about Ukrainians, their history and their culture. This sudden interest was welcomed by Ukrainians around the world, but simultaneously frustrated them: it served to confirm that Ukraine, despite having existed in Europe for more than a thousand years, largely remained a mystery to the world. Ukraine's geopolitical position between competing empires has led to its independence being challenged and interrupted throughout its history. Meanwhile, Ukraine has created a rich and vibrant culture, one that offers the world its unique perspectives, values and aesthetic expressions. Despite lacking sustained statehood, Ukrainian art has managed to survive and even thrive over the years. In fact, this lack of a consistent political presence often enlivens Ukraine's culture, as its people strive to ensure the existence of a Ukrainian identity and to protect it from repeated attacks aiming to eradicate it.

The twentieth century was a particularly devasting period for Ukrainian lands, but it was also a time when modern Ukrainian culture arose and, at times, flourished. And, in 1991, as the Soviet Union collapsed, Ukraine achieved its long-awaited independence. Finally, after many years, Ukrainian writers and other artists had the opportunity to create freely in their own land, without fear of persecution. They also had the opportunity to celebrate the past achievements of their own culture, which had been banned by colonizing powers, and to establish routes of cultural exchange with the suddenly accessible rest of the world. Since independence, figures in the Ukrainian literary milieu have acted as ambassadors, traveling the world and meeting audiences, presenting their writing and offering nuanced explorations of Ukrainian identity.

The newfound interest in Ukraine since February 2022 is unprecedented. Those institutions and individuals who have long disseminated knowledge about the country and analyzed its history, politics and culture are now increasingly being turned to for knowledge and guidance. Fortunately, Ukrainian studies has developed steadily over the years, and today there is much to offer the world on the subject of Ukraine. Myriad publications, as well as academic and cultural forums, have made Ukraine accessible to the global community. In the field of literature, translations of Ukrainian literature into various languages have gradually increased since the country's independence in 1991 and have grown significantly since Ukraine's 2013–14 Revolution of Dignity.

This volume is a republication of the 2017 book *The White Chalk of Days: The Contemporary Ukrainian Literature Series Anthology*. The book compiles literary works by fifteen of Ukraine's key writers of the final decades of the twentieth century and of the first decades of the twenty-first. The authors of these texts presented these writings publicly as part of a literature series that brought them to cultural and academic forums in North America from 2008 to 2016. Such an opportunity for cultural exchange was essential then: interest in Ukraine was growing steadily, but slowly. For years, these writers have been discussing issues that are crucial for Ukraine today. Their writing helps tell the story of how Ukraine got to this point. Many of the anthology's authors were active in the 2013–14 Revolution of Dignity, a pivotal episode in Ukraine's defence of its independence from Russia—a continued fight that unfolds on the world stage in the present day. And these writers are as involved today as they were then, volunteering at home and helping to explain Ukraine to the world beyond its borders. Their writings in this book are an important component of that effort.

The texts contained in this book offer diverse voices presenting vibrant Ukrainian perspectives on problems of universal concern. The poetry, fiction, and non-fiction present in this book, together with its introduction and the biographies of the authors, give an initiation to the world of contemporary Ukrainian literature. Addressing the increased interest in Ukraine's existence, its identity and its culture, *Writing from Ukraine* offers a path to the vitality, sophistication and beauty of today's Ukrainian literature and to the people of Ukraine, who, as they often have had to in the past, fight today for the right to exist in their own land.

Mark Andryczyk
May 2022

Acknowledgments

The success of the Contemporary Ukrainian Literature Series can be attributed to the efforts and abilities of many individuals. The idea for the series belongs to Catharine Nepomnyashchy and Blair Ruble, who were, at the time the series was founded, the directors of the Harriman and Kennan Institutes, respectively. Blair also moderated Andrey Kurkov's and Viktor Neborak's events at Kennan, and his genuine interest in the series truly helped it progress over the years. I am grateful to Matthew Rojansky, Director of the Kennan Institute since 2013, for continuing to co-sponsor the series. Renata Kosc-Harmatiy was the primary organizer of the series on the Kennan side for its initial years; when Renata left the institute, Lidiya Zubytska, Liz Malinkin, and then Joseph Dressen took over. I organized and moderated all the series events at the Harriman and moderated all but the two abovementioned events at the Kennan. I thank all my colleagues at the Kennan Institute for their cooperation in this common endeavor.

It would not have been possible to conduct the Series as we wanted to—in English—without the efforts of our various interpreters: Yuri Shevchuk, Ali Kinsella, and Lesia Kalynska at the Harriman and Oles Berezhny, Matilda Kuklish, Peter Voitsekhovsky, and Roman Ponos at the Kennan. Thanks to Andrew Bihun and the Washington Group for sponsoring receptions for many of the Kennan Series events. A special thanks to Victor Morozov for tending to many of the Series guests while they were in Washington, D.C.

I am thankful to my fellow translators whose translations make up this volume: Michael M. Naydan, Virlana Tkacz, Wanda Phipps, Vitaly Chernetsky, Askold Melnyczuk, Olena Jennings, Patrick Corness, Natalia Pomirko, Bohdan Boychuk, Myrosia Stefaniuk, Yaryna Yakubyak, Andrij

Kudla Wynnyckyj, Jars Balan, Oksana Maksymchuk, Max Rosochinsky, and Svetlana Lavochkina. Without their talents and hard work, this volume would not have been possible.

I am grateful to Suhrkamp for allowing me to include translations of Yuri Andrukhovych's essay "Iks, 1970-1986" and Serhiy Zhadan's story "Vlasnyk naikrashchoho kluba dlia heiv" in the volume free of charge. Thank you to Andrey Kurkov's publisher, Diogenes Verlag AG, for allowing me to include a translation of a fragment of his novel *Lvovskaia gastrol Dzhimi Khendriksa* also free of charge.

Some of the translations included in this volume have been published previously. My translation of the above mentioned Yuri Andrukhovych's essay, entitled "The Star Absinthe: Notes on a Bitter Anniversary," was first published by University of Toronto Press in *My Final Territory: Selected Essays* (2017). I am grateful to Sribne Slovo for allowing me to include in this volume the following translations of Viktor Neborak poems, which previously appeared in their publication *The Flying Head and Other Poems* (Lviv: Sribne Slovo, 2005): "Genesis of the Flying Head," "Monologue from a Canine Pretext," "A Drum-Tympanum," "She," "An Itty Bitty Ditty 'bout Mr. Bazio," and "Green sounds echo ... ."

I thank Litopys for giving their permission to republish translations of two poems—Viktor Neborak's "Fish" and Ivan Malkovych's "At Home"—that had previously appeared in their anthology *A Hundred Years of Youth*, edited and compiled by Olha Luchuk and Michael M. Naydan (Lviv: Litopys, 2000).

Zephyr Press allowed us to republish the translation of Viktor Neborak's poem entitled "Supper" that appeared in *From Three Worlds: New Writing from Ukraine*, edited by Ed Hogan, Askold Melnyczuk, Michael Naydan, Mykola Riabchuk, and Oksana Zabuzhko (Boston, MA, and Moscow: Zephyr Press and Glas, 1996).

The following translations were previously published in the Fall 2010 issue of *International Poetry Review*, Vol. XXXVI—No. 2: Viktor Neborak's "The Writer" and "The Poet"; Marjana Savka's "My Beloved Sun" and "Organs of Sense"; and Ivan Malkovych's "The Village Teacher's Lesson" and "The Music That Walked Away."

The following translated poems previously appeared in the online journal *Poetry International Rotterdam* (http://www.poetryinternational. com); Ivan Malkovych's "Bird's Elegy" and "The Man"; Andriy Bondar's "Jogging," "Genes," "Just Don't Push Me Away," "The Men of My Country," "Slavic Gods," and "The Roman Alphabet"; and Serhiy Zhadan's "Paprika" and "Chinese Cooking."

Much gratitude to Arrowsmith Press for allowing me to repub- lish the following Askold Melnyczuk's translations of Marjana Savka's poems which first appeared in its publication *Eight Notes from the Blue Angel* (Medford, MA: Arrowsmith Press, 2007): "From a Short History of Dance," "Who, Marlene, Who?," "Books We've Never Read," "In This City," "For Yann Tiersen," "Baghdad Night," "Boston, April 2007," and "Easter Jazz."

Vasyl Gabor's story "High Water" was first published in *Ukrainian Literature: A Journal of Translations,* Vol. 3 (October, 2011): 243-246.

Serhiy Zhadan's "Alcohol" first appeared in *New European Poets*, edited by Kevin Prufer and Wayne Miller (Saint Paul, MN: Graywolf Press, 2008) and "... not to wake her up ... " in *Two Lines World Writing in Translation* (2007). Zhadan's "Hotel Business" was first published in *Absinthe: New European Writing* 7 (2007).

A warm thanks to Ron Meyer and Nestor Gula whose careful eyes and subsequent editorial suggestions on some of the materials in this volume were a great help.

I am grateful to the Harriman Institute for rewarding this volume with a Faculty Publication Grant in 2016 which helped the book come to fruition. This volume was also co-recipient of a 2016 National Endowment for the Humanities grant. I am elated that the NEH acknowledges the importance of contemporary Ukrainian literature in the world today and am thankful to them for supporting the widening of its presence in this world.

Thank you to Academic Studies Press, its Director and Publisher Igor Nemirovsky, and its Ukrainian Studies Series Editor Vitaly Chernetsky for believing in my idea for the *White Chalk of Days* anthol- ogy and for helping me to realize it. Thanks to Academic Studies Press acquisition editors Oleh Kotsyuba, Faith Wilson Stein, and Meghan

Vicks. It was a pleasure working with them; their excitement about this project was infectious and inspiring.

I am thrilled that legendary artist Vlodko Kaufman and his unique talents are part of this anthology project and am grateful to him for providing his original drawings for the book's design. Mr. Kaufman is a visual and performance artist, and is also Artistic Director of the Dzyga Art Association in Lviv, Ukraine. His work is tightly intertwined with many branches of the Ukrainian literary scene. Connected with Ukrainian literature since the 1970s when, as a student at the School for Applied Art in Lviv, Kaufman began associating with Hrytsko Chubai, he has designed many of the publications of post-Soviet Ukrainian writers. The writers featured in this anthology have regularly presented at Dzyga over the past twenty years.

Finally, I would like to thank all the authors who participated in the Contemporary Ukrainian Literature Series for trusting me, for agreeing to take part in the Series, and for making it so pleasurable and rewarding to present Ukrainian literature in the U.S. over the past nine years.

Mark Andryczyk

The Kennan Institute/ Harriman Institute Contemporary Ukrainian Literature Series

In 2008, the Kennan Institute and the Harriman Institute's Ukrainian Studies Program at Columbia University initiated a series showcasing contemporary Ukrainian literature through events with Ukrainian writers.

Since the launch of the series, Ukraine has frequently appeared in news headlines, but too often associated with stories about continuing challenges to Ukraine's sovereignty and stability, or about the country's ongoing struggles with corruption and divisive domestic politics. In addition, much of the analytical research and writing about Ukraine coming out of the think tank and university communities has also tended to focus primarily on negative stories about Ukraine's many challenges.

This context makes it all the more important for institutions like the Harriman and the Kennan to collaborate to support the Contemporary Ukrainian Literature Series. Those who have attended our lectures, either in Washington or in New York, have come away with a sense of Ukraine far deeper and more profound than what can be gleaned from discussions of gas pipelines, Little Green Men, or IMF lending packages.

The Kennan Institute supports this series because of our enduring commitment to the study of Ukraine and its region as a whole, which must include a strong foundation of culture, history, art, and literature. In the same spirit, the Kennan Institute in Ukraine has played a key role in helping to develop the strategy for and promotion of Ukrainian cultural diplomacy in Europe, North America and beyond. In partnership with Ukraine's Foreign Ministry, the Kennan Institute's Kyiv Office held the second annual Cultural Diplomacy Forum in April 2016, with 300 participants. Over the summer of 2016, the Kennan Institute hosted a major art installation by renowned Ukrainian artist Victor Sydorenko. And President Petro Poroshenko specifically thanked the Kennan Institute for its efforts toward developing Ukraine's cultural diplomacy during his 2016 address to Ukraine's parliamentary body, the Verkhovna Rada.

The Contemporary Ukrainian Literature Series is likewise an important component of the Ukrainian Studies Program at the Harriman Institute, Columbia University. The Harriman's Ukrainian Studies Program organizes courses, lectures, and conferences in Ukrainian studies featuring an international array of specialists in Ukrainian history, politics, language, and literature. Recent conferences organized by the program have focused on non-conformity and dissent in the Soviet bloc, media in Ukraine, and the city of Kharkiv as an important center of Ukrainian culture. Events organized by the Ukrainian Film Club of Columbia University, together with the Literature Series, reflect the Program's emphasis on contemporary Ukraine. Both the Kennan and the Harriman recognize the importance in having an awareness of Ukraine's culture when analyzing the country today.

As political and economic upheavals persist in Ukraine, public life seems unimaginable without the cultural accomplishments that have continued to enliven Ukrainian society ever since the collapse of pervasive Soviet censorship on literary and artistic expression. Observing Ukraine through its literary landscape offers an opportunity to understand much of the transformation that has occurred since it gained its independence. The creative energy unleashed in Ukrainian literature in recent decades has displayed such a variety of styles, themes, and approaches that readers, many of them young, continue to be enthralled by literary depictions of Ukrainian life: the lingering vestiges of the old Soviet system, the new freedom of open borders, the unremitting turbulence of social and political life, and the individual search for meaning and fulfillment amidst these changing circumstances.

Introduction

> quietly
> the gloom
> scuttles
>
> deeper and deeper
> evening digs a well
>
> here geese
> return from the meadow:
> their procession walking through the evening
> like a white
> tunnel
>
> it's as though the geese
> are small bundles of the white chalk of days—
> God's big bottles walking to the white[1]
>
> **Ivan Malkovych**

In his poem "an evening (goose) pastoral," Ivan Malkovych sets white geese against the backdrop of the encroaching darkness of evening. The geese act as a connection to the fleeting day as a cycle of time runs its course, thus preserving the light of the day that has just passed.

---

1   This is a fragment of the Ivan Malkovych poem "an evening (goose) pastoral." It can be found in its entirety on page 239. The poem was translated by Michael M. Naydan. Unless otherwise indicated, all comments on figures, places, and cultural and social contexts in the translations contained in this volume are mine.

This book, *The White Chalk of Days: The Contemporary Ukrainian Literature Series Anthology,* also marks the completion of a cycle, as it captures the days during which thirteen Ukrainian authors shared their words with audiences in the United States, illuminating dark spots in the existence and the culture of their country. This volume is a collection of translations of literary works written by many of the leading authors that shape the landscape of today's contemporary Ukrainian literature. The poems and prose works were presented at forums in New York City and Washington, D.C. as part of a series co-organized by the Ukrainian Studies Program at the Harriman Institute, Columbia University, and the Kennan Institute at the Woodrow Wilson International Center for Scholars. The Contemporary Ukrainian Literature Series (2008-2016) hosted today's Ukrainian literati, who read and discussed their writings and also shared their views on the cultural and political developments taking place in post-Soviet Ukraine. The year 2016 marks the twenty-fifth anniversary of Ukrainian political independence. This era of independence also corresponds to a new era in the history of Ukrainian literature, which is characterized by vigor, experimentation and upheaval. The texts in this volume are vibrant examples of this period and demonstrate many of the key dynamics prevalent in the Ukrainian cultural movements that marked it.

* * *

A greater degree of freedom for artistic expression in Ukrainian literature began just before the country's political independence, in the final half-decade of the Soviet Union's existence. The policies of perestroika and glasnost led to a general loosening of the restrictions that had shackled art in the Soviet Union since the early 1930s, when Socialist Realism was established as the only officially sanctioned style of art. The Communist Party, through the Union of Soviet Writers, assigned which subjects should be treated in art (and which should not) throughout the USSR and often imposed additional restrictions on the artistic expressions of the various ethnic groups in the Soviet Union. Such curtailing allowed the colonial center to maintain stereotypical and condescending depictions of peripheral national groups in Soviet art.[2] Thus, a Ukrainian hero in a novel did not merely have to be shown working toward the proletariat's emancipation and espousing the ideals of communism, as Soviet Russian protagonists did, but he also needed to be depicted with his national traits reduced to condescending clichés and quirky peculiarities. Ukrainian writers who attempted to create outside these confines of Soviet Socialist Realism were ignored, marginalized and repressed. Some writers, of course, were able to carve out a measure of creative freedom within this system by using Aesopian language and engaging the reader to "read between the lines." It was not until the second half of the 1980s, however, that there emerged a growing aesthetic freedom in Soviet cultural policy; also at this time, much Soviet Ukrainian literature that had previously been hidden or written "for the drawer" began to be published in the open.

Alongside the widening breadth of what could be published as Soviet Ukrainian literature during glasnost came the rehabilitation of many—but not all—Ukrainian authors that had officially been branded bourgeois nationalists and thus, enemies of the Soviet people. These writers, as well as émigré authors that had been publishing freely outside of Ukraine, had been erased from the pages of Ukrainian cultural history, and their books were absent from the shelves of libraries and bookstores in Ukraine. Additionally, a new generation of Ukrainian writers would emerge in the late 1980s, a generation that would be the first to enjoy complete creative freedom following Ukraine's independence in 1991. These writers often are referred to as the *visimdesiatnyky*—the 80s generation of writers. Although the term *visimdesiatnyky* is often used in discussions of late Soviet and post-Soviet Ukrainian culture and there are several publications that group authors under that label, it is important to understand that it is not a formal group with strict allegiance or membership. Rather, it is a term that, like other generational terms, groups individuals who are varied and rather loosely linked. The murkiness and

---

2   For a thorough analysis of cultural imperialism, Russia, and Ukraine, see Myroslav Shkandrij, *Russia and Ukraine: Literature and the Discourse of Empire from Napoleonic to Postcolonial Times* (Montreal: McGill-Queen's University Press, 2001).

fluidity of the boundaries between these generations notwithstanding, such terms help to explain general developments in Ukrainian culture at this time.

In the first decade of Ukraine's independence, the *visimdesiat-nyky* focused their talents and energies on leading Ukrainian culture out of the restrictions that had been imposed on it by its colonizers. However, these writers also worked to free themselves from many of the frameworks that had been placed on Ukrainian culture by the inherited Ukrainian national tradition, which curtailed Ukrainian artists' aesthetic freedom by requiring that their art serve the ongoing cause of Ukrainian emancipation. These artists were expected to express their patriotism and to adhere to themes that were largely established by Ukrainian populist culture of the nineteenth century. Post-Soviet Ukrainian literature thus (1) experienced an onrush of creative openness while (2) being reconnected to the substantial Ukrainian cultural achievements in the twentieth century that had been banned, and (3) simultaneously explored the world outside the Soviet Union, one that it had been closed off from for many decades. All three of these exciting developments provided the 80s generation of writers with a particular zeal to dismantle the colonial and national frameworks that had been placed on Ukrainian art in the past.

And dismantle these systems they did. Several writers found post-modernism to be an attractive concept and employed many of its characteristic stylistic features in this deconstruction.[3] Having been dictated certain official Soviet truths for many years, which they knew themselves to be false, Ukrainian intellectuals found postmodern doubt in absolute truth to be quite attractive while taking on issues of their colonized past in their art. Meanwhile, other writers of various generations protested that an engagement with fashionable Western postmodernism was

---

3 One leading Ukrainian scholar uses the term "post-Chernobyl literature" to describe Ukrainian Postmodernism. See Tamara Hundorova, *Pisliachornobyl's'ka biblioteka: ukraïns'kyi literaturnyi postmodern* (Kyiv: Krytyka, 2005). Hundorova treats the Chernobyl explosion as a watershed, the catastrophic effects of which thrust Ukraine's *visimdesiatnyky* to aggressively challenge existing paradigms in Ukraine's cultural sphere.

inauthentic, and that independent Ukrainian literature should instead look inward to produce something uniquely Ukrainian. What resulted in the 1990s was a healthy, though often cantankerous, open debate on the face of new Ukrainian culture and the publication of works written on many themes and styles—particularly significant achievements when compared with literature published in Ukraine just a decade earlier.

The *visimdesiatnyky* were able to deconstruct the role of the author in a literary work in general and the Ukrainian author in the Ukrainian literary tradition in particular. The potency of language, especially the Ukrainian language, was scrutinized in their writings. These writers exposed clichéd, colonial depictions of Ukrainians and shattered the restrictions that had limited the themes that could be treated in Ukrainian literature.[4] The writers deliberately engaged with many taboo subjects, such as sex, slang, and substance abuse, and they also experimented in form and narration. The previously closed-off world, especially the West and its lofty culture, as well as its pop culture, were often referenced in this post-Soviet Ukrainian literature. This was a literature that searched through Ukrainian and world history and culture to begin assembling the fragile new post-Soviet Ukrainian identity. It was an art that also reflected the disarray and disappointment of this period as corruption and dysfunction steered the post-Soviet country. Ukrainian culture was discarded by the government, and largely left on its own to survive with minimal financial and structural support from the new Ukrainian state. The experiences of the previous generation of Ukrainian writers, sometimes called the 70s generation of Ukrainian writers (*simdesiatnyky*), were a particularly important point of reference for the *visimdesiatnyky* when they experienced such difficulties.

The *simdesiatnyky* generation came on the heels of the 60s generation (*shistdesiatnyky*), who had revitalized Soviet Ukrainian culture during the Khrushchev thaw. Closely intertwined with the Ukrainian dissident movement, the *shistdesiatnyky* organized protests

---

4   I have published a monograph that addresses these phenomena, and others, in post-Soviet Ukrainian literature. See Mark Andryczyk, *The Intellectual as Hero in 1990s Ukrainian Fiction* (Toronto: University of Toronto Press, 2012).

against systemic russification and sought to protect and develop Ukrainian culture within the paradigms of Soviet cultural ideology. Their successes in invigorating literature in the late 1950s and early 1960s, however, were met with a vicious crackdown from the state between 1965 and 1972, including repression and arrests. Inspired by the rebirth and defiance that the *shistdesiatnyky* had initiated, but frightened by the brutal response of the authorities to their successes, the *simdesiatnyky* maneuvered their cultural activity underground. Circulating banned books, including the *shistdesiatnyky*'s *samvydav* (samizdat) writings, these artists developed Ukrainian culture outside official Soviet cultural policy. In Kyiv this cultural development was led by writers of the *Kyivska Shkola* (Kyiv School), which included Vasyl Holoborodko, Viktor Kordun, Mykola Vorobiov, and Mykhailo Hryhoriv. In Lviv, its main figures were Ihor and Iryna Kalynets and a creative group centered around Hrytsko Chubai.

Hrytsko Chubai's circle also included, among others, Oleh Lysheha, Mykola Riabchuk, Victor Morozov, and later, Yuri Vynnychuk. The group would gather at one another's homes to share their new poems, songs, and paintings. In 1971, they released a *samvydav* almanac entitled *Skrynia* (The Chest), which featured original poems, translations, and an apolitical call for creative non-conformity. The authorities confiscated the journal: its contributors were repressed and their creative activity was halted. The literary works of the *simdesiatnyky* could not be published until the late 1980s. However, the *simdesiatnyky* were very influential on the subsequent generation of Ukrainian artists. Inspired by the quality of their art and by their ability to create freely outside the official Soviet centralized system of culture, the *visimdesiatnyky* absorbed many lessons that proved to be useful during the disorder that engulfed post-Soviet Ukraine.

Thus, as it turns out, during late Soviet times a generation of young Ukrainian artists—the *visimdesiatnyky*—was, in essence, being prepared for the opportunity for free creative expression that had been craved by Ukrainian intellectuals for many years. When that chance finally emerged during glasnost and then expanded with the collapse of the Soviet Union, the 80ers, together with survivors from among the *shistdesiatnyky* and *simdesiatnyky*, guided the development of Ukrainian culture in post-Soviet Ukraine.[5]

* * *

The Contemporary Ukrainian Literature Series featured writers of various generations whose literary works have helped form the face of post-Soviet Ukrainian literature. Representatives from the *visimdesiatnyky* include Vasyl Gabor (b. 1959), Yuri Andrukhovych (b. 1960), Ivan Malkovych (b. 1961), Andrey Kurkov (b. 1961), and Viktor Neborak (b. 1961). Younger writers in the series, such as Taras Prokhasko (b. 1968), Oleksandr Boichenko (b. 1970), Marjana Savka (b. 1973), Andriy Bondar (b. 1974), and Serhiy Zhadan (b. 1974) have often presented their work together with the *visimdesiatnyky,* and have been published alongside them in various almanacs and anthologies. Sophia Andrukhovych (b. 1982) and Lyuba Yakimchuk (b. 1985) are among the most prominent young writers to have made a significant impact on the Ukrainian literary scene. Works of the *simdesiatnyky* were also featured in the Contemporary Ukrainian Literature Series. Yuri Vynnychuk (b. 1952) was a guest of the series in 2010, and the poetry of two other 70ers writers, Hrytsko Chubai (1949-1982) and Oleh Lysheha (1949-2014), was present in the series through the music of Taras Chubai. Taras Chubai is Hrytsko's son, who, along with Yuri Vynnychuk and Andriy Panchyshyn, co-founded the *Ne Zhurys!* (Don't Worry!) cabaret ensemble in the late 1980s. *Ne Zhurys!* combined satire with traditional and modern Ukrainian culture throughout the late 1980s and 1990s and celebrated Ukraine's growing freedom on numerous stages, both in Ukraine and abroad. Taras Chubai wrote, recorded

---

5   For informative, in-depth investigations of this period in Ukrainian literature, see Marko Pavlyshyn, "Post-Colonial Features in Contemporary Ukrainian Culture", *Australian Slavonic and East European Studies* 6 (1992), no. 2: 41-55; Solomea Pavlychko, "Facing Freedom: The New Ukrainian Literature", translated by Askold Melnyczuk, in *From Three Worlds: New Writing from Ukraine*, ed. Ed Hogan (Boston: Zephyr Press, 1996); and Vitaly Chernetsky, *Mapping Postcommunist Cultures: Russia and Ukraine in the Context of Globalization* (Montreal and Kingston: McGill-Queen's University Press, 2007).

and performed many songs using his father's poetry, the poetry of Lysheha, and the poetry of the *visimdesiatnyky* writers as lyrics. His popularity as a rock musician greatly spread the reach of this new and previously underground poetry in post-Soviet Ukraine. As part of the Contemporary Ukrainian Literature Series, Taras Chubai performed these songs, including ones based on the poems of Hrytsko Chubai and Oleh Lysheha, at the Harriman and Kennan institutes in April 2008.

One of the goals of the Contemporary Ukrainian Literature Series was to introduce today's leading Ukrainian authors to as wide a U.S. public as possible. To that end, all of its twenty-seven events were conducted in English. With the exception of Taras Chubai's concerts, all Contemporary Ukrainian Series events consisted of a Ukrainian author reading their work and answering questions posed by the event's moderator between their readings, and a question and answer period with the audience. A handout with English-language translations of the texts was provided for the audience and, if necessary, an English-language interpreter was provided for the discussion. Sometimes existing translations were used for this purpose, but often new translations had to be made so that the writers could present their selected texts. As a result, a large body of new translations accumulated over the course of the series. It is these translations that make up the bulk of the contents of this anthology. In certain cases, translations that had appeared in previous publications and were utilized at series events have also been included. For Andrey Kurkov, who already had a great deal of his work translated into English, a translation of one as-yet-untranslated work was made especially for the anthology. A goal was to have the anthology include as many texts that were featured at series events as possible and also to have it debut new translations that were inspired by the series and had never been published before. In other words, *The White Chalk of Days* is both a collection of literary works that initially comprised and now commemorates the Contemporary Ukrainian Literature Series and a volume collecting mostly new translations of the works of many leading Ukrainian writers.

As mentioned above, in addition to the reading of literary texts, the Contemporary Ukrainian Literature Series allowed audiences in New York and Washington, D.C to hear the thoughts and opinions of some of Ukraine's leading intellectuals on a variety of issues. Another goal of the series was to help shed light on Ukraine in the West, where people are largely in the dark about the country's past and present. Most of the series discussions centered on Ukrainian cultural, political, and social issues. For example, Andriy Bondar talked about why Ukraine had not yet produced its own film based on Nikolai Gogol's story *Taras Bulba*; Yuri Vynnychuk revealed how he managed to publish his own writing in censored Soviet Ukraine by passing it off as his translations from a mysterious ancient language; Andrey Kurkov divulged in which country his most active readers reside; and Viktor Neborak spoke of the "era of festivals" that engulfed Ukraine in the last years of the Soviet Union and during the initial years of its independence. Oleksandr Boichenko pointed out that, these days, many Ukrainian writers are engaged in translating Polish fiction and non-fiction works into Ukrainian but that the reverse was not necessarily true; Yuri Andrukhovych shared stories of his experiences representing Ukraine abroad; and Taras Prokhasko spoke about the need to experiment with the Ukrainian language in literature. Serhiy Zhadan disclosed that neither Ukrainian nor Russian were spoken in the home where he grew up; Sophia Andrukhovych discussed nostalgia for the past in today's Ukrainian literature; and Lyuba Yakimchuk reflected on the appropriateness of writing poetry at a time of war. An insiders' view of the Ukrainian publishing industry was provided by three of the series guests—Ivan Malkovych, Marjana Savka and Vasyl Gabor. All three are directly involved in publishing books that have garnered many of the country's most prestigious book awards. The success of Malkovych's publishing house A-BA-BA-HA-LA-MA-HA has made him a publisher-celebrity in his country. Gabor's *Pryvatna kolektsiia* (A Private Collection), which is published by Piramida Publishers, has produced some of the most important post-Soviet anthologies of both new Ukrainian literature and key literary works that were banned in Soviet times. Savka, chief editor and co-founder of the *Vydavnytstvo Staroho Leva* (Old Lion Publishing House), has been successful in making her publishing house the most visible one in Ukraine in the past half-decade.

Most of the Contemporary Ukrainian Literature Series events that took place at the Kennan Institute were video recorded and are available for viewing on their website. Taking advantage of the presence of the series' guests in Washington, D.C., the Voice of America Ukrainian Service invited many of them to appear in its broadcasts. These resources have provided valuable tools for scholars who teach Ukrainian studies worldwide. It is my intention that *The White Chalk of Days* be another key resource for students and teachers of Ukrainian culture.

* * *

A series that lasts this long and consists of so many events is bound to run into some problems with logistics, and the Contemporary Ukrainian Literature Series is no exception. In fact, sometimes it seemed that the series was being sabotaged by a mysterious, devious force. Several incidents regarding guests of the series have now become legendary. Upon flying into JFK Airport in New York, Viktor Neborak mistakenly ended up taking a stretch limousine to his hotel instead of a standard taxi. And, in Washington, after deciding to walk from his hotel to the Kennan Institute, he got lost near the White House, showing up for his event just before it was scheduled to begin. Serhiy Zhadan too was supposed to arrive in the United States at JFK Airport. Fearing he may also get in a wrong car, I traveled from Philadelphia to meet him at the airport and take him to his hotel on Broadway. A massive rainstorm, however, intervened and his plane was unable to land in New York and instead landed—in Philadelphia. He waited in Philadelphia while I waited in New York before he finally landed in New York several hours later. Bad weather also greeted Vasyl Gabor in New York. He was able to fly into New York as scheduled, but his October 29, 2012 event at the Harriman Institute was cancelled because Columbia University, and most of New York City, was shut down by Hurricane Sandy. Gabor barely managed to make it out of Manhattan in order to travel to Washington, D.C. for his event at the Kennan Institute two days later. Taras Prokhasko set out for Lviv from his hometown of Ivano-Frankivsk on his way to New York in February 2010. Unfortunately, he slipped on a patch of ice on the platform of the Ivano-Frankivsk train station and was unable to break his fall with his hands; they were busy holding a large pot of cabbage that he was bringing to his family in Lviv along the way. Due to a badly damaged leg, he couldn't fly out of Lviv and his event had to be rescheduled. A few months later, in the spring, a hobbling Prokhasko cheerfully met with audiences in New York and Washington.

* * *

The final few years of the series coincided with a dramatic turn of events in Ukraine—the EuroMaidan of 2013 and 2014 and the subsequent war with Russia. Not surprisingly, these momentous political events influenced both the topics of discussion and some of the readings at the series events. In this manner, the series was instrumental in providing audiences in the United Sates with the point of view of several Ukrainian artists at a time when interest in Ukraine had risen.

Many guests of the series took on the duties of a public intellectual over these years and were especially active in the Euromaidan demonstrations. During the most heated days of the protests, the involvement of some of these writers in supporting Euromaidan placed them in very important and precarious positions. In an attempt to disseminate as many facts about the Euromaidan as possible throughout the world, Andriy Bondar created and ran a Facebook page entitled "Eurolution.Doc (Ukraine on Maidan)." It was, in essence, a twenty-four-hour translation workshop of articles written about the Euromaidan that took advantage of the fact that Bondar had 5,000 friends and 17,500 subscribers on Facebook and that, being a translator himself, he knew many individuals who professionally translated between various languages. Translation requests were consistently posted and translators from around the world would announce their availability and language proficiencies. The importance of this workshop was confirmed when the site was anonymously shut down three times. Writers Yuri Andrukhovych and Andrey Kurkov used their relative prominence in the West to share what they saw on the Maidan. Kurkov lives just a few steps from the Maidan and from the start of the Euromaidan protests wrote diary entries depicting what he saw. These entries were later collected and published as the book *Ukraine Diary: Dispatches from Kiev*. Andrukhovych wrote an article in January 2014, when clashes on the Maidan were peaking. It was translated by Vitaly Chernetsky and published as "Love and Hatred in Kiev," an op-ed piece printed in the *International New York Times* and found online on the *New York Times* webpage; the article was widely disseminated. Serhiy Zhadan was among the leaders of the pro-Maidan protests in Kharkiv, where he lives. One day, he and his fellow pro-Maidan protestors were stormed by pro-Russian demonstrators and commanded to kiss the Russian flag. When he refused, he was beaten, receiving a concussion. When Sally McGrane reported on the incident in a March 8, 2014 piece in *The New Yorker*, it allowed this Ukrainian intellectual an unprecedented chance to express his views in the West. These are only the most dramatic examples of the activity of the series' guests in this important period in Ukraine's history—a time when Ukrainian writers, like their fellow citizens, took to their craft for the sake of dignity.

* * *

The texts that make up this volume are varied and, like their authors, come from various periods of time in late-Soviet and post-Soviet Ukraine. As the Contemporary Ukrainian Literature Series has grown every year, each subsequent guest of the series has added another layer to its structure. The anthology begins with a fragment of the 2012 Andrey Kurkov novel *Lvovskaia gastrol Dzhimi Khendriksa* (Jimi Hendrix Live in Lviv). This novel depicts the hippie community in Lviv, Ukraine in the 1970s—a group whose existence and activity forms yet another popular myth, among many others, that circulate about that city today. Kurkov, who resides in Kyiv, wrote the novel while briefly living in Lviv after being invited by that city's mayor to write a book set there. Many of the characters in the novel were actual leaders of the Lviv hippie movement, and Lviv writer Yuri Vynnychuk makes a cameo in the story.

All of the Hrytsko Chubai poems included in the anthology were turned into songs that were written, performed, and recorded by Taras Chubai. The poems were written in the late 1960s, but were found only in the Ukrainian cultural underground until their 1990 publication in *Hovoryty, movchaty i hovoryty znovu* (To Speak, To Be Silent and to Speak Again). They vary in length and form—three are short poems, one is a fragment of a long poem, and one is a long poem in its entirety—but they have much in common. Three of the poems feature a woman who manages to go beyond the mundane into nature. Is it a search for existential meaning or is it just a private escape into a realm different than stifling reality? Either way, nature interacts mysteriously and unexpectedly with such endeavors. Chubai unfolds an intimate, secluded world whose powerful charms are not accessible to all and whose subtle revelations remain closely guarded secrets. The lone Oleh Lysheha poem that was presented at the Contemporary Ukrainian Literature Series is a lullaby that was sung by Taras Chubai. The melody that Chubai chose has a faint resemblance to George Gershwin's classic aria "Summertime." This was not accidental. There was a rumor circulating in the 1990s among Ukrainian artistic circles that Gershwin's song had been influenced by the Ukrainian folk lullaby *Oi khodyt son kolo vikon* (The Dream Passes by the Window). By referencing the Gershwin tune melodically in his own song, Chubai was playfully reconnecting it to its possible origin.

Many of Marjana Savka's poems found in this anthology were inspired by a trip she took to the United Sates in 2007. Jazz, Boston, and other exotic inspirations reverberate throughout her texts. She explores foreign locales with their strange tastes and scents, while "In This City" may have been inspired by the equally mysterious Lviv, where she lives. The anthology also includes several poems from Andriy Bondar's collection *Prymityvni formy vlasnosty* (Primitive Forms of Ownership, 2004). In this, his third collection of poetry, Bondar switched to writing entirely in free verse, composing poems characterized by irony, sarcasm, and a sharp wit. Some, such as "Genes", became crowd favorites when read on stage.

Most of Viktor Neborak's works in this anthology are from his 1990 collection *Litaiucha Holova* (The Flying Head), a publication that probably serves as the best example of the Bu-Ba-Bu literary trio's approach to literature in late- and post-Soviet Ukraine. Bu-Ba-Bu, an abbreviation for *burlesk-balahan-bufonada* (burlesque-bluster-buffoonery), and comprised of Neborak, Yuri Andrukhovych and Oleksandr Irvanets, applied a carnivalized approach to Ukrainian literature. Often accompanied by rock music, revelry, and images of sex, Bu-Ba-Bu were very popular during the first years of independence. They performed at many of the festivals of the time that celebrated both the demise of the Soviet Union and the new creative freedom. It was from those stages that the writers of Bu-Ba-Bu demonstrated their talents in performance and in engaging an audience. Neborak's selections from *The Flying Head* are wonderful illustrations of all of these elements of Bu-Ba-Bu and are now regarded as classics representative of that period of Ukrainian literature.

Neborak's fellow Bu-Ba-Bu member Yuri Andrukhovych stopped writing poetry in the late 1990s as he developed into one of Ukraine's premier prose writers. Although he did return to poetry in 2004 with the free verse collection *Pisni dlia mertvoho pivnia* (Songs for a Dead Rooster), prose, especially non-fiction, became his favourite genre. The essay "The Star Absinthe: Notes on a Bitter Anniversary" takes on perhaps the one subject for which Ukraine is best known today— Chernobyl. Passing through apocalyptic ruins there today, he sees ghosts from the Soviet past that had failed to foresee their oncoming demise. Andrukhovych, like Taras Prokhasko, resides in Ivano-Frankivsk and both writers, as well as other artists from the city, are part of a loose creative circle known as the *Stanislavskyi fenomen* (The Stanislav Phenomenon). Taras Prokhasko's contributions to the anthology are short prose works that are all of very similar length. That is because they constitute chapters (dated entries) from his book *FM Halychyna* (FM Galicia), which collects three-minute recitations the writer read live on the air for the Ivano-Frankivsk *Vezha* radio station, five days a week over the course of several months. In these brief stories, Prokhasko exudes his distinct mellow tone and his storytelling prowess. Extraordinary scenes of the writer's family's life are shared with the reader and fable-like lessons conclude many of these tales.

Both poetry and prose by Serhiy Zhadan can be found in the anthology. Zhadan's poetry portrays a post-industrial, globalized world where lonely souls search for affection and companionship. He utilizes fresh, unexpected metaphors that both infuse an aura of strangeness into his texts and simultaneously provide his reader with a sense of closeness and warmth. He also addresses this world in his prose, often injecting humor to depict an absurd post-Soviet existence. Zhadan's stories are filled with protagonists who are damaged and disoriented individuals placed into positions incompatible with their skills and personalities. As is the case with his poetry, his prose offers a search for camaraderie in a situation of dysfunction.

Like the poetry of the 1960s generation of Ukrainian poets, Ivan Malkovych's poetry is often invested with a driving passion to preserve the purity of the Ukrainian language. One of his most famous poems, "The Village Teacher's Lesson", treats that issue in a direct, yet delicate, manner. This poem, which is addressed to a child, is a wonderful example of Malkovych's remarkable ability to link children to the Ukrainian language in various captivating and masterful ways. His great success as a publisher of children's books is another example of that talent. As mentioned above, Vasyl Gabor has also enjoyed much success in the publishing field. One of his essays in this anthology tells the tale of how he came to launch his *Pryvatna kolektsiia* series of books. The other two stories are fictional accounts, one of which, "The High Water", tells the story of a family being swept away by a flood—eerily prophetic setting considering that Gabor's series event in New York was wiped out by Hurricane Sandy.

Yuri Vynnychuk's selections in the anthology are a mix of fragments from two novels and a few short stories. One of the short stories, "Pears à la Crêpe," is a humorous "day-after-the-party" tale in which the writer unleashes his ferocious wit. Similar in vein are the fragments included from *Spring Games in Autumn Gardens*, a novel in which Vynnychuk candidly shares stories of his own romantic exploits. The other selections reveal another of Vynnychuk's characteristic talents—creating fantastic fictional worlds. "A Flowerbed in the Kilim" and "Pea Soup," both written in 1988, are good examples of such writing, as is the fragment included from *Malva Landa*, a novel about a garbage dump that exists as its own world and is inhabited by myriad fanciful characters.

Oleksandr Boichenko is an essayist and columnist who is considered a "writer's writer" by his peers. His writing is erudite, cleverly constructed, and full of biting criticism and sharp humor. In "With Great Love," he takes his hometown Chernivtsi to task for an ever-growing bogusness that is in danger of destroying what is genuine in the city. In "The Lunch of a Man of Letters," he shares an experience he had in Poland, a country in which Boichenko has spent a considerable amount of time as a translator from Polish into Ukrainian. Finally, "In a State of Siege" finds the writer (and former professor of foreign literature) looking to Albert Camus during a critical stage of Ukraine's Euromaidan.

Sophia Andrukhovych's prose is rich in detail—people and objects are meticulously described. Her "An Out-of-tune Piano, An Accordion" is the story of a decaying old man holding on to the relationships and responsibilities in his life. She wraps this narrative in an eerie aura of lingering death, which creates a mood fitting to the theme.

The anthology concludes with a selection of Lyuba Yakimchuk's poems including those taken from the cycle "Apricots of the Donbas," in which she writes about the ubiquitous presence of coal in her native Donbas region. Yakimchuk imagines angelic roots for this coal, and finds it even in the fruits that grow there. Some of her poems address the war in her home region, the site of conflict between Russia and Ukraine. Yakimchuk focuses on form in her poems, actively experimenting with language, and breaking the Ukrainian language into syllables and sounds that echo the sounds of war.

* * *

The White Chalk of Days is the latest in a short but growing list of anthologies, single-author books, and journals that feature English-language translations of post-Soviet Ukrainian literature. The first anthology to do this was *From Three Worlds: New Writing from Ukraine*, a special issue of the journal *Glas* that was co-published by Zephyr Press in Massachusetts in 1996. The anthology begins with an excellent introduction by Solomea Pavlychko entitled "Facing the Freedom: The New Ukrainian Literature." Edited by Ed Hogan and guest editors Askold Melnyczuk, Michael M. Naydan, Mykola Riabchuk, and Oksana Zabuzhko, the anthology features poetry and prose by fifteen writers; mostly *visimdesiantnyky*, but also older writers such as Oleh Lysheha, Vasyl Holoborodko, and Valery Shevchuk. Twenty translators or co-translators were involved in that publication. Another anthology, *Two Lands New Visions: Stories from Canada and Ukraine,* published by Coteau Books in Regina, Saskatchewan, features two introductions, one by Solomea Pavlychko on the Ukrainian texts and one by Janice Kulyk Keefer on the Ukrainian-Canadian texts. The texts written by authors from Ukraine were co-translated by Marco Carynnyk and Marta Horban, and all come from post-Soviet Ukrainian writers. In 2000, the anthology *A Hundred Years of Youth: A Bilingual Anthology of 20th Century Ukrainian Poetry* was published in Lviv, Ukraine. This collection was compiled and edited by Olha Luchuk and Michael M. Naydan and included the work of forty-four translators or co-translators. Although it covers the entire 20th century, it includes many of the leading poets of post-Soviet Ukraine. The poetry of Serhiy Zhadan, the youngest writer in that anthology, closes out the book. Also published in Lviv, by Sribne Slovo Press in 2008, is the bilingual anthology of Ukrainian literature *In A Different Light.* Compiled and edited by Olha Luchuk with an introduction by Natalia Pylypiuk, this publication collects translations made by the translating duo Virlana Tkacz and Wanda Phipps. The anthology features mostly poetry, but also includes a translation of the 1911 Lesia Ukrainka play *Lisova Pisnia* (The Forest Song). Like *One Hundred Years of Youth,* the collection includes Ukrainian poetry from throughout the 20th century (and three poems from the 19th century, by Taras Shevchenko) and also features many writers who have been prominent in independent Ukraine. In fact, the texts found in that publication are those that were featured, over the years, in productions by the New York-based Yara Arts Group, directed by Tkacz. *Herstories: An Anthology of New Ukrainian Women Prose Writers*, compiled by

Michael M. Naydan and published by Glagoslav, features eighteen writers ranging from those who began writing in the 1950s and 1960s to those who have debuted books in the twenty-first century.

Books featuring one contemporary Ukrainian author in English translation were rare in the 1990s, but their publication has quickly picked up pace. Most of the early publications appeared in Canada. In the first years of Ukrainian independence, books were published in Toronto that featured the poetry of Kyiv School poets Vasyl Holoborodko (*Icarus with Butterfly Wings and Other Poems*, 1991) and Mykola Vorobiov (*Wild Dog Rose Moon*, 1992), both translated by Myrosia Stefaniuk. Oksana Zabuzhko's book *A Kingdom of Fallen Statues: Poems and Essays* was published in 1996, also in Toronto. The Canadian Institute of Ukrainian Studies Press published translations of novels by Yuri Andrukhovych (*Recreations*) and Yuri Izdryk (*Wozzek*) in 1999 and 2006, respectively. Both were translated by Marko Pavlyshyn. Two Andrukhovych novels were translated by Vitaly Chernetsky and published by Spuyten Duyvil— *The Moscoviad* (2009) and *Twelve Circles* (2015). Northwest University Press published Andrukhovych's novel *Perverzion* (2005), translated by Michael M. Naydan, as well as a collection of prose by Volodymyr Dibrova, *Peltse and Pentameron* (1996), translated by Halyna Hryn. Oksana Zabuzhko has had two books of prose published by Amazon. Hryn translated Zabuzhko's *Fieldwork in Ukrainian Sex* (2011), while Nina Shevchuk-Murray translated *The Museum of Abandoned Secrets* (2012). Over a dozen books by Andrey Kurkov are available in English translation, including books in his popular "Penguin" series, translated by George Bird. A bilingual edition of the poetry of Volodymyr Tsybulko, featuring translations by Yuri Tarnawsky, was published by Kalvariia in Lviv in 2001. Lately, Glagoslav has published prose by Maria Matios (*Hardly Ever Otherwise*, 2012, translated by Yury Tkacz), Yevhenia Kononenko (*A Russian Story*, 2013, translated by Patrick John Corness), Irene Rozdobutko (*The Lost Button*, 2012, translated by Michael M. Naydan) and Larysa Densyenko (*The Sarabande of Sarah's Band*, 2013, translated by Michael M. Naydan). Two of Serhiy Zhadan's novels, *Depeche Mode* (2014, translated by Myrolsav Shkandrij), and *Voroshilovgrad* (2016, translated by Reilly Costigan-Humes and Isaac

Wheeler), have recently appeared in English. Two more books by Zhadan, *Mesopotamia* (also translated by Reilly Costigan and Isaac Wheeler) and a volume of selected poetry (translated by Virlana Tkacz and Wanda Phipps), are forthcoming from Yale University Press.

Several journals, both print and online, have allowed English-language readers to get acquainted with contemporary Ukrainian literature from Ukraine. Between 2003 and 2007, the online *Poetry International Rotterdam* consistently presented Ukrainian poets in English translation. Thirteen poets, with a twenty-year age difference among them, represent contemporary Ukrainian literature in this forum. The site also provides links to interviews with, and articles about, the featured authors. In Fall 2010, *International Poetry Review* published a special issue guest-edited by Michael M. Naydan, who dedicated two-thirds of the journal to translations of Ukrainian poetry. This issue presents the post-glasnost poetry of twenty-two poets that was translated by eleven individuals. The journal *AGNI* has also often published English-language translations of Ukrainian literature. A 2005 issue of *World Literature Today* includes an essay by Michael M. Naydan on Bu-Ba-Bu and his translations of a selection of their writings. *Ukrainian Literature: A Journal of Translations* published four issues between 2004 and 2014. All of the issues are available online, and the first two issues also came out in print. This is the only existing journal dedicated fully to publishing English-language translations of Ukrainian literary works. Edited by Maxim Tarnawsky, the journal also features, among others, works by classics of Ukrainian literature such as Taras Shevchenko, Olha Kobylianska and Volodymyr Vynnychenko.

Other journals and books have also featured English-language translations of contemporary Ukrainian literature on occasion but I only mention those that have been most active in this endeavor. I am happy that the anthology *The White Chalk of Days* is the next to be included in this fine group.

* * *

Advances in science have undoubtedly made introducing people to the various cultures of the world ever easier. The possibilities of what can be presented about literature on the computer screen or smartphone are seemingly endless and exhilarating. Video conferences and recordings bring the voices and images of authors into homes and classrooms around the world. It is exciting to imagine the ways that the internet will allow my colleagues and me to connect Ukrainian literature with potential readers in the future. The online, multimedia, and interactive version of *The White Chalk of Days* that accompany this print publication is a great example of some of the ways that technology can help present literature beyond the printed page in an innovative and enticing fashion.

However, I am also happy that the anthology *The White Chalk of Days* is the result of an initiative that physically brought authors from Ukraine to the U.S. It is significant that this anthology commemorates meetings that these writers had with an audience that attended their events. These Ukrainian artists were present on the Mondays, Tuesdays and Thursdays of the Contemporary Ukrainian Literature Series, and were able to shed light on a country and a culture that is very much obscured in the West—a darkness that can lead to harmful misunderstandings. Recent events have shown once again that Ukraine is a country with an important geopolitical position in today's world. A better understanding of the country, and of the complex factors that make up its identity—a subject that is continually being probed by Ukraine's post-Soviet artists—can help determine how to better engage with it. The writings of the guests of the Contemporary Ukrainian Literature Series chronicle and comment on the key issues, thoughts and emotions that have filled the days of Ukraine's twenty-five years of independence. The writers' talents with words have helped to highlight and illustrate the subtleties of these issues. I am happy that we have an opportunity, with this volume, to collect, preserve, and share the white chalk of those series days. My hope is that its readers enjoy these well-crafted texts, find them to be intellectually challenging and personally engaging, and see how they are vibrant examples of the ways great art can help to absorb and approach the intricate and serious concerns of the world today.

A Note on Transliteration

In the body of the text, we use the conventional transliteration for names and locations. However, for the notes, bibliographic information, and terms that would be of importance to scholars, we use a simplified version of the Library of Congress system of transliteration, omitting ligatures for those Cyrillic characters that are rendered by more than a single Latin character. In addition, the Ukrainian soft sign "ь" has been omitted in the body of the text but is retained in the notes, where it is rendered with a prime. For example, Львів is transliterated as "Lviv" in the body of the text and as "L'viv" in a footnote.

ANDREY KURKOV

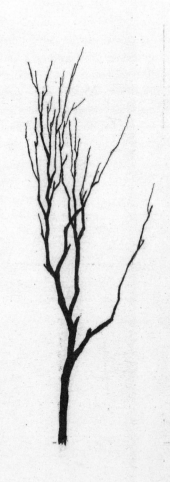

ANDREY KURKOV, born in 1961 near
St. Petersburg in the town of Budogoshch,
now lives in Kyiv. After graduating from
the Kyiv Foreign Languages Institute, he
worked for some time as a journalist, did
his military service as a prison warden at
Odesa, and then became a film cameraman,
writer of screenplays, and author of critically
acclaimed and popular novels—the first of
which he had to borrow money from friends

to self-publish and sell on the sidewalks of Kyiv. He has gone on to become one
of the most popular and critically acclaimed writers in Ukrainian history, and his
books have been translated into 25 languages.

Andrey Kurkov's events in the Contemporary Ukrainian Literature
Series, entitled *Ukrainian Literature and Ukrainian Politics: Which One is More
Dynamic?*, took place in January 2008.

From Jimi Hendrix Live in Lviv

After Alik had walked up to the closed gate of Lychakiv Cemetery,[1] about ten people stepped out from under a row of trees growing next to it. They came toward him leisurely, gathered around him, and pulled the key to the lock on the gate out of his pocket.

The key had already been slipped into the turning mechanism when the footsteps of a man hurrying pitter-pattered behind those who had gathered. Alik looked back and saw a nearly two-meter tall, slightly stooped-over giant. His long gray hair seemed to be saying: "I'm one of you."

"*Labas vakaras*!"[2] he uttered softly. "Sorry, I nearly was late!"

"Audrius?!" Alik indicated his surprise out loud, measuring the giant with his gaze from the crown of his head to his pointy shoes. "By train?"

"Yes, through Kyiv," he nodded.

Everyone clambered over toward Audrius to give him a hug.

"You've been away for a long time," Alik said, and turned toward the gate. He turned the key, and the steel shank of the padlock jumped out of its slotted hole.

They walked silently through the cemetery. After climbing onto a hill, they looked around. Alik waved his hand invitingly and led the rest behind him along a trail between graves and fences. They stopped at an iron cross that seemed to be intentionally hidden from separate gravesites behind the trunk of an old tree and two overgrown bushes. There was no fence here. The long-haired older company gathered around an unmarked grave. It was impossible to read either the first or last name of the deceased written on a rusty plate welded to the cross arm. One of the visitors squatted down in front of the cross, nuzzled his

---

1   A famous cemetery in L'viv that was established in 1787 and serves as the final resting place for many of the city's most prominent individuals.

2   "Good evening" in Lithuanian. (Translator's note)

knees onto the edge of the grave mound, and pulled a plastic bag out of his jacket pocket. He opened it, laid out a jar of white paint onto the grass, and a brush appeared in his hand.

His steady hand carefully outlined with white oil paint letters on the plate: "Jimi Hendrix 1942-1970."

In the windless silence, a branch snapped. It was somewhere nearby. Alik strained his ears. The crunch repeated. Under the feet of an approaching stranger, fallen leaves rustled plaintively.

"A guard?!" Alik thought.

Along the same route, circling around the graves and fences, a small man wearing a cap approached them. An ordinary stranger. The visitors at the grave dispassionately watched his approach. Curiosity is the realm of the young, and the gathered visitors were already over fifty.

"I beg your pardon," the uninvited guest uttered in a clear manner like a TV announcer, stopping at a polite distance from the group. "I've long wanted to... wanted to speak ...."

"Then speak." Alik calmly gave him permission.

"Don't you recognize me?" the man asked and took off his cap.

The face of the person who had come, despite the fact that it was night, was amply illuminated by the moon. A typical face, even though it was illuminated, that didn't reveal anything to Alik. An average face, billions of which the world has churned out: ears, nose, eyes, everything seemed according to a single GOST,[3] without flaws, without memorable or eye-catching highlights or defects.

Alik shook his head in the negative.

"Oh, come on," the voice of the guy with a buzz cut boomed with umbrage. "We used to be close. Not by your choice, of course. I'm KGB Captain Ryabtsev."

"Oy," tore out of Alik's lips, and he squinted, still staring into the face of his unexpected companion. "And what are you doing here, captain? You must be retired now?"

"Captain in reserve," Ryabtsev corrected Alik. "Though it's the same thing ... I wanted to apologize ... and say something."

---

3   The Soviet acronym for Government Standard.

"Well then, apologize!" Alik shrugged his shoulders. "Just make it quick. We're not gathered here to listen to you, of course," and he nodded toward the iron cross with a fresh white inscription.

The captain put on his cap and cleared his throat.

"In general terms, forgive me, guys! Both me and Mezentsev. I was just at his funeral ... bladder cancer ...."

"Do we have to listen to him?" Penzel inquired in an angry voice. He was a large long-haired and bearded man in a leather jacket, who looked more like a biker than a hippie.

"Well, we'll listen for a minute," Alik sighed. "Come on, captain, express yourself as concisely as possible! The guys are losing patience!"

"To keep it short ...." Ryabtsev began to speak in a quieter voice and less clearly. "First, I wanted to thank you for introducing me to Jimi Hendrix thirty-five years ago! He turned my life around. Thanks to him, I lost interest in my career. That's why I'm a captain, and not a colonel .... And that's why me and the boys in 1978 were able to get you a piece of his body, his hand. So Jimi would have his own little grave here in Lviv, so you'd have somewhere to commemorate the anniversary of his death!"

"What?!" Alik's eyes widened. "No way, it was guys from the Baltics who brought his hand, and they were helped by Lithuanian expats in the U.S.! Tell them, Audrius! You remember!"

"Yes," Audrius nodded. "I remember those guys. Jonas, Kęstutis, Ramūnas ...."

"Of course, they passed along the hand, and our people passed it on from the States." Captain Ryabtsev again uttered the words resolutely and clearly in military style, the way one conducts a briefing or gives a spoken order. "Moscow didn't know about it. It was me with the late Mezentsev here in Lviv who came up with a special operation in the States on the illegal partial exhumation of his body. Moscow funded it, but if they had learned the whole truth, I wouldn't be talking to you right now ...."

One of the people listening heavily sighed. The captain searched with his eyes for the one who had sighed and sustained a pause.

"I'm telling you this so you don't hold a grudge against us. We weren't stupid bulldogs. I can tell you Jimi Hendrix's biography right now year by year. I can recite the lyrics of his songs in the original. I can't sing, sorry about that! My parents didn't have money either for a piano or a guitar. As a child, I had only one musical instrument—a whistle! Am I glad I didn't become a policeman!"

"I remember you," Alik said thoughtfully. "If what you say is true, then we have to find a table, at which we all," he gestured toward the gathered crowd, "can sit. And we'll have a drink and reminisce in more detail."

"Everything I said is true," Captain Ryabtsev said. "There's no sense in deceiving you. I'm not on duty. It's been fifteen years since I've been in the service."

Alik looked down at his feet and remained silent. He turned his gaze at the cross with fresh white lettering.

"Jimi, can you hear?" he said, turning to the cross. "The authorities have put a wedge between our relationship with you again. But we're not going to reconsider our relationship with you. We haven't betrayed you, either before September 18, 1970 or after. And there hasn't been a year when we haven't gathered together here and freshened up your grave. Even when they really wanted to stop us!"

Somewhere nearby an ambulance rushed past. The siren gradually subsided.

"Well, guys?" Alik said, exhorting. "I'll begin!"

He pulled a blister pack with Phenobarbital out of his pocket, took a tablet out of it, sat down by the grave, lowered the white tablet onto the ground and, after waiting a moment, pressed it down with his index finger under the roots of the grass.

"Rest in peace," he whispered and rose up on his feet.

The captain took a step back as if he didn't want to get in the way. But he stood there motionless, observing the scene.

Bearded Penzel sat down at the grave. On his palm was a prepared tablet of the sleep medication. The ritual was repeated. Audrius was the next to sit on his haunches by the grave. He whispered something in Lithuanian. Then, with his index finger, he also pressed a white pill into the ground of the burial mound.

The sky darkened over Lychakiv Cemetery. A light rain began to drip on the not-yet-fallen leaves of the trees and shrubs. The leaves began to rustle and whisper, evoking the sensation of lurking danger.

Alik glanced up.

"Everything like a year ago," he said. "It's time ..."

They set off back toward the exit, descending down the hill, circling around the fences and graves, tombs and monuments.

Alik's eyes distinguished a large crucifix on a stone cross in the darkness. To Alik the face of the crucified Jesus Christ appeared to be momentarily happy.

After the gate had been locked shut, Captain Ryabtsev appeared right in front of Alik. The captain was a head shorter.

"Well, guys, should we look for a large table?" Alik asked, but without waiting for an answer, turned right and began to walk along the brick-lattice fence of the cemetery. The others followed him, with the captain trailing at the end.

Soon, the fence of the cemetery was left behind. On both sides of the road, the sleeping houses of Mechnikov Street now seemed gray. Alik suddenly felt a weakness in his legs. He was leading the way, showing the route to his old friends, those with whom he had been taken to the local police station in his youth. At the same time, he was thinking about the fact that he knew there was no particular large table ahead of them. And they really needed that table today. Back in the bad old days of the Soviets, even a small rectangular kitchen table, furnished with stools, seemed great. Those times and those tables are now in the "double" past: a different century and a different country. Now you wanted a full-featured chair—evidently your backside over the years began to require tenderness and comforts. But tenderness and comforts don't happen at every step.

"Maybe go to Hotel George?" My friend's warm breath filled my ear.

"Genyk's working there as a guard, he'll let us in ...."

Alik slowed his step and squinted his eyes at the guy who said that.

Right before our eyes the dark air began to stir, as if someone had cut loose a stream of cigarette smoke into it.

"The fog's setting in," said Captain Ryabtsev, who emerged to the right between Alik and the wall of the building. "It's a low-lying fog," he added in the voice of someone well-informed. "It'll inundate us today … It's better to stop."

Alik stopped. The others stopped too. In front of everyone who was standing under the 84-A Lychakiv Street house number sign, which was illuminated by a weak light bulb, the darkness filled up with the airborne milk of the fog.

Before his eyes, the sign with the name of the street and house number moved away somewhere and became invisible.

"Alik, I'm leaving," said the voice of Captain Ryabtsev. "Next time."

"Which time?" Alik asked.

"You haven't moved anywhere," the captain said amiably. "I know your address from the seventies. I'll drop by and tell you everything. Maybe even tomorrow."

The guys said goodbye and dissolved into the night fog. Just Audrius remained close by, nearly touching Alik's shoulder.

Translated by Michael M. Naydan
(with gratitude to Olha Tytarenko for her expert editorial suggestions)

HRYTSKO CHUBAI

HRYTSKO CHUBAI (1949-1982) was born in the Volyn region. A central figure of underground Ukrainian culture in Lviv in the late 1960s and the 1970s, he was harassed and repressed by Soviet authorities for most of his adult life. Chubai edited the *samvydav* (samizdat) journal *Skrynia* (The Chest, 1971), an apolitical call to non-conformity, for which the journal's contributors were supressed. His first collection of poetry, *Hovoryty, movchaty, i hovoryty znovu* (To Speak, To Be Silent, and to Speak Again) was published posthumously in 1990. A more complete collection of his work—*Plach Ieremiï: Poeziï* (Jeremiah's Cry: Poetry)—was published in 1998 followed by the definitive publication *P'iatyknyzhzhia* (Pentateuch) in 2013. Many of his poems were interpreted as songs by his son Taras, who, both as a solo musician and with his group Plach Ieremii (Jeremiah's Cry), greatly expanded access to his father's writings in post-Soviet Ukraine. A book of Hrytsko Chubai's children's poems, *Skoromovka ne dlia vovka* (Tongue Twisters Are Not for Wolves), was published in 2008.

Songs set to Hrytsko Chubai's poetry were sung by Taras Chubai at Contemporary Ukrainian Literature Series events entitled *Svitlo i Spovid: Light and Confession*, which took place in April 2008.

THE WOMAN

a sad woman who waits for no one
a sad woman who lies face-up
on a riverbank
who thinks about the river's water
flowing into the sea

she slowly becomes a river
so strangely splashing the sand
that even the fish jut their heads
out of the water to glance at this miracle
to glance at this white river
which has no bank

and where her hair flows is a mystery
and where her body flows is a mystery

Translated by Mark Andryczyk with Andrij Kudla Wynnyckyj

***

and ever so slowly looms
the darkest night on earth
and cloaks my only window

and cloaks with green eyes
cloaks the trampled red grass
which seemed like a wounded bird to me
a bird that just could not take flight

night cloaks the dried-out tree with its hands
and cloaks the scorching sun with its lips
and cloaks with deliberate words
a sad, sad melody

and now I see nothing but that night

I only hear how somewhere far-far away
beyond its eyes
beyond its arms
beyond its lips
suddenly the red grass purls its wings
and hovers above us for a while

Translated by Mark Andryczyk with Andrij Kudla Wynnyckyj

THE CORRIDOR WITH EYE-SIZED DOORS

I can't understand how the two of us entered this
corridor with eye-sized doors
I can't understand

maybe we were just chance tears
that ran into here by chance maybe it's so
and suddenly here we recalled that we're human

and there's no way back for us now there is no way
even if our tears run from here
through the doors it's here
that we'll remain

murmuring about us there beyond the walls
leaves of tongues on bodies' trees

it is the fortunate ones who can only see us
who cannot enter

it is the unfortunate ones who can only see us
who cannot enter

Translated by Mark Andryczyk

***

When your lips are but a half a breath away,
when your lips are but a half a step away—
your pupils are woven in wonderment,
your eyes are blue and wide.

You whisper something enchantingly and quietly,
and that whisper coolly cuts my silence!
And I forget now how to breathe
and how to walk, I too forget.

And your eyelids' black bird rises
and takes my confidence away.
A half-step still untaken,
a half-breath mired along the way.

Your pupils are woven in wonderment,
your eyes are blue and wide …
But your lips remain a half a breath away,
your lips remain a half a step away.

Translated by Mark Andryczyk

FROM MARIA

do not restrain her
for she remembers the cemetery and the towering rye
she remembers

she lights up the moon with her being

with her lips she lights up all sounds
over your cradle I see her weeping

over your coffin I see her laughing

only when you are falling asleep
is she happier than all of you
dancing out on the damp sand

and today
she leaves you
dancing
and utters no farewell

Translated by Mark Andryczyk with Andrij Kudla Wynnyckyj

LIGHT AND CONFESSION

For Halyna Chubai

1
a wooden cuckoo in an old clock
will sound the desertion of time

the apple tree will sever
from the heavy dew

You'll return from the well
with pails unfilled

2
I'll ask You in darkness
about when the snow fell
and an echo an abyss
will fill my every word

from a courtyard through a gate ajar
a light will step barefoot onto the trail
to leave us behind forever
but even in darkness it is clear
that You have a fleeting shadow

3
nowhere around
can You see a reflection
in which You are not
strange

find other still waters
in which to gaze at Yourself

leave behind a recording for me
a song about Your leaving

Your run begun in jest
escape now for real

4
run at midnight along the sandy beach
let the water there keep up with You till morning
in the form of a river bed

let the silvery bass carved out of the moon
run before You

lighting the water's way

5
I won't follow at Your heels
I'll shut my eyes like falling leaves

I will not see
when the tracks' leaves fall
from the time-worn branches of the paths

6
a mute cuckoo will sit across from me
with summer's hoarfrost on its beak

I'll let it sift through last year's
herbarium

which has been gathered
by the wind and by You

7

    the purest voices
    in long corridors
    recite prayers
    composed of numbers

here the hours' madonnas are dressing in white
there the hours' madonnas are hurrying off
to their clock's holy place
in order to light up by dawn
not candles below icons
but snow

8

from the window and from the pond
above the orchards and the tracks
all that flew sang
with the eyes of water

the sleds will have their hosanna
in the winter to come
and glorifying words
will arrive on their own

and now the hours' madonnas
have lighted the snow
leaving a trail behind them
only one

9

I'll run along it with a rifle
the rifle will turn into a cane

the tracks will lead into the high rye fields
the rye fields will slowly become smaller

and amongst the rye
a new year's tree
and me so little beside it

"But Daddy, don't three trees
make a forest?"

10
I don't know where
I don't know from where

a clock made of hay
its hands broken by the wind

the wheat stubble's name has been silenced by the snow
I want to forget You
the ploughed field's name has been silenced
I want to love You

11
the wind straightens out the crumpled grass
the grass straightens out and forgives us
of everything

bells ring in ant-sized
empty churches
signal the cleanest of confessions

12
and You atop the tall mountain

from which the sun is visible at midnight

starc at Yourself in a thin sheet of ice

13
You'll dream of clear water
return
fly in an airplane
to repeat the cuckoo's path
from when it first sang to when it became silent
look from up high into the empty nests
return before the light
before the birds fly south and before your voice
enters the house silently

Translated by Mark Andryczyk with Yaryna Yakubyak

OLEH LYSHEHA

OLEH LYSHEHA (1949-2014) was a poet, prose writer, translator, playwright, and sculptor born in in the town of Tysmenytsia, near Ivano-Frankivsk. He was expelled from his studies in English at Lviv University for his participation in the *samvydav* (samizdat) journal *Skrynia* (The Chest, 1971; edited by Hrytsko Chubai), and he was prohibited from publishing his poems until 1989. Lysheha served in the Soviet army in Buryatia. He

is the author of the poetry books *Velykyi mist* (The Large Bridge, 1989) and *Snihovi ta vohniu* (For the Snow and Fire, 2002), a book of selected poems also entitled *Velykyi mist* (2012), the prose collection *Druzhe Li Bo, brate Du Fu . . .* (Friend Li Po, Brother Tu Fu . . . , 2010), and is one of the authors in the anthology *Chetvero za stolom* (Four at the Table, 2004). The Ukrainian- and English-language publication *The Selected Poems of Oleh Lysheha* (1999), co-translated with James Brasfield, received the prestigious PEN Club Award for best book-length translation in 1999. Lysheha's poetry has also been translated into German, Dutch, Estonian, Croatian, Buryat, Polish, Russian, and Japanese. He translated English-language literature into Ukrainian (T.S. Eliot, Ezra Pound, D. H. Lawrence, Sylvia Plath, Mark Twain, Malcolm Lowry) and co-translated, with I. Zuiev, from Chinese (*Stories from Ancient China*, 1990). A book of his essays entitled *Stare zoloto* (Old Gold) was published posthumously in 2015, as was *Potsilunok Elly Fitsdzherald* (Ella Fitzgerald's Kiss), a collection of essays, translations, and poems that he himself compiled and edited.

An Oleh Lysheha poem set to music was sung by Taras Chubai at Contemporary Ukrainian Literature Series events entitled *Svitlo i Spovid: Light and Confession*, which took place in April 2008.

SONG 55

Sleep, my love, everything's dozing off,
after some bedtime milk from the river.
The alarm clock's face,
overgrown with dry reeds, is napping away.
Your cradle,
smiled good night
snowy-white,
now rocks in the wind,
hung from heaven on dreams.

I will weave your braids all through the night,
and lean over you, frost-covered, at morning,
ribbons bright and crimson.

Sleep my love,
in the house of reeds, a candle burns,
lit by me, the homeless one.
An ice floe above you, an ice floe below you.
Memories will thaw in its flame.

Translated by Mark Andryczyk with Andrij Kudla Wynnyckyj

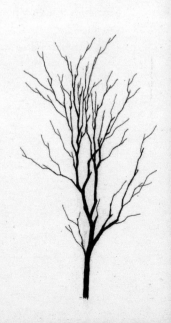

MARJANA SAVKA

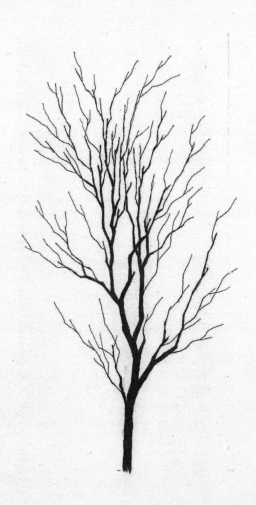

MARJANA SAVKA is a writer, publisher, community activist, and chief editor and co-founder of *Vydavnytstvo Staroho Leva* (Old Lion Publishing House). Born in the village of Kopychyntsi, Ternopil oblast, she currently lives and works in Lviv. Savka is author of the poetry collections *Oholeni rusla* (Naked River Beds, 1995), *Hirka mandrahora* (Bitter Mandragora, 2002), *Kokhannia i viina* (Love and War, 2002; together with Marianna
Kiianovska), *Kvity tsmynu* (Helychrysum Flowers, 2006), *Boston-dzhaz* (Boston-Jazz, 2008), *Tin ryby* (The Fish's Shadow, 2010), *Pora plodiv i kvitiv* (The Time of Fruits and Flowers, 2013), and the monograph *Ukraïnska emihratsiina presa u Chekhoslovatskii Respublitsi (20-30-ti rr. XX st.)* (The Ukrainian Emigre Press in the Czechoslovak Republic [1920s-1930s]). She has also written several children's books, including *Chy ie v babuïna babusia?* (Does the Baboon Have a Grandma?), *Lapy i khvosty* (Paws and Tails), *Korova kolorova* (The Colorful Cow), *Kazka pro Staroho Leva* (The Tale of the Old Lion), *Bosonizhky dlia stonizhky* (The Centipede's Sandals) and *Tykhi virshyky na zymu* (Quiet Little Winter Poems).

Savka's poems have appeared in several anthologies. She has received the Smoloskyp (1998) and International Vasyl Stus (2003) awards. Savka was also a participant in the international literature program at the William Joiner Center (Boston, 2007). She has twice been listed as one of the "100 Most Influential Women in Ukraine" by Focus magazine. Her poetry has been translated into English, including the publication *Eight Notes from the Blue Angel* (2007), as well as into Polish, Belarusian, Lithuanian, German and Portuguese.

Marjana Savka's events in the Contemporary Ukrainian Literature Series, entitled *Don't Take It Literally!*, took place in October 2008.

BOOKS WE'VE NEVER READ

Books we've never read are opening for us.
Towns shimmer in the night air.
Cold dawns. Warm autumn train stations.
The roads turn like pages. Eyes reddened by wind.

Nothing now but the bookmark of a horizon.
You hold my little finger tightly.
Dew prints ellipses on our path;
Later, coppery shadows line the grass.

The day's reborn. I yearn for longer books.
The Lord plays his music on the wind's viola.
We are as pure and strange as Sanskrit words.
We greet the sun, whom we resemble.

Translated by Askold Melnyczuk

From A SHORT HISTORY OF DANCE

Listen, child, to a wise old wolf:
in dance everything has its own meaning.
Here we've stopped—
we haven't touched,
yet our breath dances to one rhythm,
always stronger and faster.
We began with the foxtrot—but do you hear the pulse of tango?
For another minute, listen to the vibrations in silence.
Now, hold out your palm,
let's find the pressure points,
here our history begins:
from here rush rivers of mania,
a yellow heat flares
in the ruby eyes of longing,
firing a reckless tarantella in the veins.
If you dare, go all the way to the end on wire bridges
above the boiling lava.
I promise everything—
to dance with you,
to be with you in the dance,
be inside you on far alpine peaks,
in blinding green fields,
black chasms,
in the folios of Egyptian libraries,
on red silk scrolls in Chinese shops,
everywhere and anywhere,
amid the beads, amid the sands,
on cinnamon waves,
in the pleated water lilies,
on whispering sheets,
tangling time and space.
… later, though, don't pretend
you didn't want exactly this …

Translated by Askold Melnyczuk

EASTER JAZZ

Sonny Rollins
mad and bearded like god with his sax
wild as the wind
beating against the door
of Symphony hall
prophesizes that spring has a chance
to bloom
and the mindloose jazz
and my desire
and blood
blow recklessly through my veins
I go
I dance
I catch the syncopations,
Lord of Jazz,
Bless, please, this our Easter.

Translated by Askold Melnyczuk

FOR YANN TIERSEN[1]

If I were a director
I'd make a movie
about an eccentric composer
who writes music
only for his music box,
and cranks it up
only when the snows arrive in Paris
a tiny music box
with mechanical gears
and a silver key
which is turned and released
animating two lovers
miniscule as your pinky
who circle, holding hands
my childhood held no such toys
and if I'd known
such things existed
not just in stories
I would have regretted
not having such
a music box myself
maybe I wouldn't
even know about Paris
nevertheless, in dreams
doubtless I'd stumble
on the silver
music of snow-globes
along with all
those other things that *are*
I still can't name

Translated by Askold Melnyczuk

---

1   Yann Tiersen (b. 1970) is a French musician and composer. He wrote the film score
     for the popular film *Amélie* (2001).

BOSTON, APRIL 2007

this spring's a bolt of fear
    over lost time
sweat beads on black-
skinned branches
a scattering of powder
    a blue scarf blooms
I am beginning again
I step from behind the curtain
it's spring on both continents
    an a-rhythmic staccato
like a kid just jumping
    spreading her knees
I am discovering how easy it is
    to open yourself
so easy to swallow
    the jazz of these days

Translated by Askold Melnyczuk

BAGHDAD NIGHT

1

At the level of the heart—above and below,
Baghdad night, sweat and sand.
On the lips, eroded names.
Everywhere, silence and war.

At the level of the heart—the sign of the star,
Turning centuries to ash,
Gravestones, ancient scrolls.
Everywhere, silence and war.

At the level of the heart—the world intact.
Baghdad night. Sweat and sand.
And a wound without a bottom.
Baghdad silence—and war.

2

You who support the saffron-colored sky
Lord of the scarlet spirits of the desert,
of the script of filigreed knots
of the seeds of the pomegranate, blood on the dish,
You, the perfected, glare at fate
with an unwavering eye,
cleaning rusted old weapons, peering
through a sniper's scope from on high.

3

Bird-catcher, strange bird-catcher.
At the Baghdad bazaar, baklava.
The heart grows cold, and colder.
A bird fell, fell dead.
What do you want, my saffron beauty:
a dead bird, a gold wing?

Morning to morning, the bird-catcher
twines the thin threads of his traps.

4
You
I must forgive
then ask forgiveness
of myself
for asking forgiveness,
because I can do no other
than love you
but when I die
who will there be
to pray for you?

5
Oh mother my Quran,
cure me of death,
my breasts have opened
and the milk flows

Oh mother my madness,
Your warm withered arm
embittered with sweetness
the blood of your milk

Oh mother my Almighty,
whether I'm one of yours or not
save me from the night
carry me on your shoulders

And when you lose all strength,
lament with the gulls
as the warm Baghdad night
cools in my eyes

Translated by Askold Melnyczuk

IN THIS CITY

so few underground docks
in this city
and hardly any artesian wells
it's tough getting around
on such ragged oars
always late
knocking at the gate
hiding one's fishtail each morning
behind the doors of the ancient commode
turning the clock back to six
to keep you from asking inside your dream:
why are your braids so damp?
there's so little water in this city
it's rarer and rarer that the sailboats
ever return from their voyages
while in the hulls
of the coral shells on the table
ever since summer
only dry winds dwell

Translated by Askold Melnyczuk

WHO, MARLENE, WHO?

A spool of heart in a sarcophagus.
In the frames before that censored kiss
the corners of your lips rise wearily ... Marlene,
who was it wound your youth in reels,
splicing frames to taunt the hearts
of grieving fans long past their prime?
Snow heaps the unswept stairs
of the shuttered film club.
So who did *you* love then, Marlene?
Whose forehead singed your palm,
who tattooed the bomb shelter walls
with your perfect Aryan profile?
Do you hear, Lili Marlene,
this melody, this song of songs, this tolling sweetness
turning back the miles, years, departures
on the ragged movie screen, foxed with time,
your smile a palimpsest of eyes?
But who remembers who
Marlene loved?

Translated by Askold Melnyczuk

***

Some woman
fails to astonish you
Sylvia Plath
drapes the windows
and listens to the sea
to her it seems
this all is just an imitation
in truth it's not the sea
but just
sampled sounds
sound effects
no one tells the truth
to her
that there is no sea or wind
no fear
no pain
no rage
just simulations
of all feelings and hopes
other than one—
the hope of writing
to survive
either to die
or live

Translated by Michael M. Naydan

ORGANS OF SENSE

sight

with my memory's eyes
I thank you for all
that I can see
even with
eyes closed
even when you
block out the light
with your palm
the world a camera obscura
its concave mirror
reflecting
the little soul of a boy
barefoot and short-haired
and two oceans
full of heavens and clouds and eyes
of the same deep shade

hearing

you know it too
no silence
it does not exist
even in dreams
amid the most subtle vibrations
I always successfully
find
the pulse of pigeons' wings
and the rustling of trees
on a certain chestnut street
the dance of nighttime moths
encircling the fixture

the crackling of a page
which
is turned
by trembling fingers
the sighs of lovers
perhaps from the house just across
the whispers of an unknown language
in the telephone membrane
and the arrhythmia of hearts that
always fall out of rhythm
when attempting to beat in time

Translated by Mark Andryczyk

***

My beloved sun
smells of cinnamon,
evening beneath eyelashes
weaves a silver thread of dreams.
So unbelievably close,
so indivisibly home,
slouched in a time-worn armchair
with twilight at the window.

And outside the window
old cherries sway in the wind,
no more letters written
by our closest friends.
My beloved sun,
a pit lying on a saucer,
the taste of bitter cherry,
shadows thickening.

And a silver fish
flows into the net of night,
and silence lies
down on the stony bottom.
Once more alone in this world.
What else do we really need?
The cherry tastes bitter
with twilight at the window.

Translated by Mark Andryczyk

VIKTOR NEBORAK

VIKTOR NEBORAK is a poet, prose writer, literary critic and translator who lives and works in Lviv, Ukraine. He is a founding member of the Bu-Ba-Bu literary performance group, which gained enormous popularity in Ukraine during the late 1980s and the 1990s. The syllables of the group's name stand for *burlesk* (burlesque), *balahan* (bluster) and *bufonada* (buffoonery). At that time, Neborak's performances, and that of his Bu-Ba-Bu colleagues—Oleksandr Irvanets and Yuri Andrukhovych—were often at the center of mass gatherings  that celebrated the cult of the new, which were ushered in by the fall of the Soviet Union. Neborak's poems, particularly those from his ground-breaking collection *Litaiucha holova* (Flying Head), introduced a myriad of taboo topics into Ukrainian literature, including rock music and its imagery, which fed the suddenly free Ukrainian youth starved of Western symbols of freedom. His poems often feature an aspect of performance and, in fact, many of them served as texts to songs written and performed by the then-budding and now-legendary rock bands *Plach Ieremiï* (Jeremiah's Cry) and *Mertvyi Piven* (Dead Rooster).

Neborak is the author of ten collections of poetry. He has also authored the novel *Bazylevs*, a monograph analyzing Ivan Kotliarevskyi's *Eneida* (2001), and a monograph on Ivan Franko entitled *Ivan Franko: Vershyny i nyzyny* (Ivan Franko: Highs and Lows, 2016). Neborak has published four books collecting his essays and literary criticism. He currently works at the Academy of Sciences' Institute of Literature in Lviv.

Viktor Neborak's events in the Contemporary Ukrainian Literature Series, entitled *The Flying Head and Other Poems*, took place in January 2009.

From GENESIS OF THE FLYING HEAD

(a show in verse)

I. METRO FANTASY

Color is still not space you try anyway to hew through
this black night facets of light sparkle and a double
sits in the pane opposite the painted doll faded
a rapid line of movement saws his neck
an underground river dried up dinosaurs crammed together in the night
tusks bones broken mirrors voices of apparitions—
this is all the setting for a painting your neck is bleeding
and your head in the pane starts up and your head
through the thickness of a stone sea through a Dnipro River fish and
block of ice
through library stacks burning a path for itself
a minute flies solemnly to a carnival explosion
its lips move with exertion: I-am-a-fly-ing-head

III. METRO FANTASY

This is a body a murder a specter a hook
this clown takes skulls
cicero'anderthal shakespeare adolph chaplin
joseph skovoroda
peopleraven Christ 'umanobeast bug
boar-fanged-night
an even narrower tunnel draft
the black ash of faces
shadows painfully wail
a piercing moment

monsters mongrels ghosts
they howl through you in a flock

and they try on your body
like an old boot you squeak

V. METRO FANTASY. REFLECTIONS

He sees himself before himself
he sees himself transparent
he sees a transparent colored shadow
a moving shadow in the air
it utters words and all at once goes silent it utters words
he takes a step it comes to meet him
face to face eyes
overlap pass through
a mirror of glass thickens
raise my eyelids
THERE HE IS
my shadow in me

bat wings grow
fangs and fingers grow
shadow grows through the body
the stinger sniffs out blood

VIII. THE FLYING HEAD. A PRODUCTION SELF-PORTRAIT

... They assemble the flying head in my likeness

in a mine.
A brigade of vampires in overalls with banging carry

a nine-foot nose.
In the nostrils—fireworks, and wires, and paper streamers

two loud talkers gape downward.
My nose is massive, an ordinary one, a monumental

nose—not for assorted nobility!
Into the three-story carcass a control center

is lowered with a crane,

and the brain is transformed into levers, pedals, and a steering wheel.
My forehead—stuffed aluminum—welded by metal specialists,
                                        will be moved down a bit below—
there they fit my eyelids and connect
                                        the juice for the TV screen eyes.
A few more words about the mouth—some dozens of devils push
                                        the jaw-bone,
a snail-giant crawled into it, a boastful liar,
                                        his 'cellency's tongue,
the teeth stand guard, no fillings whatsoever,
                                        tongue like a sleeping bull,
two anacondas pressed together hide it,
                                        to keep from getting into trouble.
Here they fit the ears, glue on the skin,
                                        weld the joints—a roar and unbearable heat.
The engineer-lucifer-mime turns on the flame in the nozzles.
I'm in a space suit, I'm saying goodbye—let's get going—I crawl
                                        into my brain.

Half of hell runs up to watch the start.

X.

It rises up like a head,
the lopped-off head of a vagrant.
It utters words from the beyond
once, twice, and for the third time:
I AM THE FLYING HEAD!
The all-seeing flying Baroque
hangs above the city square's horde.
Blood clots drip in the air, the torn cut
casts a deep and heavy shadow:
I AM THE FLYING HEAD!
An invisible ax has entered the city,
headless bodies are thrown from the scaffold,
gawkers have drunken their fill of cheap blood,

and will scrape off the rusty smudge from the forehead
A GHOST—THE FLYING HEAD!
Are you devouring TV soaps?
You gaze at dragons behind the glass!
The wrecking ball from Fellini's *Orchestra*[1]
has come to life and breaks through your wall—
I AM THE FLYING HEAD!
Remember, you can't hide anywhere!
The square is coming to the hiding places, the square!
The feast rinses the dark cobblestones
and moves to the heavens of the Renaissance
A MASK—THE FLYING HEAD!
I AM THE FLYING HEAD!
I AM THE HE AD FLY
ING HE AD I
INGHEA I AM
AYO AY O

Translated by Michael M. Naydan

---

1   The wrecking ball that breaks through the walls in Fellini's *Orchestra Rehearsal* (1978). (Translator's note)

MONOLOGUE FROM A CANINE PRETEXT

The body of the deceased was found in a ditch
In the middle of a yard hung on
a hook and they buried him beyond the garden.

Fido's[2] hung himself—suicide dog!
Fido's soul'll be hounded from heaven.
They'll tell him: "You didn't croak the way you should have!"
Then they'll lift him up by the tail and …

Fido's hung himself on his chain at night.
The real nightly R movie[3]—rats viewers
sighing, wooing,
curling up, and lovemaking!

Fido's hung himself! Do you hear?—you!
Are you reading *Leaves of Grass*?
Márquez? Borges? Hesse? The *I Ching*? Ah?
Fido's hung himself! That's the change!

You're called a poet
        and he's—a dog.
A poem gnaws at you,
        a chain—at him.
Someday you'll be a pro poetaster,
But Fido chose not meat, but the spirit!

---

2   "Dzul'bars" in the original—a typical name for a Ukrainian dog. This particular
    canine poem has a real event as its basis. Viktor Neborak's dog Dzul'bars strangled
    himself on his chain. (Translator's note)
3   "Notsne" is in Polish in the original and refers to the practice in Soviet times of
    going to a friend's house in Western Ukraine, someone who had a strong antenna
    and could receive signals from Polish TV to watch films from the West—usually
    with a heavy dose of eroticism or horror. (Translator's note)

How much can you bark at the moon?
How long can you wait for your paycheck?
How much can you scrape your backsides?
Forever?
Till death!
What a schizophrenic profession—
to tend to chickens and goats
and send them off to be butchered?

The Constellation of the Dog
pierces through the earth and heavens!

Translated by Michael M. Naydan

A DRUM-TYMPANUM

(a sonnet uttered by the Flying Head)

—Paint a BABE naked BLUE
with lips the day looks BA
BU in dithyraMBs BU taBOO
put your teeth in BUBABU
    poetry grows from hunchBAck work
    with money BAttle in the hump
    and BUBABU will BE reBEllion
    your head's feeble from alphaBETs
        the BArd BUrsts with his labia lips
        what the world hisses with the theater screams
        you'll play a poem that's worth it all
        you'll end up in Paradise (or Paris)
            BU to death to eternity BU
            and BU and BA and BUBABU

Translated by Michael M. Naydan

SHE

(rap performance by the Kids of the Queenie)

PART 3

(crazy lady)
alone in the lilies you're walkin', walkin'
white tops wearin'
eyes on the trees you're
paintin', paintin'
you're the queen of
the cretins my crazy lady

when you walk into shrines
gates crumble behind 'em
with their claws they scratch
the cretins at a wedding

you're the queen of
the cretins
the temp's 90 degrees
don't lead me lordy
to her hot chamber

darkness falls from the soul
the wine's hot and thick
but the queenie's cryin'
over the snout of a pig

you're the queen of
the cretins
you're-a-wi-ld wi-ld qu eenie
we be dancin' in the wind
I CAN SAY-IT-A-GAIN

you're the queen of
the cretins
you're-a-wi-ld wi-ld qu e enie
we be dancin' in the wind
I CAN SAY-IT-A-GAIN

you're the queen of the cre ...

Translated by Michael M. Naydan

AN ITTY BITTY DITTY 'BOUT MR. BAZIO

(sung by Viktor Morozov[4])

he's the holy spirit of philistine walls
he's the eternal wandering jew eternal decay
he's the dust of starry lands
he's the bastard son of a king—mr. bazio

in london there's a queen
in paris gray chansonniers
in lviv bazio drinks beer
for our happiness and his—hey bazio!

he's an astrologer and culinarian
an alchemist of lovemaking and fights
with icarus on his shoulder
he mocks the guests—caw-w-w—herr bazio

princes and commoners come
saints and sluts too
who've lost their paths in life
they put their gold coins on the collection plate—devil bazio

he's paladin and mujahadeen
he's a medium number one
he's the midnight creak of ladders
he's an eternal mushroom he's the god of creatures

mr. bazio! hey bazio! herr bzaio! devil bazio!

---

4   Viktor (Victor) Morozov (b. 1950) is a well-known Ukrainian singer and transla-
     tor. He was a major figure (together with Hryts'ko Chubai, Oleh Lysheha, Mykola
     Riabchuk, and Yuri Vynnychuk, among others) of the Ukrainian underground,
     unofficial culture of the Soviet Union. He is a key contributor to Ukrainian
     culture in post-Soviet Ukraine.

a dream carries young girls in embraces
kings lead them to a throne
cutthroats drag them to underground hideaways
witches drive ravens for them to dream

and lads go to bazio
and sell their souls to him
they're drinking liquor and breaking dishes
and rush into the heavenly melee

all souls into the black folio
a millionaire a grad student
a terrorist dragged himself from the andes
plus a dentist and a grand-giant

come closer golden maidens
come closer sluts and saints
mr. bazio will show you the way
pour your gold coins onto the collection plate! …

orchestra play a march now
because the millionaire got married
because the grad student is in the lips of venuses
because the grand-giant died from love

mr. bazio … hey bazio … herr bazio … demon bazio …

Translated by Michael M. Naydan

FISH

cold-blooded beings
living out the rest of their days
in our bathtub
their long supple
bodies end in transparent tails
their eye bulging out
just as one day they'll bulge out
from their cut-off heads

they survive on the oxygen in the water
one wall separates them from my room
and another from the leaves, the mist
the streets, the buildings, the cars
among which I live

water and food are important to them
but maybe the source of light
is not important to them and it's all the same
if it comes from the sun or the socket

water and food are important to them
but maybe knowing that someday they will die
is not important to them nor knowing their family connections
to other long supple bodies

and so it goes

their bodies will quiver on the floor
sharp blows will flatten their brains
their innards will be carefully pulled out
and tossed into the trash with their scales
the living fish will be transformed into a poached or fried one
and its head will be thrown into the soup

this is not an isolated incident
all humanity is involved in this
fish processing plants run with blood
while some people write poems,
paint, or make films in protest,
most say "bon appétit"

and all this is observed by silent fish spirits

Translated by Virlana Tkacz and Wanda Phipps

SUPPER

There were seven of us
at one table
in an empty *varenyky* restaurant

the leaves drifted down in the mist

there were seven of us
quiet and talkative ones
friends and travelers who happened by
the living and the deceased

everyone was in his own time frame
everyone had his own window on the world
everyone had his own attitude
toward food

a student artist
a graduating artist who was getting ready for the army
a surreal artist with really long
hair
the drummer in a rock band with a painted brow
the keyboardist in this group
me
and a girl that I fancy

everyone sat in front of his plate
and occasionally expressed some kind of a thought

Andrii made it known that it was time to have a smoke
Petro counted off the days to his army service
Dem ate *varenyky*
Henri roared with laughter
Yurko criticized the *varenyky*

I defended them and glanced at the girl
that I fancy
she scrutinized each of us

her hair was golden
her eyes were the color of night
I would kiss her on her strawberry lips
I would have fallen for her
were it not for the cheese *varenyky*

Translated by Jars Balan

* * *

Green sounds echo
like a stream of blood
they flow
touch and vibrate
they're sensed by lovers

the spell of the green melody
stirs in their hearts

a flood of sounds
fills the grasses the trees
press your palm against the tree bark
leaves burst out along its branches

and you descend into "the Nectar bar"[5]
two meters beneath the cobblestones
amid the roots
and blue cascading water
to Italian songs
and emeralds frozen over

Translated by Mark Andryczyk with Yaryna Yakubyak

---

5   *Nektar* (Nectar) was the name of a bar frequented by members of L'viv's bohemian, artistic circles in the late 1980s/early 1990s.

THE WRITER

the day before Ivan Kupalo[6]
in two thousand and six
smack in the middle of the day
in Bakhmach
I saw Volodymyr Kashka
in the yard behind his Khrushchev-era apartment building

we showed up out of the blue
intruded on his space slid
into his alcohol-drenched gaze
in a shiny limousine

not a single wrinkle on Kashka's face
revealed his sense of surprise

he stood singularly
across from us the newly arrived

suddenly
he began to speak

he laid out the ragged map
of his life before us

every word was
like a child beaten by his father

every word was
like a sob

Translated by Mark Andryczyk

---

6   Kupalo is an ancient pagan celebration adapted by Christianity as the feast day of
    St. John the Baptist—it takes place annually in early July. Having been Sovietized for
    propaganda purposes in the past, it is experiencing a revival in post-Soviet Ukraine.
    Its elaborate ritual features the lighting of ceremonial fires. The Kupalo festival tradi-
    tionally provides young men and women with an opportunity for courtship.

THE POET

In order for
Oleh Lysheha to be able to sing
Song 212
About "superstars
overrun with reeds"
in downtown Lviv—

the Potockis built a palace
the soviets nationalized it
independent Ukraine
allowed free verse to exist
Virlana Tkacz met Wanda Phipps
and forged the Yara Arts Group
the Sribne Slovo publishing house was formed
Olha Luchuk committed herself to preparing
the anthology In a Different Light
the New York branch of the Shevchenko Scientific Society
voted to partially fund this publication
representatives of the Ukrainian diaspora
gathered in Lviv
for one of their congresses Virlana
flew in from Kyrgyzstan and Wanda
from New York for the presentation
which the organizing committee planned for
June 20, 2008 at 9:30 AM
in the Hall of Mirrors
of the Potocki Palace

and Oleh Lysheha
showed up late
(for the start for the very start)
and fortunately he was the last one
scheduled to appear

Translated by Mark Andryczyk

ANDRIY BONDAR

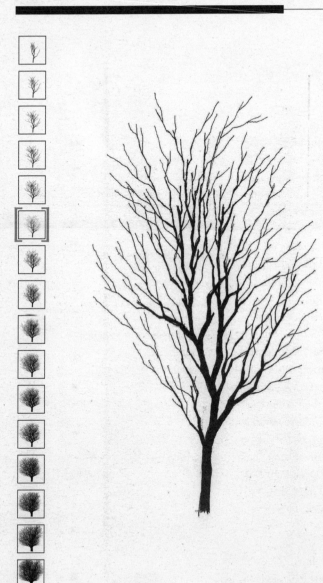

ANDRIY BONDAR is a poet and translator.
He was born in 1974 in Kamianets-Podilskyi,
Ukraine. Bondar studied history and literary
theory at the National University of Kyiv-
Mohyla Academy. In 1998, he published
his first collection of poems, *Vesinnia ieres*
(Spring Heresy), followed by *Istyna i med*
(Truth and Honey, 2001), *Prymityvni formy
vlasnosti* (Primitive Forms of Ownership,
2004), and *Pisni Pisni* (Lenten Songs, 2014). Bondar has also published the
collections of short stories *Morkvianyi lid* (Carrot Ice, 2012) and *I tym, shcho
v hrobakh* (And for Those in the Graves, 2016). He has authored numerous
stories, essays, and articles for various magazines. He is well-known in Ukraine
as a translator from Polish and English into Ukrainian. From January to April
of 2014, Bondar was an editor of the multilingual Facebook community
Eurolution.Doc (Ukraine on Maidan). Among the many works that Bondar
has translated from English into Ukrainian are: Ed Stafford, *Walking the
Amazon* (2012), Tom Feiling, *Short Walks from Bogota: Journeys in the New
Colombia* (2013), Robin Dunbar, *The Science of Love and Betrayal* (2013),
Edyta Bojanowska, *Nikolai Gogol: Between Ukrainian and Russian Nationalism*
(2013), Peter Pomerantsev, *Nothing Is True And Everything Is Possible* (2015),
Michael Spence, *The Next Convergence. The Future of Economic Growth in a
Multispeed World* (forthcoming), Anthony Pagden, *Worlds at War* (forthcoming),
and Robert D. Kaplan, *Eastward to Tartary* (forthcoming).

Bondar's events in the Contemporary Ukrainian Literature Series, entitled
Jogging, took place in April 2009.

GENES

I have very good genes
my great-great-grandfather lived to be 119 and died with dignity
simply walked into his house lay down and died
having said before this "well now I will die" and my granny and his
   granddaughter
(when I hear this story for the umpteenth time I can't stop laughing)
even calmed him down "no grandpa it's still far too early"

perhaps my granny isn't telling the truth
and perhaps she's telling the truth but not the whole truth
after all I can't dare say she is lying you can't say that about your elders
but sometimes it seems to me granny embellishes things just a bit
119 years is too much even for the early 20th century
but who knows? no one counted those peasants anyway
nor did anyone issue them any documents

but all the same, I have fantastic genes
whatever you say
I have all the chances of making it to eighty and if gerontology
will advance in its scholarly pursuits and they invent
some new pills from old age then one can live on
even to ninety

my present lifestyle and the way I test my health
is an altogether different question
how we all fuck up and shit over our health
inhale tobacco smoke drink chlorinated water
keep sleepless nights get up at noon suffer from stress
wives betray us we betray our wives
every single day we die from jealousy
shepherd our property hold on to our wallets on the bus
sit in front of computers for hours

on the one hand, ads call us to healthy living
to healthy sex and cheer us up in various ways
on the other, it's so hard to put on a condom
already at 29 it's so hard to put on a condom
it would be easier to put it on a foot no I am not saying that I have erec-
   tion problems
few people have erection problems at 29
but if I keep my laptop on top of my balls for another month
no spanish fly yohimbe or even viagra would save me

but I can't do otherwise
I will continue keeping my laptop on top of my balls and
writing my hopeless verse which people increasingly often call stories
one aging lady, a sister of a slovene poet
who has been waiting in line for the nobel prize for several years now
said precisely this, "and why do you call THIS poetry?"

no I wanted to answer her don't you worry
I am not going to compete with your brother
I am still too young for the nobel prize
I've a laptop on top of my balls and besides
I am not personally acquainted with john ashbery
and don't have english translations
so stay cool old lady don't you worry about your brother

I will go on keeping my laptop on top of my balls because
I can't do otherwise it just doesn't work out
if you like, call this stuff stories or call it dogshit
I can't do otherwise

I can no longer let myself write in metaphors
play with the tradition and write about snails
perhaps you are right and poetry died inside me
(good God a metaphor again) and I am no poet any more
even less a poet of culture or a poet of nature

I'm a poet who keeps his laptop on top of his balls
simply call me thus,
"Andriy Bondar, a poet who keeps his laptop on top of his balls"

you can't pay me a better compliment

should I explain to you what a laptop is?

Translated by Vitaly Chernetsky

SLAVIC GODS

slavic gods play dominoes
on the battered tables of their lost homeland
they are destined to eternally lay down the tiles
separate wheat from chaff
turn water into wine and wine into vinegar

slavic gods breathing their last breaths
are comfortably aware of their inability
to deal with today's climate
they remember the good old days before Christ
when sausage was cheap, yogurt cost 11 cents
televisions could be had on credit and there was total confidence
in the days to come

slavic gods quickly lose their tempers
when someone infringes
on their remaining privileges:
memories of questionable victories
subjugation of women and the humiliation of their men
lines for public toilets mineral water for hangovers

slavic gods leave their fingerprints
on tonsils they pull from mouths
gold crowns with bits of food, splinters of sunken ships
hopes for a better life memories of losses
fragments of military marches

slavic gods forget about
their unrelenting atheism only in dreams
and start to believe in god's greater plan
the influence of sun spots and social justice
as they quietly die of happiness

Translated by Virlana Tkacz and Wanda Phipps

THE MEN OF MY COUNTRY

the men of my country
give up their seats on the subway
to the handicapped the aged
and to the passengers with children
but mostly they go on sitting
since these categories of citizens
have a pronounced tendency to die out
or travel by subway less and less often

the men of my country
they are saints under a heel
with trained insect jaws
with which they gnaw their way
to deserved fatherhood
and later having untied their hands
savor children's flesh
using proscribed methods
of raising the younger generation

the men of my country
are not mutants or perverts
they are products of secondary processing
of amino acids
this is all that remains of the nation
which loves and honors its heroes
youths so roly-poly or with pit bull jaws
their love for motherhood
has outgrown all discernible limits
and become a signature style

the men of my country
wonderful specimens for an entomologist
for they are fragile like exotic butterflies

pinned to a piece of cardboard
they acknowledge the value
of every move every sound
for life is an unending crime
that has no justification

the men of my country
blow their noses simply into their hands
for the hand is the most useful organ
for such an important deed
they usually don't have any other
important deeds to consider

the men of my country
make no effort
efforts ruin the liver
and their mouths smell bad
and have they really been born
to exert efforts

the men of my country
prematurely descend into the grave
and become weightless angels
an ideal raw material
for metaphysical speculations
a superfluous argument in favor of the existence
of god or what's his name

Translated by Vitaly Chernetsky

JUST DON'T PUSH ME AWAY

behind my wall lives a modern belarusian sculptor
every day he drinks half a bottle of vodka
and still does not look like an alcoholic
andriy—his name is andriy too—
is a very spiritual person no joke
what jokes can there be if you have to drink half a bottle of vodka daily
and not be an alcoholic at the same time
what jokes can there be?

he goes to bed very early and wakes up very early and thus
our communication is limited to three evening hours
but this is fully sufficient
to open up our souls to each other
and why should we be ashamed of our souls?
what do we have to open to each other
if not our souls?

any other conversation with him turns into a mockery
sometimes it seems to me that compared to him I look
incurably soulless
I am simply a soullessness champion
compared to him

he is simple, too simple in his daily life
far simpler than I
than any of my acquaintances
he goes to his studio in the morning leaving behind
the smell of simple eggs fried in simple lard
it is a joy for me to wake up and sense this simple smell
of the modern belarusian sculptor andriy

he is even talented in some otherworldly way

"grab a power tool and pound away" he jokes and laughs at his own
joke
he works far more than I—from eight to five
and then comes home and drinks
and wonders why I don't drink and starts opening to me
his soul
and then goes to sleep
just simply goes to sleep with an open soul

every night I'm scared of his sleepy screams
I think this is his open soul screaming
when in its sleep it overcomes the resistance of the material
pours wax into forms, tones the bronze, creates the patina

sometimes I start fantasizing
that he is my husband and I'm his wife
we sleep in separate rooms because
he is afraid of scaring me with his open soul

every night I wait for him to come back from the studio
all exhausted and then open his bottle of vodka
and I will give him something tasty to eat
say mashed potatoes with milk and butter

and we'll make hot tea for ourselves
and he will again start opening his soul to me
grumble at modern art and ask for forgiveness for
disturbing me

and I always want to calm him down and I start
calming him down—no, what are you saying
don't even think this—don't even think
lean on me, don't push away, just don't push me away

Translated by Vitaly Chernetsky

ROBBIE WILLIAMS

"why are they all looking at me?
could they know that I am Ukrainian" I always wonder
as I enter another bar
"could it be so obvious could it could it be so
could it be so obvious that I am Ukrainian"

I take off my jacket (an imported one—German, I believe, but no one
      wears them here)
I leave on my jeans purchased here this year
I leave on my sweater manufactured in the country of Peru
a sweater—made of fine alpaca wool
it's of high quality and comfortable but no one wears them here
I leave on my American glasses
what else?
the shoes are somewhat sporty—they were in fashion four years ago

my look is hopeless
or maybe it just seems that way to me?
my mood wavers between fervent patriotism and punching someone in
the face
but that would blow my cover

"only Ukrainians can just punch someone in the face like that"
they suppose and they do have a point there
"only Ukrainians can sing so beautifully"
they suppose and they do have a point there
("ok, no singing today"—I decide)
"only Ukrainians can undress you with their eyes like that"
they suppose and they're not mistaken
"only Ukrainians could slaughter so many of us
in such a short period of time"
they suppose and they're not mistaken

in such a short period of time only Ukrainians could

I've got half an hour
to fulfill my historic mission

what can I accomplish in a half-hour's time over a pint of beer?

analyze the events of today
just another day for a Ukrainian in Poland
and come to a self-satisfying conclusion:

"they simply like me for who I am"

and I return the favor by buying another beer

and Robbie Williams for the tenth time today tells me what it is he needs
from life:

"I just wanna feel real love" Robbie Williams sings

he and I need the same thing

today I won't punch anyone in the face—
I take a step towards Ukrainian-Polish reconciliation
and I smile like no one here can

they can clearly see my teeth—a row of healthy white Ukrainian teeth
no one has teeth like that here

Translated by Mark Andryczyk

ST. NICK NO. 628[1]

he gave me the worst seat
that choice third-class lower seat by the wall in the last train car
by the toilet
which at least promised an interesting voyage
"seats are designated by the conductor" and there's nothing you can do
    about it

(one cannot choose one's fatherland, sons do not answer for the sins of
    their fathers
seats are designated by the conductor—
three entrenched truths everyone here is aware of)

he distributed dirty sheets but did not offer tea or a blanket
who would need a blanket in the third-class car?
it's generally filled with those who don't typically require a blanket
or tea for that matter
tea is offered in the second-class car
while coffee—that's for the bourgeois in first-class

he would close up the bathroom 10 minutes before every
minor station stop
humming "chervona ruta[2]" as he closed it
I could hear this clearly because I was closest to it

he didn't have a beard although it would have perfectly suited his
faded blue shirt and its
absolutely ambiguous insignia—
hammers weaved together in ecstasy? monkey wrenches?

1　Train No. 628 of the Ukrainian Railways network travels from Chernivtsi, the larg-
　est city in southwestern Ukraine's Bukovyna region, a region that borders Romania
　and Moldova, to Kyiv.
2　"Chervona Ruta" (The Red Rue) is an immensely popular Ukrainian song written
　by Volodymyr Ivasiuk (1949–1979). Ivasiuk hailed from the Bukovyna region.

two hammers in their eternal anticipation of a sickle?
he could be a railway army general
because between khmelnytsky and koziatyn[3] with an authoritative tone
he asked not to wake him
"I'm only human, I'm needin' some shut eye too,"
said this son of bukovyna
and who would have had the guts to wake him
between khmelnytsky and koziatyn?

he knew he was in control of the situation one hundred percent
he masterfully manipulated the fates of 54 passengers
I determined that maybe it wouldn't be so bad
if a railway employee became the president of ukraine
at least this would guarantee displacement
from point A to point B

if only for 15 hours to be in power
if only for 15 hours to be the leader of a volatile social group
of salesmen, conventioneers, students
gypsies, hutsuls,[4] romanians (which are still referred to as
moldavians in our land for some reason) pregnant girls and perpetually
traveling old ladies
in flowered kerchiefs (where are they constantly traveling to?
who awaits them? who's needin' their gifts
from plaid chinese bags?)

he awoke everyone 40 minutes before the city limits
so that 54 representatives of a volatile social group
could hastily tend to their basic bodily needs
before arrival in Kyiv

---

3   Khmelnyts'kyi and Koziatyn are Ukrainian cities that are railway stops for several
    railway lines in Ukraine.
4   Hutsuls are an ethnic group of Ukrainian highlanders that inhabit the Carpathian
    Mountains in Western Ukraine. Hutsuls are known for their elaborate dress, songs,
    dances, legends, and rituals.

thus each person was allotted about 40 seconds
he could have donned a hospital attendant's uniform
and recorded toilet-side the personal time of each passenger
you never know what to expect with Christmas approaching!

he devised a special method to deal with me

"son," he said in a half-whisper, "son, get up,
St. Nick has already left you gifts under your pillow"

he said ostensibly in jest
never imagining that I'd remember these words
for the rest of my life

Translated by Mark Andryczyk

THE ROMAN ALPHABET

I've long had
the urge
to write at least one poem
using the roman alphabet

one of my friends thinks
that if we switch to the roman alphabet
our people will steal less
and immediately
our messy byzantinisms
our obnoxious sovietisms our endless ugro-finnicisms
(sorry ugrics, sorry finns)
will disappear and something will snap in our heads
—and "voila!" we are part of europe

and another of my friends feels
that if we switch to the roman alphabet
we will automatically be better understood
by western slavs
all kinds of poles and czechs
(and even germans will suddenly respect us)
and even if they don't actually understand us any better
at least it might appear
that they could understand us better

and another of my friends feels
that we should start switching to the roman alphabet
gradually starting from Western Ukraine
where the ground, that is the soil, that is the people
are better prepared for this
since they travel to italy and portugal to work
and know europe not only second hand
but from their own experiences
doing the hardest work, filled with deepest envy, facing sheer ingratitude

and Mykola Riabchuk[5] who writes essays on politics
for whom I have the greatest respect
(notice I did not capitalize italy or portugal, but I capitalize his name)
feels that in order for ukraine to survive between east and west
it must shrink to digestible dimensions
that is to the 6 regions west of the river zbruch
I argued with him for a long time
trying to justify why vinnytsky, zhytomyrsky
and my own native khmelnytsky regions should be added to the list
but you know how smart Mykola Riabchuk is
once he thinks of something, that's that

only bukovyna[6] will find this convenient
it will automatically switch to the roman alphabet
when it becomes a part of greater romania
or even if it only joins little moldova
it will be forced to switch to the roman alphabet

if every living ukrainian poet
writes one poem in the roman alphabet
it will be possible to make an anthology
of contemporary ukrainian poetry written in the roman alphabet
what a pity that Ivan Malkovych won't be able to write a poem
about the crescent moon of the letter —
and the slender candle of the letter —

Translated by Virlana Tkacz and Wanda Phipps

---

5   Mykola Riabchuk (b. 1953) is a Ukrainian public intellectual, journalist and literary
    critic. He was active in unofficial Ukrainian culture during the Soviet years and an
    instrumental figure in the development of post-Soviet Ukrainian culture.

6   For more on Bukovyna, see Note 1.

JOGGING

I couldn't come back to my senses for quite some time
having gotten an e-mail from berlin from a friend of mine, olaf

in it besides the mandatory attributes that
are usually limited to ritual questions
about news, health, and creative plans
(as if one can plan anything about this creativity)
as it were in passing totally in the german style without any pathos but
with a very tragic feeling within just a few sentences
he said approximately this:

"yesterday I started avoiding meetings with my neighbor
we have lived side by side for twenty years already—we are the same age
and every morning
we go jogging together in a nearby park
he always seemed
a little strange to me when the chornobyl explosion happened
he started wallpapering his place with old newspapers so that
God forbid any radiation didn't penetrate his apartment and yesterday at
the landing I met his wife who told me he had leukemia
the final stage incurable, that this was the end
and I'm now afraid to look him in the eye and you know he
is such a nice person it was so good to jog with him in the morning ..."

I wanted somehow to calm olaf down immediately
talk him out of it say something like "don't take it to heart, this is fate
    after all
you'll find yourself another neighbor for morning jogs and if
you don't find a neighbor, get yourself an irish setter
you know how much they like to run? this is so much better than
with a person and besides, dogs don't get cancer" but

I don't even know why but I didn't do it
suddenly it all seemed far too literary to me
I thought this could have been a nice plot-starting point
for a novel by kundera
who loves to depict human tragedy masterfully and here all the ingredients
are ready: berlin shortly before the unification, the weird neighbor,
     twenty years
of jogging together, newspapers on the walls like a chronicle of historic
     events
that have changed the face of europe, then cancer, and you see
he doesn't know how to look him in the eye

I wrote him something completely neutral
something like "hang in there, after all you cannot help him with any-
     thing now, and you
still have to live and live, don't think bad thoughts, don't think
about cancer"

and then a completely heretical thought came into my head
I thought
that for the past ten years I've been living less than 100 km
away from chornobyl—I live here and walk down these granite and
     marble
streets and get choice portions of radiation
I am nearsighted—recently they found I have hepatitis
just as a carrier I'm not sick with it but still I have a muffled
form of gastritis which reminds me of itself every now and then I've
     been having
warts now for 15 years they don't bother me much but still they don't
     disappear
just like all the chornobyl children I have thyroid gland problems
sometimes I get a prickling pain in my heart and I'm not yet thirty
but I know for sure I won't come down with cancer

I am simply convinced that I definitely won't come down with cancer

I will live long oh I will live so long
I won't buy newspapers won't jog in the morning won't read kundera
won't walk around the city with a geiger counter won't go have a physical
I won't submit a declaration won't quit the party
won't join a party won't take blood tests won't kill won't steal

I won't leave my homeland I will climb deeply so deeply inside my
Homeland

and fall asleep

Translated by Vitaly Chernetsky

YURI ANDRUKHOVYCH

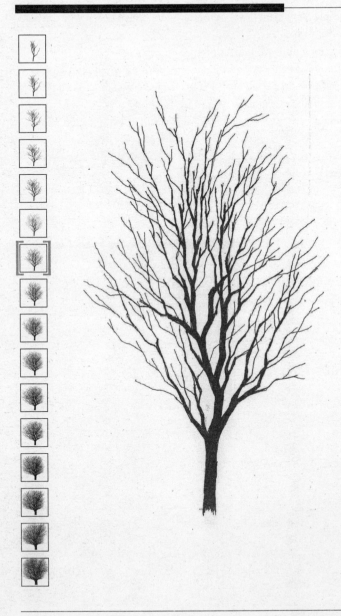

YURI ANDRUKHOVYCH was born in 1960 in Ivano-Frankivsk, Ukraine. In 1985, together with Viktor Neborak and Oleksandr Irvanets, he founded the popular literary performance group *Bu-Ba-Bu* (Burlesque-Bluster-Buffoonery). Andrukhovych has published four poetry books: *Nebo i ploshchi* (Sky and Squares, 1985), *Seredmistia* (Downtown, 1989), *Ekzotychni ptakhy i roslyny* (Exotic Birds and Plants, 1991; new editions 1997 and 2002), and *Pisni dlia mertvoho pivnia* (Songs for a Dead Rooster, 2004).

Andrukhovych's novels *Rekreatsii* (Recreations, 1992), *Moskoviada* (The Moscoviad, 1993), *Perverziia* (Perverzion, 1996), *Dvanadtsiat obruchiv* (Twelve Circles, 2003), and *Taiemnytsia* (Mystery, 2007) have had a great impact on readers in Ukraine. His book *Leksykon intymnykh mist* (Lexicon of Intimate Cities, 2011) is an experimental work of fiction structured as a cycle of stories set in different cities, arranged in alphabetical order, and his most recent book, *Tut pokhovanyi Fantomas* (Fantomas Was Buried Here, 2015), is a collection of prose miniatures. Andrukhovych also writes literary essays, which have been collected in *Dezoriientatsiia na mistsevosti* (Disorientation on Location, 1999) and *Dyiavol khovaietsia v syri* (The Devil Is in the Cheese, 2006). Together with the Polish writer Andrzej Stasiuk, he co-authored *Moia Ievropa* (My Europe, 2000 and 2001).

Yuri Andrukhovych's books have been translated and published in Poland, Germany, Canada, the U.S., Hungary, Finland, Russia, Serbia, Italy, Slovakia, Spain, Switzerland, France, the Czech Republic, Croatia, Romania, Bulgaria, and Lithuania.

Andrukhovych is the winner of five prestigious international literary awards: the Herder Prize (Alfred Toepfer Stiftung, Hamburg, 2001); the Erich-Maria Remarque Peace Prize (Osnabrück, 2005); the Leipzig Book Prize for European Understanding (2006); the Angelus Central European Literary Award (Wroclaw, 2006); and the Hannah Arendt Prize for Political Thought (Bremen, 2014). In 2016, he was awarded the Goethe Medal by the German government.

English-language translations of Andrukhovych's novels have been published as *Recreations* (1998), *The Moscoviad* (2008), *Perverzion* (2005), and *Twelve Circles* (2015). A selection of his essays in English translation, entitled *My Final Territory*, was published by the University of Toronto Press in 2018.

Yuri Andrukhovych's events in the Contemporary Ukrainian Literature Series, entitled *Werwolf Sutra*, took place in October 2009.

THE STAR ABSINTHE: NOTES ON
A BITTER ANNIVERSARY

Prypiat is the only city in the world that has such an easily calculated age: 1970 (its founding)—1986 (its end). Besides that, of all the cities that have been ruined, it existed for the shortest time—only sixteen years. That is, it was no longer a child, but not yet a young man, sort of like a teenager who has the right to obtain a passport and to participate in an election for the first time. But, instead of a passport, he is issued a death certificate. And the reason listed for death: Acute Radiation Syndrome.

No other city has existed for such a short time. And it continues to be ruined—usually by human hands. It's not just the forest that eats away at it.

An opportune digression: I wonder—how long did Sodom and Gomorrah exist? You can fantasize about this all you want, but it is impossible to imagine that they existed for less time than Prypiat did. Sixteen years could not have been long enough to bring God to such wrath. In a competition for brevity of existence, Sodom and Gommorah lag far behind Prypiat.

Moreover, with the example of Prypiat, we have a precise, final date: April 27, 1986. No, not the 26th but the 27th—the day of the evacuation, not of the accident. The existence of an exact, final date makes Prypiat comparable to Pompeii. The latter also has a precise date—August 24, 79.

The ghost of Pompeii climbed up out of nowhere into reality when we, stepping onto broken glass and rotten boards, lifting our feet like herons, entered the Prypiat Café—at one time, the coolest joint in town. The café was situated on a hill above the river docks. From there, you can observe the city's beach and the arrival of the blindingly white Kyiv passenger liners with their underwater wings. The wall of the café across from the beach was made of stained glass. Our Guide took the opportunity to share with us the fact that, according to lore, the artist who had made this stained glass wall had, at one time, created another stained glass piece that tempted fate. What he had in mind was that, among other works by that stained glass artist, there was "The Last Day of Pompeii." He did indeed curse this place. There's no way a person like that should have been asked to create any stained glass in Prypiat. Our Guide chuckled while telling us this legend.

It's doubtful that "The Last Day of Pompeii" could have become a monumental-decorative theme during, need I remind you, a time of Socialist Realism[1]—not even as a replica of Karl Briullov's work.[2] What club, hall, or sanatorium could have had any use for its catastrophism? What executive committee could have ordered a far-from-the-most-optimistic scene depicting volcanic lava and the scorn of the heavens?

One can perhaps understand a moment of the artist's weakness that resulted in a work being given birth to out of wedlock. A stained glass work made for oneself? In order to materialize random apocalyptic visions? Art that does not belong to the people? Art for art's sake? In any case, that latent decadent categorically should not have been invited to Prypiat. People such as him always drag their horrible karma around with them and meddle with otherwise happy streams of events.

Where can he be found today? How can he be made responsible for everything that came to be?

* * *

What's on the stained glass?

For starters, it's worth noting that almost half of it was ruined. That is, today, it's no longer a stained glass work, but half of one; only pieces remain intact. The other half crackles underfoot when you carelessly come too close to it. By the way—upon entering the café, the radiation meter strapped to Our Guide's shoulder began to flap madly, alerting us to a dangerous hot spot. We carefully circumvented it. You can't walk barefoot here—you'll be overexposed.

---

1   The sole officially sanctioned style of art of the Soviet Union and its satellite countries from 1932 until the USSR's demise. Its required themes were the glorification of communism and the proletariat, and its dominance was enforced by government cultural policy.

2   Russian painter Karl Briullov's (1799-1852) best-known painting is entitled "The Last Day of Pompeii" (1830-1833). Briullov was instrumental in buying Ukrainian poet Taras Shevchenko's freedom from serfdom in 1838.

So then, getting back to the stained glass. Everything that has remained gives the sense of an accented splash of colors. If one were to describe the colors of the stained glass in terms of physics, you would need to use the prefixes "infra-" and "ultra-" as much as possible. The stained glass is remarkably active. It emits. The verb "to emit" usually requires a complement in the accusative case. You can emit something, for example, happiness. Or radiation. The stained glass in the Prypiat Café on the shores of the Prypiat River in the city of Prypiat simply emits.

Its sun is multi-colored. Like the rest of the world, it's striped. The stripes are dark-red, bright yellow, blue, azure, and green. This is summer in all its fury, at its zenith, in its surplus—the singing of forests, the silence of lakes, reeds, pines, the buzzing of bumble bees among the bushes of berries, becoming one with nature, the sweet swelling of the biosphere.

A bit later, when we were already in the bus, Our Guide played an agitprop film for us about Nuclear Power Plants (NPP) that was filmed the last summer before the catastrophe. "And what's most important," a choleric guy with the rank of an engineer, in a white lab coat and glasses, says in one scene, all choked up by his own enthrall-ment—"what's most important: we live in such unity with nature here, we are the flesh of its flesh! Go swim in the river, enter the forest, walk among the pines, breathe, gather a whole frying-pan-full of mushrooms for dinner, if you want, it's all here, right next to you, we are in it, we are part of it."

About nine months later—and this fidgety, life-embracing person, with his quick manner of speech seemed cruel. But for now—the pro-paganda of success, the standard victorious context in which the words "man" and "nature" are now always written in uppercase letters, M and N, Man and Nature, NatureMan, a celebration of harmony, swim-ming in the river, gathering mushrooms, the peaceful atom,[3] the scent of pine, dialectic materialism.

---

3   According to Our Guide, the roof of one of Prypiat's buildings had "Let the atom be a worker and not a soldier!" written on it in huge letters. (Author's note)

The inhabitants of Prypiat exemplified the success of scientific communism, they embodied it: clean, naïve, and obtrusive.

Are you really sure that instead of "obtrusive" I should have written "cocky"?

* * *

Most unforgettable that day were, of course, the catfish in the canal near the Nuclear Power Plant. They were the size of dolphins, or sharks, and this is nature's categorically harsh answer to man (now in a different context—one in which both of these words are always written in lowercase letters).

Gazing at fish in water is one of my favorite and constant activities. I've had very few opportunities to do this in my life. One, for example, came in Nuremberg, another—in Regensburg. I think it was in Nuremberg that I came to the conclusion that Europe is a land in which fish live well. I would not have come to this conclusion if I hadn't been in Nuremberg precisely at that time, in the summer of 1995. If I hadn't stood on those bridges time and again and I hadn't gazed down deep into the river to see how fish slowly move just above its bottom. And I ended up in Nuremberg at that time just because Walter Mossmann[4] summoned us to come there.

And now I am recalling him not just casually, and not out of thanks, but because a few months earlier he too gazed at those very same catfish in the canal near the Nuclear Power Plant. In his report, he writes about "meter-long monstrosities with giant, flat skulls and wide jaws, and with long, waving outgrowths jutting from the left and the right of their jaws that recall the curled moustaches of the Zaporozhian Cossacks."[5]

That's a rather caustic joke, in case anyone missed it: catfish with Cossack mustaches in a sluggish radioactive canal nestled in slime, the cold blood of Ukraine, its adipose fish hearts.

* * *

---

4   Walter Mossmann (1941-2015) was a German songwriter, journalist, and activist, one of the leading figures of the German student movement of 1968. He frequently visited Ukraine in the 1990s while developing several projects of cultural exchange between post-Soviet Ukraine and Germany.

5   Zaporozhian Cossacks were a Ukrainian political and military force in the sixteenth, seventeenth, and eighteenth centuries.

Europe? A land in which fish live well?

It's doubtful—in the case of those catfish.

First of all, I'm not sure if they really live all that well. But they definitely live long: no one catches them or kills them, in fear of the undeniable danger of radiation. How long is Silurus glanis, a normal (non-radioactive) wels catfish, supposed to live? According to several sources, up to one hundred years. This fish can live longer than any other fish found in our rivers and waters. Only moss-covered carp can live longer—but that's only in Aldous Huxley's novels.

On the other hand, abnormal (radioactivus emanatos) catfish—that is, the Prypiat catfish—live eternally. And as evidenced by their size in the twenty-fifth year of their eternal life after the catastrophe, they will continue to grow eternally. And someday they'll grow into eternally living, monstrous leviathans. But will they really be living well then?

Second of all, I'm not sure if it's really Europe. In our country, Europe occasionally appears and then disappears again. It's phantasmic, like communism in the early poetry of Marx-Engels.[6] You can't touch it, it's made of mist, misunderstandings and rumors.

In April 1986, Europe was not even a topic of discussion. There was the USSR and there was the West and also China. What Europe? Central? Eastern? If "Eastern," then how can you call that Europe? Europe cannot be eastern. From our geography lessons we learned that there is only the European territory of Russia and a few adjacent republics. The city of Prypiat was located somewhere there in that European territory. But certainly not in Europe.

And really—if it wasn't for Sweden, if it hadn't created such a ruckus about the accident, then how would this have continued on? There probably would not have been any continuation, just another cover up of yet another mega-crime. They nonetheless classified as secret the oncological illness statistics, regardless of all those Swedes. What, do you think the USSR was going to change all of a sudden?

---

6   Karl Marx (1818-1883) and Friedrich Engels (1820-1895) were the founders of Marxism.

And it's good that there was a resistance to the system. It's good that Sweden made a fuss and indicated that Poland was in danger. It's good that Poland had stopped being a friend and was increasingly turning away, westward. This time it turned away from a radioactive cloud—holding its breath and fastidiously holding its nose. It's good that Poland became frightened and took up Sweden's appeal.

But France did not stop being a friend and denied everything. There is no danger, France said, there is nothing to see here. It's a good thing the European Union didn't exist then. Otherwise it would have, once again, come up with some kind of blushingly indecisive decision (please excuse the oxymoron) like the one they came up with during the war in Georgia: the most important thing is not to anger the Russians.

It's good that Germany had had the experience of the 1970s, when hundreds of thousands and even millions of people protested against the Nuclear Power Plants, led by a few poets with guitars and fifes. It's good that by May 17, 1986 the German Greens called an emergency meeting in Hannover. And it was on May 17 that I wrote these lines:

Blood will change. Blossoms will fall from the chestnut trees.
We rush to live, like after a plague.
Perhaps that is where salvation lies—to recognize this time,
as a final flowering. The Only. One.

No one understood what they were about. On the other hand, Walter Mossmann, who certainly would have understood, did not know about their existence. "And then I tried," he writes about that day, "to imagine an infected landscape, forests, pools of water, fields, villages — everything is radiating. And I wasn't able to. This is not something that can be seen in reality."

I replied to him a dozen years later: "What were our initial reactions? To understand them is to understand what it is to fear the wind, the rain, the greenest of grass, to be afraid of light." And later—concerning the presence of a different kind of death—one that you cannot sense or see, "death to grow into,[7] death so devoid of form (and, following Hegel—content), that any kind of resistance lost any sense."

But the authorities demanded that resistance be applied. They, from the first days, shamelessly hurled full echelons of poor souls rescuers into the Zone—the same way, as if in war time, they hurled, *full speed ahead*, masses of un-uniformed and unarmed men from the "recently liberated territories." The authorities were in charge of the resistance and were bringing about their own end. But no one had realized it at that time. It seemed that the end of the world would come sooner than the end of such a wonderful epoch-empire.

The resistance consisted of de-activization. Zone X was ordered to be washed of its dirt. What couldn't be washed was to be buried in the ground.[8] What could not be buried was to be left as it was.

But there was another resistance as well, which consisted of pillaging. It's as if people decided to deal with the radioactivity of the materials through the act of dividing the loot, that is, through the acquisition of things that belong to others. It's as if someone's possessions, when taken out of their home, immediately lose their deathly glow.

That's why Prypiat is a city not only abandoned but also a city robbed, a take-out city, a city taken apart, a city to go. And that is its particular attraction. No longer a city but a body, collectively raped by new gangs of rescuers-lovers each time.

* * *

In his notes on Prypiat, Walter Mossmann calls it "an installation beyond compare." I also couldn't shake the feeling sometimes that all this surrounding me was probably a fragment of an exposition that had been

---

7   And why not "on a payment plan"? (Author's note)

8   The path to Prypiat goes through the former villages of Zalissia and Kopachi. The latter has, in fact, now been buried. In this manner a name crossed paths with its own destiny. (Author's note) *Kopaty* means to dig in Ukrainian and a *kopach* is a person who digs.

especially created and then methodically developed inside some kind of Contemporary Art-and-Ecology Zone—it's just that the curators over-did it and now the dose-meter goes bonkers in some places. And not just they—that very same Walter Mossmann admits a bit later: "The entire city of Prypiat is an installation with such rich *Bedeutungsebenen*[9] that it creates buzzing in your skull."

Picking up on his skull buzzing, I attempt to list at least the high-est "levels of meaning"—as if trying to formulate a question about the semiotics of Prypiat. I've even come up with more than two levels. Here are just the first five:

Ecological
Political
Social
Lyrical
Mythological

In the case of the last one, it emerges—a friend of the people and an enemy of the gods, a superman and near-god himself, that is—a titan.

* * *

It was Prometheus, and not Sabaoth or Jehovah, who created man from clay. What word first comes to mind when we hear his name? Correct—"fire." But it should be "clay," one that is red, at least. The meaning behind the fire that was stolen from the gods for man can only be under-stood if the factor of clay is taken into consideration—that is, the con-dition that Prometheus needed to care for those that he had fashioned out of clay. By the way, I hear in the Ukrainian word for "burn" (*o-pik*) the root of the word for "to care for" (*pik-luvatysia*). Clay hardens and strengthens as a result of burning. There is no way to avoid fire here. If fire burns in a nuclear reactor, then all the more so.

---

9   Levels of meaning *(Ger.)* (Author's note)

Prometheus is a favorite of the Romantics, it is they who, one after another, as if according to plan, sang of his self-sacrificial protest against the static order of things. It is not strange that Shevchenko, in his "The Caucasus," a poem that is first and foremost concretely political, launches it with him, bound to the top of a cliff for thirty thousand years (well that's a long sentence!). And an eagle fits in here too—not necessarily a two-headed one but an autocratic devourer of a liver nonetheless.

Prometheus remained a favorite in the era of Socialist Realism as well, in the sphere of late Soviet electro-energy. He was sort of a patron of more and more electro-stations and of the residential areas tied to them. It is as if he came up with the slogan about the electrification of the whole country.

It's understood that Prypiat could not help but be one of the centers of this cult. Yet another blow from greedy and lascivious gods landed on the reactor.

*   *   *

Secondly, of course, a star or, more accurately, the Star called Wormwood. In the summer of 1986, that is, about a month after the catastrophe, we began to actively quote verses 10 and 11 from chapter 8 of St. John the Divine's Revelation. Wormwood is a very strange, a completely ridiculous, name, if one really has a star in mind—and even if by star one has in mind a comet or an asteroid. Why should a cosmic body have the same name as a field plant? It only begins to make sense when taking into account the place where the catastrophe occurred.

In that manner, wormwood is a double "a": apocalypse and absinthe. Both are extracts of sorts: the former, of a secret knowledge; the latter, of bitterness. If geographical names were to be translated, then discussions on an international level would not be about the ChNPP (the Chernobyl Nuclear Power Plant) but about the ANPP (the Absinthe Nuclear Power Plant). They would be about a technogenic catastrophe not in Chornobyl but in Absinthe.

There is, of course, a third "a"—angel (yes, the third one, the one who sounded the trumpet). Isn't that whom we see among other figures on the aforementioned stained glass in that café in what is yet another allusion to Pompeii made by the artist? The angel, although disguised as a flying girl (with breasts!), and although with invisible wings, is nonetheless given a trumpet as its main and most important sign. Angels cannot have female sexual organs, moreover primary ones, because angels are sexless. But angels can pretend to be girls. Long hair and the absence of indicators of the male sex, even secondary ones, allow for this. That angel flying on that stained glass window, perhaps, is one like that. Its author didn't really know but was trying to guess. And sometimes a guess is much more impressive than actual knowledge.

* * *

We drove down Lenin Avenue to get to the City of the Electric Sun. We exited the bus on the main square in front of the Energy-Man Palace of Culture, where Lenin Avenue intersected Kurchatov[10] Street. Actually, the epithet "former" needs to be used everywhere in these sentences— at least six or seven times. "Former" is the primary and most important characteristic of Prypiat. It makes you kick in your memory, full on. Memory has to work for everything else because nothing else remains in Prypiat.

When I was a kid, I often dreamt about the Yucatan and about cities abandoned in jungles. And although to compare Prypiat with it seems too flattering, and thus dishonest, I do compare them. It's about how nature, upon returning, takes back its own. It's about weeds, sometimes impassible, in former courtyards, about trees on the roof and on stairs, about boars or deer, that suddenly cross Friendship of Peoples Avenue (formerly: now, today—Friendship of Animals). It's about extraterrestrial and hypertrophic mushrooms filled to their caps with roentgens. Nature returned and took back a hundredfold, unnaturally.

---

10 Igor Kurchatov (1903-1960) was a Soviet nuclear physicist and director of the Soviet atomic bomb project.

The indifferent-merciless revenge of nature against the system can attest to the unnatural quality of that system. To the notion that the place where Kurchatov and Lenin intersect goes beyond the boundaries of the order of things and is horribly dangerous.

The contamination was worst in the park. It was best not even to approach the Ferris wheel. According to Our Guide, the park missed its own opening by just four days. The opening was to take place on May 1. Everything stood, just about ready, all the carousels *greased and ready to go*, all that was left to do was wave a hand, signal the orchestra, cut the red ribbon and give the command. The inhabitants of Prypiat were methodically getting their kids ready: ten, nine, eight, seven, six, five days until the opening!

That was approximately the amount of days left for the existence of communism. This was evidenced by prosperity, its growth, and by the Kyiv Cakes,[11] for which people from Kyiv would come to Prypiat. Stepping onto the broken glass and other screeching scraps, I could not help but notice the countless ranges and refrigerators in the "Rainbow" store. Well there it is, embodied in the consumer goods—this *higher*, this truly highest, as if in Moscow, category of supply!

The chief color for the city of Prypiat should have been the color of those ranges, refrigerators, and washing machines—an ideally white color, the sum total of the rainbow, an indicator of the inability to get dirty or stained, an index of absolute cleanliness and sterility, the color of lab coats, wings, orchards in late April and rapid passenger liners with underwater—also white—wings, that arrived at the city docks, one after the other.

And if we imagine the angels clothed, then it is also the color of their special clothing.

That's why, when I walked around inside the former Energy-Worker Palace I could not help but think about the third myth and, simultaneously, the phantom, of this city. His name is Harmonious Man—an exemplary creation of Prometheus, Clay Creation No. 1, the tireless, conscientious worker, a dazzling dancer, the blessed-with-perfect-pitch-

11 A dessert baked in Kyiv that was very popular throughout the Soviet Union.

and-velvety-voiced champion of the world in chess and swimming and also in acrobatics, numismatics, and gymnastics. On a heavily peeling panel in the foyer of the palace hall, the exemplary Workers, Engineers, and Scientists united in a new Trinity with the exemplary Villagers and embraced each other in a happy round dance. The concert hall continued to echo something from Leontiev, Antonov, maybe some Rotaru, her "Lavanda" [12] and other songs.

A bit later, in the workshop beside the palace, filled with portraits of members of the Politburo, I tried to recall their last names. In the army, we had to know them by heart in order to distinguish between their identically kind, good faces. But how can you distinguish between Voronov and Kapitonov? Ustinov and Tikhonov? Gromyko and Kunaev? Or, even more difficult, how can you tell the difference between Vorotnikov and Solomentsev? How can you tell the difference between the ideal and the ideal? Between the positive and the positive? Between the perfect and the harmonious? Between the good and the even better?

The city of Prypiat died because of the inability to answer these questions. The Harmonious Man could not withstand his own progress and choked on happiness.

* * *

P.S. I also remember something else that Our Guide told us. In the days before the 1986 New Year's holiday, the holiday tree in front of the Energy-Worker Palace fell down twice. Few of the city inhabitants paid any attention to such a telling sign.

March 2011
Translated by Mark Andryczyk

---

12 Valery Leontiev (b. 1949), Yuri Antonov (b. 1945) and Sofiia Rotaru (b. 1947) were among the most well known pop singers in 1980s USSR. The latter's song "Lavanda" (Lavender) was a popular 1985 duet with Estonian singer Jaak Joala.

TARAS PROKHASKO

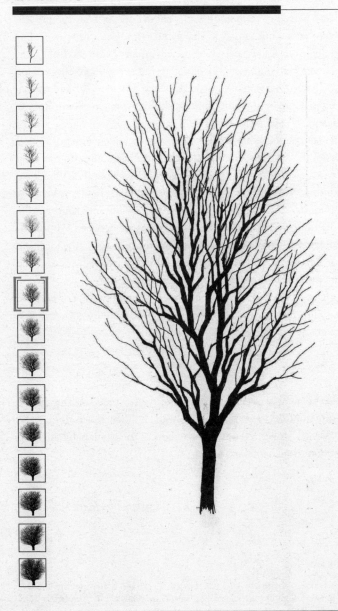

TARAS PROKHASKO studied biology at Lviv University and took part in student protests for Ukraine's independence in 1989-91. Prokhasko has worked as a radio operator, an editor, a bartender, the host of a radio program, a forester, a teacher, a gallery proprietor, a screen writer, a journalist, a video operator, and a gardener. He is the author of *Inshi dni Anny* (Anna's Other Days, 1998), *FM Halychyna* (FM Galicia, 2001),  *NeprOsti* (The UnSimple, 2002), *Leksykon taiemnykh znan* (Lexicon of Secretive Knowledge, 2005), *Z tsioho mozhna bulo b zrobyty kilka opovidan* (Could Have Made a Few Stories from This, 2005), and *Port Frankivsk* (2006). Prokhasko has also published a number of books in his *Inshyi Format* (A Different Format) series, which features interviews he has conducted with leading Ukrainian intellectuals. His novella "Necropolis" (1998) and novel *The UnSimple* (2007) have been translated into and published in English. Prokhasko's books have also been translated into Polish, Russian, Serbian, and Czech. Prokhasko is a recipient of the Joseph Conrad Award (2007) and *Korrespondent* magazine's Best Ukrainian Book Award (2006, 2007). He lives and works in Ivano-Frankivsk.

Taras Prokhasko's events in the Contemporary Ukrainian Literature Series, entitled *FM Galicia*, took place in April 2010.

Selections from FM GALICIA

18.11

For a city to be considered a genuine, traditional, European city, two elements are required, which, in fact, define it as a city. A city may lack a sewer system and it will still be a city. But it cannot lack a fortification wall or a tower—two opposing things, whose clandestine duel is the very sign of the existence of a city. The wall is necessary to make the city stand out against a backdrop of fields, to distinguish it from the surrounding area, and thus, render it a tangible, noteworthy point on a map; the tower is necessary in order to oppose any forced demarcation of a city. It is essential to look out from a tower beyond the walls and see the neighboring territories and distant landscapes and even more distant horizons. Because it's necessary to know from where the sun appears and to where it disappears to avert the thought that it just turns on and shuts off above one's head at certain times of the day.

For the sun has a tendency to rise and set in beautiful and important places—above the sea, the forest, the mountains and the rivers. Looking at these places from a tower, city dwellers realize that they too could end up over there, that they passed through these walls voluntarily, and that they can, at least occasionally, cross its boundaries.

Ivano-Frankivsk has walls. But it has no tower. That is why each one of us needs to find his own tower from which the mountains can be seen. Because we're not just a ditch lying between two rivers: we are a place, located below the level of nearby mountains. Only if they learn how to grasp the nearness of the mountains will residents of Ivano-Frankivsk obtain their tower, after which Ivano-Frankivsk will qualify as a city.

Through our urban worldview, the mountains can become streets, courtyards, squares. The mountains don't need us. They are self-sufficient and immaculate. We need them very much. If only as images and as points of orientation. Because for us, the Carpathian Mountains signify a trip southward, towards warmth and life at its fullest. For us, the Carpathians are something which cannot be captured. They are the knowledge of a safe hiding place, of the most elemental respite, of the ultimate opportunity for escape, should it become necessary. The mountains are that neglected orchard on the edge of our yard. An orchard that we have not tended to for quite some time. But all the trees in that orchard are healthy and fruitful. Its existence comforts any blows. You are aware that, if necessary, it awaits you and is ready to receive ...

19.11

Anyone who has witnessed winter, spring, summer and autumn will never see anything radically new.

The seasons exist in order to never bore us—that is why we forget about them so quickly. Over a certain period of time, the traits of the previous season are erased and the upcoming year's autumn will turn out to be as poignant as last year's.

But the seasons require attention. We can't just treat the highly refined changes that occur between the seasons as shifting weather patterns—it became cold, it became wet or otherwise unpleasant in some way.

We act superficially. Even our language demonstrates such inattentiveness. Arabs possess several dozen words that correspond to shades in the color of sand. Just for sand. While Inunits know a hundred different words that describe the various states of snow—color, hardness, pliancy. They don't have the word "snow." Their language has equivalents for one word, for example, "morning, shiny snow, which is difficult to walk upon because it is hard on top and deep underneath"—this is all just one word. And this constitutes being attentive to one's surroundings. And when we're trying to be poetic, we say—the leaves have yellowed, the yellow leaves. But can they be so uniform? Can they really just be yellow? And can they be the same yellow when on the tree, when falling, and when on the ground? And, when on the ground, don't they change color depending on whether they lie separately or are gathered in a pile, or whether they have been lying for a few minutes or several days and nights? And what if there has been frost or rain?

And autumn is not just defined by the shades of leaves. It has countless other characteristics. The fact that they have been forgotten does not mean that they shouldn't be seen and that we shouldn't try to remember them. There is no truer method for organizing one's everyday life than wisely adhering to phenology—to the flow of changes in the seasons. If you implement this methodology, you needn't worry about your mind—it will be free of confusion. And now everything that you do will contain that special joy of making sense. Food will be better, dreams more interesting, wine more healing. You need to just sense winter, spring, summer, and autumn flowing through you.

22.11

For some reason, we do not consider our territory to be a fertile land. Transcarpathia, Moldova, and, perhaps, the Kosiv region—those are the fertile lands. While all we have are potatoes, beans, some squash, and onions. But our region—the *Prykarpattia* foothills—is an apple paradise. Nowhere else are such winter apples found, except, perhaps, somewhere in northern France, but they're hard to find in the winter anyway because the whole harvest is used to make calvados. And we have the most prized Rennet apples, and winter apples can last—if treated with love and care—until summer, without losing their taste or smell, even though they leave a trace of their fragrance in spaces where they have been stored.

In wintertime, mountain orchardists make their way to the stations in snowy hordes, bringing apples to the Ivano-Frankivsk market by train. If one of their sacks should tear along the way, those yellow-red apple billiard balls might utilize that which they had absorbed from the sun to warm the whole dreary *Chervona Ruta*[1] train-car, or maybe they'll singe the hopeless frigidity of the snows with their cooled skin.

Sometimes that is exactly what takes place. And then the apples need to be gathered. But once, it so happened, that not one single winter apple, which had been spilled along the railroad tracks, had been touched by anyone. They just lay there like that and then melted through snow's thickness and eventually seeped into the ground, maybe without even having deteriorated; no one can say for sure because when the snow thawed, no traces remained. And no one picked up those apples because they spilled from a sack belonging to Mr. Boiko. Mr. Boiko was carrying a sack of red winter apples to the train station. It was still dark and freezing cold. His winter hat was tied tightly, his head bent from the weight sitting on his neck. That is why he didn't hear the train approaching from the rear, and the apples spilled out along the train tracks.

---

1   For more on Chervona Ruta, see Note 2 on page 94.

The reason people didn't gather them was not because in wintertime there were no flowers to lay at this spot, but because the apples served to remind them how difficult it was to escape one's fate. Because Mr. Boiko had been hit by trains in the past, having gotten his wagon stuck while crossing the tracks. Never had this happened to anyone else. He had always survived, unscathed, while his wagons had been smashed into splinters. For him, trains probably had been like lightning bolts.

I don't know why, but I find this story to be very optimistic. But it also reminds me that you never really know who will finish eating up the harvest you have gathered.

23.11

Once the snows came, it became more difficult to determine what this autumn had been like. It wasn't until today, upon arriving in the mountains, that I realized that it had been, it seems, a very dry one. Because where there had always been a lot of water, there now was little.

The bucket needed to be lowered to the full length of the chain. And, even then, it barely reached the surface of the water. Whether it was from the wood shavings that had crumbled off the windlass or because of something else inside, the water smelled of wood. It's as if it had been aged for a long time in a vessel made of wood prone to humidity. This is sort of the way that cognac, calvados, and rum are made. The aftertaste of the wood didn't bother me. I wanted to drink as much water as I could from this very well.

If ninety percent of my body is made up of water then, obviously, the whole state of such a system is dependent on the type of water it is. Even the brain consists mostly of water. This means that thoughts should adjust according to the type and quality of the water.

If that is so, then water needs to be adjusted. It is necessary to squeeze out the dirty water with the clean, as is usually done with a reservoir. There is, however, a complication—if you pour dirty water into clean water, then all of the water becomes dirty, and when you add clean water to dirty water, it nonetheless remains dirty. (This is one of life's truths, formulated by my son). But regardless of this complication, it's worth trying to adjust it, at least partially.

You just have to find a well that is most suitable to you, because drinking the same water as everyone else is dangerous—imagine if everyone were to become identical, the way two buckets of water are. I found my well. Not to get too poetic, but after I drank that water, I truly started to feel different, and this lasted for a long time. Because if I flood all of my internal pipes with it, then it seems to start becoming me, and I it. And this will keep me going for a while. And then later, I'll set off once again, from home to the mountains, to my well. Meanwhile, the snow will melt and the water will rise. It will no longer smell like wood. And by that time, I'll notice whether there have been any changes in me between today and that day.

24.11

When you live in the mountains, firewood becomes an important part of your life, like bread, milk, a bed, a shirt, a warm jacket. Firewood becomes an extension of you—it's as if it's a part of your body. You see condensed warmth in that timber, without which your body ceases to be yours. Upon it, in fact, your existence is dependent. And a pile of logs can be regarded as a peculiar anatomical structure that is part of your organism. That's why you can't even think of treating it as something that is foreign or supernatural; you just want to make sure there's lots of it.

Up against the walls, arranged stacks such as these transform houses into true fortresses. In such a lair, one can survive any attack. And they will come. The frost will press up against the walls so hard that the wooden framework inside will crack and, at least a couple of times, the snow will blow up against the door so that you'll have to climb out through the window, crawl over the snow heaps up to the door and shovel the snow. The wind will transform the windows into vibrating membranes and the chimney and the attic into territories settled by various unfamiliar creatures.

And then your choice is simple—don't burn it, and become one with the wind, the frost and the snow, or burn it, and transform the wood into warmth for your body.

That's after you've lived in the mountains for a while. Winter's progression, its calendar, its marked-off days—all of these are traced by the gradual shrinking of that pile of wood.

But when you only come to the mountains occasionally, firewood is not treated as daily bread but as some kind of delicacy, as gourmet food, like a cordial. My firewood, in fact, is most similar to aged cognac. Because, in addition to last year's spruce logs, I also have a stash of beech logs that has been stored for over twenty years. They are pure white, almost transparent, and sonorous. And they provide a warmth that is simultaneously intense and delicate, and, most importantly—long lasting. They've learned not to hurry. It seems to get warmer when you're just holding such a log in your hand.

In Austria, they use such aged beech to make crucial components for violins. From one of my logs, they could make about twenty. I am aware of how many violins I have burned over all these years, I am aware how much money I could have made, had I just taken one suitcase full of logs to Vienna. But I also know that I'll continue to burn them little by little, offering them to my friends and children, as one offers conversation or wine. And I'll spill the ashes onto the plot where garlic spends the winter, awaiting its time. Let it warm up as well.

25.11

After the snow has fallen and it looks like it will lie there for a while, I start to feel better about my household chores. I know that my arms and shoulders will get a break because I will be provided with transportation. Snow, in itself, is a form of transportation. It can move anything: people, barrels, sacks, logs. Actually, it only becomes capable of transporting when combined with an inclined surface. But where I do my household chores, all the surfaces are somewhat inclined. Besides the snow and the hills, I also have a sled. And that is what provides me with hope that my arms and my shoulders will be relieved.

I don't know how other people are able to do it. But I never leave my sled just lying there on the road. It lives in my house, in the best spot. That's how they used to treat livestock, letting them in the house for the winter. The sled greatly affects both the look and the mood of the house. It's especially pleasant to wake up in the middle of the night and see the sled's skeleton in my room, lit up by reddened oven tiles (for there is no other source of outer light). At first, you can't figure out where you are, at what road rest stop it is that you have paused your journey. Then you realize that indeed it is your sled that is resting for the night in your house. And it becomes very pleasant to fall asleep knowing that tomorrow there will be the day, there will be snow and there will be the sled. It is needed to take care of some very important things. Take the borrowed shredder across the river, and, while riding back, walk along the railroad tracks to find a large rock with which to press down the shredded cabbage. You have to ride into the forest and, shaking off the clouds of snow from the spruces, chop off some twigs—some thick spruce branches. They'll be needed to cover those roots left in the soil. Although these twigs aren't heavy, carrying a whole armful of them is very cumbersome. But on the sled, it's very easy. You, of course, have to tie them on with a rope. The twigs look unbelievably beautiful against the snow. I would like to send this carriage down from the mountaintop so that it would ride for a long time. May this mobile green blot intersect the snow slope's gigantic screen. Instead, I sit on it by myself and begin to steer with my boot. And I ride down to the house. I fly into a haystack which, unlike the sled, I have left outdoors for the winter.

26.11

I've understood for a while now that every person needs to be in possession of a very detailed knowledge of two or three landscapes. That provides enough concrete landscapes to enable one to think. Because a person cannot think without having placed certain pictures onto the landscape that has been fixated forever in one's mind. Moreover, these varieties of terrain suffice for the combination of dreams. Dreams always take place based on a very dear, fundamental, landscape that has been fixed, along with language, in the earliest days of childhood. The alchemy of dreams comes from the endless other fragments, witnessed at various times in various places, heaped onto the background of your fundamental territory.

I very often dream of my hill in the mountains, the house, everything surrounding it, the nearby forest, apexes, and abysses. Actually, my place grows, it becomes filled with all kinds of strange details, additions, new trees grow; the rooms get bigger, as do the number of entrances, exits, and corridors—new paths of combination become possible. Of course, all this becomes inhabited by a large number of people who, broken off into groups of interest, do their own thing. Most often, I walk from group to group.

Another typical motif—I'm home alone or with someone who is very close to me. It's nighttime, it's cold and quiet. And we know that surrounding us—in the ravines, behind the trees, perhaps already by the walls—are some sort of armed enemies. We keep the lights off, listening in. We grab makeshift weapons lying nearby—knives, scythes, ropes, pitchforks. Sometimes there's one old-fashioned musket for the two of us. In such dreams, we're almost always able to leave the house and its surroundings through one of the exits that don't exist in reality and, moving past mute figures, make it through the orchard in the direction of the forest. One time, in order to do this, it became necessary to shoot the pneumatic rifle through the glass straight into the eye of the attacker, who had attempted to look into the dark window by pressing his face against the glass. While today, for example, I had a real nightmare. I walked out at night to have a smoke, stood by the wall. Suddenly, a car came out of the darkness and flew between me and the nearest tree.

And this kept repeating. And then everything became clear—I noticed that while I had been gone, a transnational highway had been laid out through my orchard. Right through the orchard. Once a secluded house by the forest, it now found itself right by the road. This was worse than hundreds of attackers with rifles. This was the nightmare in which my world came to an end. Waking up, I said a prayer, asking not to live to see such changes. To die before our world changes in such a way.

29.11

Whenever I begin to think that my life is starting to resemble a tangled ball of thin rubber bands—many fragments with many ends, all jumbled together—I then begin to think about people who have experienced more difficult times. And most people have. A calm, unemotional comparison always exposes how cheerful my biography is when measured up to anyone else's. Dad once told me an old Hutsul[2] tale about a man who was tired of living and who, in his prayers, would ask the Lord to offer him an easier fate. God, of course, heard the pleading of the downtrodden man and led him to a giant hall in which crosses were stacked—every cross a particular fate of an actual person. Then he allowed the man to choose which one he wanted for himself. The man searched for a while and then chose the smallest and lightest one.

"But that one is your cross, it is your fate," said the Lord.

And that's the way it really is.

We are too involved with love—actually, pity—for ourselves to understand that we need nothing else but thankfulness to the Creator for every day of existence. I respect the thankful. They are joyful and good. Those who are thankful to the Creator understand that it is precisely that which is needed by others whom he has created. My aunt said that what a person needs most of all is gratefulness. In time, I proved it to myself that she was correct. For, in essence, everything is dependent on gratefulness. That is why I understand people who accept gifts with enthusiasm. That enthusiasm is made up of gratefulness, not self-assurance. That is why I also understand people who give, never accepting thanks in return. They know that the latter know to whom they are thankful. And if not, then thank God that when someone needed something, you were in a position to give.

As for difficult times—they disappear when you fathom that the day is a gift. Because just by possessing that day, you have received something. And you believe that your day is better than other possible

2   For more on Hutsuls, see Note 4 on page 95.

similar days. You just need to understand that if you are hungry today, then it is because you were full yesterday and will be full tomorrow. And it's the same with coldness, pain, despair, fear, and other real things, which let you know that you are alive. The greatest wisdom, then, is the simple, daily prayer, given to us, without any expectation of gratitude: Lord! Thy will be done, not mine.

30.11

After grandpa's funeral, I noticed that various people would approach me and, among other things, cautiously begin asking me about some kind of grass that is used for smoking. It reminded me of plots in films about secret drug addicts. I, of course, was convinced that grandpa had nothing to do with grass that is smoked and I tried to convince all those who had approached me of this. Old village men would walk away doubting my honesty.

I remember the way grandpa smoked. He had a plain but high-quality pipe and a nice little bag for tobacco. He loved to take a break from work, lean up on his hoe, shovel, scythe, or rake and smoke a bit in the shadow of the plum tree or on the knoll overgrown with sweet briar, depending on the weather. And it was by that plum tree that he had his worst asthma attack, the result of having spent many days on the Lysol-covered concrete floor of a solitary confinement cell.

After the attack, grandpa stopped smoking. For several months after, he would keep dried plums in his pocket so that he could eat them to help suppress his cravings to smoke, and a bunch of kids would follow him, asking for a plum. Grandpa left behind some almost poisonous makhorka tobacco dating back to the end of the 1950s, half a pack of Herzegovina-Flor cigarettes, and a couple of packs of small filtered Soviet cigarettes unimaginatively named "Minty." But I knew nothing about any grass. By the way, those old men would keep coming up to me, sometimes once a year, sometimes more frequently, asking that, even if I continued to refuse giving them that grass, I at least show it to them. I came to understand that all this represented some kind of secret my grandpa had had.

Several years later—in the attic, of course, among homemade Christmas ornaments, I found a little metal box of Lviv ground coffee. Upon opening it, I was astounded by the extraordinary fragrance that was released. It was the smell of an orchard in summer, honey poured over magic herbs, the most delicious fruits, and the essence of the most delicate petals. And I recalled that scent, although I had believed that a distant recollection of it was really just another childhood fairy-tale.

Grandpa would put a pinch of this herb in his tobacco and this would make the smoke very pleasant. This little box contained that grass those wise old men were searching for. As it turned out, it was a treasure more valuable than grandpa's whole inheritance. This secret mix he had discovered was a real masterpiece. It makes poor tobacco good, and good tobacco—amazing. If grandpa wanted to, and if he had lived in a different part of the world, he could have become the magnate, the champion and the hero of all smokers. Instead, he passed that chance along to me. Maybe someday I'll be up for it. But today, I just pull a pinch of herb from the little box, mix it with Dutch tobacco and throw myself a little party. And I think about grandpa. And, to this day, I don't know what grass is contained therein.

01.12

Every now and then, I enjoy reading the Lives of the Saints. There are very few books existing that contain so many amazing stories. They are a waterfall of people's fates. Besides providing instruction, they also offer a great number of fantastic narratives. I'm convinced that, in all the literatures and among all the peoples of the world, there is no such collection of stories.

But even these lives and these stories can be systematized by looking into how it is that the saints became saints. In turns out that in addition to the most important requirement—absolute faith—several other acts were also required. Chief among them was an honorable death. Martyrdom was important, but an honorable death was your guarantee that you would become a saint. The saints died in horrible ways. All the descriptions of brutality found in today's literature cannot compare with those terrible manners of dying that were assigned to the saints. The phantasmagorical imagination displayed by the authors of those deaths refute any declarations made by pessimists who contend that, in today's world, humankind has declined. Because then, at the start of the millennium, the fantasies and the industriousness of the executioners knew no borders. But the variety of deaths is only an insignificant feature of belles lettres. What is important is the conduct of those who were destined to die. None of them wavered, bowed down, or encountered doubt. They accepted their hours or minutes of death almost joyfully. Besides, there are things that our simple minds cannot fathom—parents witnessing the torture of their children and vice versa. But no one allowed themselves the opportunity to flee the situation or to be cowardly. The path of a righteous and virtuous life. Few were able to stay true to it. And those that were can be divided into two categories—ascetics and those who relentlessly helped others. Other possible paths—acts for the good of the church committed above and beyond the call of duty, or producing miracles and wonders. And the saints I like best are those who came up with something that you keep thinking about to this day.

Especially important for man's reflection and reasoning is the life of St. Simeon Stylites. A person who, out of a thousand possible ways to live, chose the strangest—20 years of prayer on top of a tall pillar, on which no stray move was possible. Day after day, for twenty years, for every minute, only in this spot. Completely ignoring that which we call life's opportunities. Just two leaves of cabbage a day for twenty years. And that's it for the food. For the rest of the time—conversations with God. No outside impressions; no journeys, meetings, or entertainment. And, most importantly: no complaints, an inhuman patience. A pragmatist might consider such a life to be useless, an escape. But actually, Simeon is among those who provide life with at least a little bit of sense.

Whenever I start to get bored and impatient, I always think about Simeon Stylites. How did he deal with it?

02.12

Today, I was subjected to a series of strange coincidences that could be considered magical. Because now and then when we think about someone, even subconsciously, we conjure up their image over and over throughout the day.

In the morning, I went to shave, or perhaps just wash my face. Looking in the mirror, I said to myself: "Bohumil! Hrabal!"[3] And before evening, I entered a winery. And there, the spirit of Hrabal crossed paths with me once again (surely, if he were to appear just like that it would be in the company of wine). In the winery, a visiting Czech gentleman told me about Hrabal's death. The story was very emotional. And it was extra appealing because it wasn't true. But the Czechs, the countrymen of the Great Bohumil Hrabal, believe in it. The Czech gentleman said the following: while Hrabal was lying in the hospital unable to use his legs, he became engrossed with some birds that were stirring just outside the window. Mr. Bohumil crawled up to the windowsill and crumbled some bread from his hospital tray for the birds. And he increasingly leaned out the window, listening in to the birds' conversation, up until the moment that he lost his balance and fell out the window, dropping to his death.

In reality, it is a proven fact that the elderly Hrabal neglected his medicine, illness, and frailty. Maybe he wanted to take on the role of that wooden angel he had described, the one that splintered into pieces in the courtyard of a Prague church. Or maybe he had been called by one of those who had often appeared to him, and to his grandfather, and to his father after a few jugs of Moravian wine—Christ, Friedrich the Great, Lao Tse.

Hrabal is probably the greatest poet in contemporary Czech culture among those who wrote down stories they had overheard. Scraps of the conversations of ordinary citizens of Prague were ground into the well-puddled-stream of Bohumil's fantasy and became masterpieces.

---

3   Bohumil Hrabal (1914-1997) was a prominent Czech writer. He died when he fell out of a fifth-floor hospital window.

The whole world knew of him, while Hrabal continued to work, either at a factory that was wreaking havoc on his brain or at a paper recycling facility to which various Prague weirdos would bring used paper. His kingdom was the enchanting Czech language, with wine, ghosts, and the tales of the half-insane and their oversaturated lives. "Bohumil! Hrabal!"—he would address his reflection with the scolding voice of his mother. The reflection was silent. And Bohumil wrote down stories. He died the same summer that those other wrinkled elders like him did—Jacques-Yves Cousteau, Bulat Okudzhava,[4] Mother Theresa.

And today, in this insinuating manner, he came to me the way that, earlier, the immortal elders had come to him.

And what's really strange—almost all people whom I admire had some kind of connection with this deceased man.

---

4   Bulat Okudzhava (1924-1997) was a poet and musician of Georgian and Armenian heritage. He is considered to be one of the pioneers of the "author song" musical genre popular during the Soviet era.

04.12

The arrival of the concept of what in Ukraine they now call by the English word "second-hand"—the market for used clothes—can be considered to be one of the most important events in recent years. It greatly affected our daily lives. Let's recall Soviet times, when clothing was rather expensive and most fellow citizens wore sad, identical suits, coats, jackets and hats. Because of this, our people were recognizable throughout the world in the way that Indians or Africans are when they wear their national costumes. Second-hand provided two or three major possibilities—to have lots of affordable clothes, to have everyone dressed differently, and, most importantly, to find something that fit you well.

But there is a great danger hidden within it. Because we know that clothing, more than anything else, accumulates the energy of its owner. Thus, every one of us, by donning something worn by the anonymous, takes on the remnants of something good or bad, calm or nervous, happy or tragic. It is not possible to ever deduce which it is; it is not possible to determine it in any manner. The grand circulation of the clothing spirits is like the massive spreading of various viruses that enter genetic codes, seeping into them, snatching for themselves something from the previous master, and then inhabiting the next person with all of this.

I thought of these things when I got dressed this morning—there was not one single thing that I myself had purchased. Everything had been given to me, everything was someone else's, everything with traces of someone else's life. A jacket given as a gift, which had been purchased at a Prague store stocked with goods hailing from various "colonies." A sweater that earlier had belonged to a famous avant-garde actress from a German youth theater. A shirt previously worn by a Kurdish freedom fighter who was also a Lviv University student. An absurd pair of pants, wide at the waist and of a stupid color, presented to me as a sign of recognition by the Maltese Order. A belt given to me by grandpa on the day I turned seven, and on which I have noted every new place where I have been. Complimentary socks obtained by an actual German count when he flew on Lufthansa Airlines. Army boots that had taken part in the storming of the palace of the President of Georgia, Zviad Gamsakhurdia,[5] Also—an earring given to me as a present, a silver ring, a watch, a knife. A Franciscan cross brought from Assisi. I did not choose any of these things myself. They came to me from various parts and they brought with them fragments of the lives and fates of others. But my advantage over the second-hand is that I know what to expect from each of these things.

---

5   Zviad Gamsakhurdia (1939-1993) was the first democratically elected president of post-Soviet Georgia. He was overthrown in a coup d'état launched in December 1991.

06.12

My great-grandfather was very strict with his children. He didn't beat them, but he gave them a very stern upbringing. At home, to this day we have a whip—a sixer (with six leather belts), which was called a quirt. No one ever beat me. I didn't experience it my whole childhood. Perhaps my dad slapped me on the wrist a couple of times, and my grandfather hit me only three times. But those three times were so unusual that I remembered them for my whole life. Actually, those three spankings were as useful as three university degrees.

Grandpa was very gentle and loving towards me, but he possessed a fiery nature. His anger was short-lived but excruciating, although it never jeopardized his relationships with others.

The first time he hit me was with a scythe handle, which caused me to fly into the ditch by the railroad tracks. And this was very timely. Because a train was approaching very fast and I, still a little boy at the time, almost stepped out right in front of it as I was crossing the tracks to go to grandpa, who was returning from the harvest.

Another time, some friends as old as my grandpa visited and sat at the table, conversing and sipping some gin. I was there too and when I was asked a question to which the answer was supposed to be either "yes" or "no," I started babbling on, not noticing that the old men had had enough. Then grandpa grabbed a link of kielbasa and hit me for a second time.

The third time was actually completely unclear to me at first. Grandpa and I sat in the house; it was raining and there was no work to be done. A member of our family stopped by and, talking about various things, asked where my father had been. Grandpa said that he did not know, but I knew that he knew that my dad had gone with his buddies to the mountains and that he was aware of the path that they had taken. I began telling this to the family member. But I didn't finish telling him because I received a very painful and out-of-nowhere blow in a certain tender place. My grandpa had learned how to do this at a special training camp in Holland. When our guest left, grandpa apologized to me and told me never to say that which is unnecessary.

I was hit infrequently. But three hits accomplished more than daily beatings would have. Now I never cross railroad tracks when a train is coming, I never interrupt those older than me and instead hear them out, I never reply to questions the answers to which no one really wants to know, and I never tell of the paths taken by those whom I love.

07.12

Today I was scolded: so-and-so or so-and-so, who raised you, would never have conducted themselves in such a way. In other words, what happened to all the guidance you received, your upbringing? At first, I was shocked—I truly did not want it to be this way. I would like to be the person I was brought up to be. But after a few hours, it hit me—my God!—well I've been raised by so many different, extraordinary people. I loved all of them, I was enamored with all of them, and I've absorbed something from, and remembered something about, each one of them. But these people themselves were so dissimilar they often had difficulty agreeing on anything. I didn't recognize this as a child, because I didn't comprehend it. I now realize that certain individuals who raised me, each of whom had the same amount of influence on me, were all equally exceptional. That's why coming to a conclusion based on one, as criminologists say, episode, is incorrect, illogical, and impossible.

And, in addition to living relatives, two irrefutable factors that have had a direct influence on me have to be taken into account—the dictate of blood, that eccentric twisting of heredities, and, of course, myths—stories about those whom I never met in my life but without whom I cannot imagine my worldview.

Take this story about my great grandmother, for example. When it became too dangerous for my great grandfather to remain here in Galicia, Sheptytsky[6] was able to get him to America. After a period of time, my great grandmother joined him there. She settled in a small town, and, being the wife of a priest, had to participate in the social life there. But my great grandmother had one important need—she was a heavy smoker. And in America at that time, a woman who smoked was looked upon with disdain. Smoking in public was simply forbidden. My great grandmother couldn't last more than half an hour without a cigarette. She truly loved her husband, but she just could not suffer such

---

6   Andrei Sheptyts'kyi (1865-1944) was the Metropolitan Archbishop of the Ukrainian
     Greek Catholic Church and one of the most important and powerful figures in 20th
     century Ukraine. Treated as an enemy by the Soviet Union, he was a hero of the
     Ukrainian national political and cultural movement.

torture. She stayed in America for a bit longer and then took her child, who had been born there, and returned to her homeland. Forever. She kept smoking and later died of lung cancer. This was foreseeable but, ultimately, not obligatory. What was obligatory was not succumbing to the decrees and dictates of social mandates. And what can be said about this? How can her conduct be logically justified, and moreover, how can all this be applied to an interpretation of my behavior? And to the fact that, in one particular episode, I did not act like so-and-so, or so-and-so, who had raised me.

09.12

I believe that most offenses should be forgiven. I believe that society should not be divided into the guilty and the not-guilty. However ... Today, I came across a manifestation of something that frightened me ten years ago. Here's what happened. It was the Ukrainian revolution. We, students from Lviv, were organizing a very risky demonstration in Kyiv. Marching toward us was a riot police brigade. This was scary, but most of us were used to it. That day, doubt had emerged within the police. So they didn't start beating us right away. Several leaders of the student corps, including me, were packed into a car and taken to the commanders of the Kyiv special forces. There were people there whose last names were the very symbols of brutality, but it's not worth listing them now because they are the ones who are in power in today's Ukraine. And it was then, at that interrogation ten years ago, that I suddenly understood: a time will come—the one for which, in fact, we are fighting now—when I will be forced to attest to these very people my allegiance to a sovereign Ukrainian state. I understood that neither my absolute belief in Ukraine, nor my indisputable patriotic upbringing, nor that which I do now so that Ukraine may continue to exist, nor all that my family has done— nothing will protect me from that situation when I will be forced to prove to all those generals and their cronies that I am for Ukraine and for its statehood. It's absurd, but absurd things such as these are precisely those that usually come to fruition. And today, I finally experienced this as reality. I am all for forgiving, I am against revising biographies, but I desire that which, it seems, is completely normal— that the forgiven understand that they have been forgiven and that the guilty know that they are guilty, and thus do not continue their offenses. I don't want to have to prove to people responsible for all sorts of malevolence back then that I am for this country and for this state. I don't want former enemies to judge what I have done for my people. And I don't want to have to answer to boys from the special services who were members of the Komsomol[7] to its dying days and who are now responsible for the safety of my country. Even though I have lost the biggest game of my life and things have not turned out the way we had wanted them to, my former brothers-in-arms and I should not have to fear the harassment of those who change colors when it's convenient.

---

7   The Komsomol, or All-Union Leninist Young Communist League, was a Soviet youth organization that served to prepare future members of the Communist Party.

15.12

Many of us possess a secret map—it could be a real map, it could be one that's been painted by hand, it could be a certain photograph or an illustration in a book, some kind of painting in an atlas, a diagram in an encyclopedia. It could be an old photo featuring unknown people or someone's painting. Sometimes this map could even be a picture of a certain author, a statue, or, perhaps, even a city-square. This map could exist in the form of an old sweater, a spoon, a beat-up knife, or a chipped cup. It could be dissolved in a certain type of wine or chopped up and ground with coffee of a certain quality. I won't even mention spices and perfumes, a few words written in a certain font, herbariums, numismatic, or philatelic collections. Or attics and basements, beds and dressers, melodies and pianos.

It could be carried in someone's face, sometimes in that of a stranger, or it could be chiseled onto somebody's tombstone. Thus, that secret map could be hidden in just about anything. What unites all of them, however, is that they all show you the path to your own lost paradise. It's a chart of your paradise and the means of getting there.

I also possess such a map. I grew up on a balcony. My aunt transformed this balcony into something that was incredible. It was large and covered with vines. It faced three of the cardinal directions. And my aunt was the most amazing floriculturist in the world. She was never concerned with the size of the flowerbed, because it was never about having a lot of flowers. She was only concerned with having a lot of different kinds of flowers. In a few boxes and reinforced large pots grew several hundred of the most exotic plants. Searching far and wide, she would find at least one seed of a certain very strange plant. One seed—one plant. That was the principle. Floriculturists from various corners of the world would send her letters containing seeds. The balcony on which I grew up was like a tropical coastline. All that was missing were coral reefs. I bathed in basins that had been set up in the sun in order to warm up the water. Later, this water, like in the jungles, was used to water the plants.

When my aunt died, I sketched a chart of her garden. I wrote out all the names. This is the map of my lost paradise. I warm myself with the thought that someday I will be able to reproduce that whole paradise on a different balcony.

16.12

While I was still a student in the Department of Biology, I realized that biology itself provides as much a fundamental foundation for education, for a worldview, and for comprehending philosophical formations, logical constructions, and even artistic creations and metaphors, as does, perhaps, linguistics. Simply put, biology can be the basis for everything the mind requires. But today I met up with a former classmate, whom I had not seen for many years—a fellow biologist who had changed professions and was now informing me about a whole system of observations he had made concerning the influence of various biological sciences on the psyche.

Entomologists (insect specialists) always become collectors. Moreover, they are collectors by nature—they collect everything, even experiences and emotions, which they carefully systematize. Botanists are a varied sort. Some almost become philologists, others become erudite practical workers—gardeners, horticulturists, mushroom-pickers, floriculturists—while the rest become experts of every corner of a certain region. They know exactly where everything grows.

A separate category is made up of all who work with a microscope. Herpetologists, ichthyologists, and physiologists constitute another bunch of weirdos. But completely apart from all of these are ornithologists—those who study birds. To decide to become an ornithologist is already a sign of an unstable psyche. Ornithologists can be recognized immediately and unmistakably. They are unique. Something pulls them from the earth up into heaven. They probably corral birds into Godknows what and travel somewhere with these harnesses. Ornithologists do not see the ground—only the sky, the tree tops. These are their roots. Just think about it: to count, based on their contours, flocks composed of thousands as they move; to plot paths between us and Africa; to put a ring on captured birds' legs and receive telegrams from the island of Java, should one of those birds happen to die there; to be able to differentiate between twenty shades of pink in the tiny feathers on a little belly. To recognize nests and eggs of various sizes and colors. To constantly look into binoculars, lorgnettes, and clear tubes. To know which trolley will get you to see a certain migrating flock on time. All these things do not lead to a normal psychic state.

I know this from my own experiences of co-existing with birds: thrushes would nibble on bushes of berries, and I would then gather them; crows always sat on the building outside my window; sparrows would not allow swallows into their nests on my balcony; a rook drowned in my bucket of water; a crow lived with me for a while; my kids found a frozen parrot that later flew freely around my house; a stork fell, weakened by a long flight, while I was on my post when I was in the army; pigeons that my neighbors would fry up on Saturdays; a crane that flew to my forest from bombarded Serbia; crows from which I stole nuts in the army... If plants are notions, and animals are pictures, then birds are symbols and signs. I was not surprised that my acquaintance had become a theologian. Because, in some way, birds are similar to angels.

23.12

Lately, I have not only lost the ability to distinguish between years, but also between days of the week. That is why the idea of a "Sunday stroll" has become an archaism for me. And it's not so strange that this Sunday stroll took place on a Thursday. Actually, it was quite a perfect day for a walk—sunny, snowy, and frosty. Snow is especially conducive to strolling because it alters the space—it makes it more porcelaneous—it becomes divided, portioned, and partitioned into its various fragments. I chanced upon the most prestigious neighborhood in my city. This is an extraordinary neighborhood with magical blocks that lies to the right of a small park and to the left of the railway tracks. The fantastic world of a different city, of quiet streets—upon which you can walk outnumbering automobiles—of villas and orchards. It is the villas that are the most interesting. This corner of the world overflows with them. There are many of them and they are all different. Each of these villas acts as an illustration to a long story. Each of these stories includes an introduction, a conclusion, a peak, a culmination. They feature stability followed by collapse, one that is unnoticeable at first but then becomes steep, and later tumbles towards ruin. So that should be the end of the story. But not in this case, because the villas are stalwart and lasting. That is why old stories are replaced with new ones. And then everything begins anew—an idea, a peak, a culmination, stability. It is also clear that a collapse is coming. Without a certain aftertaste of collapse, buildings such as these lose their taste. It is especially interesting to see these villas as the materialization of someone's concept of an ideal building. Someone came up with the idea of having his own palace. Usually, it was the reflection of certain Viennese, Praguian, Cracovian, or, at least, Lvivian dreams. But how their dream was supposed to look was imagined poorly by the owners. That is why builders took this task upon themselves. Their dramas were also notched into each building. They, these buildings, are actually the manifestation of everything that did not work out in the lives of these architects, builders, engineers, and decorators. And, nonetheless, they are very much triumphant. It is our good fortune that there is a small territory such as this in our city. And it is our good fortune that one can take a Sunday stroll there. Even if takes place on a Thursday.

15.01

Living in my home (in addition to various people) is an extraordinary plant—an araucaria. If you look through the window from the street, you can see it. The araucaria is still shorter than me, although it's over a hundred years old. They grow very slowly, these araucaria, in their Andes. For araucaria are Andes evergreens. And they live some three thousand years. They were rather fashionable in European dwellings at the beginning of the century. The Secession style adored ornaments such as these. And truth be told, it really is beautiful. It has paw-like branches, four on each level. It usually does not contain more than three levels. The rest gradually droop, die off, and are moved out of the way. And fresh millimeters begin to grow on the top. This araucaria was given to my grandma as a gift in return for some sort of successful medical treatment back in the 20s. At that time, it was no taller than 40 cm, although it was older than my grandma, who, actually, was not yet a grandma. Based on its life span, the araucaria was an infant. At first, the plant did not notice anything. Later, it became increasingly nosy of everything that went on in the house, and all our experiences came to be preserved in its tree rings. Because it's been proven that plants, especially such perfect ones—although, perhaps, not fully capable of thought—at the very least, understand, sense, and remember everything.

Sometimes it's scary to be in its presence. Because it's not so easy to have witnessed past events and then live on for a few more thousand years, having outlived us all, everyone close to it now. For it, we probably are like some kind of half-real, half-imagined childhood memory. Perhaps, it barely notices us—if one takes the difference in our life spans into consideration. Surely, it's not able to comprehend individual episodes that take place with us as they happen—in the same way that a camera with an unbelievably long shutter speed does not fix something that has moved somewhere.

In that way, trees that live slowly don't notice, cannot notice, the existence of seasonal butterflies.

I bathe it every now and then. And every time I take out the trash, I see that my trash bin is unique because it contains araucaria branches.

Not long ago, I purchased another little evergreen from the Andes. Perhaps it's as old as I am. I'm convinced that at least this araucaria will survive to see better years.

24.01

The greatest joy a person, or any other living thing, can possess is communication. No matter what some may think, it is through communication that all things having to do with happiness come together. Without communication, everything loses its sense, and no pleasures can bring it back. That is why anything having to do with poor communication always results in drama. And complete misunderstanding—in a tragedy. There are various types of misunderstanding—on purpose or not on purpose, sudden or drawn out, fleeting or endless, radical or compromising. They're all tragic. And, first and foremost, they are based on an opposition of desires and intentions—this is the first level of misunderstanding. The second level is more complicated—when interests are common but there are different world views and manners of coexistence. And even higher is the level on which everything concurs, except for an understanding of words—meanings, shades, emphases, the history of a word and its various synonyms.

These tragedies are the most unpleasant ones, and there is almost no way out of such a situation. What's the saddest is when everybody thinks that they've done everything they could to understand someone else and to make themselves as easily understood as possible. What remains, then, is nothing but sorrow, reproach and distrust. I once knew a turtle. And I knew its owners. Both the owners and the turtle were very pleasant and loved one another; they did all they could to make sure that everyone was satisfied and happy. I remember the look that turtle had when it communicated with its owners. But one day the turtle carelessly crawled to the edge of the balcony and fell helplessly down onto the pavement. Luckily, it was found right away and taken back home. As it turned out, it was still alive—the shell had been only chipped a little bit. They treated it and it seemed like everything was back to normal. But something was not quite right—happiness had disappeared. At first the turtle became indifferent and soon, as a result, so did the people.

Gone were communication, contact, and understanding. Remaining were sorrow, reproach and distrust. And that is how they lived.

On one occasion, I gazed into the turtle's eyes for a long time and came to understand everything. It had become different—having fallen, the turtle had damaged its brain. Permanently. Simply put, it had gone crazy. And we could not know what was going on in its head—perhaps total darkness, perhaps the brightest of search-lights, maybe it had forgotten everything or, maybe it had excruciating headaches every night. Maybe it tickled between its brain and its skull, or maybe all sounds and smells irritated it. We could not know. We could not come to an understanding. We could not advise. We could not save it because we could not fully communicate. It, by the way, will live for another 240 years. With all of the above, but without us.

25.01

"A fable, that's all," is what they say in the mountains when they are inferring that something is not worthy of attention or is trivial. "Tell us the latest fable," they say on the street as night approaches, when a couple of friends sit by the fountain, enjoying a few beers at the end of a day of partying. It is then that true-yet-fantastic life stories are told, having been passed along by an acquaintance. And literary scholars refer to a fable as a short, allegorical work, in which usually animals, or other natural phenomena, embody various human characteristics, traits and conditions.

For too long, people have abused that last definition of a fable. As a result, an enormous number of mistakes and superstitions have occurred that twist the truths of natural science. Animals have become erroneous symbols, strapped with the burden of human faults and digressions that are alien to them. Yet, this can be looked at from another point of view. Instead of utilizing animal-protagonists when telling human stories, we can simply study actual situations that animals find themselves in and then recognize in those situations that which has happened, is happening, and may happen to us. So here's a short and true, non-fable story about how foxes acquire dwellings.

For foxes, to live comfortably in luxurious burrows is of paramount importance. But they are incapable of, don't want to, and don't know how to dig them. Wonderful burrows are made by badgers— deep, dry, sophisticated, multi-roomed. Toilets and bedrooms are in separate rooms; corridors branch out; there are several entrances and exits. Badgers are born to be builders, while foxes need to find badgers' burrows and take them over. It is impossible to do this by force. A badger's jaw is among the most powerful, and a strike with its paw can kill two foxes, along with their babies. But there is another way, another approach. Badgers are extremely tidy animals. They hate—they cannot stand—the smell of a toilet. Foxes take advantage of this. Upon discovering a badger's dwelling, they relieve themselves right at the entrance. The first time around, the badger gathers the feces and buries it somewhere. And then the foxes do it again. And the badgers do it again. This goes on for several consecutive days. The tired and disillusioned badgers gather their whole family, including their pregnant ones, infants, teenagers and the helpless aged, and abandon their homestead. They cannot take it anymore. They prefer to go a different place and build a new, ideal home—sophisticated, dry and deep. And the trashed, vacated burrow is then calmly settled by the foxes.

27.01

A meal, any meal, has a distinct ritualistic significance, especially a common meal. A common meal is like an inner circle, a brotherhood, an exchange of confirmations and guarantees, a sign of similarity and camaraderie; it's like being involved in a crime or taking part in a heroic deed. I have shared a meal in the most diverse, and sometimes uncertain, exotic and wild situations. Holiday parties, family lunches and dinners, wakes, nighttime breakfasts, the distribution of dry rations and improvised drinking snacks with the guys, the feeding of one's own children and of others' children, friends and foes, feedings in the hospital and food in the train, the last of what is edible in the mountains and the final grains of various cereals, cooked together, sliced sandwiches, receptions of the highest order, feeding by random people who had put me up for the night. Delicious, improvised suppers and the finishing off of meat scraps in restaurants, mystical Christmas Eve dinners and Easter eggs. And countless other lofty and lowly manifestations of the ritual of common meals.

But a particular one stands out in my memory—an unforgettable breakfast in Kyiv. It was about an hour before the hunger strike demonstration was to begin on the Maidan—Freedom Square.[8] Several tens of students entered the cafeteria on the street just above the square for what could end up being our final breakfast. We ate boiled eggs, cheese, sour cream, crepes, and omelets; we drank coffee and sweet tea. Strangely, it was eerily good—calm, placid, filling, and immediate. The October sun broke through the huge windows in a special way and filled the whole cafeteria space. Less than one hour remained before the deciding moment. And then, suddenly, the doors opened and members of the riot police began entering the hall—wearing helmets and carrying

---

8   In October 1990, hundreds of students occupied Lenin Square in Kyiv, in Soviet Ukraine, demanding reforms in Soviet political and military spheres. Many of the participants went on a hunger strike. In independent Ukraine, the Square was renamed Maidan Nezalezhnosti (Freedom Square) and was the site of both the Orange Revolution (2004) and Revolution of Dignity (2013-14), the latter often referred to as EuroMaidan.

batons and shields. They entered one after another, forming a seemingly endless line.

"And in just such a primitive fashion unsuccessful revolutions come to an end," I thought to myself, "in a cafeteria, when all the participants in the rebellion are satiated and helpless."

But a minute later, it became evident that this was not the end of the revolution. Because the riot police warriors did not pay any attention to us. They too had come to eat breakfast—they had been brought in from various cities in the morning and, before tending to their duties, before the battle that was to take place in those abovementioned forty minutes, the soldiers wanted to eat. They ate eggs, sour cream, kefir, cheese, and crepes, and sat at the neighboring tables. They did not realize that they had been brought to Kyiv because of those sitting next to them. We finished the meal together. We exited in two separate groups and had a smoke after the meal. We had a smoke and dumped our cigarette butts into the same trashcan. And we parted. Within five minutes, we had run onto the Maidan and sat down on the granite, having begun the hunger strike, the rebellion, and they took up their positions, surrounding the Maidan with a ring of iron. All sorts of things happened in the days that followed. But on that first day, we ate together.

10.02

Some time ago, I came to realize that if a weapon is aimed at you it doesn't necessarily mean anything, because if it truly is aimed at you, then there is nothing you can do about it, and if it is only vaguely aimed at you, then it will not be shot. I have been aimed at many times and nothing really came of it. I needed to just stay calm, even though, in the past, I've been commanded to do some ridiculous things with a weapon pointed at me—jump out of a moving train or off a towering bridge, give up something that was very important to me, or some other impossible feat. But these are all fragments that are soon forgotten. They rarely actually fired and almost always inaccurately. I was only accurately shot at once—I almost died instead of my buddy. But nothing came of it. They missed me. And this is what bought my buddy a bit more life. I seldom had such reliable buddies. And such ideal ones. His name was Rudko. I named him. Large, wolf-like, but yellow and with long hair. With the marvelous eyes of a tiger or bobcat—amber, deep and wise. And those eyebrows. Completely human-like, brown eyebrows. He was all grown up, and with a massive collection of nasty experiences, when he showed up on our mountain. He immediately became attached to me. In the beginning, he would occasionally bark at me when I would pet him, because tenderness seemed somewhat strange and cunning to him. But he soon got used to it. Only I was capable of petting him the way he wanted to be petted. Even though he began living with us, Rudko never entered the house. I suspect that he was claustrophobic. He kept order in the yard—he didn't allow anyone into it but members of the family, he mercilessly harassed postal carriers, he barked at all the trains. He hated anything that represented the slightest change in the rhythm of our lives. And besides that, for some reason, he defended me from certain family members and determined that I should not have anything to do with them. Infrequently, he could get upset and gnaw someone. Gnaw them, not bite them. Soon, the list of those who had been gnawed was identical to the list of those who lived near us. And it was then that the older adult neighbors decided that it was time to get rid of him. One of them had a rifle; the others would stake out

Rudko. The dog sensed something and stopped visiting the neighboring territories.

I was running in the ravine when buck-shot whistled over my head. Surprisingly, I didn't fall to the ground. I peeked out of the ravine and heard a couple more whistles by my head and saw the neighbors-hunters, who were shooting in my direction. They were shooting because the only thing sticking out of the ravine was my head, which, with its color and shagginess, recalled some part of Rudko's body. After the sharpshooters had come to their senses, they kissed and hugged me for a long time. And, as if speaking to someone who had returned from the dead, they promised me they would no longer harass my buddy. Of course, as it is written in ancient books, in time, they simply rescinded their promise. I think that if they had shot and killed me that day, this would have happened even sooner.

Translated by Mark Andryczyk

SERHIY ZHADAN

SERHIY ZHADAN is the most popular poet of the post-independence generation in Ukraine. His work speaks to the disillusionment, difficulties, and ironies brought by the collapse of the Soviet Union. Zhadan's readings fill large auditoriums, and he publishes regularly. He is considered to be Ukraine's most important poet of the decade, and even one of the leading voices of the last century.

Serhiy Zhadan was born on August 23, 1974 in the town of Starobilsk in the Luhansk oblast of eastern Ukraine. He graduated from the Kharkiv Teacher's College, where he wrote a thesis on the work of Mykhail Semenko and the Ukrainian Futurist writers of the 1920s. Zhadan currently lives in Kharkiv and writes poetry, prose and essays; he also translates from German, Belarusian, Polish and Russian. Zhadan is the author of the collections of poetry *Rozhevyi degenerat* (Pink Degenerate, 1993) *Tsytatnyk* (Quotations, 1995) *Heneral Iuda* (General Judas, 1995), *Pepsi* (1998), *the very, very best poems, psychedelic stories of fighting and other bullshit* (selected works 1992-2000, 2000), *Balady pro viinu i vidbudovu* (Ballads about War and Reconstruction, 2001), *Istoriia kultury pochatku stolittia* (History of Culture at the Turn of the Century, 2003), *UkSSR* (2004), *Maradona* (2007), *Lili Marlene* (2009), *Efiopiia* (Ethiopia, 2009), *Vohnepalni i nozhovi* (Gunshot and Cut Wounds, 2012), *Zhyttia Marii* (The Life of Mary, 2015), and *Tampliiery* (Knights Templar, 2016). He is the author of the prose publications *Big Mak* (Big Mac, 2003), *Depesh Mod* (Depeche Mode, 2004), *Anarchy in the UKR* (2005), *Himn demokratychnoï molodi* (The Hymn of the Democratic Youth, 2006), *Voroshylovhrad* (2010), *Big Mak ta inshi istroiï* (Big Mac and Other Stories, 2011), and *Mesopotamiia* (Mesopotamia, 2014). In 2014, *Voroshylovhrad* received the prestigious Jan Michalski Prize for Literature and the Best Book of the Decade award from the BBC Ukrainian Service. Zhadan has also written several theater pieces, which have been staged in Kharkiv and New York. He has also compiled and edited several anthologies of poetry and prose. Zhadan's work has been translated into German, English, Swedish, French, Italian, Polish, Hungarian, Slovak, Slovenian, Serbian, Croatian, Lithuanian, Belarusian, Russian, and Armenian. He performs with the band *Sobaky v Kosmosi* (Dogs in Space). English-language translations of two of his novels, *Depeche Mode* and *Voroshilovgrad*, were published in 2013 and 2016 respectively. Translations of *Mesopotamiia* and of a volume of selected poems are forthcoming from Yale University Press.

Serhiy Zhadan's events in the Contemporary Ukrainian Literature Series, entitled *Gospels and Spirituals*, took place in December 2010.

CHINESE COOKING

This happened some fifteen years ago, if I'm not mistaken.
Right here, you know, on the next street, there's a tall building
where they rent out rooms,
well, several Chinese lived there then and, it turned out, they were traf-
ficking drugs in
their own stomachs
like some unseen heavenly caviar, capable of finally destroying this
rotten civilization.

These rooms were mostly rented out by taxi drivers and charlatans,
as well as aeronauts, deprived of their heavenly apparatus, who always
made coffee in
the kitchen
and listened to jazz radio stations
till things would start to glow with a bright light without casting shadows
while former rugby players drank beer and smoked camels as they
played cards and
talked about their damned rugby.

But something went wrong with the Chinese business, much was
written about this later,
you know how it is: one day the split wasn't right—and that was it,
so they had this terrible shoot out right there in the back yard,
scaring rats into the basement and birds into the heavens.

I stop in there, once in a while; I make a little detour on my way home,
I look up at the fire escapes and see the sky in which, if you think about
it, there's
nothing but sky,
and you know, sometimes it seems to me that people really die
because their hearts stop out of love for this
strange-strange fantastic world.

Translated by Virlana Tkacz and Wanda Phipps

HOTEL BUSINESS

In cheap Berlin hotels run by Russians
there are no candies in the lobby and in the rooms—of course—
no envelopes with the hotel's logo,
tubs yellow with age
hide fish and scorpions,
the frequent guests have seen life
and have many tales to tell before they collapse
on the bed with their liquor and old cigarette holders.

While they talk and chew the sliced ham
bought in the store across the street,
the ash from their cigarettes falls on the bed,
snow on a port city,
the moon manages to move from the street corner closer to the church,
and the cleaning ladies start their morning rounds
to find condoms in showers
and towels smeared with blood.

One day a man takes a room
in one of these hotels, he shows his student ID
to register and locks himself in his room.
In the morning they bring him breakfast and he
takes the tray, then, without taking off his clothes or shoes,
gets into the tub and turns on the water.

The cleaning ladies gossip about this endlessly
since they found him the next day
and called the police.
Did he have to swallow so many pills
to simply drown in the water?
See, death can smell of
Turkish coffee,
and what should we do after this.

Cities torn apart by the cravings of lonely women,
the moon covered with the saliva of young immigrants—
everything they talk about, all the stories they have to tell,
every gulp and every puff,
is only an excuse to continue the endless conversation.

Few guess at the limits of the visible world,
especially in this room with its toaster and night-light,
from which there is no return and no explanation,
you will not listen to the frightened cleaning lady
who first entered the room
and saw the wet currency and black dolphins
float in the water
as spiders and angels descended
from the ceiling on thin webs
to throw rose petals
into the chlorinated water.

Translated by Virlana Tkacz and Wanda Phipps

CHILDREN'S TRAIN

Get out of the rainy street into the auditorium,
in March when many of the city's insane
warm themselves in libraries and free public toilets
turning their brown eyes to light like newts;
the generous hand of time dips into its watery reservoirs and pours into
   your palms
handfuls of mussels and snails,
comets and river rocks.

There was a time when all the trains stations in my city
stopped like alarm clocks
with a thousand broken springs;
hiding beneath the sky
in which two lights flew
like a person with two hearts,
red-haired girls who held dusk on the tip of their tongues,
sang a song of coal
full of old armor, clothes, and decaying tarantulas;
and on the hill where the city ended,
you could see the train
the workers took home.

In this mining village,
so much fire, tears, and coal
burned in the lungs, sails full of wind.
Why does the sky gather all the sweets,
goods and light
only to turn its back and disappear behind the hill?

We paid with our lives
for every invisible exhaled breath of each butterfly exhausted by the night,
for every orphan folding his sheets like a parachute in the morning,
for every clarinet stuck in your throat which won't let you breathe,

transforming the voice into shadows and jazz into disease.
Hold me tighter. The experience
you gain is a scaffold
to support unsteady young lungs
with wire and chalk.

And the snow like old sheets
stuffed in the dresser drawers of heaven
won't cover your grief. Look—
gusts dance from border to border
and train stations like unexploded bombs crouch in the dark,
and lonely night express trains like lake serpents
swim through the dark beating their tails
around your heart.

Translated by Virlana Tkacz and Wanda Phipps

THE INNER COLOR OF EYES

On the university steps sits a woman
just under thirty
smoking camels.
After the rain
she wipes her skin
which is so transparent that
you can see seaweed and sand underneath.
She thinks cool blades and silver nails
are falling from the heavens once again
mortally wounding snails
cut in half like crusaders in the sands of Palestine.

It's important to talk long,
to whisper and pronounce
various words and the names of various things
so that the air around her
does not seem so empty.
After awakening,
all her men
hold their heads to clocks
like seashells
and listen to the sound of giant turtles
raising the silt
in distant lakes.

And you won't even call her when you get a chance
because sometimes it's worth dying to understand
that this was actually life
and that is why when you close your eyes you can see
on which side of the dream you find yourself;
after this change in the weather the pressure will rise again
causing capillaries to burst
in the eyes of passing butterflies

and her skin becomes warmer
and the water in her faucets and pans
turns to blood
and once again she can't
make herself tea
or even a cup of coffee.

Translated by Virlana Tkacz and Wanda Phipps

ALCOHOL

The green river water
slows in warm bends
fish zeppelins
scatter the plankton
and tired bird catchers
attempt to catch
every word.

Hold on to
the brightly colored rags and scotch tape
that bind the slashed wrists
of these heroic times.
One day you will turn off this radio,
you'll get used to her,
to her breathing
and, dressed in your T-shirt,
she'll bring you water in the middle of the night.

On the terrace the left-over cups of tea
are filling up with rain water
and cigarette butts,
you and I share a cold
you and I share long conversations—
you don't notice the morning rain
you go to sleep late
and you wake up late
I write poems about how I love
this woman, and I invent
newer and newer words
to avoid
telling her.

Translated by Virlana Tkacz and Wanda Phipps

CONTRABAND

In a broken seat, ripped out of a truck,
looking at clouds overhead
since early morning
sits the young god of European contraband
wrapped in a down jacket
listening to a gypsy melody playing on a stolen cell phone.

My countrymen, winter has come to our land
and oil shines in cellars, fish fall asleep in reservoirs,
churches and train stations are heated only by long conversations—
there is always more warmth in winter voices than content.

Tear the tanned leather of shearlings and bomber jackets;
as long as we know every saint
on our border by name,
countrymen, our sons can't be hurt by knives or bullets
or carried off by the current or blown away by the north wind.

Snow in the mountain pass
the bitches at customs
will take your weapons
will take your drugs
you will stand like a ghost in the fog, gold scattered about,
where now, lord, where are your Carpathians?

Who should I spend the night with in these fields without snow?
How can I cross to the other side, how can I stand
my fury which filled me when you abandoned me;
pull me out, lord, from this shit,
if you can see me in this fog.

> Wandering sun, roll through our quiet days,
> come, my joy, warm yourself with wine and fires.

While you suffer, winter is passing,
there's only our heat—nothing else,
between you and me—only a river
filled with fish and water.

Translated by Virlana Tkacz and Wanda Phipps

PAPRIKA

Walking through the supermarket at night
past the green flash of salads,
behind the two teens holding hands—
the girl picks out lemons and sweet peppers
and lets the boy hold them, then laughs and puts them back.
It's ten to ten, before this they argued
for a long time she wanted to leave, he convinced her to stay;
pockets full of green stuff,
gold Assyrian coins, painkillers,
sweet love, enchanted paprika.

take us out, come on, take us out, the dank soul, every dead fruit, the
   blood of
strawberries, and fish killed by old ship propellers in southern states,
   minced
with earrings and British punk pins, their gills stuffed with
caffeine, black disease, turning away from the green light, they groan as
   if begging

take us out from here, come on, take us out to the nearest bus stop, to
   the nearest
gas station, to the nearest cool ocean, they seem to signal, bending
their dank souls, till the propellers in the night skies above the supermarket
wreck the juicy air, and the caffeine stains your fingernails

take them out, well come on, hide the warm green flashes in your
   pockets, place silver
and gold coins under your tongue, take us to the nearest hiding place,
   to the nearest stadium,
blood for blood, the lord calls us, moving our fins

Since I won't ever be able to hold anyone
the way he holds her, I can't simply pass by

all this still life, I hesitated too long,
didn't have the strength to move, so now I have to follow them.

Where you are now, you must know what awaits them, right? where
you wound up, you can predict everything—two or three more years of
    golden
teenage swooning in the August grass, squandering coins on all kinds of
poisons and that's it—memory fills the place in you once occupied by
    tenderness.

Since I won't ever be able to be afraid for anyone
the way she is afraid for him, I won't ever be able to give
anything to anyone with the ease with which she places
the warm lemons in his hands;
I will follow them further
through the long exhausting twilight of the supermarket,
with yellow grass underfoot,
dead fish in hand,
warming its heart
with my breath
warming my breath
with its heart.

Translated by Virlana Tkacz and Wanda Phipps

***

… not to wake her up,
carefully stepping over the things she left
books and clothes, fragments of a May night
warm as the air; stepping over these in the silence
where walls, windows, stairways, and stagnant darkness
settle in the dregs;
stepping closer to the wet, fresh shutters,
where the solitude of plants and trees begins,
warmed by their own growth,
hearths of homes heated by the breath of entire provinces,
the breath of a country, a hot May night on the plains,
deep viscous ground actively expanding
toward its surface;
stepping over the grass, you feel how much the planets strain
to stay in balance as they stream past you,
the entire atmosphere, which accompanies you,
all the darkness of the world, the order of all things
the measure and imperceptible drift of the objects
inside themselves, your moment expands,
but not enough, to encompass
this parting in May and the alarming heat of the factories.

To begin from a different place each time,
to emerge every time from the black nothingness toward voices
and the breath of those you share life with
touching all the scars and veins on the body of your country,
all the bends in the twigs that keep their balance,
touching the warm air currents that spread over you,
washing out dreams from hearts,
so that by morning she no longer remembers
what she dreamt that night.

Light spilling from atom to atom,

straightening the roots and the stems that give them height,
dragging the slippery sap filled with bitterness
along the railroad tracks, pulling along
swallows and insects, chimneys and antennae—
the trees reach with their bodies toward those places,
where our atmosphere breaks off
and where nothingness begins,
almost reaching that point where twilight appears,
where only silence is strewn and rain forms.
And before crossing that boundary, before landing on the other side of air,
before finally untangling themselves from the dense May background
they suddenly think that even the smallest motion,
the smallest shudder of a wet twig will not go unpunished,
for stirring up the air, displacing space
and awakening her from her dream.
This is what stops them …

Translated by Virlana Tkacz and Wanda Phipps

THE LORD SYMPATHIZES WITH OUTSIDERS

I looked out at the sea and understood everything—
for three days I had been wandering up and down the empty shore
walking out onto the wetlands where raindrops hung,
and fell, you know, into these wetlands, and swam
there like fish, for three days I saw the golden light of diners, motels,
and harbor eateries packed with workers in
white T-shirts, who drowned in alcohol as their sweet saliva
colored their liquor pink,

this is what I think—
I think, Jesus was a red, he made
all this up on purpose, so you would suffer,
as you run into all the mistakes in his blueprints,
he seems to be saying on purpose—
look, he says to you,
here is your heart, here is her heart, do you hear how they beat?
you're alive, as long as you listen to all the sounds and movements deep
    under your
skin,
you're alive, as long as you see what is happening there—
inside of things or objects rising up beneath the surface.

And then I thought, you know—all these bicycles in the sand,
and all these preachers on lifeguard towers—
when you wade far out into the water and preach to all
the jellyfish and flying fish, lecturing them, as they
patiently swim around you, explaining
to them the dimmest and most terrifying entries in your
dictionary, telling them—

that Jesus was a red, with all his leftist tricks
like walking on water, all his apostles—
engineers from the local tech, who gathered at the factory

for their last supper, all those golden threads in your sweater
and scabs on your knees,

Jesus was definitely red, he counted on
the communist principles of bird flight,
and all the rest so that you would suffer,
listening to the heartbeat of trees and bicycles,
to the conversation of foremen, whose tongues are washed
down with cool liquor, like new chrome.

The green grass, which will grow on these foundations,
the green grass which no one knows yet, the green
grass, around which the heavens spin,
grass—green and damp is the reason for
everything;

this girl has such narrow veins that sometimes
her blood can't push through them,
can you hear her heart in the winter, when skin dries like a river?
her heart beats slower now,
this means that she is either asleep
or simply very calm.

Translated by Virlana Tkacz and Wanda Phipps

OWNER OF THE BEST GAY BAR

Anyone who has ever experienced true despair will surely understand me. One morning, you wake up and realize that everything is wrong, terribly wrong. Not too long ago—yesterday, for instance—you were still able to induce change, to improve things, to make your mark, but now—you stand by the wayside and no longer have an effect on events, which unfurl like bedsheets around you. This very sense of helplessness, estrangement, and disassociation is what a person feels, I guess, before death, if I correctly understand the concept of death—you seemed to have done everything right, you kept everything under control, why are they now trying to disconnect you from the twisting red wires of the system, to delete you, like a file, and cleanse you away, like a skin infection; why does life, in which you had just been playing an active role, ebb, like the sea, heading east, quickly becoming distant and leaving the sunshine of slow death in its tracks? The unfairness of death is felt most harshly during life; no one tries to convince you of the purpose of your relocation to the territory of the deceased, they simply won't have enough arguments to accomplish this. But everything is wrong, you yourself suddenly start believing in it, you fathom it and become silent and you let certain charlatans, alchemists, and pathologists-anatomists rip out your heart and display it at fairs and museums of curiosities, you let them smuggle it out for the purpose of conducting suspicious experiments and performing gloomy rituals, you let them talk about you like about a deceased person and let them fondle your heart—which has become black from love lost, recreational drugs, and a bad diet—with their smoke-scented fingers.

Behind all of this stood the tears, the nerves, and the love of your contemporaries. Tears, nerves, and love, in particular, because all the misfortune and the problems of your contemporaries began concurrently with puberty and ended with default, and if anything is ever able to silence these smoldering Slavic tongues and these strong smoky lungs will once again be capable of containing air—it'll be love and economics, business and passion, in their most improbable manifestations—I have in mind both passion and, of course, business, everything else remains beyond the flow, beyond the dark turbulent current into which you all jump, having just reached adulthood. Everything else remains scum, circles on the water, superfluous additions to a biography, dissolving in oxygen, which, although it may also seem to be necessary for life, in reality—is not. Why? Because, in reality, no one really dies from a lack of oxygen, they die from a lack of love or a lack of cash. When, at some point, you wake up and realize that everything is terribly wrong, that she's gone, that yesterday you still had a chance to stop her from leaving, that you could have fixed everything, but that today—it's too late, and now you're left on your own and she won't be around for the next fifty or sixty years, depending on your desire and ability to live without her. And from this realization you suddenly became enrobed with vast and endless futility, and beads of sweat prance upon your hapless skin, like clowns at a circus, and your memory refuses to cooperate with you; but then people don't die from this either, it's actually the opposite— all faucets are flipped on and all manhole covers explode, you say that everything is okay, I'm fine, I'll get through this, everything's good and you painfully battle on, ending up in those vacuums, which were created in the space where she had been, into all these wind tunnels and corridors, which she had filled with her voice and in which the monsters and reptiles of her absence begin to nest, everything's okay, you say, I'll get through this, I'm fine, no one has died from this yet, one more night, just a couple more hours in territories sown with black pepper, shattered glass, on hot sand mixed with bullet casings and bits of tobacco, in clothes, which you both wore, beneath the sky, which is now just yours, using her toothbrush, taking her towels with you to bed, listening to her radio, singing along during especially significant parts—the ones she never sang, singing those parts for her, especially when important things are mentioned in a song, like life or one's relationship with one's parents, or religion, for that matter. What can be sadder than this singing alone, which, occasionally, is interrupted by the latest news—and then a situation arises in which each upcoming news update could really be your last.

The only thing that could be sadder than this is the situation with money. Everything that has to do with finances, with the business which you conduct, with your personal financial stability, leads you into an increasingly darker and more hopeless corner from which there is only one way out—into a black, little-known space, in which the region of death is found. At which point you wake up and realize that, in order to prolong life, you need outside support and, hopefully, this support comes directly from the Lord God or from anyone within his closest circle. Well forget about support. Put this word out of your mind. Everything in this world revolves around you, so you've got to pull it off yourself, be wary of business and love, sex and economics— yes, yes, economics—that prostate of the middle class, that tachycardia for the boy scouts of the stock markets; a couple of unsuccessful policy decisions and you are a soon-to-be drowned person, in the sense that they'll definitely drown you, probably in cement, and fatal cement waves, the color of coffee with milk, will overcome you, distancing you from life, and even from death, because, in this situation, you don't deserve a normal, peaceful death, whether you pull it off or not, it doesn't matter, financial debt hangs above you, like a full moon, and all you can do is howl at it, attracting the attention of the tax inspectors. So many young souls have been swallowed up by the inability to come up with a good business plan, so many hearts were torn by privatization politics; wrinkles on their wizened faces and a yellow, metallic reflection in their eyes are all that remain after the long battle for survival—this is our country, this is our economics, this is your and my path to immortality, the presence of which you sense, waking up at some point and unexpectedly realizing that, in life, there is nothing but your soul, your love, and your, goddamn it, debt, which you will never be able to pay off, at least not in this life.

And that's precisely what we're going to talk about.

The story about the nightclub was told to me directly by one of its founders. I had heard about it for quite some time but I hadn't crossed paths with him, which isn't so strange, considering the specifics of the establishment. Rumors of the city's first official gay bar had been circulating for several years, various names and addresses were mentioned and, because no one really knew where it was actually located, every place was considered to be suspicious. The place where the nightclub was most often discussed was at the stadium—the city's right-wing youth staunchly condemned the appearance of establishments with such a profile, they promised to burn down this nightclub together with all the gays that gather there for their so-called soirées. Once, during the 2003–2004 season, they even burned down the Buratino café, which is located right next to the stadium, but the police, rightfully, did not trace a connection between this incident and the existence of a gay nightclub, because, just think about it—what kind of gay nightclub could be established in a Buratino café, the name of which, itself, is xenophobic. On the other hand, the nightclub was often mentioned in mass media outlets, in various chronicles of cultural events, or in features about the city's vibrant nightclub scene. Usually, stories on the city's nightclub scene recalled letters from the front lines—television reports on this theme featured various toasts being announced which were then followed by machine-gun shots, and sometimes, if the cameraman didn't neglect his, let's say, professional duties, in other words, if he didn't get shit-faced off of the complimentary cognac, the machine-gun shots would ring in unison with wedding toasts and parting gestures, and the pulsating bullets would poke holes in the warm Kharkiv sky, like a salute to faithfulness, love, and other things rarely seen on television. In this context, news about the gay nightclub was intriguing because of the lack of any clear picture or of any mention concerning the direct ties between the government and criminals, it was just that there was a party, it took place in a gay nightclub, the public behaved in a civil manner, there were no casualties. In any case, rumors about the nightclub kept spreading but, in reality, the wave of interest fell, which wasn't hard to predict from the start—our city has much more exciting establishments, like the Tractor Plant, for example. And, generally speaking, who's really interested in the affairs of sexual minorities in a country that has such a substantial foreign debt. And even the fact that the nightclub, according to rumors, was part of the governor's racket, didn't create any special resonance—this is what they expected from the governor. Everyone, in essence, runs his own business, what's most important is a clear conscience and the timely submission of tax forms.

San Sanych and I met during the elections. He looked like he was about forty years old but he was actually born in 1974. It's just that one's biography is stronger than one's genes, and Sanych was a prime example of that. He would walk around in a black, squeaky leather jacket carrying a piece—a typical, mid-level mafioso, if you know what I mean. Although, for a mafioso, he was rather melancholic, he seldom spoke on the phone, occasionally calling his mother, and, as far as I can remember, nobody ever called him. He introduced himself as San Sanych when we first met and gave me his business card, on which "San Sanych, Lawyer" was written in gold letters on vellum paper, along with several phone numbers with London area codes; Sanych said that they were office phone numbers, I asked whose, but he didn't answer me. We became friends at once; Sanych pulled the piece out of his pocket, said that he is a supporter of free elections, and mentioned that he could get a hundred of these pieces, if necessary. He added that he has an acquaintance working for the Dynamo sports club, who takes starter pistols and transforms them into normal guns in his home workshop. "Look," he said, "if you file down this thingy"—he was pointing to a place where, obviously, the thingy was once located, having earlier been filed down —"you can load it with normal cartridges, and what's most important is that you won't have any problems with the police, it's just a starter pistol, right? If you want, I can get you a set, it'll run you forty bucks, plus ten more to file down that thingy. If necessary, I can sort you out with a Dynamo worker's card, to make it fully legit." Sanych loved weapons and he loved talking about them even more. In time, I became one of his closest friends.

One time, he told me about the nightclub; he just happened to mention that before becoming a lawyer and a supporter of free elections he had been in the nightclub business and, as it turns out, he was directly involved with the first official gay nightclub—that very mysterious establishment that the city's progressive youth unsuccessfully spent so much time trying to burn down. That's when I asked him to tell me more about it and he agreed, saying, okay, no problem, it's all in the distant past, why not tell the story.

And his story went something like this.

It turns out that he was a member of the Boxers for Fairness and Social Adaptation Association. He told me a bit about it; they grew out of the Dynamo sports club as a people's organization of former professional athletes. What Boxers for Fairness and Social Adaptation actually did, nobody really knows, but the fatality rate among members of this organization was quite high, every month one of them would be shot and then pompous memorial services would take place, which police officials and members of the regional government would attend. Occasionally, every couple of months, Boxers for Fairness and Social Adaptation would organize friendly matches with the Polish national team, at least that's what they called it; several buses would pull up to their office, they'd fill them up with boxers and a large array of domestically produced electronics, and the caravan would set off for Poland. The regional directors and the trainers would travel separately. Having arrived in Warsaw, the boxers would go to the stadium and would unload the whole freight, after which they would celebrate yet another victory for the national Paralympic movement. What was interesting was that Sanych was not a boxer. Sanych was a wrestler. Not as in a wrestler for fairness and social adaptation, but as in a freestyle wrestler. His grandfather introduced him to it; at one time, his grandfather was quite serious about wrestling and even took part in a competition featuring all the peoples of the USSR at which he had his hand broken, which he was quite proud of—not of the broken hand, that is, but of his participation in the competition. And thus, his grandfather brought him to Dynamo. Sanych started out doing quite well. He took part in city matches, he showed much promise, but after a few years he also had his hand broken. At this point he had already finished his studies and had begun setting up his business, but was having difficulty, especially with the broken hand. And that is when he came to Boxers for Fairness and Social Adaptation. Boxers for Fairness and Social Adaptation looked at his hand, asked him whether he supported fairness and whether he supported social adaptation, and, having received an affirmative answer, accepted him. Sanych immediately joined a brigade that dealt with the markets in the Tractor district. It turned out that making a career in this business was not so hard—no sooner had your superior been killed than you immediately filled his position. Within a year, Sanych was put in charge of a small unit, again he showed much promise, but he didn't really like the business: Sanych did possess a higher education and dying before he turned thirty from a dealer's grenade didn't tickle his fancy. Even more importantly, business took up all of his free time and he had no personal life, if you don't count the prostitutes which he would personally pick up at the markets. But Sanych didn't count the prostitutes, they probably didn't consider it as being a part of one's personal life either, it's more like one's societal-economic life, which may be the best way to put it. And thus, Sanych began to seriously contemplate his future. The incident with the bulletproof vest was the turning point. One time, in the midst of a prolonged alcoholic stupor (obviously it must have been some kind of holiday period, the Birth of Christ, I believe), Sanych's underlings decided to give their young boss a bulletproof vest. They had gotten the bulletproof vest from the workers of the Kyiv regional militia in exchange for a latest-model copy machine. They partied for a while to celebrate the gift and then decided to try it out. Sanych put on the bulletproof vest, his boys got a Kalashnikov. The bulletproof vest turned out to be a pretty reliable thing—Sanych survived, having only gotten three semi-serious bullet wounds. But he decided that this would be the end—a career as a freestyle wrestler didn't work out, a career as a combatant for fairness and social adaptation also wasn't progressing in the best manner, it was time for a change.

Having licked his wounds, Sanych went to Boxers for Fairness and Social Adaptation and asked to leave the business. Boxers for Fairness and Social Adaptation correctly observed that it's not so easy to leave the business in this line of work, not alive, at least, but they eventually took Sanych's battle wounds into consideration and agreed. In parting, they expressed their hope that Sanych wouldn't sever his ties with the association and that, in life, he would continue to serve the ideals of the fight for fairness and social adaptation and, in the end, they wished him a speedy recovery and set off to load the bus with stacks of domestically produced electronics. In such a manner, Sanych ended up on the street—with no business or personal life, but with a wrestling background and a higher education; the latter, though, was of little interest to anyone. And in his time of crisis he meets up with Hoha—Heorhii Lomaia. They had been classmates, after which San Sanych went into wrestling and Hoha went into medicine. They hadn't seen one another for the last few years—Sanych, as has been noted earlier, was actively involved with the movement for the social adaptation of boxers, while Hoha, being a young specialist, went to the Caucasus region and took part in the Russian-Chechen war. But it was unclear with which side he was actively involved because, in the capacity of a middleman, he would purchase drugs from the Russian health ministry and would then sell them to the administrations of the Georgian rehab centers where Chechens were being treated. His downfall, however, came with the anesthetics, when, having purchased too many of them, he induced the health ministry officials to raise the buying price and to pose a completely reasonable question: why does the regional children's medical center, to which the funds were allocated, need so many narcotics? Because of this, Hoha was forced to return home, getting into several shootouts with offended Caucasian dealers along the way. Having returned, he immediately picked up several shipments of gypsum boards. Business was going well but Hoha became obsessed with a new idea, which occupied an increasingly larger part of his imagination and ambitions—he decided to go into the nightclub business. And it was precisely at this anxious time that our protagonists met up.

"Listen," said Hoha to his childhood chum, "I'm new to this business and I need your help. I want to open a nightclub." "You know," his old friend replied, "I really don't know much about any of this, but, if you want, I can ask around." "You misunderstood," Hoha said to him, "I don't need you to ask around, I already know everything, I need a compadre, you dig? I want you in this business together with me, it's better for me that way, you see—I've known you since childhood, I know your parents, I know where to find you if I need to, should you decide to bail on me. And, most importantly, you've worked with everybody here. You're a true compadre." "What," asked Sanych, "you really think you'll make some money off of this?" "You understand," answered Hoha Lomaia, "I can make money off of anything. You think I'm doing this for the money? Hell, I've got five freights full of gypsum boards at Balashovka, I could sell them right now and it's 'Cyprus here I come.' But you have to understand why I'm so enthralled with this idea—I don't want to go to Cyprus. And do you know why I don't want to go to Cyprus? I'm almost thirty, just like you, by the way. I've done business in four different countries, I'm being pursued by the law agencies of several autonomous republics, I should have been lying dead from a disease in the tundra long ago, I've been under artillery fire three times, I had President Basaiev as my client. I was almost shot to death by a Krasnoyar special forces unit, once, a lightning bolt hit a car which I was driving, I later had to replace the battery. I'm paying alimony to a widow in Northern Ingushetia—she's the only one of 'em getting any money from me—half of my teeth are implants, once I almost agreed to sell off one of my kidneys, because I needed to buy up a shipment of machine lathes. But I've returned home, I'm in a good mood and I sleep soundly, half of my friends have been killed, but half are still alive, like you, you're alive, but the odds were against you. So you see, somehow it turned out that I stayed alive, and once I was still alive, I thought to myself—hey, okay, Hoha, okay, now everything is alright, now everything will be good, if the Krasnoyar special forces weren't able to wipe you out and the lightning bolt didn't kill you, well then what do you need Cyprus for? And then I suddenly realized what I had wanted my whole life. And you know what?" "What?" San Sanych asked him. "My whole life I wanted to have my own nightclub in which I could sit every night and out of which no one could throw me, even if I started puking all over the menu. And what did I do? You know what I did?" Hoha chuckled. "I just went out and bought that dreamed-about fucking nightclub, you understand?" "When did you buy it?" Sanych asked. "A week ago." "What kind of nightclub?" "Well, it's not really a nightclub, it's a sandwich shop." "What?" Sanych asked, confused. "Yeah, the Sub, you know it? There's a shitload of work to do but it's a great location, in the Ivanov neighborhood, I'll unload the gypsum boards, renovate it, and all my problems will be behind me. All I need is a compadre, you dig? What do you think?" he asked Sanych. "I like the name." "What name?" "The nightclub's name: the Sub."

And so they agreed to meet the following day in the nightclub. Hoha promised to introduce his compadre to the proposed art director. San Sanych arrived on time; his school chum was already there, waiting outside by the entrance to the Sub. The Sub was in bad shape, it must have been thirty years since any renovations had been done here, and, taking into account that it had been built about thirty years ago, it can be said that the place had never been renovated. Hoha unlocked the door and let San Sanych in before him. San Sanych entered a half-lit space furnished with tables and plastic chairs and he sadly thought to himself—well I guess I should've stayed with Boxers for Fairness. But it was too late to do anything—Hoha followed him in and closed the door behind him. "The art director will be here shortly," he said and sat down at one of the tables. "We'll wait for him."

The art director's name was Slavik. Slavik, as it turns out, was an old druggie, he looked to be about forty years old, but it could have been the drugs. He was a half hour late, saying that there was a lot of traffic, and then later saying that he had taken the subway—in other words, he was talking shit. He was wearing an old jean jacket and big, nerdy sunglasses, which he categorically refused to take off, even in the dark basement. "Where'd you find this guy?" Sanych asked quietly, while Slavik was walking around and checking out the space. "My mom recommended him," Hoha replied, also quietly. "He was an art instructor at the Pioneer Youth Cultural Center, but was later thrown out for, I think, amoral conduct." "Well, obviously not for his religious convictions," said Sanych. "Well then," Hoha replied, "all right." "So," he shouted to Slavik, "what do you think?" "I like it, in theory," Slavik replied anxiously, coming up to them and sitting on a plastic stool. Just try not to like something you asshole, Sanych thought to himself, and even turned his phone off so that no one would bother them, and because no one ever called him anyway. "Well then," Hoha was visibly excited about the situation, "what do you say, any ideas?" "Okay, here's the deal," Slavik dramatically exhaled and pulled out a cheap cigarette, "here's the deal." He remained silent for a bit. "Heorhii Davydovych," he finally addressed Hoha, "I am going to be frank with you." What a moron, thought Sanych. Hoha was joyfully relishing in the depths of the sandwich shop. "I'll be frank," repeated Slavik. "I've been in show business for twenty years, I've also worked with the Ukrainian Concert Organization, musicians know who I am, I have contacts with Grebenshchikov's[1] people, I organized a U2 concert in Kharkiv...." "U2 played Kharkiv?" San Sanych interrupted him. "No, they shot down that idea," Slavik replied, "and here's what I want to say to you, Heorhii Davydovych," intentionally ignoring Sanych, "the fact that you bought this nightclub is a *fabulous* idea." "You really think so?" Hoha asked, in doubt. "Yes, it really is a *fabulous* idea. I'm being frank with you, I know everything about show business, I organized the first rock jam in this city." At this point he, apparently, recalled something, lost his train of thought, and became silent. "And?" Hoha asked, unable to contain himself. "Yes, yes," Slavik shook his head, "yep." Man, this guy must be totally wasted, Sanych thought emphatically. "What do you mean, yes?" Hoha didn't understand. "Yep," Slavik again shook his head, "yep...." San Sanych, out of options, went for his phone; in principle, at his previous job, he would just whack someone like this, but this was a different situation, a different business, let them settle this on their own. "This, Heorhii Davydovych, is what I have to say to you," Slavik suddenly began to say, and, to everyone's surprise, came up with this gem—

"The nightclub business," he began from afar, "is a real shitty affair, first of all because the market has already been established, you understand what I'm getting at?" Everyone looked like they had understood. "It's all because of mid-level business, it, goddamnit, this mid-level business developed first. So, you bought a space," he addressed, more

---

1   Boris Grebenshchikov (b. 1953) is a Russian musician. He is considered to be one of the founders of Russian rock music. His band *Akvarium* (Aquarium) was immensely popular in Soviet times and remains relevant and respected today.

than likely, Hoha, "you want to set up a quality nightclub, with a quality clientele, with a cultural program, blah, blah, blah." "Come on, Slavik, cut the bullshit," Hoha interrupted him. "Fine," Slavik agreed, "but what is it that is most important? What's the most important thing in show business?" Hoha gradually stopped chuckling. "What's most important is—the format! Yep, yep," Slavik merrily nodded, even clapping his hands once, "yes, that's it...." "Well what's the deal with the format?" Hoha asked after a long pause. "The format is a real fucking problem," Slavik replied. "In this business, all the spots have been taken, all the spots," he chuckled. "The market has already been formed, you understand? You wanna do fast food—go for it, but there are already a hundred fast-food joints in the city, you want to have a fancy restaurant—go ahead, I'll organize a cultural program, you want a dance club—let's do a dance club, you want a pub—let's do a pub. But you won't make dick off of it, Heorhii Davydovych—you'll have to excuse me for being so direct— you won't make dick." "And why is that?" an offended Hoha asked. "Because the market has already been established and they'll crush you. You've got nobody backing you up, right? They'll just burn you down together with your nightclub." "And what's your proposition," said Hoha, visibly upset, "do you have any ideas?" "Yep," Slavik smugly said, "yep, there is one *fabulous* idea, a truly *fabulous* idea." "Well, what's the idea?" asked Hoha, wary of where this was leading. "We need to fill a vacant niche, if I'm expressing myself clearly. And in this business there is only one niche—a gay nightclub needs to be opened." "What kind of nightclub?" Hoha couldn't believe his ears. "Gay," Slavik replied, "in other words, a nightclub for gays. That niche needs to be filled." "What, are you completely fucked in the head?" Hoha asked after another pause. "Are you serious?" "Well, why not?" Slavik asked defensively. "Wait, you seriously," Hoha was getting fired up, "want me, Heorhii Lomaia, to open a gay bar in my space? That's it, you're fired," he said and hopped off the table. "Hold on, wait, Heorhii Davydovych," now Slavik was getting nervy, "nobody's going to write 'Nightclub for Fags' in big bright letters on it, right?" "Well then what will you write?" Hoha asked him, putting on his overcoat. "We'll write 'Nightclub of Exotic Leisure,'" announced Slavik, "and we'll just give it an appropriate name. For example—the Peacock." "Moose-Cock" said Hoha, imitating his voice. "Who's going to come to your Peacock?" "But that's just it, lots of people," Slavik assured him. "It's like I said, there is a niche to be filled, in a city of two million people and not one gay bar! We're sitting on a pot of gold. You won't even have to work to draw a crowd, they'll come on their own, just open the door for them." After these words, Hoha grimaced and once again sat on the table but didn't take off his overcoat. Slavik saw this as a good sign, got another cigarette, and continued: "I myself was stunned when I came up with this idea. This is capital, lying right on the street, just pick it up and it's yours. I still can't believe that no one has thought to do this yet, another month or two and they'll steal this idea, you can bet on that. Mark my word!" Slavik was becoming increasingly edgy, perhaps truly fearing that they'll steal it. "In essence, we'll have no competition! Tell him," he finally turned his attention to San Sanych, looking for his support. "Okay," Hoha said at last, "on the surface, it's not a bad idea." "Are you being serious?" Sanych asked him. "Well why not, it's doable." "Of course it's doable!" Slavik cried fervently. "Hold on," Sanych interrupted him and once again addressed Hoha. "Listen, you and I are friends and all that, but I'm against this. I worked almost two years for Boxers for Fairness, they'll destroy me, are you kidding me? We agreed to set up a normal business, not some peacock." "Would you forget about the peacock," said Hoha, "nobody is planning on calling it the Peacock. We'll come up with a good name. Or we'll leave the old one." "What old one?" Sanych didn't understand. "The Sub! Of course," said Hoha, now once again becoming jovial. "It sounds great: 'The Sub: A Nightclub of Exotic Leisure.' What do you say Slavunia?" Slavunia nodded and then nodded again. It was difficult to expect any more from him. "Don't sweat it," Hoha said to his compadre, "the gays will be dealt with by that guy over there," he pointed at Slavik, "our job is to finish the renovations by summer, and then we'll see." And you know what, he was thinking out loud, why not a gay bar? At least there won't be any whores there.

And everybody went to work. Hoha unloaded the gypsum boards, Sanych introduced him to some necessary people, and they began renovating. Slavik, on his part, came up with the idea to register the gay bar as a youth nightclub, in order to avoid coughing up money as a commercial enterprise. As it turned out, everybody did indeed know Slavik, evidenced by their determined efforts to avoid him. In the morning, Slavik went to the Cultural Events Committee, visited their cafeteria, drank tea there, talked about the weather with the ladies working at the cafeteria, and then went to the office of cultural affairs. They wouldn't let him in, he became offended, rushed off to the nightclub, argued with the workers renovating it, hollered that he has been in show business for over twenty years, and threatened them that he would invite Grebenshchikov to the opening. And, by the way, about the opening—spring had passed, the renovations were completed, the nightclub could now be opened. Hoha once again gathered everyone, this time in his own, freshly renovated office. "Well," he asked, "anybody have any ideas for the opening?" "Okay, here's the deal, Heorhii Davydovych," Slavik began in a very official tone, "there are several ideas. Firstly, fireworks...." "Give me the second idea," Hoha interrupted him. "Okay," said Slavik, not being distracted, "I propose we serve Japanese food." "And where will you get it?" Sanych asked. "I have some acquaintances," Slavik replied, not without dignity. "They're Japanese?" "No, they're Vietnamese. But they pretend they're Japanese—they have two freight wagons at the Pivdennyi train station, in one of them they sew fur coats and in the other one they run a kitchen." "What else you got?" Hoha again interrupted him. "A circus striptease show," Slavik haughtily offered. "What kind?" Hoha asked. "Circus," Slavik repeated. "I've got some contacts, four chicks in bikinis, they work twenty-four-hour shifts, every third day, they can't work any more often—they moonlight at the Pioneer Youth Cultural Center." "Alright," Hoha cut him off, "not gonna happen, I said—no whores in my nightclub. It'll be bad enough with the gays," he added worryingly and once again addressed Slavik. "Is that all you got?" Slavik got a cigarette, lit it leisurely, blew out some smoke and began: "Well then, fine, fine," he made a distinct pause, "okay, Heorhii Davydovych, I understand what you're getting at, okay, I mean, I'll talk to Grebenshchikov if you want me to, but I don't think he'll do it for free, even for me...." "Enough," Hoha waved his hand, "Sanych, be a pal, get me a few musicians, any musicians, okay? And you," now addressing Slavik, "think about who we will be inviting." "What do you mean who?" Slavik asked, animatedly, "the fire department, the tax collectors, anybody from the cultural affairs office. We'll make a list, in other words." "Good," Hoha agreed, "but you make sure that, besides all those fags that you mentioned, there will also be some cool gays there."

The nightclub opened at the beginning of June. San Sanych got a vocal-instrumental ensemble that regularly played in the restaurant of Hotel Kharkiv; their program was well rehearsed, they don't ask for a lot of money, and they don't drink on the job. Slavik put together a list of invited guests, a hundred or so people, Hoha spent a lot of time studying the proposed list, crossed out the names of the ladies working at the Cultural Events Committee cafeteria and of four workers from the Pioneer Youth Cultural Center, the rest of the list was agreed upon; Slavik tried to argue the case for including the cafeteria ladies but gave up after a long debate. Hoha invited his business partners, middlemen, to which he had sold gypsum boards, some childhood friends, and the Lykhui brothers. San Sanych invited his mother; he wanted to invite an acquaintance of his, a former prostitute, but then thought of his mother and gave up that idea. The opening ended up being quite pompous. Slavik got drunk within half an hour, San Sanych asked the security guards to keep an eye on him, Hoha told everyone to relax—it was an opening, nonetheless. San Sanych's mom did not stick around for long, complaining that the music was too loud; Sanych hailed her a cab and returned to the festivities. The middlemen took off their neckties and raised toasts to the owners, Slavik sang loudly and kissed the representatives from the tax administration; in essence, out of everyone there, he was the only one who was acting gay, at least the way that he understood it, and he did this entirely on purpose, in order to engage the guests. The guests, finally, became engaged, and in the end, the Lykhui brothers got into a fight with the middlemen in the men's bathroom, basically a good old fisticuffs—in essence, that's what they're paid to do; from the bathroom one could hear an offended Hrysha Lykhui's shouting, "You're the one that's a faggot!" His brother, Sava Lykhui supported him. The fight was quickly contained, Sanych separated everyone, and the drunk middlemen set off to continue their drinking at a strip club, because the Sub wasn't offering a striptease show. The drunk representatives of the tax administration also set off for the strip bar, not taking Slavik with them, in order not to spoil their reputation. All the guests were almost gone, except for a girl who was sitting on a stool by the bar and two middle-aged men whispering in the corner, who kind of looked like the representatives of the tax administration, in other words, it was hard to find something that was memorable about their appearance. "Who's that?" Sanych asked Slavik, who was beginning to sober up and was now recalling whom he had kissed. "Well, they," he said, focusing his look at them. "I don't want to offend anyone here but, I think, they are authentic gays." "Do you know them?" Sanych asked, just in case. "Yes, I do," Slavik nodded his head, "it's Doctor and Busia." "What kind of doctor?" Slavik replied, "I don't know—a doctor, come on, I'll introduce you. Greetings, Busia." He was addressing the guy who looked younger and looked more like a representative of the tax administration. "Howdy, Doctor," he shook the hand of the guy who looked more together, in other words, he looked less like a representative of the tax administration. "I would like to introduce you, this is Sanny." "San Sanych," a fearful San Sanych corrected him. "He's our manager," interrupted Slavik. "Nice to meet you," Doctor and Busia said and invited them to sit down. Sanych and Slavik sat down. Everyone became silent. Sanych became nervous, Slavik reached for his cigarettes. "So, Slavik," said Doctor, trying to relieve the situation, "so you're here now?" "Yep," said Slavik, lighting his cigarette and putting out the match in their salad, "my friends asked me for my help and I thought to myself, why not, I've got some time to spare. Of course, things aren't running all that smoothly just yet," Slavik continued, taking Doctor's fork and pricking the salad with it, "let's look at tonight's opening, for example: in essence, we could have taken the high road and had a cultural program, I had already cut a deal with

Grebenshchikov.... But, it's okay," he placed his hand on Sanych's shoulder, "it's okay, I'll advise them, a little bit here, a little bit there, everything will be fine, yeah...." Sanych carefully moved Slavik's hand off of his shoulder, stood up, nodded towards Doctor and Busia, implying—have a nice time, we'll talk again later—and went up to the bar. "What's your name?" he asked the girl, who had just ordered another vodka. She had a piercing on her face and whenever she drank, the metal balls would clink against the glass. "I'm Vika," she said, "what's your name?" "San Sanych," San Sanych replied. "Gay?" she asked, seriously. "Owner," Sanych defended himself. "I see," said Vika, "can you give me a lift home? I got pretty trashed here." Sanych once again hailed a taxi, and bidding farewell to Hoha, escorted the girl outside. The taxi driver turned out to be some kind of hunchback, Sanych had seen him here before, and now it turns out that they're riding together; the hunchback joyfully looked at them and asked them—"Did you order a pickup at the fag bar?" "Yeah, yeah," San Sanych replied uneasily. "Where to?" he asked Vika. Vika started getting head-spins in the taxi. "You aren't going to puke are you?" the hunchback asked. "Everything's fine," Sanych said, "we're not going to puke." "As you wish," the hunchback said, somewhat disappointingly. "So, where are we going?" Sanych put his arm around Vika, pulled her towards him, reached into the inside pocket of her biker's jacket and pulled out her passport. He looked at the address listed in it. "Let's try this," he said to the hunchback, and they set off. It turns out that Vika lived very close by; it would have probably been easier to carry her home, but who knew? Sanych pulled her out of the car, asked the hunchback to wait for him and carried her into the entrance of her building. He stood her up on her feet by the door. "You gonna be okay?" he asked. "I'm fine," she said, "fine, give me back my passport." Sanych remembered that he still had the passport, pulled it out, and looked at the photo. "You look better without all the piercings," he said. Vika grabbed the passport and put it in her pocket. "If you want," Sanych said, "I can stay with you tonight." "Dude," she replied, smiling smugly, "I'm a lesbian, don't you get it? And you're not gay, you're just the owner. You dig?" Vika kissed him and disappeared behind the door. Sanych tasted coldness and felt a piercing on his lips. It felt like his lips had touched a silver spoon.

The tribulations of everyday business started to kick in. The tribulations lay in the fact that the nightclub was wholly unprofitable. The target audience doggedly ignored the Sub. Hoha was infuriated, Slavik tried to stay out of his line of sight, and, when he wasn't successful in doing this, he would loudly holler about the niche, about the Ukrainian Concert Organization, and about the Vietnamese diaspora, he even proposed to turn the Sub into a sushi bar that would focus exclusively on the Vietnamese diaspora, after which he received a smack in the face from Hoha, and, consequently, stopped showing up at the office for some time. Hoha would sit in his office nervously trying to solve crossword puzzles published in *Accountants' Review* magazine. San Sanych tracked down Vika and invited her to a dinner date. She told him that she was going through her period and asked to be left alone, but then added that someday she'd stop by the Sub. The summer was hot. Juice trickled down from the air conditioners.

Slavik showed up. Diligently trying to hide his black eye, which was still visible behind his sunglasses, he entered Hoha's office. Hoha asked Sanych to come in. Slavik was seated, sadly shaking his head and not saying anything. "How long are you going to keep sitting there without saying anything?" Hoha asked, smiling joyfully. "Heorhii Davydovych," Slavik began, carefully selecting his words, "I understand, okay—we were all very upset, I was wrong, you flipped out." "Me?" Hoha asked, continuing to smile. "You know, we are all professionals," said Slavik and then adjusted his glasses. "I understand—business is business, and we have to save it. I'm used to everything being up front, yeah.... And if you have a beef with me—I'd like to hear it, I won't be offended. But," Slavik continued, "I understand completely, maybe we don't fully agree on some matters, perhaps our ways of seeing things are not always the same, okay, that's just the way it turned out, I understand—you're new to this business, that's why, no, everything is okay, I'm part of the team, everything is fine." "Slavik," Hoha said to him, "it's absolutely fantastic that you are part of the team, but the problem is that our team is being kicked out of the big leagues." "Yes," said Slavik, "yes. I understand—you have every right to say this, I would have said the same thing if I was in your shoes, I understand, everything is okay...." "Slavik," the boss addressed him again, "I'm begging you, give me something to work with, I'm in the red, that's not how businesses are run, you understand?" Slavik continued to shake his head, talked about how great this team to which he had returned was, mentioning his belief that, if they had been in his shoes, they would have done the same; he bummed some cab money from Hoha and said that he'd return tomorrow with some good news. He called the following morning using somebody else's cell phone and enthusiastically shouted that, at this very moment, as it turned out, he was at the Cultural Events Committee office, and that at this time, decisions were being made on a regional level, regarding the idea of awarding them the right to host this year's Embroidered Rushnyky![2] "What?" Hoha asked him. "Rushnyky," Slavik patiently repeated, you could hear the phone's legal owner grabbing at the phone and trying to get it back, but Slavik just wouldn't give it up. "Embroidered Rushnyky! Hey, would you just back off for a second!" he yelled on that side of the conversation and, once again commanding the phone, continued: "It's a talent competition for children and youth, backed directly by the governor; it gets funded by the budget, if we pull this off—they'll give us the status of an artistic center, and then the tax police won't fuck with us." "But are you sure that this a good fit for us?" Hoha asked him, just in case. "Well of course it is," Slavik yelled, "this is exactly what we need—painting on asphalt, a children's fashion show, older schoolgirls in bathing suits, fuck, we'll come up with a program, we'll run the dough through the accounting office, we'll give the firemen a cut so that they'll include us in the budget next year, and that's it—we'll be talent-showing for the whole year on the public's money, ze show mast go on, Heorhii Davydovych, I've been in this business

---

2   A *rushnyk* (pl. *rushnyky*) is a ritual towel that is one of the most widespread popular symbols of Ukraine, and, as such, can often function as a representative of Ukrainian kitsch. Traditionally, however, it has been an important element of the Ukrainian folk tradition. Among its powers are the abilities to secure a marriage and to protect one's home from intruding evil.

for twenty years, goddamn it!" This was, probably, shouted into empty space, because they had indeed managed to take the phone away from him. Hoha sighed heavily and returned to his crossword puzzle.

In the afternoon, four guys in sweat suits came in, but they didn't look like athletes, unless they all played for a goon squad. The security guard asked them what they wanted but they knocked him down and went to look for the director. Hoha was sitting with Sanych and finishing up a crossword puzzle. Sanych saw the four of them and quietly turned off his cell phone. "Who are you?" Hoha asked, already knowing the answer. "We're the Copy Kings," the first one, the one in the blue sweat suit, replied. "Who?" Sanych asked. "What are you, deaf?" The second one said, also wearing a blue sweat suit. "'The Copy Kings'. That building across the street from this joint, it's ours. The parking lot around the corner—ours." "And an office at the Pivdenyi train station as well," the first one, wearing blue, again entered the conversation. "In essence, we are the leaders in this market, you got it?" Now this was said by the second guy wearing blue. The third, wearing green, turned awkwardly, and a sawed-off shotgun fell out from under his sweat jacket, the green guy quickly bent down, picked it up, and put it back, apprehensively looking around. "We have a network of wholesale dealers," the first one said, "we receive direct deliveries from Sweden." "What," said Hoha, trying to prolong the conversation, "you want to sell us a copy machine?" The foursome disconsolately became silent, sternly moving their glances from Hoha onto Sanych. "What we want," the first one finally began to say, wiping his sweaty palms on the blue fabric of his sweat pants, "is for everything to be sorted out the right way. You guys are new here, you were not here before. This territory is ours. You gotta pay up." "We do pay up," Hoha tried to joke, "to the tax police." The third one once again turned around awkwardly and his shotgun once again clanged onto the floor. The fourth one flicked him in the face, bent down, picked up the weapon, and put it in the pocket of his crimson sweat pants. "Yo, *brother*, you didn't get it," the second one again started speaking, putting all his disgust into the word *brother*. "We're the Copy Kings, we control the whole region." "What do you mean?" San Sanych asked. "Hey, don't interrupt, alright?" the first one said sharply and turned to the second one, "Go ahead Lionia, continue." "Yeah," said Lionia in reply, "we've got connections in the administration. This is our territory. So, you gotta pay up." "Well we're not complete strangers here either," Hoha tried to say something, "I could say that we are known around these parts." "Yeah, well who knows you, *brother*?" the second one exclaimed, making a fist, but the fourth one took him by the elbow, as if to say—easy there, Lionia, easy, they don't know what they're doing. "So, who knows you?" "What do you mean, who?" Hoha tried to buy some time. "I deal with gypsum boards, I know people in the Balashovka district plus I've got connections in the tax administration. The Lykhui brothers, for example...." "Who?" the second one asked, and Hoha immediately realized that it was better for him not have mentioned the Lykhui brothers. "The Lykhuis?! Those morons?!! Yeah, they got a set of printers from us, from Copy King, and resold them to some dorks from the Tractor district! They claimed that they were copy machines for the next generation! And the latter guys, for their part, resold them to the militia academy, together with our warranty! We barely got out of that one!!! The Lykhuis!!! The Lykhuis!!!" The second one was tugging at his blue sweat jacket and was hollering, for the whole nightclub to hear, that accursed last name. "Well that's not it," added Sanych, just to add something, "we're also on the Cultural Events Committee...." "What?!" The second one didn't let him finish. "On what Cultural Events Committee?!! You want to tell me that you're also under the protection of the Cultural Events Committee?!!! Are you standing by your words?!!!!" The fourth one resolutely reached into his pocket for his weapon. Shit, thought Hoha, it would have been better if those Krasnoyar special forces had killed me, it wouldn't have been as revolting. All four of them began approaching threateningly, blocking off half of the room with their bodies. And it looked like neither Hoha Lomaia, nor, even less so, San Sanych, could expect anything other than serious bodily injuries from this situation.

And, at this point, the door to the office opens and Slavik walks in, merrily smiling and waving a stack of xeroxes like a fan. The foursome, with raised fists, stopped in their tracks. Hoha slowly sat down onto a stool, Sanych shrunk himself and touched the phone in his pocket. Everyone turned to Slavik. "Hi, hello," Slavik called out, failing to notice the surrounding tension, "hello to all!" He walked up to Hoha and shook his lifeless hand. "Partners?" said Slavik, playfully referring to the foursome and, smiling, shook the hand of the one on the end, the one in the blue sweat suit. "Voila!" he shouted emphatically, tossing the stack of xeroxes in front of Hoha. "What's this?" Hoha asked, barely able to speak. "We got it!" Slavik emphatically called out. "Embroidered Rushnyky!" "Embroidered Rushnyky?" Hoha asked distrustfully. "Embroidered Rushnyky?" Sanych asked, walking up to check out the copies. "Embroidered Rushnyky, Embroidered Rushnyky," the foursome whispered in fear, backing out of the office. "Embroidered Rushnyky!" triumphantly repeated Slavik and, leaning down to Hoha, confidently said, "So here's the deal, Heorhii Davydovych, I sorted everything out with the fire department, we'll run the money through their account, I figured it out, we take the cash and write it off as an overhead expense," he anxiously giggled, sharply cut off his laughter, and, turning to the foursome, commandingly asked them: "Can I help you with something, gentlemen?" Hoha also inquisitively looked at the foursome, but lacked the guts to ask them that very question. "Brother," the second one finally said, zipping up his blue jacket, "you're gonna tell me that you're really under the protection of the governor?" "Yep," Slavik impatiently answered him and whispered to Hoha, "we'll list the deficit as an expense for the children's choir, I settled it with the administrators, they'll register it in the quarterly report as a one-time payment to the orphans." The foursome nervously lingered by the door, not knowing what to do. The fourth guy tried to give the shotgun back to the third guy but the latter guy glumly spurned him. "What, leaving so soon?" Slavik turned to the foursome. "By the way, Heorhii Davydovych, are we inviting these gentlemen to Embroidered Rushnyky?" "Embroidered Rushnyky, Embroidered Rushnyky," the foursome groaned and slid out of the office. When the door behind them closed, Hoha sighed heavily. "Give me a smoke," he addressed Slavik. Slavik pulled out his cheap smokes and stretched one out to Hoha. Hoha grabbed the cigarette with trembling lips, Slavik instantly gave him a light. The boss took a drag and immediately coughed. "What just happened?" Slavik didn't understand. "Slavik," Hoha addressed him, "you're a guy who has seen his share of things, right? You've been in show business for twenty years. You know, what's his name...." "Grebenshchikov," Slavik helped him. "You organized U2's Kharkiv concert, you've worked with the Pioneer youth. Now tell me—does God exist?" "Yes, he does," said Slavik. "Of course he does. But it doesn't really matter."

Vika stopped by the Sub. "Howdy gayboys!" she said to the compadres who were sitting by themselves at a table. Hoha grunted. "Okay," he said to his partner, "I'm heading home." "Alright, I'll close up," Sanych promised. "Ah, sure you will," Hoha laughed and, timidly letting Vika pass him, went outside. "Haven't seen you in a while?" Sanych asked. "What do you care?" Vika answered. "What happened to that piercing you had?" Sanych inquired. "I sold it," Vika answered. They then set off to drink some vodka, Vika cried and complained about her life, saying that she broke up with her girlfriend, who had left the country for good. "So why are you still here?" Sanych asked. "Well, what about you?" Vika countered. "Well, I've got a business," he said, "plus, I don't know any foreign languages." "Neither does she," Vika said, "she's an actress, her body is her language, you understand?" "Not really," Sanych honestly replied. "Listen," Vika asked him, "you're almost thirty. Why haven't you gotten married yet?" "I don't know," Sanych said, "I've been busy with business. I've got three wounds. Plus, a broken hand." "Just find yourself a gay guy," Vika suggested. "You think it will help?" Sanych doubted. "Probably not," Vika said. "Hey, let's go to your place," he proposed. "What, you wanna fuck?" "Well, maybe not fuck," Sanych said, "we can just...." "We can just—not," Vika authoritatively declared." And then added, "Yeah, it's too bad you're not gay."

Then they just lay on the floor of her room for a while. The air was dark and warm. Vika counted his gunshot wounds. "One," she counted, "two, three. That's it?" She asked somewhat disappointingly. "That's it," Sanych said apologetically. "It's kind of like having a piercing," she said, "except that they don't heal." "Everything heals," he answered. "Yeah, yeah," Vika didn't agree, "my girlfriend would also say that. And then she takes off for Turkey." "That also counts as an experience," Sanych said philosophically. "Uh-huh," Vika replied with anger, "you know, experiences like that are like those things on your body—you can always track how many times somebody has tried to kill you."

Things weren't going well for the nightclub. And even the successful presentation of Embroidered Rushnyky—during which Slavik almost got beaten up by the older pioneer youth, because he had entered the dressing room where the older girls were changing without knocking— didn't save the situation. Hoha would spend his evenings in the office, computing their debt on a calculator. Sanych fell into a depression, Vika wasn't calling him, she wouldn't pick up the phone, he was running out of money. Sanych smoked by the nightclub entrance and looked on jealously as the Copy Kings began constructing a penthouse on top of their building. Business was obviously not happening, it was time to return to Boxers for Fairness.

One morning, Slavik showed up and said that he had some good news. "We're going to present a show," he said. "You didn't want a strip show," he addressed Hoha, "so be it. Let it be. I respect your choice, Heorhii Davydovych, I do. But I've got something that will amaze you." Hoha became tense. "I," Slavik said lazily, "have made arrangements with Raisa Solomonovna. At first, she categorically refused because, as you know, she has a very busy schedule, but I got through to her using my connections. She'll be here soon, it would be nice if everything was very civilized here, well, you know what I mean," and Slavik threw a concerned glance at Sanych. "And with whom is it again that you have made arrangements?" Hoha asked him. Sanych laughed. "With Raisa Solomonovna," Slavik repeated somewhat vociferously. "And who is she?" Hoha asked carefully. "Who is she?" Slavik smiled arrogantly. "Who is Raisa Solomonovna? Heorhii Davydovych, are you kidding me?" "Alright, alright, take it easy, answer the question," Hoha interrupted him. "Well," Slavik said, "I don't even know what to say. How could you have gotten into the nightclub business without having heard of Raisa Solomonovna? Hmmm ... Alright. You gotta be kidding me ... Raisa Solomonovna—she's with the gypsy municipal ensemble, an award-winning Belarusian actress. You must have heard of her," Slavik confidently yelled out and then reached for his cigarettes. "So she's coming here to pick up something she left behind?" Hoha asked with dissatisfaction. "Well that's what I'm trying to explain to you," said Slavik, taking a drag, "we're going to present a show. On Tuesdays. She can't do it any other day, she's got a very busy schedule. I've made all the arrangements. Everybody has heard of her, we'll fill a niche." "Are you sure?" Hoha asked without enthusiasm. "Of course," said Slavik, sprinkling ash onto a crossword puzzle that had just been solved. "So what does she do, this actress of yours?" Hoha asked, just in case. "She has her own repertoire," Slavik informed seriously. "An hour and a half long. To pre-recorded music. Gypsy romance songs, and movie hits, about gangster life." "And in what language does she sing?" Sanych inquired. "In Belarusian?" "Why Belarusian?" Slavik was offended. "Well, I really don't know. In the gypsy language, I guess, it is a gypsy ensemble." "Is she going to perform alone," Hoha asked, "or with bears?"

Raisa Solomonovna arrived around one p.m., out of breath because of the heat. She looked to be forty-five years old, but she wore a lot of makeup, so it was tough to tell. She was a skinny, dirty-blonde in leather go-go boots and wearing some kind of see-through slip, explaining that she had come straight from a concert she had performed at an orphanage, adding that she'd brought along a poster, to illustrate. Printed on the poster, in large red letters, was: "The Kharkiv Philharmonic Invites You. The Award-Wining Belarusian Actress Raisa Solomonovna in 'Twilight Shout-outs.'" At the bottom were the blank lines reserved for 'Time' and 'Price of Admission.' "Alright then," Raisa Solomonovna said excitingly, "show me the nightclub!" Everyone went into the main hall. "So what do we have here," the actress asked, "a fast-food joint or a pub?" "What we have here is a gay bar," Hoha replied, uncertainly. "Fuck yeah," Raisa Solomonovna said and climbed onto the stage. Slavik, being a show-business pro, turned on the pre-recorded music.

Raisa Solomonovna began with songs about the gangster life. She sang loudly, addressing the imaginary audience and waving her arms emphatically. Surprisingly, Hoha liked it; he smiled and started singing along, obviously having been familiar with these tunes. Slavik stood edgily behind the mixing board and monitored his boss through the corners of his eyes. Sanych watches all of this perplexedly. After the fifth song, Hoha clapped his hands, said that it was time to take a break, walked up to the stage and, offering the singer his hand, led her to his office. Sanych hesitantly followed them. "Good stuff," Hoha said to Raisa Solomonovna, "real good stuff. Raisa, what's your...." "Solomonovna," she helped him. "Yes," Hoha complied. "Let's have a drink." "What, we won't be singing anymore?" the singer asked. "Not today," said Hoha. "Let's agree that today we will drink to our having met." "Okay then," Raisa Solomonovna agreed, "but, if I may, I'd like to change my clothes, it's so hot in here." "Whatever you want," Hoha said merrily and, dialing up the bar, order two bottles of cold vodka. Raisa Solomonovna took off her go-go boots and pulled a pair of slippers from her bag that looked like puffy cats. Hoha looked at the cats and opened the first bottle. Sanych understood where things were heading and sadly turned off his phone. Slavik was not invited to come to the office. He came anyway.

First, they drank to celebrate their acquaintance. Then they started singing. Hoha suggested that she get back up on stage, Raisa Solomonovna agreed, and slid back up onto the show business stage, as she was dressed, in house slippers. Hoha followed her onto the stage, wearing her leather go-go boots. Wearing go-go boots and in his silk, fake-Armani shirt he looked like a nineteenth-century Russian intellectual. Slavik turned on the pre-recorded music. Raisa Solomonovna returned to the mafia-themed material, Hoha sang along. The go-go boots glistened in the stage lights.

Upon entering the bathroom, Sanych found Slavik in there. The latter wasn't feeling very well, he was splashing water onto his face from the faucet and breathing heavily in the hot air. "You feel like shit?" Sanych asked him. "I'm fine," Slavik groaned, "fine." "Slavik," San Sanych said, "I've been meaning to ask this for a while, maybe this isn't the best place for such a conversation, but, you know, I'm not sure if we'll get another chance—what, in general, is your opinion on gays?" Slavik stuck his head under the cold stream, breathed out and sat up against the wall. He remained silent for a bit. "I, San Sanych, will tell you this," Slavik began speaking, trustingly, spitting out the water. "I am not thrilled with gays. But," he lifted his pointer finger, "there are reasons for that." "What reasons?" Sanych asked; he didn't feel like returning to the main hall, that's why he decided to linger here. "The reasons are of a *personal* nature," Slavik informed. "I've got allergies. People like me are constantly popping pills. I, for example," Slavik said and pulled out a cigarette, "am a pill popper. For ten years now. My doctor used to write me prescriptions. They, however, stopped having any effect, you understand? But my sister works for a pharmaceutical company, they opened a factory just outside of Kyiv. The Germans gave them a half a million worth of equipment and they constructed an entire lab as part of a rehabilitation program. They promptly divvied it all up and threw an extravagant grand opening for the factory. Joschka Fischer[3], the president of Germany, came for the opening," Slavik nervously exhaled some smoke. "The ex-president," he added. "So, they began working, they created a sample batch and then the attorney general's office says: fuck this—it does not meet the necessary standards, it has too much morphine in it." "Too much of what?" Sanych didn't understand. "Morphine," Slavik repeated. "The whole problem was that the equipment was theirs, while the raw materials were ours. And because their machinery is geared for non-waste production, in other words, it produces no waste, they ended up producing massive quantities of half-strength drugs. The whole program, obviously, was shut down. The factory went bankrupt. The unions raised a ruckus, our environmentalists backed them. They wrote a letter to Joschka Fischer. But he did not write back. So, to make a long story short, they laid off everyone, my sister included. And, in order to ease the tensions with the unions, the workers were paid with the product which they had produced. These days, they stand by the side of one of the main roads leading out of Kyiv and sell these tablets to tourists, along with squeezable toys. And my sister brought me a couple of boxes. So, I have allergies, just so you know...." "What does this have to do with gays?" Sanych asked after a long pause. "Well, hell if I know," Slavik disclosed. "Here, take this," he said and offered Sanych two tablets. "It's good stuff. It'll knock your socks off." Sanych took the pills and

---

3   Joschka Fischer (b. 1948) was, in fact, vice chancellor of the Federal Republic of Germany and its minister of foreign affairs (1998–2005).

swallowed them, one at a time. It can't get any worse, he thought to himself. It didn't get any worse.

Raisa Solomonovna got completely drunk. She ripped the microphone out of Hoha's hands and began singing movie soundtrack hits. She put her red wig on distressed Slavik's head. Hoha tried to take the microphone away from her but she grabbed him by the hair and began screaming. Slavik tried to pull her away from his boss but was unsuccessful—Raisa Solomonovna was holding on tightly to Hoha with one hand, while trying to poke his eyes out with the other. At first, Hoha tried to push her away but then, later, also got riled up and started blindly waving his fists. With his first punch he knocked Slavik to the ground. Slavik grabbed his bruised jaw and once again tried to pull Raisa Solomonovna away. Raisa, having met resistance, became incensed and attacked Hoha with renewed strength. After a few attempts she connected with his left cheek, leaving bloody scratches and breaking off her press-on nails. Hoha bellowed, stepped back, and kicked Raisa Solomonovna right in the stomach with the toe of his shoe. Raisa flew back and, together with Slavik, who had been holding on to her, stumbled into the main hall. Hoha, cursing, wiped away the blood. "Sanych," he yelled to him, "do me a favor, lug that witch outta here. And turn her music off," he yelled. Sanych walked up to the singer, grabbed her, and pulled her to the exit. Running in the tracks of all the crying was Slavik, still wearing the wig. Hoha looked at all of this from the stage and cursed. "A witch," he yelled, standing in the middle of the stage, "the devil's witch!" Sanych hailed a cab, slid Slavik some cash, and returned to the nightclub. Hoha was sitting at the edge of the stage, wiping away blood with his silk sleeve and drinking vodka straight out of the bottle. "A witch!" he cried, and buried his nose in Sanych's chest. "What did she do that for? Damn witch!" "It's okay, buddy," Sanych replied to him. "Let me take you home." They went outside. The hunchback was standing by his car, looked at Hoha in go-go boots, shifted a ponderous glance at Sanych and silently got behind the wheel. Nobody spoke on the way home, except for Hoha's occasional sniffling. "You know, I have a gay neighbor," the hunchback tried to get a conversation going. "Big deal," Sanych said sullenly. "My apartment building is full of homos."

In the morning, Hoha woke up at home, in bed, fully clothed and wearing go-go boots. Ponderously looking at the go-go boots, he tried to remember everything that had happened. He couldn't. Shit, Hoha thought, what the hell am I doing? Soon I'll be thirty, I'm a good, established businessman, chicks throw themselves at me. Well okay, chicks may not throw themselves at me, but nonetheless—what is it that I need this nightclub for, that I need these gays for, that's worth ruining my life over. He grabbed his phone, dialed up his middleman buddy, and hastily bought a batch of gypsum boards.

Sanych arrived at the Sub sometime in the afternoon. A frightened security guard stood at the entrance. "San Sanych," he said, "Heorhii Davydovych is in, uh...." "We'll sort it all out," Sanych succinctly replied and entered the nightclub. The main hall was littered with a bunch of boxes. They were all over the place. The tables were folded up in the corner. The bar was closed. Sanych went to see Hoha. Hoha was sitting, with his legs propped up on top of the table, and cheerfully conversing with someone on the phone. The go-go boots were on the table in front of him. "What's all that?" Sanych asked him, pointing at the main hall. "What?" Hoha asked him, calmly. "Oh, the stuff in the main hall, they're gypsum boards. I got a good deal." "Well, what about the Sub?" Sanych asked him. "Not happening," Hoha replied. "It's useless, this Sub. I'm in the red, Sanych, fuck the Sub. Soon I'll unload these gypsum boards and I'm off to Cyprus." "Well what about the exotic leisure?" Sanych asked him. "Yeah, what about the exotic leisure?" Hoha nervously smiled. "We just don't have the mentality for this, you understand?" "Well then what kind of mentality do we have?" "Hell if I know what kind," Hoha answered him. "Our mentality is that we gotta have vodka and a babe for exotic leisure, right? And, with these gays, you can forget about vodka. Let alone the babes," he added sadly.

A piercing scream could be heard coming from the main hall. The doors flew open and Slavik raced into the office. "What?" he yelled. "What's all that?" He was dejectedly pointing towards the main hall. "Heorhii Davydovych, Sanych—what is all that?" "They're gypsum boards," Sanych told him. "Gypsum boards?" "Gypsum boards," Sanych confirmed. "What do you need gypsum boards for?" Slavik didn't understand. "Gypsum boards, Slavik," Hoha explained to him, "are for building architectural structures." "Heorhii Davydovych is shutting down the business," Sanych explained to Slavik, "from now on he's going to be dealing gypsum boards in Cyprus." "In Cyprus?" an affronted Hoha disagreed, but Slavik was no longer listening to him. "What?" he asked. "He's shutting down the business? Just like that? What about me? What about our plans?" "What plans?" Hoha nervously interrupted. "Oh okay, I get it," Slavik breathed in, "I saw this coming from the start. For you guys it's *like*—today we open it, tomorrow, we close it, that's just what it's *like* for you guys. I understand you, if I was in your shoes I would act just *like* you did. Sure. When you need something, when you need to put on Embroidered Rushnyky, then it's—Slavik, take care of it. Or when you need someone to invite Raisa Solomonovna, then it's Slavik, no problem." "Your Raisa Solomonovna is a witch!" Hoha responded, yelling. "The devil's witch!" "Oh yeah?" Slavik, for his part, yelled, "Raisa Solomonovna is an actress! She has her own show! And you kicked her in the stomach." "What do you mean I kicked her in the stomach?" Hoha was confused. "Yes! You kicked her! In the stomach! And she has her own show!" Slavik couldn't contain himself, dropped onto the chair, and, grabbing his head in his hands, bellowed. A rotting silence took hold. "Sanych," Hoha finally began speaking, "Sanych, what? Is it true? Did I really kick her in the stomach?" "Well, you were just defending yourself," said Sanych, looking away. "I can't believe it," Hoha whispered and also grabbed his head with his hands. San Sanych went outside. Across the street stood two Copy Kings in green sweat suits who blended nicely with the July greenery.

Maybe Hoha was just reacting to this whole story about the stomach, about Raisa Solomonovna, that is. Something clicked inside of him after all of this, maybe it was because he felt shameful in front of this group, but, the next morning, he unloaded the gypsum boards to the director of the amusement park and asked Sanych and Slavik to come over for a talk. Sanych was beset with depression but he collected himself and came over. The last to show up was Slavik, who was quite together and had a stern look about him. Hoha tried to avoid making eye contact with him. The go-go boots were still on the table, it seems that Hoha just didn't know what to do with them. Everyone sat down. No one said anything. "May I?" Sternly, and in a somewhat school-boy manner, Slavik raised his hand. "Please, go ahead," Hoha allowed, trying to move things along. "Let me go first, Heorhii Davydovych," Slavik began. "I created this mess and it's up to me to save this project." San Sanych looked at him with despair. "I understand," said Slavik. "We all made a lot of mistakes. You guys are new to this business, maybe I didn't stay on top of it as I should have. So then. No need to point the finger of blame," said Slavik and then looked directly at Sanych. "But not all is lost. I always have an ace up my sleeve." "Well now," he said, "they should be here any minute." "Who?" Hoha asked in horror. "The Bychkos!"

And Slavik told them about the Bychkos. He found them through the strippers from the Pioneer Youth Cultural Center. The Bychko duet—father and son—were circus clowns but, a few months ago, because of the financial difficulties that the city circus was having, they were laid off and began focusing on their solo career, according to Slavik. According to him, they had an *awesome* show program, an hour and a half long, with music, acrobatic numbers, and card tricks. Slavik laid everything on the shoulders of the Bychkos, they wouldn't disappoint them.

And so the clowns arrived. "Bychko, Ivan Petrovych," the older Bychko introduced himself and shook Hoha's and Sanych's hands. "Bychko, Petia," the younger one, lacking the guts to shake their hands, greeted them. Hoha invited everyone to sit down. "Well, then," Bychko Sr. began talking, pulling off his glasses and wiping them with a hand-kerchief. "I was told about your dilemma. I think that Petia and I can help you out." "What's your show like?" Hoha inquired. "Our show is all about dysentery," Ivan Petrovych said. "Dynasty," Petia cor-rected him. "Yes," Ivan Petrovych agreed. "We have a circus dynasty, from the year one thousand nine hundred seventy-four. It was then that my older sister applied to circus school." "Was she accepted?" Hoha asked. "No," Ivan Petrovych replied, "—so then, for us, the circus—it's a family thing. I, just so you know young man, back in the year one thousand nine hundred seventy-three, received second prize at the all-republican competition of young stage performers in Kremenchuk. With my number 'Africa—A Continent of Liberty' I caused quite a furor during the inter-regional shindig in Artek, in one thousand nine hundred seventy-eight. No," Ivan Petrovych abruptly contradicted himself, "it was in seventy-nine. Yep—it was in one thousand nine hundred seventy-nine, in Artek!" "So you're," Hoha tried to join the conversation, "so you're proposing to present the 'Africa—A Continent of Liberty' show for us too." "No," Ivan Petrovych calmly countered, "no, young man. We always try to stay in touch with the new trends. Petia and I have a show, we perform for an hour and a half, any overtime will cost you extra, debit or credit, everything is legitimate, everything is legal. You may wire the payment, but then you must pay an extra ten percent service fee." "Well, okay," said Hoha, "that's clear. But do you know about the specifics of our establishment?" "Well what specifics?" Ivan Petrovych asked, throwing a displeased look at Slavik. "We operate a gay nightclub," Hoha told him. "That is, a nightclub for gays, you understand?" "So let's see, what do we charge for gays," Ivan Petrovych pulled a tattered notebook out of his sport coat. "Eighty dollars an hour. Extra for overtime. Plus ten percent service charge," he added, as a decree. "But have you ever performed for such an audience before?" Hoha continued to doubt. "Ahem, ahem," Ivan Petrovych coughed heavily. "Recently we did an office party for a consulting firm. Well, that audience, I must say, was quite special. And, just imagine if you will, the executive director walks up to Petia and I and says...." "Alright, alright," Hoha interrupted him, "I know that consulting firm." "So then," Slavik voiced. "Are we booking the Bychkos?" "We'll book them, we'll book them," Hoha replied, "but how do you see all of this coming together?" "Okay, here's how it'll be," Slavik grabbed the initiative. "Heorhii Davydovych, I thought of everything. How's your calendar look?" "Well, what do you got?" Hoha asked him. "Kupalo![4] We'll do a gay Kupalo celebration!" Slavik said, and cheerfully laughed. The Bychkos also laughed—Ivan Petrovych's laugh

---

4   For more on Kupalo, see Note 6 on page 80.

was rough and congested while Petia's was ringing and clueless. Hoha also laughed, his laugh was particularly nervous and uncertain. Later, as they were leaving, Ivan Petrovych turned away from the door. "Are those yours?" he asked Hoha, pointing to the go-go boots. "Yep," Hoha said. "My friends sent them to me. From Cyprus. But they're the wrong size." Bychko Sr. walked up to them and felt one of the go-go boots. "Quality material," he said, well versed in such things.

They prepared for the gay Kupalo celebration particularly earnestly. Hoha no longer trusted Slavik and personally took care of the task of attracting an audience. Once again, among those invited were business partners, middlemen, childhood friends, and the Lykhui brothers, of which, however, only Hrysha showed up because Sava had gotten beaten up during a fight in the Tractor district and he was lying at Regional Hospital #4 with broken ribs. Slavik was given permission to invite the workers from the Pioneer Youth Cultural Center, all four of them. Besides them, a whole bunch of unknown people packed the place, who were enticed by God knows what, but definitely not by a gay Kupalo celebration. Providing the main event for the evening, were, of course, Ivan Petrovych, and Petia, Bychko. As they had mentioned, they had put together a program especially for the celebration entitled "The Fires of Cairo", which, according to Slavik's—who had been at the dress rehearsal—indisputable affirmation, would blow everybody away. The Bychkos appeared on stage wearing pharaoh costumes, which they had rented from the amusement park. The music sounded. The stage lights went ablaze. Petia Bychko bent down backwards, forming a bridge with his body. Ivan Petrovych flexed, grunted, and also made a bridge. The audience applauded. Hrysha Lykhui, who was already drunk upon arrival, even jumped to his feet but lost his balance and knocked over a waiter. The security guards attempted to lift him up and lead him out, but Hrysha resisted. He knocked one of the security guards on his ass and was able to free himself of the other. Sanych noticed the fight and tried to break it up. The middlemen, who had already managed to take their neckties off, saw that Hrysha was being roughed up and, forgetting the recent past, set out to help him. Meanwhile, Hrysha tossed the second security guard onto the stage, and the latter cut himself on a truss on which the lights were hanging. The truss collapsed and fell onto Ivan Petrovych who was still bent over in the form of a bridge. Bychko Jr. saw none of this because he too was bent over in a bridge. The public leapt to pull Ivan Petrovych from under the truss but Hrysha was in their way, fighting both the security guards and the middlemen, not ready to give in to either of them. At that moment, Bychko Jr. finally turned his head and saw his dad, lying under a mound of metal beams. He stretched towards him but his father commandingly lifted his hand, as if to say, go back, onto the stage, you are an artist, so get to it—enchant the audience! And Petia understood him, he understood what may be his father's final command. And he once again formed a bridge. And the audience also understood everything and restrained Hrysha Lykhui and took him to the bathroom to splash him with cold water. "Go ahead Petia, go ahead my son," Ivan Petrovych whispered from under the truss and then a blast sounded—Hrysha Lykhui was offended at everybody and, not having any strength left to resist, pulled a hand grenade from his jacket pocket and threw it over into the last toilet stall. The toilet exploded like a crushed walnut, smoke drifted out of the stall, the audience fled for the exits. Sanych tried to gather the beat-up security guards, Hoha stood by the stage and didn't understand what all the noise and smoke was about. "Heorhii Davydovych! Heorhii Davydovych!" Slavik ran up to him, out of breath. "It's mayhem, Heorhii Davydovych." "What happened?" Hoha asked, confused. "The cashier!" Slavik yelled out. "The cashier, that bastard, he took off! With all of the proceeds!" "Where did he go?" Hoha didn't understand. "He's not far from here!" Slavik continued yelling. "That's it. He must have gone off to blow the money on slot machines! Let's go, we can still catch him!" And Slavik ran for the exit. Hoha, not really wanting to, followed him. Sanych left behind the bruised security guards and joined them. Already waiting for them outside was the hunchback: "Hurry up!" he yelled, "Get in the car!" Besides Slavik, Hoha, Sanych, two workers from the Pioneer Youth Cultural Center, and Petia Bychko, a deafened Hrysha Lykhui, reeking of smoke, also, somehow, piled into the car; the latter was yelling louder than anyone else, as if it was his money that had been stolen.

The hunchback floored it, Slavik was showing the way but he was being interrupted by Hrysha, whose jacket, missing one sleeve, was still smoking. The hunchback was angry but kept flying, the workers from the Pioneer Youth Cultural Center were shrieking with every turn, until, finally, the hunchback lost control of the steering wheel and the taxi, having crossed over the oncoming lane, slammed into a newspaper stand. Newspapers flew all around, like startled geese. It was four a.m., all was quiet and calm. A truck drove by, hosing down the street with water. The doors of the taxi creaked open and the passengers began crawling out. The first to crawl out was Hrysha Lykhui, wearing a jacket missing one sleeve; he saw a stack of newspapers, grabbed one paper, and walked down the street. Behind him, with snake-like dexterity, crawled out Petia Bychko, wearing the pharaoh costume. Behind Petia, San Sanych stumbled out pulling out the two workers from the Pioneer Youth Cultural Center. Pushing the two workers out of the car was Slavik. Then they pulled out Hoha. Hoha had lost consciousness, probably from anguish more than anything else. The hunchback was able to get out on his own; it seemed that his back became even more hunched. Actually, one of the workers from the Pioneer Youth Cultural Center, Anzhela, had probably got the worst of it—Hrysha Lykhui had knocked out one of her teeth along the way. San Sanych walked off to the side and pulled out his phone, which had been turned off since yesterday. He tried to turn it on. He looked at the time. Four fifteen. He checked his in-box for new messages. There were no new messages.

Within a month's time, Hoha renovated the place again, paid off his debt and filled the Sub with arcade games. The hunchback was now working as his new cashier. Slavik, together with Raisa Solomonovna, set off for the Far East. Sanych left the business. Hoha had asked him to stick around, stating that they would soon make some money off of the arcade games, and begged him not to abandon him alone with the hunchback. But Sanych said that everything was okay, that he didn't need a cut of the proceeds and that he simply wanted to leave. They parted as friends.

But that's not all.

One time, at the beginning of August, Sanych ran into Vika on the street. "Hey," he said, "you've got some new piercings?" "Yes, I didn't even wait for the scars to heal," Vika answered. "Why haven't you called?" Sanych asked. "I'm flying to Turkey," said Vika, not answering him. "I'm gonna try to convince my girlfriend to come back. It sucks without her, you know?" "Well what about me?" asked Sanych, but Vika just caressed his cheek and, without a word, set off for the subway.

A couple of days later, Sanych received a message from Doctor and Busia. "Dear Sanych," they said, "we're inviting you to our place to celebrate our beloved Doctor's birthday." Sanych reached into his stash, took the remaining cash he had in there, bought a plastic amphora at the gifts store, and set off for the birthday party. Doctor and Busia lived in the suburbs, in an old, private building, together with Doctor's mother. They greeted him joyfully, they all sat down at the table, and started drinking some dry red wine. "What's new with the Sub?" Doctor asked. "The Sub is no more," Sanych replied, "it sank." "That's a shame," Doctor said, "that was a nice place." "So what are you going to do now?" "I'm going into politics," Sanych said. "Elections are coming up." Unexpectedly, the phone rang. Doctor picked up the phone and got into a long argument with someone, after which he curtly excused himself and disappeared, slamming the door behind him. "What happened?" Sanych inquired. "Oh, that would be mom," Busia laughed, "that old hag. She's always getting on Doc's case, she wants him to ditch me, she sneaks off to the neighbor's house and calls from there. But Doctor doesn't give in. Good for him!" Busia slid closer to Sanych. "Listen, Busia," Sanych said, after having thought a bit, "I wanted to ask you something. So, you and Doctor are gays, right?" "Well ... ," Busia began saying diffidently. "So, fine, you're gays," Sanych interrupted him. "And you live together, correct? Well, and of course you love one another, if I understand everything correctly. But explain one thing to me—are you physically satisfied with one another?" "Physically?" Busia didn't understand. "Well yeah, physically, you know, when you're together, is it good?" "And why do you ask?" Busia was lost. "No, I'm sorry, of course," Sanych answered, "if this is an intimate topic, you don't have to answer." "No, no it's fine," Busia was even more lost.

"You understand, Sanych, what I want to say is that, in essence, it's not so important, I have in mind, the uh, physical side, you understand? What's most important is something else." "What then?" Sanych asked him. "What's most important is that I need him, you get it? And he needs me, at least it seems so. We spend all our days together, we read together, we go to the movies together, we jog together in the mornings—did you know that we jog?" "No, I didn't," Sanych said. "We jog," Busia confirmed. "But physically, I honestly don't really like it, well, you understand, when we're together. But I never told him this, I didn't want to upset him." "The reason I'm asking," Sanych explained, "is that I've got this acquaintance, she's very cool, except that she drinks a lot. And once we spent a night together, can you believe it?" "Well," Busia said unobtrusively. "So, I'm in the same situation—it was great being with her, even without the sex, you understand? Even when she was drunk, and she would be drunk all the time. And all of a sudden she gets up and takes off for Turkey, can you believe it? And I just don't get it—where's the justice, why can't I, a normal, healthy guy, just be with her, why does she take off for Turkey and I can't even stop her?" "Yeah," Busia replied, deep in thought. "Alright," Sanych looked at him. "I thought that at least with you guys, with gays, everything works out okay. But you gays have to deal with the same bullshit." "Yep," Busia agreed, "the same deal." "Well then, I'm off," Sanych said. "Say hi to Doc." "Wait up," Busia stopped him. "Just hold on for a second." And he ran off to the kitchen. "Here, take this," he said and handed Sanych a bundle of something. "What is this?" Sanych asked. "A turnover." "A turnover?" "Yes, an apple turnover. Doctor baked it, especially for me. It's just that there are things that always make me cry. This turnover, for example. I know that that he baked it especially for me. You asked about sex, well, I'll tell you. How can I leave him after this? You know, I had an acquaintance who explained to me the difference between sex and love." "What is it?" Sanych asked. "Well, generally speaking, sex is when you're fucking and afterwards you want her to get out of there as soon as possible. And love, correspondingly, is when you're fucking and after the fucking you want her to stay for as long as possible. Here, take this," he extended the bundle to Sanych. "So what," said Sanych, after thinking for a bit, "so this is justice?" "No, no, it's not justice. It's just a pastry."

And he set off toward the bus stop. Along the way, a dog began to tag along with him. And that's how they walked, up front was Sanych with the turnover, behind him, the dog. The warm, August twilight unfolded around them. Sanych got to the stop, sat down on a bench and began to wait. The dog sat across from him. Sanych stared at it for a while. "Alrighty," he said, "you mutt, today is your lucky day. In honor of International Gay and Lesbian Day, you're getting a turnover!" The dog was licking himself with approval. Sanych pulled out the bundle and broke the turnover in two. Each of them got about half.

Translated by Mark Andryczyk

THE PERCENTAGE OF SUICIDES AMONG CLOWNS

A person is a trusting being requiring an ideal and in need of stereo-types, surrogates, and satisfying facsimiles of things. Men tend to be more trusting, women—less so; however, it is women who suffer most from trust, perhaps because male trust is given only to males, it is not extended to women. As an example, I would like to share this story.

Everyone knows how secluded and isolated actors' circles are. No one hides from the world within their fantasies and rituals as passionately as actors do. And thus, in the mid 1990s, in those difficult times, when the national currency was not considered to be currency at all, a group of male actors from a certain independent theater received an invitation to a festival in Lublin that was dedicated to the idea of erasing bor-ders. The concept of erasing borders itself could have applied to almost anything but this particular group of actors was offered a proposition to perform a circus-themed act. At first the actors were offended, but then the abovementioned trust and the satisfying facsimiles kicked in. The actors thought to themselves—well why not, maybe this is our big chance, perhaps it's the start of something new? And they sent a reply to the organizers stating that they could bring an act entitled "Clowns on the Beach." Bystanders immediately came to understand that this was not the start of something new but, more likely, the continuation of something old and endless, a continuation that, for that matter, was rather shitty. And so they found a clown kit, bought a big rusty tuba after selling off some booze they had, and set off for the border. There were five of them. Four of them believed in the power of art and were hoping to make some coin. The fifth one believed in show business and was just looking to hang out.

In Lublin they were settled in a dormitory. Donning their clown garb, they set off for their performance. The last of them, the fifth one, man-aged to score some weed and was happily dragging the tuba along behind them. The concert was attended by municipal authorities, representatives of the Ukrainian diaspora and a few feminists, who looked at the tuba with open aggression. After their performance, they were immediately dragged off to the after-party, not having been given the chance to change clothes. At the party, the actors immediately got drunk and struck up a conversation with the feminists. They ashed their cigarettes right into the tuba. Four of them, those who believed in the power of art, immediately became testy and got into a serious argument with the feminists. And then they began arguing with the representatives of the diaspora, who refused to pay them because their piece "Clowns on the Beach" had lacked the necessary national call-to-arms and ethnic coloring, not to mention that they had also precariously omitted the concept of erasing borders in their act. On the other hand, the fifth one managed to meet a representative of the municipal authorities who was responsible for international relations and even managed to share a few drags with her. She was a young woman with hair dyed red and dressed in a short black dress and black fishnet stockings. After the first joint, they switched to a more informal manner of speech and, after the second, they switched to English, which neither he nor she really knew how to speak.

Meanwhile, the group of four clowns, having had a serious argument with representatives of the diaspora and having beaten up two municipal clerks, abandoned this esteemed gathering in disappointment, remembering to take the tuba with them. "Assholes!" they shouted in the direction of the organizers, "Fucking feminists!" And right then and there, without even taking off their clown makeup, they got on the first bus heading for the border.

On the other hand, their forgotten colleague managed to switch to Polish, a language which he did not know, and, together with the chick in the black stockings, set off to go club-hopping. Sometime between three and four a.m., they stopped the car and started making love, right in her car, tearing clothes off of one another and smearing makeup off of one another. By morning they fell asleep—he at the steering wheel, she—on the back seat.

And at this time, the foursome of clowns, drunk and pissed off at the world, made it to the border town. The clowns immediately decided that they needed some booze and traded the tuba for three liters of moonshine.

The Polish customs officers, having seen at the border crossing four clowns with an unfinished, three-liter container of moonshine, started flipping through their customs declarations and suddenly noticed that the tuba, which had been listed as an object of art in the declarations, was missing. The customs officers decided to play it safe and placed the four of them in a cell, so that they could sleep it off. The clowns were placed on beds in their giant clown shoes.

Meanwhile, their buddy, whom they had left behind, woke up—in a strange car and in clown makeup; he pulled out another cigarette, woke up his partner, had a smoke with her, and asked her to drive him to Ukraine. The chick, gazing at him with dreamy and loving eyes, agreed to help him. And thus, on that bright sunny day, they approached the Polish border.

The customs officials, having now seen at the border their fifth clown that day—one who was sitting next to a chick in torn pantyhose and with diplomatic license plates—decided not to test the patience of the heavens and let this odd couple cross the country's border without further delay.

Arriving at the nearest set of kiosks, the clown procured some booze, and then, later on, said the following to his girlfriend: "You know," he said, "what it is that I don't like about contemporary art? It lacks the spirit of tragedy, that all-encompassing play, of death, the way it really is. We all live with illusions, surrogates," he said to her, drinking his booze straight out of the bottle, "most of us are simply afraid to look reality in the eye, but instead look away, and don't say the truth. And the truth is that real clowns don't wear wigs—they're born with such hair. Like my hair, for example, you see?" And she sat there and agreed with everything. And so we have this story which, if you think about it, isn't really all that extraordinary, because chicks always love real clowns. But they end up marrying acrobats.

Translated by Mark Andryczyk

IVAN MALKOVYCH

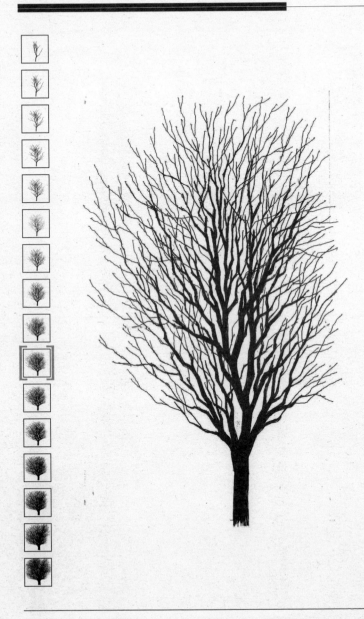

Poet and publisher IVAN MALKOVYCH was born on May 10, 1961 in Nyzhnii Bereziv (Ivano-Frankivsk oblast, Ukraine). He graduated from the violin class of the Ivano-Frankivsk Music Institute (1980) and from the philological faculty of Kyiv National Taras Shevchenko University. Malkovych has been a member of the Writers' Union of Ukraine since 1986.

At age 19, Malkovych was voted best young poet in a clandestine vote among several hundred Ukrainian writers. The publication of his first poetry collection was lauded by the legendary Ukrainian poet Lina Kostenko, who wrote: "Each of his poetry collections would become a phenomenon of literature discourse...The neomodern poetry of Ivan Malkovych became an example of the generous taste of 'new wave' poetics." (*Mala ukraïnska entsyklopediia aktualnoï literatury*).

Malkovych, who lives and works in Kyiv, is the author of seven poetry collections: *Bilyi kamin* (White Stone, 1984), *Kliuch* (The Key, 1988), *Virshi* (Poems, 1992), *Zianholom na plechi* (With an Angel on My Shoulder, 1997), *Virshi na zymu* (Winter Poems, 2006), *Vse poruch* (All Is Near, 2011) and *Podorozhnyk* (The Traveler, 2016).

The poetry of Ivan Malkovych has been translated into English, German, Italian, Russian, Polish, Bengali, Lithuanian, Norwegian, Georgian, Slovak, and Slovenian.

In 1992, Malkovych founded the first privately owned Ukrainian publisher of children's books, A-BA-BA-HA-LA-MA-HA. He is the editor, compiler, author, and translator of several dozen children's books. It has been suggested that he "is maniacally devoted to the idea of 'the Ukrainian book of special quality'" (*Knyzhnyk-review*, no. 1, 2002).

Ivan Malkovych's events in the Contemporary Ukrainian Literature Series, entitled *All Is Near*, took place in October 2011.

***

"Stand up and look
how I walk without you now"
she says to me
"and cry and cry …"

I cry
and sob quietly:
"And what will I do now
without you?"
I ask hopelessly

"And you will bathe in tears"
she says, stressing the word "tears"

my cry borders on a laugh

"Cry in a way
that I'll like"
my favorite, 3-year-old niece, Yaya
orders me

The entire family
is trying to hold back their laughter
I can't hold it either—I burst out
and thus end up ruining
our traditional
staged farewell

Yaya is not satisfied
so I lift her up and
toss her to the sky

at first she screams
but then laughs

I seat her in the car
and drive her back home

On the way
I ponder how in every trait
in every little intonation
of this little girl
there flows an enchanting
and unsparing woman

good luck to the men in her life
I think with a smile

and then I recall her latest phrase
and I pause, overwhelmed:

what an amazing title
for a book—

Cry
In a way that I'll like

Translated by Mark Andryczyk and Yaryna Yakubyak

BIRD'S ELEGY

children
are most like birds
brothers to angels

they still haven't learned to fly
safely fluttering about in their nests
chirping revealed in their voices

you remember of course children's
puzzling passion: burying birds
beneath the earth and constructing

a make-shift cross at the head of a grave
(as if in the frozen bird's mound they created
a sanctuary for their own bird-like spirits)
. . . .

but remember the dilated pupils
those eyes wide with grief
for the bird—then isn't the madness

of cruelty lessened in children—and tenderness
suddenly and stealthily streams into what
we call the soul—his is the greatest moment

when an angel becomes a person—
achieving perfection ...

ask your friends then let them ask
to your amazement you will
comprehend the number

of birds' graves filled by the hands
of children—in other words how much
tenderness should exist on earth—so tell me

where does it go? why doesn't it grow with us?
why is it given to everyone only once
and only a handful to the soul?

so all masons that inhabit the vertebrae
stubbornly lift our bones
raising our heart higher and higher

(as if our heart could see further)
. . . .

through the years only this inconsolable sadness
limitless sadness with the eyes of children
that slips into us—slowly but steadfastly

substitutes itself for our ruined soul—
fills it and immediately reigns on its own
over our quiet hearts
. . . .

every time in testament
we leave a sadder soul

more alone more despondent
become the generations of

people
birds
trees

Translated by Olen Jennings

***

happiness
returns
with the smile of a child
who is starting to feel better
and for now
is smaller than a little umbrella
which too
has folded its wings
and is sick with the flu

the whirligig in the corner also has the flu
too weak to bang its foot
to fan out
its colorful
skirts

with a fever of
one hundred
the whole house
has become silent

and only
two sad creatures
helplessly pace about
the room

shuffling their lowered
wings
along the floor

Translated by Mark Andryczyk and Yaryna Yakubyak

FUTILE PEOPLE

you too have left that gloomy paradise
of the not very deep mine of chromosomes
where—like living dew—together the invisible
seed of people quivers
        (in invisible honeycombs)
and you yielded pusillanimously to life

you came—blossomed—and withered—
and—in a flash into the earth . . . .

everywhere in the earth
slightly deeper than potatoes
you stretched out naked before the Almighty
the exact same inventory of bones
        (as if the only expediency on earth—
        was to grow your own bones)
the trite hieroglyphs of people
like matches stacked
by a child's hand . . . .

futile people whose faces
even God can't remember

Translated by Michael M. Naydan

THE VILLAGE TEACHER'S LESSON

This may not be the most essential of things,
but you, o child,
are called upon to defend with your tiny palms
the fragile little candle of the letter "Ï",

and also,
stretched out on your tiptoes,
to protect the small crescent moon
of the letter "Є",
which was carved out of the sky
along with a tiny bit of thread.

Because they say, o child,
that our language is like a nightingale's song.

And they are right.

But remember,
that one day
the time may come,
when our language
will not be remembered
by even the smallest of nightingales.

That is why you cannot depend
only on nightingales
child.

Translated by Mark Andryczyk

* * *

Nothing is right here, you see:
morning flooded the valley,
in the forest a pine hedgehog
carried the sun on its back.

A woman goes to the river
to wash her thinning sheets,
in a minute the regiments will descend—
turning the river gold.

Look closely: for in a second—
the river will carry them away.

Listen, do you hear how blood courses
through horses and soldiers? . . .

Translated by Olena Jennings

AN EVENING WITH GREAT-GRANDMA

when I was
five years old
a little devil
moved into
our pantry

I brought him food
I talked with him

occasionally
when many guests
would visit us
I would even lend him
dad's necktie

now
I cannot die
until I pass him along to someone else
until I hand him over

so I lay
suffering
I cannot die
everyone is afraid
to shake my hand

please invite me
to dance

Translated by Mark Andryczyk

***

The black parachute of anxiety grows
in your chest and opens up—and clenches so much
that it squeezes your heart through your throat …

Out of the shell of the body little brother Brutus
breakfasts on my soul (on purpose even
using a tiny silver spoon): you are tasty, little Ivan.

Bloody ants. Sweet briar. A slaughterhouse. Lechery.
I close my eyes—it grows dark in my head,
the light disappears: from the depth the wicked
sickle of the moon turns silver. Above your ear. Somewhere here.

Translated by Michael M. Naydan

***

There is much—I know—sadness
and the unavoidable ahead. Namely:
fear, illness, death, the cicada's song

in my own abandoned home, involuntary betrayals,
and awakenings, and the lure of stars ...
O heart, that from behind ribs, like from behind gratings,

gazes into this mad game,
why did you find your way to me,
to be tormented in this tedious body,

so that once again I would bend over the river,
and my face would fall and disappear beyond the water,
and so that I would sob in mute despair ...

Translated by Michael M. Naydan

THE MAN

He puts on a jester's mask—
they recognize him.

He dresses in the robe of a merciless judge—
they implore:
"Stop it, you can't fool us."

He changes into a fox—
they yell:
"We recognized you long ago.
Enough."

He wraps himself in Don Juan's cloak—
they laugh:
"Wrong style."

He stretches on a chameleon's mask—
and tears off that façade himself:

comical
lost man—
he can't understand
that every mask
has a slit
for eyes.

Translated by Olena Jennings

THE MUSIC THAT WALKED AWAY

When she was still young, her hair in braids—
Why, violin, did you turn away?
How could you let this music go barefoot,
Into such a strange, seductive night?

O bow, and where were you looking?—
Gray hairs now shedding from her shoulders—
How could you let this music go barefoot,
Into such a strange, seductive night?

I'll grasp a slice of earth
And go wander through the world—
Let only a light wind blow
Along my scattered path ...

Mommy, daddy, if they ask you,
Whether your son has disappeared, out of sight—
Just say: he's searching for that music
That barefoot walked into the night.

Translated by Mark Andryczyk

AT HOME

Again I'll visit for a day or two,
won't help with anything again,
nervous, distracted conversations
will just distress my parents.

What will I find next time
I come? Everyone there?
As I leave: father and mother in the window
like Hutsul[1] icons on glass.

Translated by Bohdan Boychuk and Myrosia Stefaniuk

---

1   For more on Hutsuls, see the note on page 95.

***

I gaze at my mountains
as if I were dying tomorrow

I want to absorb all there is

even this little potato plant
which has laid something
into the ground
like a chicken

and this poppy
like a carnival

Translated by Mark Andryczyk and Yaryna Yakubyak

***

Tonight
you are approaching Kyiv in a green train

but there is no train, or maybe it can't be seen
and I only see your body above the tracks
a sleepy little comet
flying horizontally above the ground
and it shines, shines at me
from afar;

I worry about you so:
will you get lost in the middle of the night?
will you succeed in flying over
the packs of stray dogs,
that rummage hungrily about the steppes?

How in the world did it come to be,
that I cannot protect you in any way;
it's as if you have been fated to fly forever
in an invisible train
following the very quiet chugging of your heart.

Translated by Mark Andryczyk and Yaryna Yakubyak

CIRCLE

You can't put a straightjacket on your soul.
All the same—it's spring, and you can see,
just before evening, tiny white threads hang in the wind:

you approach, stand up, clasp your shoulders—
not holding back, you pull at the thread—
and the wooden circle falls

to your hand, and you sketch the circle,
stretching it to the very edge:
o, how cramped it is in that circle all around,
and people live in it, are joyful, and die

Translated by Michael M. Naydan

AN EVENING (GOOSE) PASTORAL

quietly
the gloom
scuttles

deeper and deeper
evening digs a well

here geese
return from the meadow:
their procession walking through the evening
like a white
tunnel

it's as though the geese
are small bundles of the white chalk of days—
God's big bottles walking to the white

they walk from the meadow
they strain to hear inside themselves
the swelling
that becomes round and grows
that clangs from side to side
that sways the geese

look closely:
white ripens in the white—
even whiter than white

and yolks become furious—
eternal seedlings of the sun

Translated by Michael M. Naydan

A MESSAGE FOR T.

in the grasses of life
I'm such a child at heart
that I believe: the constellation Sagittarius
isn't pointing its arrow at me
From early poems

It was long ago that I left that tree
at home, behind which the sun
set for me. Maybe you will want

to go back there: to the room and the window
with a good view of it; maybe you will want
to return to it when your fatigue dissipates …

Behind it—there was a mine full of sun
in which, as if in a furnace,
there slowly shaped, melded,

and blended in boiling gold
gigantic orbs of sunlight—
on every God-given day of my life …

Now there is—yarrow—
bow to it for me, to its waving stalks—greet
its waving with a wave and ask

about the snails (they are each alike—
a snail Gundertwasser: their belfries
without any bells in them ring out loudly …)

Visit them, hand them some small
things from me: this bit of lime
I brought from Hellas for them . . . . .

Aside from that,
I also ask—that you bow
to the gray turtledove for me: she

lives in luxury at the very peak,
of a house surrounded by an earthen bench, beyond its threshold
a heavenly field filled with the sun and God.

(By the way, don't alarm my turtledove
for I failed to get a gift for her—
what gift is appropriate for turtle doves?)

. . . . Listen
what a long mysterious song

emerges from the throat of the turtledove
as it coos and calls in the night: as if the Lord himself
is blowing into a clay cuckoo . . .

Go there, when it grows dark,
stand on the hill: you'll see—it glimmers,
there, way down below . . . like a phosphorescent map,

scattered in a ravine . . . some sort of cosmic symbols . . .
like children's dreams . . . . Fireflies light their souls
on boughs of yarrow.

This—is reading meant for angels; personages,
that we will sometime be able to attain from heaven
but into us—those that are here—something else will flow

that, which destroys all of our secrets
and distant memories, something quiet and precious
that has flown here for hundreds of years,

where a firefly is still a firefly,
and a turtledove—is still a turtledove, and a snail
is still a snail.... And no further description
is needed.

Don't return from there ...

Translated by Olena Jennings

VASYL GABOR

VASYL GABOR was born on December 10, 1959, in Transcarpathia, in the village of Oleksandrivka (previously Shandrovo), Khust raion. He is currently Head of the Foreign Periodicals Research Department at the Scientific Periodicals Research Centre of the Lviv Vasyl Stefanyk National Scientific Library. In 1997, Gabor defended his PhD thesis and also became a member of the Ukrainian Writers' Association. He has been awarded the Kurylas Family Prize (1994) and the Lesya and Petro Kovalev Literary Prize (2006).

Gabor currently lives in Lviv, and is well known in Ukraine as an original short story writer. He has also compiled the widely recognized anthologies *Pryvatna koleksiia: vybrana ukraïnska proza ta eseïstyka kintsia XX stolittia* (A Private Collection: Selected Ukrainian Prose and Essays of the End of the 20th Century, 2002); *Neznaioma: antolohiia ukraïnskoï 'zhinochoï' prozy ta eseïstyky druhoï pol. XX – poch. XXI st.* (The Unknown Woman: An Anthology of Ukrainian 'Female' Prose and Essays of the Second Half of the 20th and the Beginning of the 21st Century, 2005); *Dvanadtsiatka: Naimolodsha lvivska literaturna bohema 30-kh rokiv XX stolittia: Antolohiia urbanistychnoi prozy* (The Twelve: The Youngest Lviv Literary Bohemians of the 1930s: An Anthology of Urban Prose, 2006); *Bu-Ba-Bu (Yurii Andrukhovych, Oleksandr Irvanets, Viktor Neborak): Vybrani tvory: Poeziia, proza, eseïstyka* (Bu-Ba-Bu [Yurii Andrukhovych, Oleksandr Irvanets, Viktor Neborak]: Selected Works: Poetry, Prose, Essays, 2007); *Ukraïnski literaturni shkoly ta hrupy 60-90-x pp. XX st.: Antolohiia vybranoï poeziï ta eseïstyky* (Ukrainian Literary Schools and Groups of the 1960-90s: An Anthology of Poetry and Essays, 2009) and others, issued under the auspices of the *Pryvatna koleksiia* (Private Collection) modern literature publishing project by Lviv's Pyramid Literary Agency.

Vasyl Gabor is the author of a collection of short stories entitled *Knyha ekzotychnykh sniv ta realnykh podii* (A Book of Exotic Dreams and Real Events, 1999; 2nd ed. 2003, 3rd ed. 2009) and a collection of writing entitled *Pro shcho dumaie liudyna* (And That Which People Are Thinking, 2012).

He is one of the authors of the book *Chetvero za stolom* (Four at the Table: Anthology of Four Friends, 2004), and is also the author of the essays and literary investigations found in *Vid Dzhoisa do Chubaia* (From Joyce to Chubai, 2010), the historical and bibliographical research project *Ukraïnski chasopysy Uzhhoroda (1867-1944)* (Ukrainian Periodicals in Uzhhorod [1867 – 1944]], 2003), a brief summary of the life and the work of Ivan Kolos entitled *Ivan Kolos—Poet Karpatskoï Ukraïny* (Ivan Kolos—Poet of Carpathian Ukraine, 2010), and of a local history essay entitled *Moie Shandrovo* (My Shandrovo, 2003). In 2000 Gabor re-issued the previously self-published literary journal *Skrynia* (The Chest, 1971). In 2007, he compiled the biographical and bibliographic reference *Dariia Vikonska (1893—1945)*.

Several short stories by Gabor have been translated into English, German, Serbian, Slovak, Croatian, Czech, Japanese, and Bulgarian.

Vasyl Gabor's event in the Contemporary Ukrainian Literature Series, entitled *And That Which People Are Thinking*, took place in November 2012.

THE HIGH WATER

And it was here, in this very place, in these mountains reaching up to the skies, that I began to be pursued by the high water. I could hear it getting closer. If I closed my eyes for an instant, I could see a colossal wall of muddy water overwhelming me and engulfing the mountains at incredible speed. I saw the massive volume of water destroying everything in its path, spinning around in a wild maelstrom: uprooted trees, roofs torn from buildings, and all manner of household implements, livestock, and domestic animals—cows, pigs, chickens, dogs, and cats. Amidst all this, human beings, dead and alive, were also being whirled round. The living desperately clutched at the branches of trees, planks of wood, and logs that were floating in the water in an instinctive attempt to save themselves and their dear ones. But could anyone survive under the pressure of such deep water? The roar of the water grew louder and louder; it sounded as though some gigantic wounded beast was approaching. I could even hear the cold breathing of the watery beast, and then I quickly opened my eyes to see my last moments. Suddenly the vision disappeared, and peace and quiet reigned all around. From time to time, it was interrupted by the deep buzz of a bumble bee or the pleasant hum of a honey bee. The blue mountains could be seen in the distance, and above them an eagle was circling, a tiny dot scarcely perceptible against the clear sky. Only the birds will survive the high water, I thought. But who knows whether they will be able to remain airborne for such a long time. As their wings become stiff with exhaustion, the birds will plunge like stones into the water's bottomless depths. For there is no escape from the high water.

I try to fathom what it is that is disturbing me, why I began to have this vision of water, purifying water, water that brings people into the world and carries them away. Can it be that the very water that created the world will also cause it to perish? Terrified, I close my eyes and again I see the gigantic wave, like a wide wall many kilometers high. Roaring, it is rushing towards the mountains, and I think of my parents, my brother and his family, I think of my wife and our children, all of whom I left behind in the valley. I run after them. I arrive, quite out of breath. And they are all very peacefully sitting around in the dining room, calm as you like, chatting away happily while sitting at the table and enjoying their food and drink. I call out to them that the high water is coming, but they look at me in surprise, almost as though there were something wrong with me.

I see only the fear in my wife's eyes—not for herself, but for our children. I ask my father and brother to bind together with wire and chains the planks that have been lying in two piles in the garden, drying in the sun, for years now. My brother gives my father a quizzical look, but the latter gives him a nod, indicating that he should do as I ask. We only just manage to tie together the two piles of planks and get on the raft, taking with us a little bread and two axes, when we hear the frightful roar of the high water. Nobody has seen anything like it before. People begin to rush about crazily, hurrying to untie the cattle and bring in or out some valuables, while others do the opposite, shutting themselves indoors.

Father ties us all to one rope and then to the raft, and just then we catch sight of the gigantic wave, so high it half blots out the sky. "Nothing will be left of us when that wall of water falls on us," I think involuntarily. Amazingly, the water engulfs us and then lifts us, raft and all, and in a crazy maelstrom throws us up to the surface. And we all survive, though we are swamped by filthy, salty water. Oh God! All sorts of stuff is floating about—so much of it! In the whirling maelstrom we see people and terrified cattle, but we can't hear either human voices or the bellowing of the beasts above the water's roar. We push away the tree trunks and drive away the frightened livestock from our raft to prevent them from capsizing it. Under the weight of our bodies, the raft is already sitting quite low in the water, and the waves submerge it time and again, so if it were not for the fact that we are tied to it, we would be swept away into the inky black depths.

Survivors spotting our raft begin to swim toward it from all directions, their eyes blazing maniacally. To them our raft is the last hope of salvation. We realize that if they climb aboard we will all perish, because the raft will either capsize or sink. We exchange glances among ourselves. We all know that if we want to survive, we will have to repel the people from our raft—our neighbors, our kin, and our best friends. We will even need to use the axes, because the poles will not be enough—the people we drive off will keep trying to clamber onto the raft again and again. We know that once we raise the axes against someone, we will become murderers. Is it worth surviving, in that case? And then, even if we manage to survive, I think, won't we be merely prolonging the agony of dying? After all, our bread will run out and we will be left alone in the middle of the sea created by the filthy, salty high water. What will our fate be then?

The shouting of the people gets louder, and dripping wet hands grasp at our raft as the first people begin to clamber onto it.

"Push them off! Push them off!" shout our womenfolk inaudibly. "Save our children!"

The axes tremble in our hands.

"I can't do it!" shouts my brother. Like them, he is shouting, but I can't hear his words.

"Neither can I!" says my father, shaking his head.

We drive the terrified people off with the poles. We are soaked in sweat and water, and they keep swimming towards the raft. Our arms are already becoming numb, and all our strength is deserting us.

"Oh God, if they get onto the raft we'll all perish," shout the women. We still can't hear their voices above the roar of the water, but we can read their words on their lips and in their eyes, full of despair and terror.

And we know it will be as our women say, since there are crazed looks in the eyes of the people who want to be saved, and wild, hoarse screams struggle to escape from their throats. All that is left of our former fellow villagers, our best friends and neighbors, is their human form. The high water has turned them into animals. But wait a minute, are we really any better? Perhaps we are the animals, because we are cruelly driving people away from our raft instead of offering them a helping hand.

And then our father falls, and they start to drag him into the water. How fortunate that he is tied to us by the rope. We rush to his aid and strike at the arms of the attackers with the butts of the axes. We rescue our father, but he is hardly breathing. Blood is flowing from the scratches on his face. The women are crying.

"Leave our raft alone!" we keep shouting, but our attackers don't hear us and clamber up.

We know that our raft is an uncertain means of survival, yet it gives us at least some faint hope. But more and more people are trying to get aboard.

I can't watch this frightful vision any longer, and I open my eyes. The vision disappears, but I can still hear the roar of the rushing high water in the distance.

I can't understand why it is pursuing me. I try to think about something else, to get it out of my head, but it steals up on me like a gust of wind, making itself felt like a gentle breath of air that is enough to strike fear into my very soul. It seems to me that I used to experience feelings like this when I was fifteen years old. For a long time then, I kept having the same dream again and again. I dreamt that I was being led through a cemetery by someone who was very close to me and yet was a stranger, who was showing me the graves of my descendants. I saw the names of members of my family carved on the headstones, with the dates of their birth and their death below: the year 6500, the year 6900. I was surprised and gratified to see how prolific our family turned out to be, but I was terribly afraid to look around, since I knew that my own grave was behind me. I was gripped by fear at the very thought that I would see the date of my own death on a headstone. At that point, I started to run. First I ran through the whole cemetery, then through the town. The town was large and empty, like the cemetery—its buildings and roads were black. Only when I collapsed, exhausted from running and not far from our house, did I see that the road and our building were different in color. At this point I always woke up, with incredible relief and joy in my heart that I had not looked round and seen the year of my death on a gravestone.

Ah, I thought, so this dream was not pointless—it was a premonition of danger. In those days of my youth, that alien force could not get the better of me, and it left me in peace. But now it had returned and was trying to force the vision of the high water on me. Of course, I knew very well that it can end only in death—but does anyone want to see their own demise, or that of other people?

True, initially the idea of committing suicide had come to my mind, so as to obliterate the vision of the high water absolutely. But, I thought, in that act I would discover only my own powerlessness and weakness and in the end, would not avert the coming of the high water. What disturbed me most was that by this act I would not only distress those dearest to me, but I would leave them to face the high water on their own. When it comes, I want to be by their side—and my sense that it is approaching is ever more keen. In despair, I wipe my face and squint. Once more I see myself with my family and my brother with his family and our elderly parents on the raft, driven by the waves to the furthest edge of the wall of water that extends over many kilometers. It begins to dawn on me that the high water is carrying with it all that is living and non-living on the earth, like a wheel destroying everything and crushing everything into a mire. Is it really our turn now to hurtle into the black abyss? No, no! I shake my head, banishing the vision as my heart starts to race and my hands tremble. Why should it be me that suffers all this? Why can't I get rid of these terrifying premonitions? And why did the vision of the high water start to appear here, of all places, in the mountains, which one would think cannot be threatened by any water? Are they the first to sense our demise, and are they already weeping over our final days?

Don't come, high water, I whisper faintly, and I find that I am ridiculous: for it is already on its way and nothing can stop it now ...

Translated by Patrick Corness and Natalia Pomirko

A STORY ABOUT ONE DOLLAR

This is a true, not a made-up, story. When I set off for America, my father, being completely convinced that America is a fantastically rich country with dollars lying around everywhere, even on the street, strongly advised me, although we laughed at him, to take a large shovel with me so that I could gather as much money as possible. Having arrived in a small, provincial town, I immediately wrote father to advise him not to be too upset that I hadn't taken a shovel with me because, in America, money doesn't just lie around on the street. Moreover, I was indeed hoping to earn a little money but, because I didn't have official permission to work in America, no one would hire me; and it looked like I would return a half a year later, to everyone's chagrin, not with overfilled pockets but with empty ones.

But God took pity on me. In three months, I obtained the right to work and, with fervent energy, I began making up for lost time. I took on two jobs, working all Saturdays and Sundays, often during the night shift, sometimes only sleeping a few hours a day, and the work was very intense and at a pace not unlike that with which I would disassemble and assemble an automatic rifle while in the army. But the earnings in that small town were meager, which discouraged me. I even ended up working on Easter Sunday (Gregorian calendar). And it was on that very day that something happened to me that affected me greatly and, as I can now say, changed me drastically. On that day I received a gift from God.

And this is what happened. When the number of customers in the fast-food restaurant had died down, I took a seat by a wide window to drink a cup of hot coffee with milk. It was warm and quiet in the restaurant, but it was windy outside. The wind whistled loudly by the window, swaying the tops of trees and whipping a path of random trash around the restaurant: newspaper shreds, crumpled plastic food wrappers, dried weeds. "Looks like I'll have to go out and sweep again," I thought unhappily and set off to the task. But then, suddenly, I saw that the wind was tossing directly at me, along the asphalt road and across the flowerbeds, a green banknote. It was difficult to make out what kind of bill it was, but I immediately became happy that God had not forgotten about me, even though I was in distant America, and had sent me a gift right on Easter Sunday. It turned out to be only a dollar bill, but this did not disappoint me in the least bit; conversely, it cheered me up. Because a thought instantly popped into my head that God, tired of hearing me pleading for help, had sent me a dollar so that I could use it to buy a lottery ticket with which I would win the jackpot, rendering me materially comfortable for the rest of my life. But then this thought made me laugh, because God and money are discordant. More likely, God had sent me a sign: He calmed me so that I wouldn't be so concerned with making money, because money is nothing but trash that gets blown along the street by the wind. And I did calm down, and I don't even remember what I spent that dollar on—whether I spent it on a bus ride or whether I just added it to a larger sum when buying something at a store. But nonetheless, a devilish voice then said: "You should have bought a lottery ticket with that dollar, because it certainly would have been a winner." I don't know, maybe it would have. But that's not the point—this found dollar taught me not to be overly concerned with money and not to tremble over every hard-earned penny. That is why, upon returning home, my close friend and I had the guts to set off on a risky venture—we put up all of our hard-earned cash to publish the "A Private Collection" anthologies. We could not cover all the printing costs, we borrowed money to publish the book, and our debt was so high that we basically would have had to sell both of our houses in order to just settle it. Today, it seems that our initiative really was insane, but without it a whole series of books published in Lviv under the title "A Private Collection" would not exist. And all of this was influenced by one dollar.

I like to tell my friends this story, and some of them think I am exaggerating a bit about the effect one dollar had on my life. But no, I counter, I am like my father, who likes to say that he only truly feels good when he is being thrifty, when he's sitting on a bit of money. And I now have an alternative: I can sit on a stack of published books ...

Translated by Mark Andryczyk

FIVE SHORT STORIES FOR NATALIE

The Fifth Story—the Last One

THE LOVER

He too, the chairman of the council, the most respectable man in the village, was seduced by the charms of the young widow. After dark, when his exhausted wife and little children had fallen asleep (the two elder sons slept on straw in the barn), he quietly left by the front door and made his way across the gardens to The Hump, where the widow lived. He didn't want anybody to see him, so he crept along like a criminal, crouching in the bushes for a long time whenever he heard the slightest sound. It was a peculiar sensation for him to hear his heart pounding in his chest, perhaps from a fear of being found out, because he had never been afraid of anything in his life. His heart had pounded like that when he first saw the drop-dead gorgeous young widow—it would have been a sin not to call on her, so he dared to do it. Not immediately, it's true. At first, he spent a long time searching for a pretext. His preference would have been for the young widow to get into some kind of trouble—nothing serious, mind—so the responsibility of sorting it out would fall to him. He would have gone to see her as a representative of the authorities, and the widow would have been well-disposed towards him; indeed she might even have taken a liking to him, which would have made life easier in a situation he found it difficult to handle. The thing is, he simply didn't know how to get into conversation with a strange woman and steer her, without being too blatant about it, in the direction he wanted. But the widow gave him no pretext and today he was going to see her with no particular idea in mind; he was just driven by sheer lust. Perhaps there was one thing that worried him: the chairman of the council usually goes to see people on official business in broad daylight, not at night when it's dark. And when he gets to the young widow's, what if one of her lovers is there? How should he react? Shout at her: "Why are you living in sin? Why are you breaking God's commandments?" And what if the young widow's lover asks him: "Well, what are you doing here at this time of night?" He had a response ready for such an eventuality: "I am the chairman of the council, and the chairman of the council is supposed to see order is kept at night-time as well as during the day." But if he came across an argumentative lover who asked him: "Then why have you come on your own without witnesses as the chairman of the council ought to have done at this late hour?" he would reply, "Your wife asked me to catch you at it, you old layabout. Without making a big fuss though, because that would be embarrassing for her in front of people and in front of the children." At first, he was satisfied with his presence of mind, but when he considered how he should behave towards the young widow after that, he became uneasy, his resolve weakened and his legs began to give way.

Perhaps he should give her a fright, saying he would tell the priest, who would condemn her dissolute behavior from the pulpit and make her do penance. This would alarm the widow, and on her knees she would start to beg him, the chairman of the council, not to do it, and he would lift her up from the floor and begin to reassure her, stroking her curly tresses, her lovely face and her ample shoulders. At the prospect of feeling her firm breasts too, his face flushed and he shook his head, saying to himself: "Christ, Yura, how childish is that, you daft old goat. Just go home to your wife and pray; these are the temptations of the devil." But he did not have the strength to return; he was utterly feeble in the face of the force that was driving him towards the widow. He crept towards the darkened windows of the widow's house, imagining that inside, in the deserted house, on the bed—on those white sheets—a young woman was lying alone, unable to sleep without a man's caresses, and his desire to get into the house grew stronger. He began to scratch at the window with a finger-nail, whispering softly:

"Eufrusina, open the window for a moment."

But nobody came to the window, so he went to the door and began knocking gently, continuing to whisper Eufrusina's name. He recalled that when it was freezing cold, his dog whined piteously, begging to be let indoors, just like this. This made him, the chairman of the council, the most respectable man in the village, uncomfortable in his

indecision. So he went back to the window and knocked on it loudly.
A light immediately flashed in the house, shining straight at him, the
chairman of the council, causing him to recoil into the darkness of the
night. He heard the young widow asking in an annoyed voice:

"Who's there?"

He quite forgot his momentary dissatisfaction with himself, trotting
up to the window and whispering with delight:

"It's me, Eufrusina, the chairman of the council. Open the door."

"But what if someone is in the house and has heard everything, and
spreads rumors all round the village?"—the thought suddenly crossed
his mind and it was as though somebody had poured a bucket of cold
water over him. But he immediately recovered and coolly, as though in
somebody else's voice, shouted out:

"Open the door, Eufrusina. It's me, the chairman of the council.
I've come to see you about a certain matter."

The young widow opened the door, carrying a gas lamp. She wore
a linen blouse, revealing her full breasts; her full head of hair was let
down, flowing as it was caught in the light and the chairman of the
council found it arousing. The young widow looked relaxed and there
was not the slightest sign of fear in her eyes. On the contrary, they radi-
ated a happy playfulness and she had a smile on her lips.

He went indoors. When he saw her lover sitting at the table, his jaw
dropped in surprise and everything he had been ready to say to the illicit
lover flew right out of his head, because it was his eldest son Mitro who
was sitting at the table, no old layabout yet but just a lad with his moth-
er's milk scarcely dry on his lips, looking at him quite unconcerned. It
was actually the fact that his son was looking at him so calmly that took
his breath away. He showed his son the door and he left unhurriedly,
while the chairman of the council, shifting from one leg to the other,
stayed on outside the house for a while and then followed his son.

On the way home, he considered that he ought to give his son a
good hiding, because then it would mean that he had come for him in
person, the chairman of the council and the father, and now the widow
would realize why he had visited her so late at night. But perhaps it was
better that she should not know that.

In the morning, he told his son:

"Mitro, if you walk over to see that widow, I'll break both your legs. Got it?"

"Yes, Dad," his son replied. Suddenly—and this was a considerable surprise to the chairman of the council—the son's eyes sparkled with amusement and the lad found it hard to avoid laughing out loud.

"Watch it! Don't you dare to laugh about it," said the chairman of the council severely.

The son kept his promise never to walk over to see the widow, but every night he was at her house.

When darkness fell, the young widow would come to the village from The Hump and carried Mitro home on her shoulders. Hiding in the orchard, the chairman of the council was surprised to see the widow carrying the boy. She followed the winding path, passed the well, went round the grove of hornbeam trees up to the old wild apple tree. Here she stopped for a moment to turn Mitro round and settle him better on her shoulders, then she climbed up to the cottage on The Hump. The chairman of the council watched all this spellbound. O Lord, how he wished he could carry the young widow off to her cottage like that, on his shoulders, but she had eyes only for his own lad. Sometimes he, as chairman of the council, considered going to the widow's and giving his son a good hiding, but at the thought of how cleverly he had fooled him and still managed to keep his word, an involuntarily smile would come to his lips. After all, this wasn't just anybody, it was his own flesh and blood, his son, who had gotten away with it so resourcefully. He heard the neighbors calling to one another in surprise:

"Look, look, Eufrusina has carried off the chairman of the council's Mitro on her shoulders again."

The chairman of the council found this amusing too, but he could not forget the young widow; he still dreamt of her at night and he gave a deep groan when his wife, alarmed by his moaning, woke him and asked if he was in pain.

"No," he replied feebly, "go to sleep, love, go to sleep …"

Translated by Patrick Corness and Natalia Pomirko

YURI VYNNYCHUK

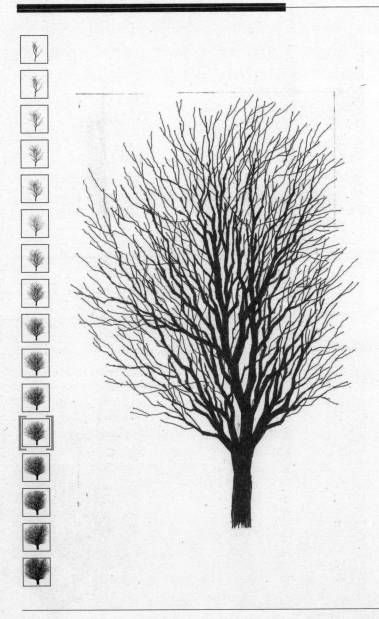

YURI VYNNYCHUK, one of independent Ukraine's most popular writers, was born in the city of Ivano-Frankivsk in 1952. Unable to have his own works published until the early 1990s due to Soviet cultural policy, Vynnychuk would publish them as "translations" from ancient languages (Old Irish, Old Welsh) or even made-up languages, such as "Arcanumian". Vynnychuk even invented a whole Arcanumian civilization in the 1990s and convinced others of its existence.

Unable to obtain employment as a philologist, Vynnychuk worked as a freight handler and a painter. In 1987, he co-founded the cabaret theater *Ne Zhurys!* (Don't Worry!), writing songs and scenes for its performances. Since 1990, Vynnychuk has worked as a journalist, and in 1999, he received the honorary title of *Halytskyi Lytsar* (Galician Knight) for his weekly article series published under the pseudonym *Yuzio Observator* (Yuzio the Observer) in the *Post-Postup* newspaper.

In 1990, Vynnychuk began to publish everything that he had written over the years that had remained unpublished. This has included poetry, short stories, and the novels *Malva Landa* (2003), *Vesniani ihry v osinnikh sadakh* (Springtime Games in Autumn Orchards, 2005), and *Tango smerti* (Tango of Death, 2012). *Tango smerti* was awarded the prestigious BBC Ukrainian Book of the Year prize for 2012. He has also authored many popular publications covering the history of the city of Lviv; his immensely popular two-volume set *Lehendy Lvova* (Legends of Lviv) is republished almost every year. In 2015, he published the novel, *Aptekar* (The Apothecary) and, in 2016, another novel, *Tsenzor sniv* (The Dream Censor). Vynnychuk's works have been translated into English, French, German, Japanese, and all Slavic languages. Two books containing Vynnychuk's Ukrainian translations of Czech writer Bohumil Hrabal have been published: the novel *I Served the King of England* (2009) and a volume of selected short stories, *Kooks* (2003).

Yuri Vynnychuk's events in the Contemporary Ukrainian Literature Series, entitled *Tango of Death*, took place in November 2013.

THE FLOWERBED IN THE KILIM

On the wall in the living room hung a multi-colored kilim on which a flowerbed was woven; behind the flowerbed was a little orchard, and in the orchard—a small house under a red cherry tree. The little house was so charming that, every time I looked at it, I was struck with a strange and insurmountable sadness. I wanted to find out who lived in that little house and whose flowerbed it was. The flowers that grew there were truly remarkable—even Auntie's flowerbed didn't have those kinds of flowers, nor did her straw hat.

When I put my ear to the kilim, I heard the rattling of moths and the buzzing of bumble bees, while my nose caught the intoxicating scent of flowers, dew, and honey. But no matter how often I gazed at the little house, I was never able to see a living soul there. Yet somebody had to live there, because, looking at the flowers, it was obvious that someone was diligently taking care of them, weeding and watering them.

Sometimes, when I pressed my ear right up against the little house, I was just barely able to hear the clamor of human voices. I wasn't, however, able to make out exactly what it was they were saying.

The strangest thing was that the seasons would change on the kilim as they would in nature. In autumn, flowers would break off and leaves would fall, leaving the branches bare. Every now and then rain would shower down, and the colors on the kilim would fade. The little house would lose its elegant and fabulous appearance, and the sky above it would spill down like gray lead. In the winter, snow would fall and solidly cover the orchard, weighing down heavily on its branches. And then tiny footprints could occasionally be seen along the snow. Smoke rose from the chimney and the scent of resin would take wing. And, at night, a light would shine in the window, and a dark shadow would spread along the curtains.

I really wanted to end up in that little orchard in the kilim and peek into the little house, but no matter how much I tried to fulfill my dream, the kilim remained just a kilim and would not let me enter it.

A large wall clock was hanging right beside the kilim in a wooden case and behind glass. The wall clock would always stand still, and I never ever heard it tick. Its hands were always stuck in one spot, displaying five minutes before twelve o'clock. The wooden case was locked, and I didn't know where the key was, otherwise I would have tried to set the correct time long ago.

I would have never noticed any connection between the kilim and the wall clock if it hadn't been for a certain strange incident. One time, having opened the door to the living room without warning, I saw a male mannequin frozen in an unusual position by the kilim. He stood, bending over and extending his arm as if he wanted to pick a flower. But as I got closer, I saw that he was not trying to pick a flower, but, instead, was trying to pick up a key from inside the flowerbed. I had never noticed any key on the kilim before. And now, it seemed, somebody had lost it.

I pretended that I hadn't noticed anything and walked out of the living room. After some time, I re-entered the living room and saw that the mannequin was in his usual position and that the key had disappeared. You didn't have to have an especially wild imagination to figure out where it was.

I bravely walked up to the mannequin and pulled the key out of the pocket of his suit jacket. He ferociously blinked his eyes but didn't dare to budge.

Now there was only one thing left to do: put the key in the wooden case and see if I'd guessed correctly. But as soon as I attempted to do this, there was a loud squeak. The mannequins turned their heads toward me and popped open their eyes in fright. I saw they were afraid of me.

I turned the key, and the case—creaking and screeching—flung wide open. Then I lifted the lever and the clock moved. The room filled with new sounds, and it seemed like they gave life to all the objects in the room, because they also immediately began making sounds, each in its own way, and, just like that, the whole living room was abuzz. The faces of the mannequins cheered up, anger disappeared from their eyes, and the corners of their mouths were smoothed out.

And not only did the living room come to life, but the kilim, too, seemed to have woken up from its winter slumber—I saw how leaves on trees shook from the wind, how petals shivered, and how the scent of flowers rose up into the air. Everything now looked like it was on a movie screen. I tried brushing my hand along the flowers, but all my fingers could feel was the thick wool of the kilim.

And then, suddenly, everything changed. The wall clock let out a heavy groan, something clanged and made a grinding noise, and the first stroke of the clock sounded. At that instant my hand forcefully broke through to the flowerbed. Without stopping to think, I jumped into the kilim and ran along the path that leads to the little house as fast as I could. Behind me I once again heard that sound.

Right on the third stroke, I ended up by the door and turned the doorknob, but it was locked. I ran up to the window and looked inside. The house was cloaked in twilight, but I was immediately able to recognize several things that had been familiar to me since birth. There on the table was the bowl that I had once broken accidentally, and there was Grandma's vase with its peculiar rhododendron—it had dried up after Grandma died, so Mom threw it out. And there was our cat lying on the pillow, a cat that also had died long ago. There was the bench on which Grandma used to love to sit. And the eyeglass case with her glasses, and her embroidery … And all the walls here were decorated with various embroideries. One of them was of me, as a little boy, playing with a kitten.

And the clock behind struck two more times.

I couldn't pull myself away from the window, recognizing one object after another, and most peculiar was the fact that every one of these objects was connected, in some way or another, with Granny.

Well then, where was she?

I ran behind the house and saw that a yard stretched from behind the bushes all the way down to a narrow little river where ducks were quacking. From the little river, a path climbed up the hill, cutting through the yard, and along this path a hunched-over figure carrying buckets was ascending. I recognized this person immediately and, shouting in turn with the menacing grumbling of the wall clock, I yelled:

"Gra-a-an-dma-a-a!"

At first, she thought she was just hearing things and even stopped to look around her. Then she put down her buckets and, after I yelled again, raised her head.

Initially, her face lit up with joy, but then it immediately was overcome with horror. She waved her hands and screamed:

"Run away! Run away at once!"

The clock now struck for the eight time. I don't know why I was counting these rings.

"Grandma!" I yelled. "I'm coming to you!"

She became even more horrified and started running up the hill, repeatedly imploring me:

"Run away! Go back! Before it's too late!"

I looked back and saw the frightened mannequins, who were also waving their arms at me, surrounding the kilim.

"BONNGGGG!" The ninth ring sounded.

I didn't want to leave my Grandma and this delightful orchard! Nevertheless, I saw something in her face that convinced me and, when "ten" sounded, I finally moved and dashed home. As I ran, tears flooded my eyes, and I could hear Grandma's voice behind me:

"Faster! Faster!"

"BONNGGGG." "Eleven."

I tripped over a rock and flew headfirst into the flowerbed. The flowers crunched beneath my feet and squirted dew in my face.

"O, Lord!" Grandma screamed.

Gathering my strength, I was barely able to push myself off the ground and thrust my body forward. The wall clock, with a certain despair and groan, struck "twelve" just as the strong hands of the mannequins caught me and laid me down on the floor.

I looked at the kilim and saw a familiar scene. Everything now was as it was before. Except that the flowers were a bit squashed. But Grandma would tie them up, straighten them out, sprinkle them with fresh water and, God willing, Auntie wouldn't notice anything.

I once again immobilized the wall clock, returning the big hand to five minutes before twelve; I closed the wooden case and placed the little key in the mannequin's pocket.

Tears spilled from my eyes and, for a long time, I was unable to free myself of sorrow over the fact that I didn't stay with Grandma and with my beloved kitten.

Translated by Mark Andryczyk

PEA SOUP

My aunt often cooked pea soup, which her late husband used to love to eat. Nowadays, when she finished preparing it, she would always fill up a bowl and place it on the windowsill. At night, her deceased husband would come and eat up the soup.

I was always fascinated by how clean the bowl was when I saw it in the morning. Because everybody knows that it's impossible to finish a bowl of pea soup without leaving behind a yellow film. Unless … unless, of course, he licked it clean.

And although I was not especially fond of peas in general, just the fact that someone would lick the bowl clean after eating it enchanted me for some strange reason. I, too, wanted to lick the bowl after eating the soup.

When my aunt became aware of this, she dropped her washcloth and, for a moment, gave me a frightened stare. Maybe she had imagined that the spirit of her late husband had entered my body. But when my aunt looked into my eyes, she saw nothing strange, just the clever eyes of a young hooligan looking up at her, and she was able to calm down.

Nonetheless, the pea soup continued to intrigue me—and it dawned on me that there must be something beyond taste that would drive my deceased uncle to lick the bowl clean.

From that day on, I began to gaze much more attentively at its murky, yellow waters, in which finely chopped carrots and onions would swim. And when my aunt would pour a handful of golden croutons into the soup, they would make it even cloudier, and a pale, yellow slime would begin rising from the bottom.

One day, I realized that strange creatures lived at the bottom of the pea soup, who, just at first glance, looked like minced dill weed—thin, branchy, and akin to people, with arms, legs and something resembling a head. These tiny, green dill weeds submerged and then resurfaced, swimming and overtaking one another as part of some kind of race. When I gathered a spoonful of the soup, the tiny dill weeds, as if they had been scalded, shot down to the very bottom, and settled in the slime like a school of fish. But not all of them were able to rescue themselves, not all. Those that ended up in my mouth struggled in despair—I could feel them bustling, tickling my palate and tongue.

At one particular moment, I swish about the pea soup, together with all of its inhabitants, in my mouth, delighted at my absolute supremacy, tossing the despair of the poor little dill weeds against my palate with my tongue and then, finally, I swallow, feeling the pea soup stream down in a hot waterfall and hearing the screams of these strange creatures.

Spoonful after spoonful, I pour their fatherland—all of them together with the graves of their ancestors—into me.

Everything disappears in my mouth—all of their dreams and imagination, all of their hopes for a better life, all of their plans and intentions … It's the death of their civilization—a civilization that hasn't yet had the chance to fully blossom.

Pea soup is not a suitable place to live, but the tiny dill weeds don't understand this, and choose it time and time again.

Translated by Mark Andryczyk

From SPRING GAMES IN SUMMER GARDENS

selections

PROLOGUE

1

The dark waters of sleep spread so slowly and softly—the flow carries me to the surface rocking, and though my eyes are shut, even so, I see everything beautifully—I see the Arabian dance of the underwater plants and the silver glimmering of the tiny fish, the sorrowful twinkling of the water and the undulating beams of light that penetrate the water from above and below, stealthy shadows and the flashes of a shell—it seems I am so tiny in my mother's cradle and it's so warm and peaceful that a baby bird wouldn't want to wake up, and I remain happy in this balmy water rocking on the waves, but some inexorable power pushes me out from the depths to the surface grabs me brutally by the hair and I don't don't don't want to wake up—I don't want to go to the surface I want to go back into the depth into the silence there into the half-shade into the balmy water into the soothing rocking …

2

The winter sun gnaws through squinting eyelids, the rays painfully bore your brain and open the damaged cupboards of memory, pull out the drawers, shake them out with a clamor, and then he begins to remember what had happened before now, with which thoughts he had fallen asleep, and why his head was buzzing like a tambourine … This kind of awakening is so horrible … as if it were a plunge into glacial water. Back, back into the balmy water of dreams, into a warm mirage, into a world without pain and sorrow, into meadows filled with flowers … But the eyes are incapable of closing, the brain has become fixed on the transition from dreams to wakefulness, there's nowhere to retreat, the dream is disintegrating, like mortar on an old building, baring the surrounding world—your eyes glide along the room, filled to the brim with book-shelves, drooping lower to islands of papers, magazines, books, empty bottles, eyes wander, sinking in the thick pile of the rug, to the doors, beyond which dead silence lurked, for a certain amount of time your ears try to capture at least the hint of a sound, a strum, a clink, but the silence is dead—it is never more dead … Together with the conscious-ness of awakening from a dream, something else appears—painful and unpleasant, filled with despair and a sense of being lost, consciousness of complete ruin … All the fortresses crumble all at once and the towers have fallen to ruins, the smashed armies have fallen to their knees and lowered their banners, everything that surrounded him till now, every-thing behind which he continued to live in a cozy nook and in safety disappeared in a single instant.

3

In the middle of the night and into his dreams, the ringing of the tele-phone reverberated, it burst into his brain like a dashing train, rat-tling and giving off sparks, it seems his head would crack in another minute, split into two halves. What's this? Who is it? In the middle of the night! He tears from his bed, stumbles on the books strewn all over the floor, slips on piles of manuscripts, nearly falls, but he manages to grab onto the table, finally blindly with a trembling hand groping for the receiver, and first before putting it to his ear, in which the warm sea of dreams still continues to splash, and not everything is still sufficiently distinguishable between mirage and reality, he shouts out: "HELLO!"—so loudly, as if he needed to be heard on the street.

The morning recollection of a telephone conversation is like read-ing a palimpsest. Did it really happen? Or did he dream it? But your gaze falls onto the table—there were two bottles of champagne, and both of them empty. They were drunk up during the night. Right after the phone conversation. And this is reality, which it is impossible to doubt. His memory retained several fragments of the conversation; all the rest is torn, shredded, and submerged in the wine.

The call was from the U.S. She suggested getting a divorce. And she added: "It'll be better this way." Better for whom? He couldn't manage to ask her, he was so stunned that he was incapable of squeezing a single complete phrase out of himself. Eventually, this wasn't all that strange, because he was asleep, and the phone call had awakened him. A phone call in the middle of the night has its peculiarities. It always forces you to shudder, it forces the heart to beat faster, it fills you with anxiety. The one making the call is in a better state because she knows what she wants, has had time to think out what she has to say, she knows what she wants, but the one picking up the receiver is absolutely unprepared for a conversation. What kind of conversation can there be when someone calls from the U.S. and to save money babbles hurriedly, chokes on her words, swallowing individual syllables without any pauses, that would allow anything to be grasped—the sleepy brain is unable to digest all this, to comprehend it, to counter it …

"… it'll be better this way."

These words stung my brain and will never be effaced, all others—will wither, will crumble, but these will remain and will prick for years and years, will shoot out in sprouts of couch-grass and wound.

The conversation lasted for a short amount of time, he mostly listened, and she quickly set out everything in its place, arranged everything onto shelves, numbered and sealed everything. And then she threw down the receiver: somewhere far, far away on Long Island in New York. And he heard her slam the receiver down. And he even dreamt that he had heard her words that were directed not at him, but at another man, who the entire time was next to her listening to their conversation. She said: "Well here … ," and the man also said something hoarsely, it was hard to make out the words, maybe it was all said in English, in the dark room only the rustle of his voice wafted, and then silence came, and he stood next to the telephone and didn't move away, as if he were continuing to listen to the receiver gone silent, waiting for another call, though he understood that the conversation had come to an end, no one would call, but all the same there was some kind of invisible thread that linked them across the ocean, it continued to vibrate, continued to link them, refused to be broken, and until he stopped hearing its vibration, he didn't move from where he was standing.

And in a moment the vibration disappeared, and in his ears silence again dawned, but it was restless and dreadful, clenching his heart with a burning sadness. Back, back into sleep … gropingly, scraping his brow with his hands, diving and swimming, further, further from that place, further from that time, to return everything from the beginning, to fix it, to rewrite it, to save it … Actually, to save it—he needed to rush beyond the seas and oceans to foreign lands and to free the princess, whom a wicked sorcerer had imprisoned in a tower without windows, to snatch her onto a winged horse and, pressing her to himself ever so tightly, to fly home … In his head, a noisy carousel swirled and assorted colors twinkled. This lasted for several long wearisome minutes, until outside the window it began to drizzle, a fine, miserable, winter rain, but he sensed a certain strange gratitude to this rain that finally destroyed the silence, forced him to move from where he was standing and turn on a light. In his head, the carousel of words continued to swirl, separate sounds, pauses and breathing … He uncorked a bottle of champagne, fell into an armchair and drank glass after glass, and at that time around him the walls fell and a wasteland appeared. Time after time he replayed that conversation, trying hard to recreate it in its entirety, but the champagne set in all too quickly; for every new recollection, something was lost, words were confused, order was lost, he was annoyed mostly by the fact that just when he had immediately grasped something, he could answer this or that reproach. The words faded, were replaced by others, and the more he got drunk, the less and less memory of the conversation remained, and just one phrase refused to fade and continued to circle in his ears: "It will be better this way."

Maybe it really will be better this way? Wine saves you from sorrow and covers everything with a semi-transparent film of paraffin. If not for the wine, he would have never fallen asleep after that conversation.

The man finally crawls out of bed and shuffles heavily to the bathroom. The cold water washes away dreams from his eyes. He squeezes out onto his toothbrush an entire mountain of toothpaste and, when he begins to brush his teeth, his gaze falls into the mirror. In the mirror he sees the sullen, unshaven face of a forty-year-old man, he sees swollen bags under his eyes, he sees disheveled hair, he sees sadness in his eyes.

And at that moment with horror I suddenly become conscious of the fact that this man in the mirror is—me! And it was I who had had a conversation on the telephone with my wife who called from the U.S., and then—again it was me—who downed two bottles of champagne, and now it was my head aching, and not somebody else's.

A mirror is always indifferent to whose kisser it is reflecting. My kisser half-awake had a sour taste. To somehow sweeten it, I brushed my teeth, combed my hair, washed my eyes, then I crawled under the shower, shaved, got dressed—but anyway I still looked like a squeezed-out lemon. It's always this way. Waking up in the morning after a drinking bout, I always feel like a cat run over by a car. But my nighttime drinking bout was of a particular kind—I drank out of despair. When you drink out of despair, it's a completely different feeling, because then you usually drink alone. You drink alone with yourself late into the evening, when all the sounds around you grow quiet, and when midnight passes, you're finally the way you need to be, you're drunk, you're no one's, and here right then, right in that state you can finally speak with yourself, openly and candidly, to cut out all your insides, all your intestines, hang them all up nicely and make a diagnosis. And, this is always the most interesting, to create plans for the future. Well, what can you say—plans at such moments simply bloat your head, and everything looks so courageous, so rosy, that despair disappears, hides itself in the deepest recesses of memory, so that it can rise to the surface tomorrow, but it will be tomorrow, not today, and today you just feel like swimming along the waves of daydreams.

Translated by Michael M. Naydan

THE PILGRIM'S DANCE

PART 1

1

You really begin to understand women only when they leave you. It's right then that they finally illuminate some kind of higher truth unknown to you to that point and with it slay you on the spot. You might have lived with a woman for forty years, but just as that moment arrives when she tells you she's leaving, you find out something about yourself that had never occurred to you. And this, by the way, can be some totally inane thing, a complete nothing, nil, that at any other moment would have elicited just wild laughter, but not then, not at that moment, when she tosses it out at you as she's saying good-bye. And the main thing is that she tosses it out! Something at which you just want to wildly burst out laughing. What? At such idiocy? Yes, strictly speaking, at it. Thus, it sounds like a verdict, like a final judgment that is driven into your forehead with a nail, into the very center of your forehead, right here between your eyebrows, and from that time on you have to wear this nail in the middle of your forehead, to touch it and think quite hard what it really all meant and what in actuality stood behind it.

From every young lady with whom I've been close, I've learned something new. Strictly speaking, at the time when we broke up. Perhaps someone might call this masochism, but when I've wanted to break-up with a young lady I've never said such a thing to her. I couldn't have pasted together words such as these: "Pardon me, but I've fallen in love with someone else," or "Everything's over with us. Let's break up." I've listened with astonishment to several of my friends' stories about the strange scenes that they've played out with young women they've broken up with. Some even arrange a farewell dinner that ended again with such similar farewell endearments. Oh no, that's not for me. I did it in a simpler way. I have in mind simpler for me, and not for the young lady, for in fact all this was not simple for her. I did things so that they would break up with me. I began to play the role of a scoundrel—this isn't a simple role if in your heart you're actually not a scoundrel—but you want to come out dry from the water, you don't feel like enduring any scenes, explaining your relations, maybe even earning a slap in the face, anything you feel like. All this so that the young lady will tell you to go to parts unknown and that the windy rhetoric will turn out to be shorter, that's better for you. But, in reality, it never turned out short. It always lasted a long time. Always the young lady's fault. It's superfluous to say that I never guarded myself against slaps to my kisser. Finally understanding what kind of scoundrel she was dealing with, the young lady exploded into an uninhibited fountain of accusations that uncovered for me such bizarre facets of my "self" that it was impossible to comprehend even a single one of them: and why did you, my little dove, waste so much time with such a monster?

And do you know what? It made no sense to ask the irate young lady any such question. The answer would always sound like this: "I thought I could make you better!"

In the relations between two people, can there be a nobler wish than to make someone better? At the very moment of utterance of such a sacred intention, fanfares, flutes, and trombones enter, at such a moment you feel like embracing the young lady by her knees, kissing her shoes and begging: "Keep trying, make me better!" But no, if you've seriously aimed at breaking up with her, don't relax, because all this is a fiction, no one will ever make anyone better in reality. You can mold from clay, but not from sand. You will remain the very same as when you first met, the only thing that can be expected from you is that when at some point you accommodate the young lady, you'll strive to rid yourself of habits that irritate her, but only at those times when she's there next to you. Certainly you in fact can become what the young lady thirsts for you to be, but if for you she is not a gift from heaven and you feel just a physical attraction, just her butt interests you, you can merely sneeze at all the conventions and you are the way you are in reality: inattentive, imprecise, unfaithful, ungrateful, dishonorable, unreliable, ill-bred, mendacious, insolent, unsocial, conceited, shameless ....

The main thing here is not to get depressed and to take these accusations seriously. Otherwise, a vile thought might really steal in to allow yourself to be saved, to give in to reeducation and, constantly improving yourself on the wings of love, to become exemplary, to become ideal, and sometimes, stepping out on the balcony, to listen to the rustle of the wings behind your back.

Usually, my method of breaking up with a young lady will stick out to some as a bit protracted, but the process of becoming a scoundrel can't last just a number of hours, or even days or weeks. But, nevertheless, I've been lucky with the young ladies, for some reason fate for the most part has constantly provided me with explosive frenetic women, ready at any suitable moment to scratch out my eyes, tear out a handful of my hair, scald me with boiling water, or tear my manuscripts to shreds. It is strictly speaking the manuscripts and books that for some reason evoke in them—evidently for a long time—a pent up ferocity: it was only literature that stood as an obstacle to complete possession of me. Consciousness of the fact that there is something more important and more valuable for me than their vagina, their butt, their breasts, their loving heart, than their lips with droplets of sperm, for their kitten-like caresses and even for their plum-filled fried dumplings, elicits in them aggression directed right at what is most valuable and dearest, by which a writer lives, and then at moments of hysteria they grab papers and tear them up, tossing bits of your writings in every direction, with their feet they step on half of a book, and with a wild scream pluck the other half upward—and where do they get such strength?—in ecstasy they're ready to help themselves with their teeth, and here into the air a plundered Baudelaire flies down, and after him—Rilke, and after Rilke—Svidzynsky,[1] and you, as though you are mad, try to save what's nearest and dearest to you, and, helpless, you must revert to your strength, twist her arm, knock her to the floor, rip her nightgown, and tearing her underwear with the very same ferocity that she had ripped up Rainer-Marie Rilke, you screw

---

1   Volodymyr Svidzins'kyi (1885-1941) was a Ukrainian poet and translator. He died while under arrest during the evacuation of Kharkiv.

her, while she's all tearful, sobbing, howling, moaning, agonizing, in front of the plundered Charles, Rainer-Marie, and Volodymyr.

Actually, with frenetic women who love to drink and smoke, it's considerably easier to split up. Draw them out of their equilibrium— then spit once. It's enough just to refuse to do something that you've done to that point without excess words, but beside that give such a shaky reason for your refusal that it grates the ear. For example, if you have constantly made coffee for her, but one time growl out to her request: "Make it yourself—I'm busy," then you can be sure that at that very instant you should abruptly duck, otherwise a cup will crack right on your forehead. The very same reaction awaits you after a negative answer to the question: "Will you go along with me?" Then, in the best case, a slipper flies at your head, and in the worst—a shoe.

I don't know how others react, but when I listen to groundless accusations from my beloved, then I feel offense, sadness and despair, as well as absolute helplessness, inasmuch as I am not capable of answering with the same astonishing fountain of words. The words are strewn out in such a way as if they were hurled into my face not individually, but in entire handfuls: they scorch and blind me, they jam my lips and span the air, and if in the first minute any kind of timid attempts to defend myself appear, to hide behind any of my own words, perhaps, and not so sharp and painful ones, then in the next minute—unexpectedly for me, I begin to feel in my heart a slight crust of responsibility, and in an instant I'm already unable to come to the conclusion that I'm not guilty of anything, and it begins to seem that these accusations are completely just, and I am being insulted not undeservedly, but with justification. And here I already discern in those words a note of indulgence; actually, I'm left the small apartment with the door open, a quite tiny apartment, but I can take advantage of this magnanimity and fly into it with arms crossed over my chest uttering: "Forgive me! Forgive me!" However I never did this, inasmuch as everything went according to plan. And it was only that nighttime ring of the phone that wasn't according to plan. It stunned me with its unexpectedness.

2

Everything began completely innocently, and not because I had to hear what kind of swine I was. At first, my wife set off for the U.S. on some kind of shaky invitation to have just as shaky an exhibit of her paintings. We said good-bye with intense embraces and nearly with tears in our eyes. She didn't hide the fact that she intended to remain there, to find work and tried to convince me to go after her, inasmuch as I had an invitation to Canada. I didn't take it seriously: for me to live in the U.S., there'd have to be at least a return of Soviet power in Ukraine.

My last vivid memory of her is a kiss through the air. But after that, a strange situation began: she disappeared, and for half a year I heard no news from her. Besides one—the shaky invitation turned out to have been so shaky that no one met her on arrival and she was barely able to find an artist acquaintance of hers and took up residence in his studio where she slept right on a table. A woman who had just returned from the U.S. passed along this disconcerting news to me. My wife's parents, of course, got letters from her, but they told me they didn't have any news. Right at that moment, she phoned me and announced that we needed a divorce. And here, strictly speaking, I heard something about me that I never would have guessed: I didn't have a clue that I was some kind of philanderer, that I chased after every skirt, that I slept with all my female colleagues and God knows who else, that I may even have hit on her mother, but that now at last I could fashion an idyllic existence with ... and here she named about a half-dozen of my female colleagues, whom I not only hit on, but dreamt of marrying. The cascade of absurdity poured onto my head so unexpectedly that I couldn't find a single argument to counter it, I choked on the nonsense the way a fish gasps for air. As for the fountain of her accusatory words, I managed only to gurgle out something inarticulate, and then she didn't try to hear me out, but prattled like a machine gun, tossing out of herself a hundred words per second. That's why it's not surprising that I couldn't remember a tenth of what flew into my ears later.

From what I remember anyway, a rather unattractive picture arose. For monsters such as me, there simply was no place on earth. There is nothing sacred! There was no hope to fix things up. I flirt with everything of the opposite sex on two legs. I'm a monster! A maniac! A vampire! I suck out energy, I drink blood and get enjoyment out of the torments of others.

After this, there were several phone conversations, just as agitated, in haste, she attacked, I defended myself without knowing that her attacks already made no sense whatsoever, she was just searching for justification for herself because during that time when I continued to live alone, she already had found a cozy little nest and was living with a dentist near New York. When I found out about it, I sensed a heavy winter's ice floe slide off my chest and it became easier to breathe. I grew weary of fighting and understood all that I needed now—which was, strictly speaking, to turn into what she said I was: a maniac and a vampire. But for the purity of the experiment, I needed to convince myself that she never was.

Translated by Michael M. Naydan

PEARS À LA CRÊPE

Waking up in the morning in Vynnyky on the outskirts of the city of Lviv, you don't hear either the piercing screeches of the tramcars or the rattling of cars on the cobblestones. Instead, the frolicsome chirping of birds, the buzzing of bees, and the lazy cackling of chickens will tickle your still semi-somnolent ears. Every morning. And at night, you'll fall asleep to the rhythmic croaking of frogs and the delicate chirring of crickets. I won't even speak about the dizzying scent of gillyflowers and lilac.

The sun's rays slowly penetrate through closed eyelids, and the gray cover of drowsiness crawls from your eyes to reveal this quiet sluggish world of the house. A morning like any morning. It could have been like countless other ones. But it wasn't. Because when I woke up, my sensitive ear caught someone's rhythmic breathing. Someone was lying next to me, and warm breath touched my cheek in just barely perceptible waves. Who could it be? I strained my brain that was still mellow after sleep and suddenly came to the conclusion that it could only be a woman. If it were a man, then he would have been sleeping on another bed, because I'm not queer. So—it definitely had to be a woman. But my thoughts further ran into a solid wall. I couldn't remember at all where she had come from.

I tried to examine her, but this didn't give me anything, because her head was covered. For some reason I've only been lucky with girls who cover their heads in bed. Why they do that, I've never been able to figure out—for the simple reason that this happens with them completely subconsciously. Because when you ask a young lady why she always covers up her head, the very same answer resounds: "Really?"

Imagine— even they are surprised at this. The only thing they distinctly remember is what they're sleeping in. Women here are divided into two more or less identical halves: those who sleep in their panties, and those who don't. They have one answer to the question: "I'm used to it like that." At least you can understand that habit. Therefore, don't even try to re-educate them. It's the same as trying to teaching a cat to bring your slippers. A woman, when she gets used to something, won't part with that habit till death. One half of them before going to sleep won't take them off under any circumstances, the second won't ever put them on.

The young lady who was snuffling next to me that day could have belonged to either half. To be honest, the ones who upset me the most are those who, after passionate lovemaking, slip on their panties as if they hadn't taken them off. I could never fathom what that's supposed to mean. That she's already accomplished her mission and the gates are closed for the night? That she's afraid I might rape her in the middle of the night? Or maybe, the underwear for her is something like a garland of innocence?

Was this one in her panties? I slipped my hand under the covers and felt a hot female body. My fingers touched her springy bottom and I sighed with relief. It wasn't enough that I finally remembered her. I lifted myself up on my elbows and looked around the room. Carefully folded jeans and a white tee shirt lay on an armchair. My clothes were scattered all over the floor. This was just like me. Sometimes I toss them on the table. This time, the table was cluttered with bottles of champagne, Hungarian wine, *horilka*,[2] and beer. O Lord! It's not odd that my memory was knocked out of me.

Was it just memory? Somehow, I couldn't remember a single moment of sex from last night. Did we make love at all? It was logical to assume yes, for when two people of the opposite sex lie in bed, it's not for discussing the latest decisions of our parliament. The quantity of empty bottles struck me. What was the occasion for the party? Where was everybody else? What were we doing all evening?

If the chairs and table were not in the middle of the room, but by the walls, then people must have been dancing. I glanced at my watch. Half past noon! Well... It's all clear. The party had been till early morning. At six a.m., when the buses started running, the warm company had made its way to the bus stop. I'd be interested knowing, did we make love after that? It's hard to imagine that after an all-night party. I carefully crawled out from under the covers, grabbed my shirt from the

---

2   Ukrainian vodka. (Translator's note)

floor and dragged myself to the bathroom. Neither hot nor cold water returned my memory to me. I still couldn't figure out who was lying in my bed. When I went to the kitchen, I fell into a stupor. Everything was clean and tidied up. The table was no longer littered with dishes, little boxes of seasoning and crumbs of bread, and the floor shined and glistened. And, as if this were not enough for total happiness, all the dishes used for yesterday's party shined and glistened.

That was 1992, when I turned forty and became a bachelor again. After the regular concerts with the "Don't Worry!"[3] comedy troupe, a cheery bunch often inundated my place, one that I had to see off the next day no earlier than lunchtime. But this regular flood of guests miraculously left behind a clean house. And, additionally, this time, a certain mystery person.

I boiled some coffee in a Turkish pot and, drinking it pensively, stubbornly tried to imagine the way she looked. Tall. I figured that out when I accidentally touched her stretched-out leg. She didn't snore. And slept without her undies. She hung her clothing carefully on the chair, though in ecstasy she might have flung it onto a lampshade. And she undressed herself, because if I had undressed her, then everything would have not been hanging on the chair. In my opinion, too many positive qualities here. And once again, we need to divide women into two halves. Those who get undressed themselves, and those who wait for you to undress them. The entire fact of the matter, however, is that even when you break it down, all the same you won't figure out who she is, your young lady. The fact that she doesn't undress herself, but shyly gives in to your hands doesn't entirely mean that she's doing this for the first, second, third, or eighth time. There are young ladies who just love it when you peel off all their husks and are prepared to be in ecstasy from it for the one thousand and first time as much as the first. There are those among them who do this not from ecstasy, but to rouse you

---

3   *Ne Zhurys'!* (Don't Worry) was a cabaret group founded in 1987 by Taras Chubai, Andrii Panchyshyn and Yuri Vynnychuk. The group presented satire of Soviet politics and life and unearthed Ukrainian cultural achievements that had been suppressed in the Soviet Union. It also included, among others, Victor Morozov, Stefko Orobets', and Kostiantyn Moskalets'.

up, and when you ask them how many men they've had, you can have no doubt there will be a single answer: "You're my second." Therefore it's stupid to ask about such things. You won't hear the truth anyway. And because, when she whispers to you in moments of tenderness: "Ah, how long it's been since I've done this," accept her words with gratefulness, as if you have no clue about anything else.

A young lady who undresses herself does this for two reasons: a) she doesn't give a damn about your sorry butt and doesn't care what you think about her, b) she doesn't give a rat's ass about you and doesn't want to play a dummy.

With great satisfaction I came to the conclusion that the young lady doesn't give a rat's ass about me, because if she did, she wouldn't have tidied up in the kitchen. Though this doesn't testify to her passionate feelings. Maybe just by nature she can't tolerate a mess. There are also these types. Mostly they turn out to be colleagues of my friends and, tidying up my kitchen, they're striving to make an impression not on me, but on the person they came with.

But it's one thing to tidy up the table, and another to wash the floor. Maybe she didn't love me, but to wash the floor while not giving a rat's ass about me, that's already pathological. I'll be damned, but I won't believe she loves me.

The only thing that bothered me was—when did she have time to do this? And the more I thought about this, with even more dismay I comprehended this shameful picture for myself. But she didn't go to bed until after she had tidied up everything. That was very praiseworthy. It showed her best side. But if I don't remember it, it means I was sleeping. I conked out. And she, poor girl, finished this ordeal, and with hope took off her panties and lay down next to me. Maybe she even cuddled up, maybe she whispered something tender in my little ear. And I barely comprehended it. What a scoundrel I am! I grabbed my head with my hands and intensely got lost in thought. And what was there to think about here! Just now it dawned on my completely cleared up head: I was in my underwear. Well, that was it, I'd disgraced myself forever. I had no justification. It's clear that the night had passed full of chastity and lazy snoring.

And despair shook my soul with such power that I decided to do something nice for this girl. In my understanding of nice—something tasty. Breakfast in bed. And what do young ladies like for breakfast? Innumerable thickheaded men offer their young lady garlic sausage for breakfast, an omelet, fried potatoes, or yesterday's Salad Olivier with a great big chunk of bread.

O horrors! O the wrath of God! This is an awful mistake, this is a blow to the system and the crashing of all expectations. With this kind of breakfast you can ruin everything that was built up over the evening and night. During the night you could have demonstrated the pinnacle of sexual prowess and in the morning it will all go to waste. No! No! Three hundred times no!

Write this down, ignoramus. A person's life is given one time, and you have to live it in such a way that you don't ruin your future with one little breakfast. Therefore, the main thing this is: a young lady doesn't like to chew anything in the morning. No garlic sausage, ham, stuffed pig stomach, smoked lard, or macaroni. Breakfast has to be light and airy, it needs to melt in her mouth, run along her gums and not get stuck in her teeth. And with the first mouthful of coffee, her lips should overflow like the song of a Carpathian Hutsul[4] woman over green mountain tops.

What doesn't get stuck in your teeth? Well? I ask you! For example, flat pancakes don't get stuck in your teeth, or filled rolled ones, or apples à la crêpe. You whip up two eggs with a glass of milk, sugar and flour, you dip apple slices into the mix and then fry them in a frying pan, or bake the stuffed rolled pancakes and spread them all over with jam, preserves, fruits, marmalade, chocolate, with memories about last night, sunny little bunnies, and your own secretions. And here a sacred moment arises. At the first sounds of the awakening of your lady to active life, you carry in a tray with coffee, rolled pancakes or apples à la crêpe to the room. This historical sight will never be effaced from her memory; she will carry a recollection of it throughout all the calamities of her life. And when she will be parting from this befouled world, from her darkened lips words will fly directed at her

---

4   For more on Hutsuls, see Note 4 on page 95.

husband: "You never brought me apples à la crêpe in bed." He, poor guy, will immediately give a start, will grab her by the shoulders and say: "Who! Who has done that for you? Who?!" In response, he'll just get a bitter smile—the last one of her life.

I didn't have apples. But I did have juicy pears. But pears à la crêpe—write this down! —are even more tasty than apples.

And this is how that morning began. I fried the pears in crêpes, my young lady was sleeping in my bed, and it seemed that even the rumbling of an empty water truck wouldn't wake her.

Life was beautiful. The sunny morning filled my soul with inexpressible joy. I already imagined that after breakfast we'd dive again into bed, and then we'd gather up some food and something to drink and start off toward the lake.

I sifted through all the girls I knew in memory and tried to figure out which of them could have ended up in my bed. So it would be easier to figure out who my young lady was, I took my notepad and on a separate sheet wrote out all the names of my female colleagues, then began to check them off one by one. Half of them abruptly dropped off the list because I never would have invited them to my place even skunk drunk. Several other eligible bachelorettes looked at me like a serious target of attention, and to get them to bed I'd just need to put a stamp in their passport. In the worst case—I'd just need to go to the marriage registration office tomorrow.

I pondered. Did I need to go so far in my thirst for love? Who knows? At times you feel like saying something nice to a young lady. It ends with the fact that one wonderful morning you look into the kitchen and realize you're already married. Maybe this was just such a fatal morning.

I didn't want to believe it. I didn't believe it. That's why with a light heart I crossed off the eligible bachelorettes. Several individuals remained whose appearance in my bed would have been most likely.

Here they are, in order of probability. Olyunya gets crossed off because she took off for the beach. I got into an argument with Maryana forever and we'll make up in a week when her parents run off to a resort. Vira exclusively spends her weekends with her fiancé. Lida came over last week without warning and ran into Marta, who peacefully was sunbathing in the garden, I don't even want to bring up how that ended. We'll cross both off the list. Lesya, Oksana and Ulyana were left.

On the table, a full plate of pears à la crêpe was steaming. I made fresh coffee, put it on the tray and concentrated. Who ... Who ... Who ...

Oksana, may I kick the bucket right now, doesn't wash floors, that's already for sure. She'll sit around the entire evening staring at the TV. Or she'll lie around. Ulyana doesn't undress herself. Not for anything will she do that in her life. Besides that, she always puts on her panties. That's her style. Well then, I'll cross them off.

Lesya's left. My God! What a scoundrel I've been in the way I treat her! How many times I've deceived her, led her on, made promises. One time I even prattled on about love. And she believed me. She's generally trusting and a very kind person. I'm just not worthy of her. I suddenly felt like falling on my knees before her, kissing her feet and begging forgiveness. For just everything. Even for this too.

She! Just she could be an ideal wife. She talks so little. That's it, enough of these adventures for me, this disorder, unwashed dishes, scandalous stories, and explanations of my relations with their husbands, who, thanks to me, grow buck horns. That's it. I'll look in right away and say. What will I say? Damn... Let's get married, what do you say? No, not that way. First I should repent. I'll tell her everything. No, that'll take too long. I'll tell her in general terms. Without naming names. And I'll burn my notepad completely. Oh! What an idea! I'll burn my notepad in front of her. It won't cost me much because I have one more. And then I'll tell her, say, let's ...That is, we'll get married.

In the meantime, the first sounds of her awakening echoed from the room. I immediately felt a fervent desire to end up next to her and embrace her hot, deeply stirred body.

And here I grab the tray and with a smile from ear to ear fly into the room.

"Lesya-baby!" I call out, all hot and bothered from the unexpected flash of thirst and love. "Look what I've brought you!"

And if right at that moment Vesuvius erupted under my windows, it would have stunned me considerably less than when from under my snow-white covers shouted out to me not the angelic little head of Lesya-doll in golden curls, but the great big shaggy and bearded snout of Stefko Orobets.[5]

My knees were wobbly, and I sensed I was losing my potency for the entire next week.

"Can you shut the hell up?!" Steftsio thundered, scratching his broad chest with all five of his fingers.

"Ste…Steftsio!" I muttered. "Where did you come from?"

"From my show, 'For you, Morons'."

"But … why are you in my bed?"

"Because you, shithead, got sloshed and didn't want to put out sheets for me on the couch."

"But … why are you naked?"

"Because that's the way I sleep, you imbecile! And there's no reason to feel up my butt, you queer!"

"But who tidied everything up?"

"Leska."

"But where's she now?"

"She left with Orko."

"Who the hell is that? Why with Orko?"

"Because you, idiot, told her you're getting married. And invited her to your engagement party."

"Me?! I'm getting married?! To who?"

"Ask the champagne. And stop getting under my skin! What do you have there? Some kind of pancakes? What's with you—you couldn't fry me some garlic sausage with eggs? And where's last night's Salad Olivier?"

Translated by Michael M. Naydan

---

5   A popular cabaret singer and comedic television personality in L'viv. See Note 3 on page 279.

OLEKSANDR BOICHENKO

OLEKSANDR BOICHENKO is a literary critic, essayist, columnist, and translator who lives and works in Chernivtsi, Ukraine. From 1995 to 2008, he taught world literature and literary theory at Chernivtsi University. Between 2002 and 2010, together with writer Yuri Andrukhovych, Boichenko co-edited the Internet journal *Potiah76*. He has received the Gaude Polonia scholarship from Poland's Ministry of Culture three times. In 2003, his book *Shchos na kshtalt shatokua* (A Sort of Chautauqua, 2003) was awarded top prize in the creative essay category by the Knyha Roku (Book of the Year) competition. Boichenko is also author of the books *Shatokua plius* (Chautauqua Plus, 2005), *Aby knyzhka* (To Have a Book, 2011), *Moï sered chuzhykh* (Mine Among Strangers, 2012), *Bilshe/Menshe* (More or Less, 2015), and *50 vidsotkiv ratsiï* (50 Percent Correct, 2016).

His published translations from Polish into Ukrainian include a collection of stories by Tadeusz Borowski entitled *At Our Place, in Auschwitz*, Daniel Odija's novel *The Sawmill*, several plays by Michał Walczak, Małgorzata Sikorska-Miszczuk, Paweł Demirski and Michał Zadara, and short prose works by Marek Hłasko, Józef Hen, Andrzej Stasiuk, and Olga Tokarczuk, among others. His translations from Russian into Ukrainian include Viktor Yerofeyev's novel *The Good Stalin* and Igor Pomerantsev's story *The Basque Dog*.

Oleksandr Boichenko's series events, entitled *A Sort of Chautauqua*, took place in October 2014.

OUT OF GREAT LOVE

Among certain, one may say, narrow circles of my limited countrymen, the notion exists that I don't really love Chernivtsi that much. That's a lie. I do love it. But not all the time. For example, I recall that about twenty years ago I had to spend a week in Donetsk. Well, that whole week, I really, really loved Chernivtsi. And I loved it when I was in Magadan, and in Yakutsk and in the village of Bykovo in the Moscow region … But when I return to Chernivtsi, of course, after a day or two, I love it less. That is, a day or two after returning from the village of Bykovo. When returning from Prague or Krakow, however, then it's a day or two before that.

Sometimes I get uncomfortable because of my capriciousness. I mean—didn't Nobel Prize winner Czesław Miłosz[1] compare his pre-war Vilnius with my Chernivtsi? Yes, he did. And didn't Zbigniew Herbert[2] call it "Europe's last Alexandria?" He certainly did. And what did Adam Michnik[3] say just a few years ago? "Well if this isn't Europe," Adam Michnik said, "then where is Europe?" Moreover, a century before Michnik, the Austrian journalist Georg Heinzen[4] considered Chernivtsi to be not just Europe, but "the unspoken capital of Europe, where the most beautiful coloratura sopranos sang, where cabbies discussed Karl Kraus,[5] where the sidewalks were swept with bouquets of roses, and where there were more bookstores than cafes." Well who cares about cabbies and coloratura sopranos! We even had, according

---

1 Czesław Miłosz (1911-2004) was a Polish poet, novelist, translator and diplomat. He lived in Vilnius as a student before World War Two. He received the Nobel Prize for Literature in 1980.

2 Zbigniew Herbert (1924-1998) was a Polish poet and dramatist who was born and lived in L'viv (Lwów) but was forced to leave the city because of its Soviet occupation in 1944.

3 Adam Michnik (b. 1946) is a Polish historian, former dissident, essayist, public intellectual and editor-in-chief of Poland's largest newspaper, *Gazeta Wyborcza*.

4 Georg Heinzen was a journalist who wrote about Chernivtsi.

5 Karl Kraus (1874-1946) was an Austrian writer and journalist known for his satiricial writing.

to Rosa Ausländer,[6] "a mirror carp/ seasoned with pepper/ silent in five languages."

And what conclusion can be drawn from all this? An obvious one: in order to talk about Chernivtsi with such passion, one has to have never been there—like Miłosz and Herbert, or has to have visited merely as a tourist—like Michnik and Heinzen, or has to have emigrated and delved into nostalgic memories—like Rose Ausländer and tens of artists and scholars who truly did make Chernivtsi famous in this world, but who first had to escape from this wonderful city.

Meanwhile, if one is to believe not poetic sketches but social surveys, almost 80% of Chernivtsi's inhabitants today are, in one way or another, proud of the city in which they live. On the one hand, I am, as much as this is possible, honestly happy for them. But on the other hand, I find it a bit difficult to understand the reasons for such pride. Yes, I know that Paul Celan[7] was born here, and that Olha Kobylianska[8] died here, that Ivan Franko studied here, that Yuri Fedkovych[9] worked here, that Mihai Eminescu[10] wrote his first poems here, that Traian Popovici,[11] when he was mayor, saved Jews from the Holocaust here. I would just like to understand how we, today's residents of Chernivtsi, are connected to all of this?

The reconstructed façade of Paul Celan's building? Almost. Because, as it turns out, Celan lived not in that building but in the one next door.

---

6 Rose Ausländer (1901-1988) was a Jewish poet who wrote in both German and English. She was born in Chernivtsi (Cernăuți, Czernowitz) and lived there for much of her life before finally leaving the city in 1944.

7 Paul Celan (1920-1970) was a Jewish poet who wrote in German. He was born Paul Antschel in Chernivtsi (Cernăuți, Czernowitz) and lived there until 1945.

8 Ol'ha Kobylians'ka (1863-1942) was a Ukrainian writer and feminist. Originally writing in German, she later switched to Ukrainian and became one the leading Ukrainian early Modernist writers. She lived in Chernivtsi for most of her life.

9 Yuri Fed'kovych (1834-1888) was a Ukrainian Romantic writer who lived in Chernivtsi from 1876 until his death.

10 Mihai Eminescu (1850-1889) was a leading Romanian Romantic poet who lived in Chernivtsi (Cernăuți) as a student.

11 Traian Popovici (1892-1946) was as Romanian lawyer and the mayor of Chernivtsi (Cernăuți) during World War Two. He is known for saving 20,000 Jews from being deported from the Bukovyna (Bukovina) region.

But, because they mistakenly registered the wrong building, that's the one shown to tourists. It's not difficult to delude tourists—I've done it myself many times. I show them the forged carriage on Kobylianska Street and the clock made of flowers on the reconstructed Turkish Well Square and lead them to "The best café at the intersection of Universytetska and Skovoroda Streets" (this is a veiled advertisement, because the café is owned by my friend and publisher). "Europe," the satisfied tourists say. "Aha," you reply to the tourists and bite your tongue to resist telling them, in detail, how the European inhabitants of Chernivtsi regularly like to shit in that carriage, how they break that clock's hands and how they vandalize the exhaust in that café's attic.

Or, perhaps, is our contribution to European culture today the statue of Fedkovych, which teenagers well-versed in cartoons correctly called, on the day that it was unveiled, a Transformer? But there is a positive: a local politician built a rather quirky restaurant next to it that bears the so very typical Chernivtsi name "The Sorbonne." I'll be blunt: in all of the world's architecture, I've never seen anything more disgusting than this thing, this dream of some stoned pastry chef materialized in the historical district of our "Little Vienna." And so, as a result, standing next to this "Sorbonne," even the Transformer-Fedkovych has somehow begun to look a bit nicer.

And, concerning politicians. Until recently, it seemed that Chernivtsi was a Western Ukrainian city and that most of the local politicians had political beliefs consistent with this. Not anymore. Because I now fully realize that most of the local politicians have no beliefs, just private interests. And because in the era of the Lout from Yenakievo, these interests can only be defended with political prostitution, the oppositional majority in the city council has transformed itself into a pro-government majority. As a result, the mayor, who had just been elected by the direct vote of the citizens, has been ousted. The citizens, as is most often the case today all over Ukraine, swallowed this and are waiting to see what will happen next. Can this possibly be what famous Bukovynian tolerance looks like? I don't think so. Even if the problem is limited to political raiding—I still don't think so. It really is much deeper than that.

Let us recall: in Austro-Hungarian times, a so-called "idea of Bukovynism" was given birth in Chernivtsi—a particular Bukovynian identity that gently swaddled an entire bouquet of various national and religious identities. There probably were some minor misunderstandings in practice, but, theoretically at least, it stated that what was most import- ant was to feel that you are a Bukovynian and that being also a Ukrainian, a Romanian or a Jew was secondary. In this manner, a tolerance toward an Other was cultivated, about which, for example, Krzysztof Czyżewski[12] writes in his essay "Chernivtsi—a Forgotten Metropolis at the Edge of the Hapsburg Monarchy": "An Other is a part of us and a part of a com- munity to which we feel a sense of belonging. An Other cannot be some- one who is absent, someone about whom we are indifferent. If we wish to consider, for example, a dervish from Bukhara to be an Other, then we can only do this if we comprehend his belonging to that same community that we deem to be living and crucial for our fate."

When looking at the present, however, I'm afraid that Czyżewski is incorrect. Ukrainians, Romanians, Moldovans, Jews (those who have remained), Russians (those who replaced the pre-war Jews and Germans) really do co-exist in today's Chernivtsi without any visible conflicts. But also without any particular contact among cultures. For the "average" Ukrainian inhabitant of Chernivtsi, the Chernivtsi Romanian or Jewish culture is probably no dearer to them than the culture of the Bukhara dervishes. Simultaneously, these cultures (including Ukrainian) have not produced anything praiseworthy for quite some time and, thus, do not threaten one another. In this manner, it is not life's force and an interest in the Other, but weakness and apathy that lie at the foundation of the tolerance of today's Chernivtsi.

Of course, something positive can be found in such a situation. For example, to recognize that even apathetic tolerance is a major achieve- ment compared to passionate "Yugoslavian" hatred. But it's a real shame to observe how apathetic Bukovynian society gradually loses its once-attractive face. Too weak to apply its old model to all of Ukraine, today Chernivtsi itself, politically (and culturally as well) is drifting in the direction of the village of Bykovo.

Translated by Mark Andryczyk

---

12 Krzysztof Czyżewski (b. 1958) is a Polish author and director of the Center "Borderland of Arts, Cultures and Nations" in Sejny, Poland.

THE LUNCH OF A MAN OF LETTERS

Nobel Prize laureate William Faulkner once admitted that he had become a writer because of his jealousy of Sherwood Anderson. According to legend, Faulkner, back in that time—that is, 90 years ago—protested against Prohibition by engaging in the physically exhausting and legally dangerous practice of distributing contraband Cuban alcohol. On the other hand, Anderson would eat in a restaurant daily and did not look overly tired. Responding to the question of what field of work allowed him to live such a worry-free life, Anderson replied: literature. "Well there's a good job," Faulkner thought, "maybe I should take a stab at it."

I don't want to insult anyone, but that young Ukrainian poet—whose keyboard tapping floats over to me through the wall during quiet, scholarship-funded nights—and I are somewhat well known. In Poland, at least. Well if not in all of Poland then in Warsaw, at least. Well if not in all of Warsaw then, at least, in the corner store at the intersection of Jana Pawła and Solidarność Streets. Having realized—no matter what anyone else might say—this indisputable fact, we decided that it was no longer appropriate for us to prepare our meals ourselves. Not with our status. Especially considering that I don't know how to cook and that the poet, exhausted from his nighttime creativity, usually woke up right around lunchtime.

It didn't take us long to find a suitable establishment. Because at the end of Krakowskie Przedmieście Street in Warsaw, there's a restaurant named "Literatka" that features a summer terrace with a view of the royal castle and the square in front of it. The Polish PEN Club and the Union of Writers are located upstairs in this building. Perhaps I'll drop in someday. And because the restaurant is named "Literatka" and because both the Union and PEN Club are above it, they serve an "obiad literacki."[13] That meal costs about as much as a cup of coffee in downtown Kyiv. But that's only if you're a writer. More specifically—only if your waiter believes that to be true. And he will indeed believe you if you confidently look him in right the eye and say,

---

13 Meaning "literary lunch" in Polish.

almost without an accent, "obiad literacki." And for a person who has spent much time practicing this and who is very hungry, it's not a very difficult thing to do.

Some of the waiters there, by the way, are not at all indifferent to the fundamental issues of literature. Not long ago, one of them dramatically tossed a spare rib onto the table and directly asked: "Gentlemen, would you agree with me that the duty of a writer, his—using my words—eternal mission, is to paint the conflicts of the human heart while simultaneously strengthening this heart, giving it hope and raising it above everyday life?" "Can't argue with that," we replied, "you took the words right out of our mouths." "So then where, may I ask you, can such writers and such literary works be found today?" "We're working on it," we replied, "but first we need to take care of lunch."

Besides these literary discussions with waiters and the literary pricing, we also really like this place because it gives us the opportunity to passively, and with impunity, mess with the large number of tourist groups that pass by us during their excursions to and from the castle. The groups lift their heads, read the sign "Literatka," look at those pensive people sitting at the table and think: "And there they're sitting— the engineers of human souls, masters of the word and the conscience of the nation." And it's us sitting there.

Occasionally, some of the passers-by approach us. For example, yesterday a man came up who had so much of the world's sadness in his eyes that I realized I had to give him something. The man politely asked whether he could have a moment of our time, and then pulled out two tomatoes and said: "Tomatoes ... what do you think, can something like this save somebody's life? No, it can't. But a writer can always come up with a good word and a few coins."

Yes, a good word and a few coins—that's probably all that plain folks need from writers today. And come to think of it, that's what writers need from plain folks.

Translated by Mark Andryczyk

IN A STATE OF SIEGE

Sometimes strange moments occur that have been treated many times in literature, during which a person takes part in some kind of important or even groundbreaking event while simultaneously looking at themselves from the side or from somewhere above. Joyce's autobiographical protagonist Stephen Dedalus, for example, experiences such an out-of-body experience when he's on a first date. Something similar happened to me on the Maidan on the night of December 11. And, actually, I was also on a first date then—with a member of the Berkut riot police. But there was no close physical contact then.

And so I stood there, gazing at myself with a stranger's eyes, looking over the borrowed tanker's helmet on my own head with amazement and thinking about Albert Camus. Honest to God. I stood there and thought about Albert Camus, fully comprehending how absurd, in an existentialist meaning of that word, the situation was—standing on the Maidan and thinking about Albert Camus. Not about Cossack glory, not about our numbskull "enemies" or about "dew on the sun,"[14] and not even about Faulkner and Salinger, whom I think about most often when the subject of Ukraine comes up. No, I stood there and thought about Albert Camus, about his novel *The Plague*, and about the novel's protagonist, Dr. Rieux.

Because it's quite clear what it is we think about these days. And we ask one another: "Listen, be honest, do you really believe in our victory?" To be more precise—personally, I don't ask. And I try not to answer. Not because I don't believe in this particular victory, but because, after a certain age, "a belief in victory" begins to sound too cruel. A belief in victory? Wonderful. If you're an athlete or a military academy cadet, then you have to believe in victory. Because how else could you endure your whole life spread out before you, one that is destined to pass by in wasted anticipation of that vital moment that will never come anyway? But if you've lived on this earth for a while and

---

14 This is in reference to the Ukrainian national anthem line "Our enemies will perish, like dew on the sun."

have observed it for a bit, then in place of your belief comes a realization: people are not destined to be victorious. Well, forget about being victorious—people are not destined to compete. They're destined to walk out onto the battlefield of life and to wander over it, wander in order to become aware of their helplessness, their insanity, their despair. Well, at least that's how one of Faulkner's protagonists saw it.

And one—the most famous—of Salinger's protagonists surmised, while still a young man, that it's not worth playing someone else's game according to their rules. Especially if it seems that there aren't any "hot-shots" (that's the term he used) on your side. However, if you look at it simply and sincerely, Salinger's most famous protagonist, to put it bluntly, did not experience misfortune. Because in his America there are at least some rules and the outcome of the game depends on the quantity and quality of the hot-shot players. Conversely, in our parts, the results are determined by degraded scumbags, all those yanyko-vychs and azarovs, all those kliuievs and zakharchenkos, the dobkins and the kolesnichenkos;[15] the mere fact of co-existing with them on one common territory and in one common period of time becomes unbearable. What kind of game and what kinds of rules can we even talk about here? And what kind of belief in victory can there be? A belief in God (if, for some reason, you still have it)—it's not a sin to lose that too when you look at all those degenerates and at their loyal voters.

To make a long story short, lately any time the idea of our chances for a better future pops up, I immediately recall *The Sound and the Fury* and *Catcher in the Rye*. But that night on the Maidan, in search of some kind of inner support, I thought of Dr. Rieux from Camus' *The Plague*. Although one would be hard pressed, of course, to consider either him or Camus himself to be an optimist. But that's just who I needed then, because in the company of optimists I feel even more hopeless than I do in the company of pessimists.

So then, Dr. Rieux. Unlike his naïve-optimistic or just simply far-removed-from-medicine fellow citizens, he recognizes the plague at a

---

15 Mykola Azarov, Andrii Kliuiev, Vitalii Zakharchenko, Mykhailo Dobkin, and
    Vadym Kolesnichenko were all leaders in Viktor Yanukovych's regime, which was
    ousted from power in Ukraine by the 2014 EuroMaidan Revolution.

stage long before it becomes a full epidemic. And he fights it with all his might. He realizes that the disease is stronger than he and that it is capable of wiping out almost half of the population. He knows that the serum is not working yet and that the plague will not subside until it attains the peak of its power, at which time, maybe, it will begin to choke on its own excessiveness. Yes, Rieux does not believe in victory. Or, more precisely, he doesn't at all clutter his head with such nonsense. But he continues to fight. If only because he would lose his sense of existence if he didn't. And also because, in one's world view, there are axioms that are self-evident. Including: regardless who ends up winning in the end, a person, if he or she wants to remain a human being, cannot, in any circumstances, take the side of the plague.

These are approximately the thoughts with which I cheered myself up, and then I suddenly noticed that the sky above Instytutska Street had become red. There were more and more of us, more and more often I saw the faces of acquaintances and friends. And later, dawn arrived on the Maidan. The bacilli, following orders, retreated to their epidemic hearths. Victory, as is always the case, was very far away. But that night, we definitely did not lose.

Translated by Mark Andryczyk

SOPHIA ANDRUKHOVYCH

SOPHIA ANDRUKHOVYCH was born in 1982 in Ivano-Frankivsk, formerly known as Stanislav. One of the cultural centers of western Ukraine, the city is known for what has been termed the "Stanislav phenomenon" because of the curious fact that this rather small town is home to an unusually large concentration of postmodern writers. Andrukhovych has to date authored five books of prose: *Lito Mileny* (Milena's Summer,

2002), *Stari liudy* (*Old People*, 2003), *Zhinky ïkhnikh cholovikiv* (Wives of Their Husbands, 2005), *Somha* (Salmon, 2007) and *Feliks Avstriia* (Felix Austria, 2014). The latter was awarded the BBC Ukrainian Book of the Year prize in 2015. Her works have been translated into English, Polish, German, Czech, and Serbian. Also a translator, Andrukhovych has translated into Ukrainian Manuela Gretkowska's novel *The European Woman*, J.K. Rowling's *Harry Potter and the Goblet of Fire* (co-translated with Viktor Morozov), *A Visit from the Goon Squad* by Jennifer Egan, *Flat Earth News* by Nick Davies, *Poisoned Peace* by Gregor Dallas, *Never Let Me Go* by Kazuo Ishiguro, and *Talking to Terrorists* by Peter Taylor (co-translated with Halya Karpa). She served as coeditor of the literary journal *Chetver* (Thursday) from 2003-2005, and is currently a columnist for the online journal Zbruc.eu.

Sophia Andrukhovych's events in the Contemporary Ukrainian Literature Series, entitled *So Who Is Felix?*, took place in December 2015.

AN OUT-OF-TUNE PIANO, AN ACCORDION

When air becomes denser to the touch, when celandine's wet yellowness appears above pockmarked musty needles on the forest floor, when trash between the naked, sucked-bare pine tree trunks forms a white shimmer like giant flowers of a cosmic-sized apricot tree, then you can rest assured—the wandering ghost camp is already here, close by, in our forests.

It's your choice whether to believe in it, you can make your cute skeptical grimace: puffed lower lip like a moist cherry, an obstinate horizontal fold between the eyebrows, wrinkles on your little nose with its semi-transparent wing-like nostrils; now you'll shake the morning dew off of them, spread them out sleepily—and take off into the air, into the light-blue broth of the sky, swimming next to Boeings and globs of sour cream.

The night exhales the first mosquito swarms, opens its jaws full of warm muck. A coarse crone with a jelly-like body, nearly blind and hopelessly slow-witted—just think what its drunken grin and cloudless joy are worth.

Flowers fall off pear trees with a dry rustle; self-satisfied caterpillars lazily munch on arugula leaves, and irises—these crystal ritual daggers—fold like origami, Japanese boats and lanterns, and shine from the inside with a meager cold light.

Then you won't be mistaken: the wandering ghost camp has arrived. An indistinct melody spreads above the trees, multiplied by echo—like a tune from a victrola or an old cassette player that constantly chews up tape. Girlish laughter resounds together with teenage shouts and giggles, with piercing playful cries. An insincere feminine voice declaims something solemnly into a microphone; you can distinguish lines of poetry, rehashed jokes, and mechanical reading off a page, but you can't make out the words. Every evening up until late at night, when the cooperative dacha settlements die down, hold their breath, and their dwellers sidle up to one another in pitch-black darkness, their expansive bodies sun baked to a meaty shade of pink, the sounds of eerie amateur performance seep through the double panes.

From the forest thickets a menacing stench and an otherworldly smoke come swirling, flashing with fuzzy shimmering lights that circle around the tree branches.

You can never tell precisely where they are now—at Krasna Poliana, near Poroskoten, or in the Babka Valley[1]—their manifestations are omnipresent yet so uncertain, their music resounds, it seems, from tree trunk hollows and badger burrows, they spy on us from behind currant bushes, they rustle in the grass around the cesspit, their elongated greenish faces reflect in the glass walls of hothouses like in stagnant water.

Everything quiets down only at dawn, when the contours of trees slowly become clearer, birds shake their wings and clear their throats, and the air gets saturated with nanodroplets of moisture, invisible beads of a necklace—they refresh and make things easier. The shroud of stupor and fear falls off, the gaze becomes clearer.

Viola sits on a cold wet terrace, her head thrown back, her mouth wide open. Her red eyes stare unblinkingly at one spot. She is exhausted, drained, finished. Her large soft body has spread in the armchair like melting butter. Her wet dress sticks to her, its contact with skin unpleasant. Renat comes closer, dragging his left leg, and covers her with a yak-down blanket brought from the Himalayas.

Renat is eighty. His left leg does not obey him; he has a glass left eye. It shines mutely, its pupil directed at you no matter where you go, wherever you retreat—the way icons, especially old ones, worn, damaged by woodworm and dry rot, look at mortal sinners. Renat's right eye, squinted and sly, darts about and peeks under the lining: what's hiding there? Renat's teeth are crooked and dark (he refuses to get dentures as a matter of principle, saying that nowadays bodies already do not decompose); his wide grin is open and scary at the same time; his face is a puzzle made of hundreds of wrinkles; his hoarse ingratiating voice that of an old beast, once strong, and now simply warming itself in a sunny spot.

---

1   Krasna Poliana, Poroskoten and Babka Valley are all places in Ukraine located west of Kyiv.

Renat always knew how to enjoy life. The start package of his life included starched white shirts with wide cuffs and gold cufflinks, fragrant cigars, recliners, fancy building materials acquired through connections, the smiles of flight attendants, banquets in hotel restaurants, and also apartments, dachas, antiques, laundered linens, offices with lacquered furniture, cars with the latest sound systems, yachts, Cuban women, snorkeling, gravlax, getting to see the doctor without waiting in line, special deals, precious jewels, massages, yachts again, they really eat this stinky cheese, it costs how much? I'll be damned! …

Even now, weathered and worn by life, lacking one eye, crooked, wrinkled, and dented, Renat hasn't lost his luster. He's like an old Steinway with a cracked frame. A 1954 Rolls Royce Phantom with a broken headlight and clumsy body and doors that don't close tightly—still, its interior preserves the scent of Queen Elizabeth: lavender, clary sage, vetiver, lemon mint, and patchouli; the luxurious leather-clad seats creak heavily like balding gentlemen coughing at the opera after an intermission.

His first wife was the same age as he. They lived quietly together for thirty years, producing a couple of kids along the way, up until Renat met Viola. She was forty then, and she still remained striking and attractive: curvaceous, blond, and languid; ripe, juicy, and soft like a plum (you bite through the deep purple, almost black, skin and the purplish inside reveals itself moistly). Renat, understanding everything well (I am sixty, she's forty, I have two kids and six grandkids, real estate and savings; she has alcoholism, infertility, a room at a boarding house, and a messy personal life)—in fact, precisely because he understood everything so well—opened his embrace to her with luminous calm. He so loved watching her expose her face to the wind when riding in his yacht, try to eat correctly an oyster on a half shell, pretend to be a society lady, chasing champagne with strawberries. Her buttery voice and mannered way of talking moved him the way a child's babble can move you. She laughed loudly like a boor, opening widely her mouth covered in bright lipstick and throwing her head backwards—and he, choosing a strategic seat beside her, magnanimously squinted his one eye, smiled quietly to himself and mumbled something, paying no attention to the confusion and disapproval around them.

He, the kindly sixty-year-old daddy, showed her the world. At the dacha that Renat succeeded in wrestling from his first wife, they made an alpine garden to which they kept on adding stones brought from various corners of the world. It was surrounded by plaster gnomes—once so bright and cheerful, with the bright red cheeks and noses of drunks (which is the reason they had conquered Viola's heart), but decades of rain, snow, and piercing wind had bleached them and worn them out; paint peeled off them, and the noses of a few of them were missing.

In the spring, Viola, dressed in tight pink britches and a revealing blouse, crawled on all fours across their sizable garden with a jar of paint and a brush, refreshing the collection of plaster beasts and fairytale characters. Their well-tended lawn spread like a silk rug. The decorative bushes stood all covered with flowers.

As soon as she married Renat, Viola tried to become a good housekeeper. She studied reference books for home gardeners, bought seedlings, and planted several varieties of tomatoes: Aurora, Hussar, Turandot, and Calif. She tended them thoroughly, selflessly: that year Viola felt especially sharply her hopeless unrealized maternal instinct. The tomatoes reciprocated: their elastic stems bent under the weight of plump red fruit.

And then she cried, loudly, uncontrollably, choked on tears, howled and yelled over sixty buckets full of sweet vegetables.

"What shall I do with them, Renat dear?" she screamed in an unrecognizable voice. "To whom can I give them? We won't be able to eat so much. I won't go to the farmers' market! I won't give them to strangers! To no one! They'll rot!"

The next day, shortly past noon, Viola was barely able to open her swollen, hurting eyelids. She had a piercing headache, her throat was burning, her neck hurt from the bottle of Greek brandy.

When she was finally able to focus her gaze, she saw Renat in front of her. He was holding in his arms a kitten, black, with a triangular white patch on the chest. This was Methodius.

Oh Renat, how much did this sly old fox of a man love them, his kids. His short fingers dug into the edge of the table, so that the tips hurt—this is how much he craved to stay just a little bit longer here, next to them.

Squinting his eye, he caressed with his gaze this corpulent woman in a bright skimpy low-necked dress, her shapeless forearms covered in freckles, her puffy hands ending in sharp claws painted with sparkly enamel, her swollen face covered by the purplish-black mesh of blood vessels, her misshapen nose, tiny bleached eyes that twenty years ago were still so blue, so full of surprise—and now hidden behind butterfly-shaped glasses. Methodius, as always, spread himself over her knees, his pink neutered belly up in the air, and purred like a freshly started engine. This was like the purr of the granulators, agglomerators, and shredders made by Berlingtong, the Japanese company whose sales rep Renat was (just one capsulator sale—and a trip to Sri Lanka is guaranteed!).

"He is so smart, so smart, you have no idea, gentlemen!" Viola clapped her hands like a giant newborn. "He goes number one in the bidet, and opens doors with his little hands, like this, grabbing the latch, just imagine!" Viola tried to show with gestures how Methodius opened doors. "Our little son, I cried so much when he came back home all injured."

Methodius, the impertinent tomcat, went everywhere his heart desired. Neither someone else's territory, nor unhappy owners, nor guard dogs could stop him. He entered other people's kitchens and sipped broth right from the stove; he munched on parsley and scallions on vegetable beds, leaving stinky piles instead.

That morning Renat found him by the fence. Methodius was lying on his belly spread-eagled, his hind paws unnaturally twisted. His left eye was closed and a dark streak came down from it. The cat was maimed, badly wounded. Renat let out a sob, got on his knees in front of the cat—the way he did when pulling the heads off dandelions—and carefully pressed his forehead against the tiny skull.

"You are a strong boy, you won't get away from us," whispered Renat.

Methodius thought the same. He recovered, regained his health—yet he did not get a glass eye of his own.

"Only a human could have done this," said Viola, gesticulating wildly. "Neither an animal nor a car could have damaged him so much. I don't know where such cruelty comes from, gentlemen. But this must be a local, one of ours ..."

Viola waited for the oppressive silence to thicken, scratching Methodius behind the ear. And then she continued coquettishly,

"The boy has been with us for eight years now. This is the second man in my life. He won't let anyone offend me, my knight in shining armor." With her bright-clawed hand she lifted the cat's head, puckered her lips, and kissed the cat on the nose with a loud smack. Her voice is sweet, candied, with flies swimming in it. "Just like Renatie, isn't it right, my kitten? Do you remember, honey, how I almost got kidnapped in Istanbul? Just in the middle of the day, at the market, in a crowd of people. Renatie was walking slightly ahead of me, I was a step behind him, having stopped to admire a lovely, unbelievable coral necklace— and suddenly some man, short, below average height, grabbed me by the arm and pulled. He seemed so small but held me so tightly I couldn't pull myself free. He pushed me down some stairs, to some basement, opened the door—and then Renatie turned around, saw me and was next to me, my friends, was right next to me—and that man disappeared into thin air … Right, Renatie? I will never ever get away from you."

Renatie was losing strength. With each passing day he felt that he was melting more and more into thin air, becoming semitransparent, like smoke from burnt grass. Sitting in a cool room, he listened to Viola outdoors continuing to imitate society life, greeting people cheerfully, her voice all sugar and honey, as always,

"I am just so happy to see you! Have you been well? Perhaps you could drop by our place for a glass of wine?"

Fortunately, no one dropped by. Viola bawled next to him, sobbing like a little girl, and he first tried to calm her down, stroking her head and promising never to die, and then, finally, barked at her and chased her away, for she did not calm down and only continued to wail in a thin voice of a little bird in a large, worn-out body.

Feeling offended, neglected, Viola for half the night darted back and forth through dark rooms, threw pillows and dishes, smoked on the sofa, drank from the bottle. And then, having grabbed in her palm an uneven quadrangle of broken mirror, she thickly put on lipstick, wiped the running mascara off her cheeks and quickly, in a determined fashion, left the house, shuffled over the gravel path, and disappeared into the forest, among the creaking melancholy pine trees that gently swayed like pendulums.

Soon the dispersed little blue lights started gathering around her. Viola passed by a gazebo filled with immobile hushed shadows. The path, paved with stones, led somewhere through the prickly thickets of sweetbrier. From someplace nearby came the musty, smothering scent of blossoming bird cherry; Viola's head was spinning.

Nobody sat on the benches under the unlit streetlamps; plaster children with lidless, never-closing eyes rose on the pedestals. The clearing in front of the building was likewise empty—but from somewhere, God knows where, resounded the familiar indistinct melody: too-too-too-tah-too-too, an out-of-tune piano and an accordion.

Viola stopped in front of a broken fountain, its basin full of dry leaves, and picked at a piece of whitewash with her nail. The wide-open entry doors beckoned with their gaping orifice.

Empty hallways covered with smashed bricks breathed stuffy moisture. In the rooms, through the cracks in the floor and the walls, plants broke through, little twisted pines, ferns, lichens in puddles of stinky brownish water. Iron beds with nets, bent, sagging like a tired udder. Decomposed sheets, saturated with the stink of decay.

The melody sometimes quieted down, then again crackled at full volume, its tempo quickening. Somewhere a window frame creaked nervously—although at times it seemed to Viola this was a ball hitting the floor further up. In one of the rooms, it seemed that somebody wheezed or coughed in the corner. Viola started gazing into that direction till her eyes hurt, but the darkness only grew thicker and stuck back together, safely hiding everything behind itself.

Viola decided to follow the tune. She wandered for a long time, passed though the same gap in the wall several times, until she finally found herself in a large hall with rotted parquet floor, holes gaping in it here and there.

The accordion stood on a sports bench by the wall bars. Viola looked at the immobile instrument and continued to hear a melody. At the piano, with her back to the guest, sat a little stooping woman with curly hair. Her dark, shapeless clothes blended with the surrounding darkness, and only two pale arms, like empty sleeves of a white blouse, continued darting back and forth above the keyboard.

Viola closed her eyes and made the first step. Her body was light, weightless; she no longer felt her weight, forgot her clumsiness and exhaustion. It was as if there was no floor beneath her feet, it seemed to Viola she was swimming through the air, thick and tender, which carefully enveloped her, caressing her skin. The woman began spinning on an axis, a pleasant hum appeared in her head—no effort, but she spins like a top, and this makes her feel so cheerful, so joyful and light, that Viola couldn't hold herself and burst into clear, loud laughter, delighting in its echoing all around.

Nearby, someone readily joined in her cheer. However, the laughter of those others was muffled, like a rustling. As if from all directions at once, plastic bags crept towards the woman in a bright dress who, forgetting herself, spun under the ceiling, her legs not touching the floor.

Sensing a dull pain near her neck, Viola opened her eyes. This boy, tall, abnormally thin, with an elongated face, with heavy lids weighing over his eyes, looked somehow familiar to her. He embraced her and led her into a dance, peering intently into her face. His bloodless lips were curled in a whining grimace. The boy held Viola tightly with his strong bony hands, so tightly that it was impossible to break out, there was no strength left even to breathe—much more tightly than the short Turk who once grabbed her elbow—and the spinning grew so fast that a vortex appeared around Viola, an icy whirlwind it was impossible to resist.

And when Viola's pulse started beating so fast that in a moment it surely would fail—right at that moment resounded a mad, piercing, wild scream, and somebody small and fierce jumped at Viola's partner and, twitching wildly, clawed and bit at the alien void of the gaping hole, up until the melody cut off, yelping with a torn string, and the accordion several times twitched convulsively, drooping halfway.

Renat woke in the middle of the night in an empty bed and, groaning heavily, got up on his feet. Viola was nowhere to be found. He passed one room after the other, the heart was beating anxiously, air came through the alveoli like through a dirty filter, the leg hurt as if white-hot knives had sliced it. But his baby was nowhere to be found—neither in the garden, nor on the path behind the fence. And Renat, the old diseased predator, dragged his hurting body into the pitch-dark space of the forest.

He gazed, feeling the path in front of him with a stick, passing the palm of his hand over the pine tree trunks. He looked up—the black treetops formed extravagant Baroque ornaments against the sky.

Viola sat on a pile of dry leaves, staring at the space in front of her. Next to her, Methodius lay, bloodied and exhausted, in an unnatural pose. From his throat came muffled wheezes.

"What's with you, children, what's with you again?" Renat dropped on his knees in front of them, sinking into the pine needles covering the forest floor. "Let's go home."

… Viola, the large white butterfly of a woman, sips sherry on the terrace. An opened tome of Pérez-Reverte[2] chills on the table nearby. Viola thinks: septic amber brings Sept-ember, and this, kids, is a no brainer. Viola, oh butterfly-brained woman. God, when will You let her go! When will You come to this Earth—it seems You did rise from the dead, right? Viola looks for miracles at the bottom of a greenish bottle. Her exhausted hips tremble, like a sandwich with toothpicks assembled; it seems, it was too much of a gamble: Viola, the lady bramble, Viola, an ear of grain …

"… And we'll never ever leave each other," said Renat, covering Viola with a blanket. The cat was lying nearby; its pink belly calmly rose and fell with breathing. "It'll be time soon, kids."

Translated by Vitaly Chernetsky

---

2   Spanish novelist Arturo Pérez-Reverte (b. 1951) is best known for his popular novels about the seventeenth-century Spanish soldier Captain Alatriste.

LYUBA YAKIMCHUK

LYUBA YAKIMCHUK, a Ukrainian poet, screenwriter and journalist, was born in Pervomaisk, Luhansk oblast, Ukraine and currently lives in Kyiv. She is the author of several full-length poetry collections, including *iak MODA* (like FASHION, 2009) and *Abrykosy Donbasu* (Apricots of Donbas, 2015), and wrote the script for the film *The Word Building*.

Yakimchuk has received many literary awards, including the International Slavic Poetic Award, the Bohdan-Ihor Antonych Prize, and the Smoloskyp Prize, three of Ukraine's most prestigious awards for young poets. She is also the winner of the International Literary Contest "Coronation of the Word". Yakimchuk's poems have appeared in journals in Ukraine, the U.S., Sweden, Germany, Poland, Israel, Lithuania, and Belarus. Her poems have been translated into English, Swedish, German, French, Polish, Hebrew, Slovak, Lithuanian, Slovenian, Romanian, Serbian, Belarusian, and Russian, and her essays into English and Swedish.

Yakimchuk performs in a musical and poetic duet with the Ukrainian double bass player Mark Tokar; their projects include *Apricots of Donbas* and *Women, Smoke, and Dangerous Things*. Her poetry has been performed by the singer Mariana Sadovska (Cologne) and improvised by vocalist Olesya Zdorovetska (Dublin).

Yakimchuk also works as a cultural manager. She organized the *Rik Semenka* (Semenko Year) project (2012) dedicated to the Ukrainian futurist writer Mykhail Semenko, and was curator for the literary programs Cultural Forum "Donkult" (2015, Lviv) and Cultural Forum "GaliciaKult" (2016, Kharkiv).

Lyuba Yakimchuk's events in the Contemporary Ukrainian Literature Series, entitled *Decomposition*, took place in October 2016.

APRICOTS OF THE DONBAS
THE FACE OF COAL

With eyes sea blue
And hair flaxen yellow
Faded a little
It's not a flag
But my father
Standing in a pit
Water up to his knees

His face like coal—
With the imprint
Of an antediluvian field horsetail
Trampled by years
The sea hardens like salt
The grass hardens like coal
And my father turns like feather grass
Gray
He's a man
And men don't cry—
So they say in the ad
His cheeks are like trenches
Chopped up by the pit
And the coal taken
From my father's face
Burned in Donbas bonfires
And ovens

And somewhere high up
A pit heap stands
Snarling
Like a dragon
Like a sphinx
Defending its Tutankhamun

And it's only I who knows
That the pit heap in the middle of the steppe
Is nothing but corks from bottles
That my father drank
And ashes of cigarettes
That he smoked

THE SLAG PILES OF BREASTS

These stalks are
Like colored chalk
Stuck along the road
Just now and then a truck will pass
Amid the steppe in the grove
Donbas! Donbas!
The smokestack hisses
Into the sun's ear whorl

You stand
In the uniform
Of a coal agent
And smell perfume-like
Of reagents:

—I'm a woman
My element is water:
It's not only for making tea
Or washing dishes—no!
Though women don't work in the pits—
They work well at factories
Handling coal
I wash the coal
The way I wash my braids
I crush the coal
The way I cut potatoes
Or grind meat
In the factory blender
And sprinkle it over with oil
Melted—
That is, over this borsht
I pour reagents

Listen, all these compliments
To Donbas girls on their beauty
Make sense
If you see those factories
If you descend into the pits
Or bathe in the poisoned waters
Of the sumps
Where the broth is dumped
From this borsht of mine
If you climb up the slag pile
And tumble under its blanket
To be more exact, down its colon,
And before that
See the apricot blossom
The lithe white apricot blossom
And in the fall
See their yellow curls
From the height of the mine trolley's flight

APRICOTS IN HARD HATS

The apricot blossoms of Donbas
Grew pale in all the hues of the sky
The apricots put on hard hats
Spring already passed by

Twenty
Good men
Under thirty ...
The laws of equation
Reduced them to twenty
But there's nothing to equate them to:
They held
To the steel thread
Of the wire
In their cage, they stood
As if in Noah's Ark
After the deluge

A ton of concrete
Fell down on the cage
They fell out
They were crushed in free fall,
Broke free
Yes, free
Like apricot trees
Ripped out by their roots

They were twenty
And twenty were left
Eyes left, eyes right
By the laws of equation
When the row was continued
At the cemetery

But my father failed
To keep step
He got caught in the coal
As they rose higher and higher
In their rubber boots
And with flasks with no water
With bodies like flasks
They rose to the angels
Yonder …
And now grandmothers tell
Their grandchildren a tale
About apricots
Wearing hard hats

MY GRANDMOTHER'S FAIRY TALE

When tears
Turn to rock salt
When the sea in the stomach
Turns into a coal mine
Mammoths die
And hearts are born on the sleeves
They swap mettle for liquor
And are hired for labor

Wait!
This coal mine will swallow you
This ebony beauty
Of stone
Maybe it was for her that the Cumans carved statues
Unshaven like miners in the steppes,
Wait!
She'll give birth to a dead sea
Her waist is not sixty centimeters
Her breasts droop to her belly
Don't go inside
You may not return
Like the child of a mother
Who doesn't want to give birth

He plunged into her once
And came back with tears in his hands—
He plunged into her—a second time
And came back with salt in his hands
He plunged into her—a third time ...
And hands full of coals
He was pulled down to the bottom
Of the underground sea

Apricot trees stretched their hands to the sky
Apricots put on hard hats, yellow-hot
And now when you eat apricots
You find coals in their core
This is the end of the tale

THE BOOK OF ANGELS

Your teeth dark and holey
Like spoil tips
Your eyes gray and spicy
Like the upturned fibrils
Of the smoke of Alchevsk[1]
That grow upward
Take root everywhere
Like willows
—My health is lousy
But I don't need pity
I pluck grass but not just any grass
Stone grass from under the earth
From under the sky:
Once, a sea was here
Here grew gigantic grass
On it, angels swayed
The grass listened to them speak
Committed the words to memory
And pressed itself into the turf
The turf squeezed out its water and
Became the essence of the universe
Got covered with fresh twigs
And some other woodblocks

These angelic words
Could not be transmitted by air
So they turned into shingle
Into stony grass
That is, turned into coal,
And now every coal pit
Is a book

---

1   The city of Alchevs'k is a major industrial center in Ukraine's Donbas region.

Of angelic words
The pages of which
Burn in the forge
They are giant candles
Scattered
In swards

That is why the Donbas plants
Shoot colored fumes into the sky
Not giving a damn
About the smoking ban
In public places
Because on factory plazas
They are at home
Where
As everyone knows
Even cats
Smoke as much as their masters do

Choo choo
Goes the train
Choo choo

Translated by Svetlana Lavochkina with Michael M. Naydan

THE EYE OF THE SLAG HEAP

each time I end up home
as though under a warm shower
a slag heap observes me out of habit
in the chink of its triangular eye—
I take off my dress
my undergarments
and stand beneath the shower
with shoulders straightened like a cross
just in my own skin
that I'm not planning to take off
I throw on just the lace of recollections
and look through them at the slag heap and sun
right into their faces
into the round eye of the sun
and the triangular slag heaps—
and from the shower head onto my wet skin
it's not rain falling, but snow
in long threads of rays
a gossamer snow of rites of spring songs
that descend from the spider sun

Translated by Michael M. Naydan

DECOMPOSITION

all is quiet on the eastern front
well, I've had it up to here
at the moment of death, metal gets hot
and people get cold

don't talk to me about *Luhansk*[2]
it's long since turned into—*hansk*
Lu had been razed
to the crimson pavement

my friends are hostages
and I can't reach them, I can't *do netsk*
to pull them out of the basements
from under the rubble

yet here you are, writing poems
ideally slick poems
high-minded gilded poems
beautiful as embroidery
there's no poetry about war
just decomposition
only letters remain
and they all make a single sound—rrr

Pervomaisk has been split into *pervo* and *maisk*
into particles in primeval flux
war is over once again
yet peace has not come

---

2   Luhans'k, Donets'k, Pervomais'k, and Debal'tsevo (Debal'tseve) are all cities in
    Ukraine's war-torn Donbas region.

and where's my *deb, alts, evo?*
no poet will be born there again
no human being

I stare into the horizon
it has narrowed into a triangle
sunflowers dip their heads in the field
black and dried out, like me
I have gotten so very old
no longer Lyuba
just—ba

Translated by Oksana Maksymchuk and Max Rosochinsky

EYEBROWS

no-no, I won't put on a black dress
black shoes and a black shawl
I'll come to you all in white—if I have a chance to come
and I'll be wearing nine white skirts
one beneath the other
I'll sit down in front of a mirror
(it'll be draped with a cloth)
strike up a match
it'll burn out and I'll
moisten it with my tongue
and draw black eyebrows
over my own, also black
then I'll have two pairs of eyebrows
mine and yours above them
no-no, I won't put on a black dress
I'll put your black eyebrows
on me

Translated by Svetlana Lavochkina

I HAVE A CRISIS FOR YOU

you lit up a cigarette
but it wouldn't burn
it was summer
and girls would light up from any passerby
but I didn't light up for you anymore

"our love's gone missing," I explain to a friend
it vanished in one of the wars
we waged in our kitchen
"replace the word war with crisis," he says
because crisis is something everyone has from time to time

do you remember the second world crisis?
respectively, the first one as well
the civil crisis—to each his own
I forgot about the cold crisis
it seems there were two of them
also the liberation crisis should be mentioned
it sounds so good—
the liberation crisis of 1648–1657
write it down in textbooks
a crisis that liberates
releases forever
my great-grandfather died in the second world crisis
possibly at the hand of my other great-grandfather
or his machine gun
or his battle tank
but it's unclear
how they fought this crisis with each other
or whether it was the crisis itself that killed them, like a plague
for no one is to blame for a crisis
it is inexorable as death

and when our own domestic war
turns into a crisis
does it get better?
does it hurt less?
do birds return to us from the south
or maybe, do we go to meet them?
why is our language like that—
we lack words to describe our feelings
only crisis and love are left
as antonyms

but if love is so complicated
with these blazes and smoldering
like blood and pain
(and blood is not at all like one's periods
but some new feeling of mine)
(and pain is yours)
if love is made up of two different feelings
then soon love will also be called crisis

I have a crisis for you, darling
let's get married

we've got a crisis
we'd better split up

Translated by Svetlana Lavochkina

FALSE FRIENDS AND BELOVED

even a translator's false friends
become just friends one day:

you say "kochana"—"my beloved"—
and a blast inside me forms a mushroom cloud
I ask, are you drunk?
do you know what this word means in Ukrainian?
because there is the word "kochanie"—"cutie"
you said to me yesterday
like you were talking to a little girl

you reply that I'm sweet
that I'm just sweet and not your beloved
you express not in Ukrainian but in Polish
that I'm your "kochana"—that is
a friend, to say it more precisely, a girlfriend
you know, I say, in Belarusian they also have problems with love
in Belarusian it's not like ours at all
their "liubov" is calm and tasty, like love for food
like love for a country when it's not at war
how on earth can they live without love
as we have it?

you say:
love is like a gust of wind
you'll never guess what will happen to it tomorrow
for example, in French, "baiser"—
is not "to kiss" anymore
now it means "to make love"

what if you spoke French not Polish
and said the word "baiser" that you had been taught incorrectly at school
and I agreed

because at school I also had been taught incorrectly
what would happen?
for the body knows language better than the mind
the body will not let you down

my beloved!
this relationship is so uncertain
all this love changes so much from language
to language today kiss—tomorrow lovemaking
today romantic love—tomorrow—love for a country
beloved, je t'embrasse—
I kiss
I only kiss you
on your cheek
false
lover of a translator
that is of a bad translatress

Translated by Svetlana Lavochkina

SUCH PEOPLE ARE CALLED NAKED

For Henri Michaux

you took off your t-shirt
I pulled off my dress
you unbuckled your belt
I unhooked my bra
you dropped your pants and kicked off your socks
I freed myself from my panties, so sassy
it's better to call them sassies
and now we lie in bed
two strips
like two white loaves of bread
facing each other

you touch my cheek with your hand
you lower your hand on my neck
you drive your fingers along my upper back:
"how nicely everything is put together here!" you utter
but suddenly
from behind your shoulder your mom peeks and says,
"Andryusha, did you wash your hands?"
you turn to face her, show her your hands
she offers you fruit compote and goes to the kitchen
you turn back to me
put your hand back where you previously stopped
from my back it slides down to my breasts
softly as sea sand
and then I feel my dad's breath on my neck:
"think with your head, baby"
he whispers loudly
I turn away from you
and see his unshaved face quite close
and reply that I always think with my head!

I turn to you
and already my hand slides along your chest
and its thin hair bends under it
and then
behind your back the bed creaks:
"Andryusha, have some fruit compote"
you turn away from me
kiss her sonorously and say:
"mom, I want to be alone for a bit!"
and she replies, offended:
"it doesn't look like you're alone!"
and she goes somewhere again
and now you are with me again
and your hand on my belly
glides down slowly
so it gets so close and so tender
so it gets so
and then
I hear my grandmother's groaning
she says loudly into my back:
"you're not a virgin anymore
see how your expression changed!"
and I take your hand away from my belly
turn halfway to my granny
with the same hand of yours
I straighten her purple kerchief
and say loudly:
"I'm still pure, gran,
and will remain pure forever!"
I turn back to you
and here, over your shoulder
an old lady in a yellow kerchief peeps
this time, your granny:
"what kind of female name ends with a consonant
as if it were a man's?" she asks

mine does, but I'm silent
and I take your hands off my hips
snow falls between us
and like two toy soldiers
we lie like this till morning

when a cleaning lady comes
throws away the snow mounds between us
and I look into your green eyes for a long, long time
and you keep looking at my nipples
then I say:
"let's get undressed"
and I take off, one by one:
my dad
my granny
my mom
my sister
and you take off, one by one:
your mom
your brother
your granny
your childhood friend
your pick-up experts
and we now wear nothing at all
such people are called naked

Translated by Svetlana Lavochkina

MARSALA

It was clear to me it was you
by the way you stroked every one of my toes
as if I'd never had them before
and you'd created them out of nothing

fingers are for work
toes are useless,
I thought and doubted
but you insisted
that one should just have some things

touch after touch
you created something new in me:
a tiny birthmark on my neck hidden by my hair
a large mole on my left breast
covered by the cut of my dress
you reshaped my eyebrows—
they are different beneath your kisses
than they are beneath warm tap water—
and on my back you spread uneven circles,
diving into it deeply
and trembling fish-like

and I stand in front of the mirror
my dress like marsala wine
my glance befuddled
and I see
a birthmark under my dress
a birthmark on my neck
soft fuzz on my back
your lips still creating a world
and I'm a little fearful of Saturday's arrival

Translated by Svetlana Lavochkina

MARK ANDRYCZYK is the administrator of the Ukrainian Studies Program at the Harriman Institute, Columbia University and lecturer in Ukrainian literature at the Department of Slavic Languages and Literatures at Columbia, where he teaches courses  on Ukrainian literature and culture. He holds a PhD in Ukrainian Literature from the University of Toronto (2005). Andryczyk's monograph *The Intellectual as Hero in 1990s Ukrainian Fiction* was published by the University of Toronto Press in 2012.

A Ukrainian edition of that monograph, *Intelektual iak heroi ukraïnskoï prozy 90-kh rokiv XX stolittia* was published by Piramida in 2014. Since 2007, Andryczyk has organized the Contemporary Ukrainian Literature Series (cosponsored by the Harriman and Kennan Institutes), which has brought leading Ukrainian literary figures to audiences in North America. He is an active translator of contemporary Ukrainian literature into English, having translated, among others, H. Chubai, O. Lysheha, S. Zhadan, Yu. Andrukhovych, V. Neborak, K. Moskalets, T. Prokhasko, M. Savka, A. Bondar, I. Malkovych, Yu. Pokalchuk, I. Rymaruk, V. Gabor, D. Lazutkin, O. Boichenko, and S. Andrukhovych. Andryczyk has translated eleven essays that will be included in the forthcoming collection of Yuri Andrukhovych's essays in English translation *My Final Territory: Selected Essays* (University of Toronto Press). Under the name Yeezhak, he has recorded three studio albums in Ukraine (1996, 1998, 2006) and has performed a series of concerts in support of these recordings.

Translators

Mark Andryczyk is Associate Research Scholar at the Harriman Institute, Columbia University.

Jars Balan is Coordinator of the Kule Ukrainian Canadian Studies Centre, Canadian Institute of Ukrainian Studies.

Bohdan Boychuk was a poet, playwright and translator.

Vitaly Chernetsky is Associate Professor and Director of the Center for Russian, East European and Eurasian Studies at the University of Kansas.

Patrick John Corness is Visiting Professor of Translation at Coventry University.

Olena Jennings is a poet, fiction writer, and translator.

Svetlana Lavochkina is a novelist, poet, and translator.

Oksana Maksymchuk is Assistant Professor of Philosophy at the University of Arkansas.

Askold Melnyczuk is Professor of English, College of Liberal Arts at the University of Massachusetts Boston.

Michael M. Naydan is Woskob Family Professor of Ukrainian Studies and Professor of Slavic Languages and Literatures at Penn State University.

Wanda Phipps is a New York writer, performer and translator.

Natalia Pomirko is a translator and Professor of English at the Ukrainian Catholic University, Lviv, Ukraine.

Max Rosochinsky is a translator and poet from Simferopol, Crimea, currently working on a monograph on Marina Tsvetaeva's poetry.

Myroslava Stefaniuk is a writer and translator.

Virlana Tkacz is the artistic director of Yara Arts Group, a theater director, and translator.

Andrij Kudla Wynnyckyj is a translator, editor, and writer.

Yaryna Yakubyak is a musician and translator.

Praise for *Writing from Ukraine*
(previously *The White Chalk of Days*)

The White Chalk of Days comes out at a time of acute urgency for discovery of Ukraine's rich culture – and it answers this challenge by presenting contemporary Ukrainian literature in its diverse, changing, and becoming nature. The anthology's editor, Mark Andryczyk, accomplished a difficult yet exciting task: not to present a transparent hierarchy of a literature deserving of our attention, or to attempt a rendering of a canon, but instead to offer a glimpse into a literature where established authors (such as Oleh Lysheha, Serhiy Zhadan, Yuri Andrukhovych) participate in a conversation with emerging voices (such as Luba Yakimchuk, Sophia Andrukhovych, Marjana Savka, Andriy Bondar and others). For both the curious reader and the interested scholar, this anthology presents the unique opportunity of observing the literary momentum in its making and of enjoying a radical and exciting variety of genres, thematic approaches, and political and aesthetic positions.

Polina Barskova, Associate Professor of Russian Literature, Hampshire College

The White Chalk of Days invites us to enter the world of contemporary Ukrainian literature as it grapples with its past and designs its future. In these poems and stories, the present is a palimpsest of national history and identity. The translations in this anthology succeed in awakening readers to the sensuous and musical world of a literary history that deserves to blossom and be known to all.

Lillian-Yvonne Bertram
Professor of English in the College of Liberal Arts, University of Massachusetts Boston, and the author of *Personal Science* (2017)

The White Chalk of Days will serve as an indispensable, near-comprehensive introduction to contemporary Ukrainian literature. The topics, styles, and unique voices of the thirteen modern Ukrainian authors create a rich mosaic reflective of that nation's diverse and vibrant culture. The anthology brings together the authors who entered the literary scene in the 1970s and those born in the 1980s, thus covering the entire period of the Soviet collapse and Ukrainian independence. Mark Andryczyk's in-depth introduction and commentary help to make sense of the political and cultural context behind this creative exuberance.

Serhy Yekelchyk
Professor of Slavic Studies at the University of Victoria and the author
of *The Conflict in Ukraine* (2015)

The White Chalk of Days: The Contemporary Ukrainian Literature Series Anthology is a remarkable accomplishment, bringing together selections by fifteen writers to provide sharp and necessary insight for English-speaking readers. Some of the treasures here include Serhiy Zhadan with 'the starlight that falls into our chimneys / and the emerald green of the garlic leaves / that grow on our soccer fields'; Ivan Malkovych's three-year old niece predicting that in her absence 'you will bathe in tears'; and Sophia Andrukhovych giving us trash as 'a white shimmer like giant flowers of a cosmic-sized apricot tree,' while Lyuba Yakimchuk lets us see 'a tiny birthmark on my neck hidden by my hair / a large mole on my left breast / covered by the cut of my dress.' These translations give attention to sound as well as sense, allowing us inside these fresh perspectives, a world away.

Jill McDonough
Professor in the MFA program at UMass Boston and the author of
Reaper (2017)

There are anthologies that are exhaustive in their attempt to be representative, and there are anthologies that attempt to suggest the sensibility of a generation. *The White Chalk of Days* is the latter in its attempt to straddle the Soviet/post-Soviet era in Ukraine. What emerges from these pages is a generation that is wised up to the dangers of the Great Idea, the Grand Scheme, and the World Historical. These are local intelligences trying to keep a sense of perspective that is personal without being parochial, skeptical without succumbing to cynicism. Among the many fine writers represented, Askold Melnyczuk's translations of Marjana Savka's poems—lyrical, exuberant, but underwritten by a tough-minded skepticism—and the satiric fierceness of Yuri Andrukhovych's prose seem to me to sum up this middle generation's difficult and lasting achievement.

Tom Sleigh
Distinguished Professor, Hunter College MFA Program, City
University of New York

The White Chalk of Days is an impressive collection: translations of recent Ukrainian prose and poetry. It brings together work reflecting the past, be it historic or sordid, and the vibrant present, collective or idiosyncratic individual experiences, often humorous or deeply moving. Bravo to the gifted writers whose series of visits to New York and Washington sparked this volume—and bravo to editor Mark Andryczyk and his sixteen fellow translators.

Sibelan Forrester
Professor of Modern and Classical Languages and Russian,
Swarthmore College and the author of *A Companion to Marina
Cvetaeva* (2016)

The White Chalk of Days is an inspiring effort by Mark Andryczyk—who served as its editor, wrote an extensive introduction, and translated what seems like the lion's share of the pieces—to establish a body of reference for contemporary Ukrainian literature. The general introduction and valuable author introductions speak forcefully to the need to explain Ukraine's journey, especially since the Soviet Union's collapse, and many of the texts engage the country's post-Soviet history and politics, and the authors' geographical spread pointedly reflects Ukraine's cultural multi-valency. Sharing space with established names like Andrey Kurkov and Serhiy Zhadan are appealing new-to-me names like Taras Prokhasko and Sophia Andrukhovych.

Marian Schwartz
Translator of Andrei Gelasimov's *Into the Thickening Fog* and Polina Dashkova's *Madness Treads Lightly* (both 2017)

As the attentive reader will discover in the acknowledgements, the animating spirit for this volume took flight on a gentle evening when the Director of the Harriman Institute (the indomitable Catharine Nepomnyashchy), the editor of this volume (Mark Andryczyk), and the Director of the Kennan Institute (me) lamented the failure of scholarship to capture the depth, complexity, diversity, and fluidity of contemporary Ukraine. The astonishing works collected by Andryczyk for this volume – and the seminars and literary readings which supported this project – reveal how today's Ukraine sustains one of our era's most interestingly innovative literary landscapes.

Blair A. Ruble
Vice President for Programs, Woodrow Wilson Center

This anthology, like any good buffet, overwhelms the consumer with its variety and abundance. The master chef, Mark Andryczyk, and his collaborators have prepared a marvellous spread of treats that reflect the extraordinary richness and diversity of contemporary Ukrainian writing. The meat-eater, the vegetarian, the gourmand, and the dieter will all find irresistible temptation in the selection. The hungry reader will not run out of tasty morsels, and the dilettante will have trouble putting down the volume. Ukrainian literature has much to offer, and is very well represented in these very capable translations. *The White Chalk of Days*, unlike the geese in a poem by Ivan Malkovych, will not disperse at sundown.

Maxim Tarnawsky
Professor of Ukrainian Literature, University of Toronto,
and the editor of *Ukrainian Literature:
A Journal of Translations*

Some of the liveliest and most moving literature in the world is also some of the least known in English. So blessings on editor and translator Mark Andryczyk and the team of expert and eloquent translators he has assembled for bringing us this abundant new anthology of poetry and fiction from Ukraine of the Soviet and post-Soviet periods. It's a great public service to enlarge our acquaintance with this indispensable work, an act of moral generosity. But what the reader will be most grateful for is the sheer pleasure of it.

Lloyd Schwartz
Poet and Pulitzer Prize-winning critic

A lively collection of poems interlaced with dominoes, sunken ships, extraterrestrials, weightless angels, a gypsy melody playing on a stolen cell phone, and pithy stories that jump from secret maps to the Roman alphabet, hotel rooms, and a tribute to Jimi Hendrix's hand. The twelve men and three women anthologized here through the efforts of seventeen translators bring us playful, wistful humor infused with tragedy, irony, caprice, and wisdom.

Ellen Elias-Bursać
Literary translator, most recently of *The Judgment of Richard Richter*
by Igor Štiks

The White Chalk of Days is a rich and dramatic anthology that covers predominantly the post-independence period of Ukrainian literature, bringing together writers from a host of generations and genres. From authors whose work has become synonymous with Ukraine's modern-day cultural revival—such as Yuri Andrukhovych, Victor Neborak, and Yuri Vynnychuk—to an array of new voices representing the emerging literary vanguard, this masterfully translated, lucid, and engaging selection showcases the extraordinary power, vitality, and diversity of writing in contemporary Ukraine.

Maryna Romanets
Associate Professor in the Department of English and Women's and Gender Studies Program at the University of Northern British Columbia, Canada

When it comes to writing, freedom is often assumed to mean the freedom to write on political themes without fear of state reprisal. In the formerly Communist countries of Europe, however, the freedom not to write on political themes can be just as meaningful. These fifteen authors bring us stirring reflections on nature, hilarious morning-after surprises, touching spiritual insights, rich family histories, computers and snowy mountains and gay bars and slag heaps. In short, the sheer variety of experience on display will be exhilarating for anyone, but especially for the English-speaking reader coming to Ukrainian literature for the first time.

Alex Zucker

Translator of Czech authors Jáchym Topol and Petra Hůlová, former co-chair of the PEN America Translation Committee

The White Chalk of Days, an anthology of contemporary Ukrainian writers, is the harvest of a new flowering of one of the world's great literatures. These excellent translations into English remind us how consequential the resonances of poetry and prose can be. *The White Chalk of Days* is a celebration of the triumph of the imagination and the human spirit. It is an invaluable gift to literature.

Stuart Dischell

Professor in English Creative Writing, MFA Program, University of North Carolina at Greensboro, and the author of *Standing on Z* (2016)